THE Prodigal Daughter

PRUE LEITH

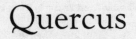

First published in Great Britain in 2016 by Quercus
This paperback edition published in 2017 by

Quercus Editions Ltd
Carmelite House
50 Victoria Embankment
London EC4Y 0DZ

An Hachette UK company

A CIP catalogue record for this book is available
from the British Library

PB ISBN 978 1 78429 019 1
EBOOK ISBN 978 1 78429 020 7

10 9 8 7 6 5 4 3 2 1

Typeset by CC Book Production

Printed and bound in Great Britain by Clays Ltd, St Ives plc

For James and Penny

PART ONE

1967

CHAPTER ONE

Laura was aghast. Plastic vines and raffia-covered Chianti bottles fixed to garden trellis covered the walls of the restaurant's bar. More vines snaked through trellis on the ceiling, and fake grapes hung thickly overhead. Mario, at the top of a ladder, fixing the last bunch, saw her. '*Porca vacca*, Laura, I wanted to finish it before you came. As a surprise.' He jumped off the ladder, his handsome face wearing a grin.

'What on earth are you doing, Mario? Don't you understand anything? Why would I want plastic rubbish all over the bar?'

Her nephew's face fell. 'But it looked so bare, so cold!'

'We have the best restaurant designer in the business, and you want his clean white walls to look like every mamma-and-papa Italian joint in London?'

'I just thought –'

'You thought? Mario, one thing you don't do is think.' She took a deep breath, made an effort to drop her voice to somewhere near normal. 'I'm sorry, Mario, but you must get rid of it. All of it. Now.'

She turned to leave. Mario made to follow her. 'But, Laura—'

'No buts, Mario. Please. Just do it. And if there are any holes in the wall, or marks on the ceiling, they'd better be fixed by lunchtime.'

Laura walked out of the bar and stood in the passage, trying to regain her equilibrium. Mario drove her mad. He always had. Ever since he'd arrived at the age of eleven with his mother and brother, Silvano, from Abruzzo, he'd been a liability – thoughtless, over-confident and getting into trouble, then sliding out of it with charm, flattery and, often, the help of big brother Silvano.

How different those two are, she thought. Her husband Giovanni's nephews had always been chalk and cheese. Silvano was studious, quiet and sensible, the opposite of his feckless father, who had abandoned the family. Now twenty-six, Silvano was the head accountant for the family's ice-cream business, the Calzone cafés and the new Giovanni's restaurant. Mario was full of ideas but his enthusiasms faded fast. If she could, she'd employ only Silvano, but Giovanni, with typical Italian loyalty to his family, had insisted Mario be given a job. Giovanni's sister, Carlotta, had refused point-blank to have her son in her kitchen and eventually Laura had agreed that he could man the bar, a decision she regretted already.

Still, Laura thought, she shouldn't have been so rude. He was only trying to help. He thought of himself as artistic and imaginative – he'd have been hurt by what she'd said.

Really, she could have done without this. Tonight was the official opening of Giovanni's, and she was only just holding at bay the panicky thought that they'd never be ready. She continued her tour of inspection. In the first dining room she found her husband surrounded by upturned tables to which he was attaching the legs and castors. 'They were supposed to come assembled,' he said.

'God, darling, how long will that take? I've got the waiters coming in to lay up at twelve.'

'Silvano's asking a few to come in early to help. We've got the other dining room to do as well, and we still have to unpack the china and cutlery.'

Silvano walked in. 'Hello, Laura,' he said, kissing her on both cheeks, 'The big day!' Then to Giovanni: 'Three of the waiters are on the way. It'll be fine.'

'Silvano, darling, I'm afraid I've just been very unkind to your brother. He got it into his head to improve on the bar décor and I shouted at him.'

'Don't worry, Laura. If he's upset, he'll soon get over it. I'll go and see him.'

Reassured, she went through to the cool pastry kitchen to find Carlotta surrounded by pasta drying on racks stacked six deep. Now she was making pistachio ice cream.

'Here, Laura, try it. This new machine is a wonder. It works so quickly – and the ice cream tastes like my mother used to make in a bucket! We had to put salt and ice round the sides and turn the handle for hours.'

Laura scooped up a teaspoonful of the pale-green mixture and popped it into her mouth. 'Carlotta . . . you've excelled yourself. It's the best I've ever tasted.' She ate another spoonful. 'Is everything on track?'

'The desserts and pastas will be ready. And the *focaccia* is in the oven. Not sure how the boys are doing, though. There's a lot of swearing coming from in there.'

Laura left her and went into the main kitchen. The chefs looked organized enough. They shouted a lot, but they knew what they were doing. At the big double sink two lads were scrubbing mussels and behind them the fish chef was cleaning squid. At the larder end another boy was coating thin slices of cooked veal loin in tuna mayonnaise for *vitello tonnato*. Such an odd dish, she thought, fish with veal, but it had suddenly become fashionable and was their most popular takeaway dish.

The head chef, Dino, was tipping a bag of charcoal into the well of the grill. 'Signora, look,' he said, indicating a sack beside him. 'We have vine prunings from a vineyard in Somerset. I'm going to cook the veal chops on them, like in Italy.'

'How on earth did you find them? We don't deal with English winemakers.'

'Luca, the new commis, he was picking down there during the *vendemmia* and they had a huge pile they were going to burn so he rang me to ask if we wanted any. He chopped off all the thicker wood and stuffed it into the back of his van. The English! They haven't a clue!'

The enthusiasm of the cooks, the quality of the produce, and the air of anticipation were exciting. Laura went into the big cold room where she found the dishes for the first course – tiny stuffed peppers, grilled Mediterranean vegetables, sliced mozzarella with chopped rosemary and olive oil, aubergine with cheese, avocado and prawn terrine, seafood salad, finely sliced prosciutto and salamis, real Italian mortadella. The simple Italian antipasti would look so enticing, so beautiful on the trolley.

At first Giovanni had objected: 'We don't want an hors d'oeuvre trolley! So old-fashioned!'

'But ours isn't going to be like that. We'll serve food like you get in summer in Abruzzo. Like you and Carlotta make at home. Nothing English, nothing from a tin. Our dishes will be fresh and irresistible! You'll see.'

6

Now, looking at glistening *peperonata* and shiny black olives, Laura had a sudden memory of Giovanni starting out in the fish-and-chip shop in Billingsgate. He'd had no real kitchen, just a bank of deep-fryers behind the counter. They'd come a long way since then.

Even now, twenty years on, thinking of those early days could unsettle her. It had been a classic war-time story. She'd fallen in love with Giovanni, who had embodied everything her father didn't want in a son-in-law: a penniless Italian ex-prisoner of war, a lowly cook, who had made his precious daughter pregnant.

Laura shook her head in an attempt to dislodge thoughts of that baby, given up for adoption. With an effort she forced them into the part of her brain that she could ignore. She had to concentrate on their successes. The fish-and-chip shop had become a warm and delightful Italian café. Others had followed, as had market stalls, the Calzone coffee shops, two Deli-Calzones selling Italian groceries, and now the restaurant, Giovanni's.

It was called Giovanni's but it had been her vision. She had been the one who believed that the public would patronize a top-class Italian restaurant as they did the French *haute-cuisine* establishments, like Le Caprice or the Coq d'Or.

Satisfied with what she had seen in the cold room, she went back into the kitchen. There, she was struck once more by the expanse of stainless-steel benches, the charcoal grill, the huge Falcon range, the rack of copper pans – and a shaft of anxiety: they had sunk so much money into Giovanni's, hiring the best designer, stocking the cellar with the finest Italian wines, buying quality equipment and employing experienced staff. What if it didn't work? But the orderly bustle cheered her and the unease passed.

7

In Reception she glanced through the bookings register. Most of the tables were reserved for family, friends and the press. Forty-five altogether. They could take another twenty but, thought Laura, it would be no bad thing today if they weren't full – less strain on waiters and kitchen staff.

Angelica, Laura's daughter, was sticking numbers to the coat hangers in the cloakroom. 'Darling, have you got the tags to give the guests?' Laura asked.

Angelica reached under the counter and produced a box of metal discs embossed with numbers on one side and 'Giovanni's' on the other, stacked in numerical order. She asked, 'Mamma, why do they have to be so big and heavy? They must have cost a fortune. Wouldn't a card have done?'

'No, because the guests lose anything like that in their hand-bags or pockets and we have to give them a coat or bag with no proof it's theirs. Big ones cut down the risk.'

'Groovy.'

Laura smiled. Angelica wasn't always so agreeable: a lot of the time she was downright bolshy. Still, she'd been the same herself when she was seventeen.

'Mamma, why can't I be in the kitchen? You know I'd rather.'

'Because we need you on Reception, darling.' She touched her daughter's cheek. 'You'll be the first thing the guests see as they come in. Tonight you'll look gorgeous and give them your famous smile, because then you'll get more tips.'

Angelica brightened, as Laura had known she would. Her daughter loved miniskirts, knee-high Biba boots and her Mary Quant haircut: she'd make sure she looked good.

Next stop on the inspection tour was the Ladies. Inside Laura stopped dead in front of the wall facing her, which was covered

8

with framed photographs of famous people, most of which were signed: John Gielgud, Joan Collins, Richard Burton, Elizabeth Taylor, the Beatles, Lulu, John Betjeman, Princess Margaret . . . She turned on her heel and dashed into the Gents across the corridor. Sure enough, there were more photographs: David Niven, Julie Christie, Muhammad Ali, Peter Finch, Peter O'Toole, Twiggy, Oliver Reed . . .

She tried to think. Terence, the designer, would never have bought them. The pictures suggested that all these people ate at Giovanni's, which was clearly impossible. And why hadn't she been consulted?

The penny dropped.

Mario.

She stalked back into the bar. Mario was filling the holes that his vine-and-trellis arrangement had made in the ceiling.

'Mario, the lavatories – those photographs. That was you, wasn't it?'

'Sure. Don't say you don't like them either? They're wonderful. Everyone will love them.'

'But they're a fraud! You're telling customers that these people eat at Giovanni's and we aren't even open!'

'We're not saying they eat here. Sure, people might think they eat at other Angelotti places, and I didn't write, "What a lovely restaurant" or "Thank you for a perfect meal," just their names.'

'You forged the signatures?'

'I had to—'

'Mario! What if Lulu or John Gielgud or, God forbid, Princess Margaret comes in and—'

'They'll be flattered. And we can say we bought them ready-signed.'

He hasn't an honest bone in his body, thought Laura. She took a deep breath. 'Has Terence seen them?'

'Not as far as I know. But he'll like them, I'm sure.'

'*I'm* sure he won't. And *I* don't like them, which is more to the point. How did you pay for them? They look expensive – proper prints, good frames.'

'They came from that Celebrity Souvenirs shop in Soho. The bill is coming to the restaurant.'

Laura shut her eyes briefly while she took control of herself. Then she went to find her husband.

Giovanni persuaded her to leave the photographs – there was no doubt that the customers would love them. He'd talk to Mario, make it clear that any more such interventions would mean his dismissal. Then he took her shoulders and kissed her. 'And, my darling Laura, we have more important things to get through before tonight.'

As Laura predicted, Angelica charmed the arrivals, who loved the clean modern décor, the quirky tractor seats on the bar stools, the informal country flowers, the back-lit wine racks and the deep turquoise carpet on the ceiling, studded with spotlights directed to the tables. It was far removed from the usual Italian restaurant, just as she'd meant it to be.

The biggest table, a long oval in the window recess, was reserved for the family. During dinner only eight people occupied it, with space for the working Angelottis to join them later. The restaurant's backers, George and Grace, the Earl and Countess of Frampton, were there with Grace's twenty-seven year-old daughter Jane, expensively dressed but with her usual

discontented expression. Laura's older brother, David, and his wife, Sophie, had come up from the Cotswolds, with their fifteen-year-old twins, Richard and Hal, and David and Laura's mother, Maud, as energetic as ever in her late seventies. This being the English side of the extended family, the atmosphere was decorous until a few bottles of Sangiovese had been drunk.

The other dozen or so tables varied from those for two in discreet corners to round six-seaters in the middle of the room, the majority seating three or four.

Laura talked to her customers, trying to distinguish between British reluctance to complain and genuine satisfaction. It particularly pleased her that the guests clearly enjoyed the first and last cold courses, wheeled to the tables on huge trolleys, and that they approved of their innovative (and, in Giovanni's opinion, mad) pricing policy. Laura had reckoned it was not so much the dishes people ordered that should determine what they paid but the fact that they were occupying a seat. If someone sat all evening with a salad and a glass of water, it was, she reckoned, costing her lost income from a heartier appetite. To make things fair for the customer, and profitable for her, she decided on a fixed price, to cover whatever was eaten, with no added extras other than drinks : no cover charge, no supplements, and with service included.

'Laura,' Giovanni had protested, 'that could bankrupt us. We'll attract only the greedy who will eat, say, a great plateful of antipasti, then lobster risotto, then a fillet steak with truffles, then a huge selection of cold puddings and a hot soufflé, followed by a great plate of cheeses, then start all over again.'

'Darling, our customers are not going to eat like that! The men will have probably had a business lunch and won't even be hungry and women don't eat like horses. They'll want exquisite food, not mountains of it. I just want to take some of the angst out of choosing. Yes, a few young men will overdo it, but most customers, I bet, will eat two, maybe three courses.'

The price was two pounds eight shillings, all in. And she calculated that wine and other drinks would bring the bill per person to about four pounds ten shillings – more expensive than any other Italian restaurant and almost matching the top-end French ones.

When Laura flopped down between Jane and David at the family table, her face was flushed with pleasure at the effusive compliments all of the customers had uttered. Now she basked in George and Grace's congratulations – Grace was raving about her Lobster Thermidor 'You've really pulled it off, little sis,' David said, hugging her. 'Smart décor, smart food, smart staff and smart customers. It's wonderful. Don't you think so, Sophie?'

'Of course I do. Laura, darling, I thought being a GP, a mum and farmer's wife was tough – but look at what you've managed! I'm bowled over.'

Laura laughed. 'Good! Always wanted to impress my oldest friend.' She turned to Jane. 'What do you think, Jane? Did you have a good dinner? What did you eat?'

'I had the avocado salad from the trolley, then the grilled squid. Both delicious, Aunt Laura.'

'No pudding?'

'I don't eat pudding.' But she was smiling for once and Laura smiled back.

The best moment of the evening came at two in the morning

when, after helping the staff with the clear-up and having a congratulatory drink with them in the bar, she walked between her husband and daughter to their car. Giovanni said, 'Angelica, aren't you proud of your mamma?'

Angelica put an arm round her mother's waist. 'I am,' she said, 'and one day, Mamma, I'm going to be as good a restaurateur as you, only I'll be the cook, not the manager.'

CHAPTER TWO

Sophie never ceased to be amazed by her mother-in-law. Maud had refused the offer of a taxi from Giovanni's: 'I've been sitting all day and I'll never sleep if I don't stretch my legs a bit.' She and David each took one of the old lady's arms and the three set off down Westbourne Grove.

'Aren't Hal and Richard coming with us? asked Maud.

'They've gone dancing,' said Sophie.

'Jigging about to records,' explained David. 'Hal fancies himself as a disc jockey.'

After ten minutes Sophie thought Maud was getting tired, which she'd never admit to. She suggested a taxi and David promptly hailed one.

As they sat down, Sophie said, 'We could stay in town for an extra day, couldn't we, David? You'd like that, Maud, wouldn't you? We could go to a show, or an exhibition.'

'Mm.' David looked sideways at her. 'Do I smell a shopping trip coming on?'

Sophie laughed. 'He always sees through me, damn it.'

'Out with it!'

'It's that dinner jacket. You've been wearing it for twenty

years at least and I dare say your father wore it for twenty years before that.'

'What's wrong with it?' asked David, fingering the lapel. 'I'm rather proud of the fact that it still fits me.'

'But the trousers are shiny and the jacket's going brown at the edges.'

'What do you think, Mum?'

'Well,' said Maud, 'a modern one would be lighter and more comfortable.' She patted his arm. 'And you might make less fuss when you have to wear it.'

'I don't remember ever seeing Dad in it, though I must have. He used to wear his RAF uniform at a formal dinner, didn't he, Mum?'

'That was what he liked.' Maud smiled at the memory. 'And very handsome he looked in it, too.'

Sophie smiled to herself, thinking how true the cliché of time being a great healer was. She knew Maud had had a difficult time with her husband, but now she spoke of Donald with humour and love. And, she thought, David, now so content, had been devastated at his first wife's death, had rejected the twins for almost a year. He'd been, she thought, close to suicide. And then he'd only married her because she'd be a mother for them. And yet, within a couple of years, he loved Hal and Richard more than life itself. And, she thought, he finally fell in love with me. And still is.

Silvano was sitting in Deli-Calzone, near the British Museum, drinking coffee. He'd been there for fifteen minutes and his brother was late. He made a conscious effort to banish his irritation. If he was to get his message across he must stay friendly and cool.

Suddenly Mario was breezing in, all smiles, no apology. Silvano signalled for two more coffees and Mario sat down, immediately swinging away from him to look at the shop's counter, stuffed with Italian delicacies. Silvano followed his gaze. Behind the overloaded display cases were boxes of pannetoni, tied in Christmas ribbon, piled high. His mother had insisted they import them from Milan and try to persuade the English that they were better than mince pies or English Christmas cake.

He breathed in with pleasure. 'Smells like the real thing, doesn't it? Coffee, garlic, salami. Italy should give Laura a medal, don't you think?'

'And she's not even Italian. Giovanni must have taught her well.' He followed Mario's gaze. 'But this place only just breaks even. It makes half the sales of the King's Road.'

Mario blew on his espresso. 'So, brother, you didn't get me out of bed to talk sales returns, I'm sure. What's up?'

'Actually, it's Laura.'

'What about her?'

'I just want to warn you, bro. Lovely aunt that she is, Laura is a tough professional, and she's a lioness when it comes to her babies. Both of them.'

'Both of them?'

'The new restaurant is her baby too.' Silvano spoke gently. He didn't want a Mario-outburst. 'She'll do whatever it takes to make Giovanni's exactly as she wants it. And if you go in for any more DIY design, or reckon you can break her rules because you're family, you'll be out on your ear.'

'I got that message last night.' Mario laughed. 'Don't worry, I'll do as instructed. Though she was so unkind about my beautiful vines in the bar. All those empty walls are so cold.'

16

'They're *her* walls. And now to her other cub, the beautiful Angelica.'

'Well?'

'If you value your job you'll stop flirting with her. She's only seventeen, much too young for you. But even if she was twenty-four, she'd still be the boss's daughter and out of bounds.'

'Oh, Silvano, it's only a bit of fun and Laura doesn't mind.'

'That's not the point. The point is, Angelica is young enough to take you seriously. She might get hurt.' As he said this, Silvano suddenly realized it was true. Angelica might fall for the handsome Mario. The thought was uncomfortable and he pushed it away.

Mario might have read his mind. 'Hah! You're jealous, aren't you? I've seen you looking at Angelica. Just because you haven't asked her out, I don't see why I shouldn't. She's pretty and good fun. Maybe I—'

'Don't you dare.' With an effort Silvano kept his voice level. 'I can promise you one thing. If any of us – and there's a dozen young cooks and waiters drooling over her – makes a move, Laura will sack him.'

The next morning, Laura took her mother and Sophie to Deli-Calzone in the King's Road for breakfast. She felt guilty about Maud: what with the business, Angelica becoming an increasing handful and Giovanni's, she'd not been down to Chorlton for months. And it was only four years since her father had died. Maud never complained and was always cheerful so Laura had told herself that her mother was fine. Anyway, she lived at her beloved Chorlton with David, Sophie and the twins. But she was still suffering. When Maud thought she was alone, the sadness in her face told the truth.

Laura was proud of Deli-Calzone's new Gaggia machine, and insisted her mother try a cappuccino rather than her usual tea. For herself she ordered an espresso, and they all plumped for scrambled eggs, mushrooms and crisply fried pancetta. All delicious.

'You must try our English-Italian compromise, Mum. Carlotta is on a mission to convert the English to Italian bread and cake. But since our customers can't do without toast and marmalade for breakfast all the Calzones serve toasted panettone with butter and marmalade.

'Goodness darling, I can't keep up with you and Giovanni.' Maud looked at the logo on the menu. 'What's a Deli-Calzone? I thought they were all called Calzone. Is there a difference?'

'Sure there is. The Calzones are straightforward Italian coffee shops. You know, like the first one in Billingsgate. Basically a coffee bar, but with table service and simple meals served all day. The Deli-Calzones are smarter. Similar menu, but open in the evenings, licensed – we sell a lot of Italian wine – and with a food shop at the front. Like here.' She pointed towards the entrance, where the stacked breads and cakes, the chilled cabinets of takeaway dishes and cheese, the wine bottles, the hanging salamis and strings of garlic had already attracted a little queue of shoppers.

'And how many are there? I lost count ages ago.'

'We'll open our fourteenth Calzone, in Dulwich, next month."

They were soon talking about Giovanni's and last night's dinner again. 'I'm so proud of you, darling,' said Maud, 'and your father would be too.'

'I do so wish he'd been there. Even though he's gone, I still want to please him. Last night, standing at the door watching customers streaming in, I was thinking, There you are, Dad! We aren't useless. And Giovanni's a wonderful husband. Childish, isn't it?'

Her mother smiled, but sadly. 'No, it's natural. Donald misjudged Giovanni, and was very unkind to you. Of course you'd have liked the chance to prove him wrong. He was jealous, of course, and furious at losing his beloved daughter.' She looked into Laura's eyes. 'Sometimes I wonder why I miss him so much. He was so difficult – proud, intolerant – so *wrong*, and so maddeningly convinced he was right.'

'He loved you, Mummy. Everyone needs someone who loves them more than anyone else. Dad knew you were the anchor in his life, even if he'd never have said it.'

Maud seemed cheered by that. 'Strangely, he did say it – one day when the morphine was working and he was feeling better. It made the next few weeks more bearable for me.'

Her father's lung cancer had spread to his bones and his breathing had become so laboured that Laura could hear its rasping sound as she'd climbed the stairs to his bedroom. Maud, drawn and pale, had hardly left his side. Once Laura had found her in Donald's dressing room, sitting on the single bed there, weeping. She'd sat down beside her, put her arms around her and held her close, conscious of the reversal in their roles. Maud's sniffling had become sobs.

'I can't bear it. He says I have to sleep in here. We've never slept apart, except when we quarrelled. I feel he's banishing me when we need each other most.' Laura had reached over and pulled one of Donald's hankies out of the drawer. Maud had buried her face in it. 'And he won't talk to me. He just turns to the wall. He's cutting me out.'

She'd said, 'Maybe Daddy hasn't the energy to cope with your grief as well as his pain.'

Now her mother went on, 'For two years after he died, it just seemed that all the colour had gone out of my life. I felt so empty, purposeless. But now I find there are some advantages to widowhood.' She smiled. 'Donald was *so* demanding – I seemed to spend all my time trying to please him, reasoning with him or soothing people he'd upset. At least I don't have that any more. And I don't have to starch dress shirts till they're stiff as a board. Or put up with crumbs in the bed.'

They both laughed.

Three nights later the restaurant was packed, the telephone ringing non-stop. There'd been a rave review in the *Evening Standard* and a less excited but still good one in *The Times*. For the sake of a new kitchen brigade still finding its feet, Laura had decided to limit the bookings to one sitting per table, which meant a maximum of about sixty-five covers, and to try to stagger the timings.

The kitchen was running smoothly: no customers were having to wait long, and Laura's rule of no swearing or shouting seemed to be holding. She walked through the two dining rooms to the bar, a now familiar thrill running through her: her own restaurant, as she'd dreamed of it, full, relaxed, convivial.

She took the couple of steps down to the bar and was surprised to see the banquette and both bar tables jammed with people, two more waiting at the bar. Mario was mixing cocktails and Laura went up to him. 'Mario, what are you doing?' she asked quietly. 'We can't take these people. Every table is full.'

'They know that, but they arrived on spec and they're prepared to wait, so I thought, Why not?'

'Because I said no to double booking tables."

'But the kitchen's managing fine, isn't it? You don't want to turn down the business, do you?'

Laura had no option but to leave it. 'We'll talk later. Meanwhile make sure they know they might be in for a long wait.'

At ten o'clock when some diners were leaving, the head waiter Paolo came to collect a foursome from the bar. As they stood to follow him into the dining room, Laura saw one of the men slip Mario a folded note. So that's his game, she thought. She'd already established her no-bribes-for-favours policy and that all tips were to go into the communal *tronc*.

Worse was to come. Back in the dining room, Paolo stopped her. 'Signora, table twelve is refusing to pay. The young lady says she's the daughter of the owner and she doesn't have to pay. I didn't like to tell her I knew she wasn't your daughter. What must I do?'

It could only be Jane. Laura followed him and saw she was right. Jane, Grace's daughter, was obviously tipsy. She waved and called loudly, 'Hello, Auntie Laura. So glad you're here. This fellow' – she waved a hand to indicate Paolo – 'seems to think I should pay for our dinner.'

'And don't you think you should?' Laura kept her voice mild, but firm.

'Of course not. owns this place. I know it's called Giovanni's, but who put up the money? Certainly not Giovanni.' She turned to Paolo. 'My father is the Earl of Frampton. Daddy owns this establishment. I'm not paying that bill.'

Laura was torn between laughter at Jane's pomposity and

anger at her attitude to Giovanni and rudeness to Paolo. One of Jane's guests tried to intervene but Laura cut him short, speaking in a straightforward polite tone so as not to ignite Jane's famous temper: 'Jane, let's not have a scene. It won't look good for you in the William Hickey column, and I hate scenes in restaurants, don't you? George hasn't said anything about paying your bills, but I'll tell you what we'll do. You just sign the bill and we'll sort it out in the morning.'

'Why should I?'

The young man intervened again: 'Jane, just sign it. Then we'll go on to Annabel's and dance. I can get us in, I'm sure.' So Jane, with a theatrical sigh, signed the bill.

Laura watched her leave, and found herself feeling both irritated and sorry for her. Jane had everything money could buy, but she was unhappy. Although she was in her mid-twenties, she'd never had a proper job or a serious boyfriend, and Laura suspected her friends were mostly spongers. Hugh, Laura's much older brother, had married the scatter-brained art student, Grace, before the war and Jane had been born in 1940. But he had been a bomber pilot and was shot down over the Channel when Jane was still a toddler. Grace had indulged her every whim, seldom corrected her and allowed her to grow up believing herself the centre of the universe. And when Grace and George had married, the future Earl of Frampton adopted Jane, and made her his heir. Her self-importance increased with every passing year. What she needs, thought Laura, is to suffer a knock or two that would teach her a little humility.

Next day, when the waiters were laying up for the lunch service, George came in to see Giovanni and Laura. 'Well, you clever things,' he said. 'If you go on like this, Giovanni's could be our best investment yet. Congratulations.'

Laura reached up to kiss his cheek. 'And to you, darling George. None of it would have happened without you.'

They sat down at a table in the bar. When the Gaggia – the success of the first in Deli-Calzone had spawned requests for one from all the managers – had gone through its gurgling and hissing routine and they each had a cup of espresso in front of them, Laura told him about the fracas with Jane. His forehead rumpled in an anxious frown. 'I'm so sorry, Laura. That girl seems to be having a late adolescence. She's always been difficult, very demanding, but as a child she did apply herself to her riding and studies. She excelled at school and Oxford. Now she does nothing but spend money, drink and dance.'

'Daughters are hard work,' said Giovanni. 'Our Angelica would be down the King's Road every night if she could be. And she's only seventeen.'

'Maybe Jane needs a husband to keep her in order,' George went on. 'God knows Grace and I are hopeless at it. She runs rings round us both.'

'Or maybe she needs a job,' said Laura. 'You should make her earn her living, George.'

He smiled. 'Too late for that, I'm afraid. I set up a trust for her years ago. Since her twenty-first birthday she's been independent – she's got quite enough money not to work at all, and certainly to pay her restaurant bills. She was probably just showing off last night.'

George promised he'd get Jane to settle her bill or would cover it himself. He refused another cup of coffee and left for the City, looking, thought Laura, unusually sad.

*

'Poor man,' Giovanni said. 'I know how he feels.'

'What do you mean? You're not really worried about Angelica, are you? Isn't she just being a normal teenager?'

'Well, if it's normal for her to rebel, wear skirts that barely cover her bottom and play pop music at full volume, it's also normal for her father to object, isn't it?'

Laura laughed. 'I suppose so. But she's a good girl, really. She works six days for Carlotta, and does three nights on Reception. I'm worried she'll wear herself out.'

'*Cara*, she has the energy of youth. Too much of it. Last night she wanted to go to a club with Mario after the restaurant closed. I'm not having that! She's too young for nightclubs and he's too old and unreliable to take her.'

'You didn't tell me. That explains why she was so sulky on the way home.'

That afternoon Laura lay in her bath, grabbing an hour for herself before the evening service. She poured an extravagant splash of Wiberg essence into the bath and watched the water go a milky green, then lay back and closed her eyes, the better to smell the heady scent of pine.

She wanted to relax, enjoy this brief moment, but something was scratching at her mind. She supposed it was Giovanni's anxiety about their daughter. Well, Angelica was never going to be easy. She had inherited Giovanni's determination and was as emotional as both her parents. But she was also hardworking, beautiful and enthusiastic. They were lucky. Imagine having spoilt Jane as a daughter.

If she was honest with herself, though, it wasn't Angelica who was troubling her but Angelica's brother, the baby she had given away. She didn't think of him as much now as she used to years ago when she'd had to find somewhere dark where she could be alone to weep.

The worst of it was that she'd had to hide her unhappiness from Giovanni, who had long ago forgiven her for giving up their son without consulting him or adequately explaining why she'd done so. She'd told him it was because they were penniless, homeless and couldn't look after him, all of which was true. She hadn't told him that she feared the baby wasn't his.

That baby boy would be eighteen now. She imagined a young man in his prime, the apple of his father's eye, learning the business at Giovanni's side. Tears trickled down her cheeks and she sank under the green water. Then she surfaced, shampooed her hair, rinsed it under the hand shower, stepped out of the bath, towelled herself and switched on the hair dryer. No more thinking, she told herself. It's bad for you.

Angelica was helping Carlotta fold thin circles of pasta round tiny blobs of nutmeg-seasoned ricotta and spinach to make tortellini. She could do it almost as fast as Carlotta now, but she had to concentrate. Carlotta didn't even watch her hands, chatting happily while the tray of tortellini filled, and the bowl of ricotta emptied. 'They're also called Venus's navels, and you can see why,' she said.

'I love that. In my Larousse, there are lots of funny names. Like *negresse en chemise*, which is a chocolate pudding half covered with cream. And *poulet crapaudine* for a spatchcocked chicken – it does look a bit like a toad.'

'Larousse? Are you deserting our Italian cooking for French, *cara*?'

25

'I think I am, Aunt Carlotta. I love our food but I want to learn French cuisine too. It seems more sophisticated, more delicate.' She was talking fast now, increasingly earnest. 'And I think to get on in the restaurant trade you need to be able to cook French. I want to work for Paul Bocuse more than anything in the world.'

'Paul Bocuse? In Lyon? You want to go to France?'

'Oh, yes! He's the best chef in the world. I wonder if Papa would let me do a *stage* with Bocuse?'

'I don't think so, *cara*. He's very proud of you, but I don't think he'd see the need for you to train in French cooking. Anyway, sweetheart, Bocuse wouldn't have you. Those top French restaurants don't employ women except to peel potatoes.'

'Why not?'

'It's the same here. Same in Italy. There are women cooks, good ones, all over Europe. But they're in family places. The top restaurants and hotels, where the grandest cooking goes on, those kitchens are men only.'

'I don't believe it! How am I to learn then?'

'If you really want to learn French cooking you could go to the École Gastronomique. It's a cooking school in Paris. They take girls. But it would cost a fortune. I doubt Giovanni would agree.'

They worked in silence for a while, shaping the tortellini. 'Aunt Carlotta,' Angelica said, 'you've got to help me persuade Papa. I *will* go to that cooking school, and then I'll work in a top restaurant. I'll *make* them give me a job.'

Carlotta looked at her. 'Ah, you're your father's daughter, so determined. But you're far too young to live in Paris on your own. In a few years, if you are still obsessed with *la cuisine française*, then I'll try to talk him into letting you go.'

'But, Aunt—'

'*Basta*, Angelica. Enough. Now go fetch the porcini for the tagliatelle.'

Angelica adored her cousins, especially Mario, who was livelier than Silvano. When they'd been little his teasing had made her cry and Carlotta would clip him round the ear. But now, even though she was younger than him, she could give as good as she got, and Mario treated her as a grown-up. Well, most of the time.

He was good-looking too. Her school friends mooned over him as if he were a film star. They envied how she lived, with her cousins in the Paddington mews. Her father was part-owner of the row of seven cottages. When she was little she and her parents had lived in two of them, knocked together, and rented out the rest. But gradually the family expanded down the mews. Papa had his office in one cottage and when her Italian cousins moved in next door, they created a great big ground floor kitchen. Her uncle David's family rented the smallest house as a *pied a terre* and everyone met in the kitchen, often including Italian apprentices living in the attic. Once Mario had made pizza for Angelica and her friends, who had never forgotten it. They were always angling for a repeat invitation. Sometimes, walking with him in the street, Angelica liked to pretend that he was her boyfriend.

One Saturday at breakfast, he said, 'Angelica, would you like to go to the King's Road or Carnaby Street this afternoon?'

Her father frowned, so she jumped in quickly. 'That'd be fun. I'd love to.' She got up and kissed her father's bald patch. 'Don't worry, Papa, I'm seventeen and he's my cousin. You can hardly object to that, can you?'

Her mother cut in. 'Mario, you'll look after her properly. No nonsense.'

They came out of the tube at Sloane Square and walked down the King's Road, past the Deli-Calzone and on towards the trendy shops. Strolling along the pavement, trailing through the stores, marvelling at the psychedelic fabrics and the diaphanous skirts was fun. She was carefree, hanging loose, doing her own thing.

Angelica gazed with longing at the high white plastic boots, laced in black to the knee, the miniskirts and tight tank tops, the pictures of models with dark eyes and pale lipstick. Mario flipped through Beatles-style jackets in Burton's and tried on shoes in Russell & Bromley. They couldn't afford to buy anything, but that didn't stop them browsing.

Mario encouraged Angelica to try on a Foale & Tuffin trouser suit. The Nehru jacket was long, in a dark green fabric and lined with peacock satin, light as air. The matching trousers were narrow, flaring slightly over her boots. The jacket slithered on and fitted perfectly. She looked like a model, she thought. Her hair, short at the back, longer at her cheeks, was sleek and sophisticated and her eyes glittered. And she wanted that suit.

Mario stood behind her, appraising her in the mirror. 'So grown-up and trendy,' he said. 'You look great.'

But she couldn't afford it.

When the shops started to close they went into the Chelsea Potter where they met two of Mario's friends, Dan and Ronald. The men drank beer and Angelica asked for Babycham. She didn't like it but didn't want to admit it. At home she was often offered a glass of red wine, and indeed had been drinking it watered down since she was about twelve. She found Babycham, which wasn't wine, rather sweet.

Angelica felt very grown-up surrounded by three men, all older than her. At about nine, they left the pub together, a little wobbly. She and Mario walked with the two young men to their basement flat off Flood Street. 'There's nothing to eat,' said Ronald, 'but I think we've got some beer.'

There were only two rooms, both bedsits. Dan's had two mattresses on the floor and an open wardrobe with clothes falling out of it. A portable record player sat in the corner and Dan took charge of the music. There were Beatles, Rolling Stones and Seekers albums, and a stack of singles, few of them in covers.

'Ooh!' Angelica exclaimed. 'You've got this! They're great, aren't they?' She handed him a single. 'Can we have it? I love it.'

He looked at the cover. 'Sure,' he said, slipping off the cover. 'Procul Harum. And as it's brand new, maybe I'll change the needle.'

He scrabbled around in the pile of records and found the box of needles. Moments later 'A Whiter Shade of Pale' filled the room. Angelica leaned against the wall and closed her eyes to enjoy it.

As the record ended, she opened her eyes to see Ronald bringing in a crate of Fuller's beer and passing Mario a packet of tobacco with a small canvas bag. Mario squared his back against the wall and opened his legs wide so he could tip out the contents of the bag onto the carpet between them. There was a packet of cigarette papers, a little Rizla roller, two soup spoons, and various little packages, one wrapped in foil. To this pile he added his cigarettes and lighter.

Angelica was now nervous, but determined not to show it.

Obviously they were going to smoke marijuana, and she'd be offered some. She'd never had a joint and didn't want to look like a baby.

'Don't worry, babe, it's only a spliff. Mostly tobacco with a little bit of hash. You don't have to have any. But don't tell Mamma! Your mamma or mine.' He laughed and Angelica felt reassured. Maybe the Babycham helped. She began to relax, but she couldn't take her eyes off his preparations.

He removed the foil from the tiny package. 'Got to warm it up first, otherwise it's rock hard,' he said, putting the small brown lump, like a toffee, into one of the soup spoons, and warming it with his lighter. Then he used the second spoon to crush the hash and his fingers to rub it all to fine crumbs. It's like cooking, she thought.

He fitted first a cigarette paper, then a filter tip, into the Rizla roller, broke open one of his Gauloises cigarettes and teased the packed tobacco into loose strands. He used it to fill the roller, then sprinkled crumbs of hash evenly on top and tamped the mix down firmly. Angelica watched as he carefully licked along the edge of the paper. He must have felt her eyes on him because he looked up and smiled at her as he turned the roller to make the cigarette. It looked just like an ordinary one.

The whole process was efficiently and neatly done. He's very practised, she thought, but I've never seen him do this at home. Too scared of Carlotta, I suppose.

Mario lit the cigarette, took a deep drag, eyes closed, then passed it round. The men took it in turns, pulling on the cigarette and holding the smoke in their lungs for a few seconds. Dan passed it to Angelica without comment. She had smoked a few fags in her time – most of the girls smoked intermittently at school – and she knew not to inhale too hard for fear of coughing.

Gradually the four of them spoke less as they smoked and the music seemed to Angelica to fill her head. She had never thought much of Tom Jones's 'It's Not Unusual', but now it sounded like a magical anthem. She felt utterly content and rather sleepy. She smiled at Mario. He seemed very glamorous with his tousled hair and dark good looks. She wondered what it would be like to be kissed by him. But he was in a world of his own.

At some point he staggered off and Angelica wondered vaguely where he'd gone. She wasn't worried – in fact, she felt adult and confident. She and Mario's friends, whose names she couldn't remember, shared another spliff and one turned on the television. The black-and-white picture stuttered into life to reveal a pair of ballet dancers. The little dancing figures were magically beautiful. She'd never been to a ballet and didn't listen to classical music, but now she suddenly understood. The ballerina seemed light as air as her partner effortlessly lifted her over his head. Angelica felt she *was* that ballerina: it was *her* back arched over his arms, *her* head thrown back, *her* arms and legs making perfect patterns in the air. As he slowly brought her down, she melted into him like cream into coffee.

Sometime later, Mario returned with hot dogs. The smell made Angelica realize how hungry she was.

'Oh, this is delicious,' she said, her mouth full. 'Where did you get them?'

'From that stall outside the nightclub. He does a roaring trade with late-night revellers.'

'I've never had such a delicious hot dog in my life. I can't believe it.'

Mario laughed. 'I'm surprised you've had one at all. I never had one till I was old enough to escape Mamma's home cooking. These aren't really that good. It's just that hash makes everything taste better.'

Angelica had no idea what time it was when they got home. Her father and Carlotta met them in the hall. They were both furious. Her aunt, who hardly came up to Mario's shoulder, nevertheless took him by the lapels and shook him. 'You idiot, Mario! What do you think you were doing? Giovanni has been half mad with worry. Angelica is a child. She's still at school.' She reached her face up close to his, then pushed him away. 'And you've been drinking. Angelica is under age. Have you taken her to a pub?'

Giovanni grabbed Angelica's arm and pulled her into the kitchen, where her mother was sitting at the table, her head in her hands. She turned as the door opened and leaped up. Then both her parents were shouting at her.

Angelica couldn't quite take it all in. She was looking at them as if through gauze. She could see they were both really upset, but she had to force herself to explain that she wasn't a child, that it wasn't a big deal. Nothing terrible had happened. They'd just had a beer or two and some hot dogs and watched television. But she didn't want to fight. Sleep was what she needed.

Her mother marched her up to her room, prodding her back as she climbed the stairs. 'No, you don't,' she said, as Angelica flopped onto the bed. 'Get undressed first.' She pulled her daughter into a sitting position and tossed her pyjamas at her. 'I'll be back in a minute.'

Laura, at first sick with worry, then furious, was now struggling not to be sympathetic. Poor Angelica – she'd not done anything too disastrous, and everyone had to have a first time when they drank too much. Mario was the real culprit. Persuading Angelica to stay out late was typically irresponsible. He could at least have telephoned.

She fetched a bucket. When she got back to Angelica's bedroom, the girl hadn't moved. She looked so forlorn and young, like a chastised waif, sitting there. But she hardened her heart. She put the bucket by the bed. 'If you're sick, make sure it's in the bucket,' she said. Then she helped her daughter to undress, but not tenderly. I'm behaving like a gaoler, she thought.

She went downstairs. 'Right, that's it,' she said to Giovanni. 'Mario can go and live with one of his no-good friends. I'm not having him in my restaurant or in this house another night.'

CHAPTER THREE

For months Angelica had pestered her parents to let her go to the École Gastronomique in Paris, but they remained adamant that she was too young. Then, suddenly, they relented, announcing that now she was eighteen she could go.

She knew it wasn't Aunt Carlotta's support of the idea that had changed her father's mind. He wanted to get her away from Mario. Ever since the day they'd gone window-shopping in the King's Road, she'd been spending her free time with him and his friends. They were all older than her, Mario's age, and most of them didn't have proper jobs, but they knew how to have fun. They lived a wonderfully free and easy life. When they had money, they went bowling, skating or drinking, and when they didn't, they sat around smoking pot while Mario played his guitar and sang, or they would listen to records. Then they'd gone to a Hollies concert, got rather high and drunk, and Angelica had fallen asleep in someone's flat. For Giovanni that had been the last straw. Carlotta had sent Silvano to track them down, and when Angelica had got home, her father had gone on as if the sky had fallen in: she was keeping bad company, he'd shouted, Mario was a bad influence, she was irresponsible, they both wore ridiculous clothes and . . . He'd gone on and on. And then one morning he'd announced that they'd enrolled her in the École Gastronomique and she'd be going to Paris after Christmas.

She couldn't believe her luck. Laura found her a room in a flat near the school, and off she went, nervous but excited.

At first she saw little of the city, just the bit between her room off the Avenue George V, and the school. Even that was a delight. Paris smelt nothing like London. The aroma of roasting almonds or frying pancakes would hit her as she walked past street vendors, the warmth and smell of Gauloises and garlic would envelop her as she stepped down into the Métro. The weather was bitterly cold, but the air was clear and crisp, and she could hardly believe she was seeing the Arc de Triomphe, the Place de la Concorde and Les Invalides almost every day. She loved wandering through Prisunic where everything seemed so desirable and cheap. On her first weekend, when there was no school, she'd eaten at a Self, joining the self-service queue to select little plates of grated carrot, radishes with butter, or cooked leeks doused in French dressing. It was all fascinating, and so different from London.

She fell in love with Paris, but things started badly at the École. She didn't like her tutor, Chef Berger. He barked orders in French and ridiculed the students, many of whom were foreigners and didn't understand when they got things wrong. She was homesick too, but she didn't admit that to her parents.

On her second week, she had her first confrontation with Chef Berger. 'What are you doing in my advanced class?' he wanted to know. 'You are just a spoilt little English girl, who knows nothing about cooking. No one in England knows how to cook. The food it is *dégoûtant* in your country.'

35

Anger overcame fear. 'Chef, I am half Italian. And I was accepted on the course because I have cooked with my mother, my father and my aunt who are all restaurant chefs.'

Chef Berger glared at her, then walked very slowly towards her, his eyes popping with anger. 'Mademoiselle, the first thing you must learn in a French kitchen is that the only answer, the *only* answer, you give to the chef, is "*Oui, Chef.*" Nothing else.' Angelica's heart quailed but she met his gaze, her chin up. '*Comprenez-vous?*'

'*Oui.*'

'*Quoi?*'

'*Oui, Chef.*'

Later that week, she split her mayonnaise, and he reduced her to tears. It was shameful – she had to run out of the kitchen and blub in the loo. But then she'd dried her eyes, summoned her courage by glaring at herself in the mirror, and returned to the kitchen.

Chef Berger straightened up and put his hands on his hips. 'Ah, so *la petite madame* has deigned to return. Well, shall we see if she can manage a mayonnaise without curdling it?' He turned to the other students, who were keeping their eyes down. 'Mademoiselle Angélique, go and fetch more eggs and start again. And don't split it this time.'

He was speaking French, and though Angelica understood perfectly, she answered in English: 'Chef, if you won't tell me what I did wrong, I will probably do it wrong again.'

'Are you telling me how to teach, young lady?' He strode towards her.

She stood her ground. 'If the cap fits, wear it,' she said.

Chef Berger didn't understand this. '*En français, Mademoiselle,*' he barked. 'This is a French kitchen.'

Angelica did not know how to say it in French and, anyway, she was losing courage. She lowered her eyes. He turned away with a shrug.

When Angelica had fetched the eggs and oil and returned to her station, Chef Berger was waiting for her. He thrust a large white soup plate towards her and dropped a fork into it. 'You will make the mayonnaise with these,' he said. 'And make sure you do not waste this abomination.' He indicated her bowl of curdled mayonnaise.

'What do you mean? I don't understand.'

He gave a slow shrug, half closing his eyes in contempt, and walked away.

Angelica, close to tears, was wondering where to begin, when the star of the class, French-Canadian Nicole, put an arm round her shoulders. 'Don't let him upset you. He's a brute.'

'But what does he mean? With the fork and plate? And not wasting this disaster?' She tipped the bowl with the separated oil and egg to show Nicole. 'And I still don't know why it curdled.'

'You probably added the oil too fast.' She followed Berger's progress through the kitchen. 'Look, he's going off to the staff room – probably to put a slug of brandy in his coffee. He drinks, you know. Come on, I'll help you.'

She separated two eggs, took the whisk out of Angelica's failed mayonnaise, and started to whisk the new yolks. 'I know,' she said, 'how we can speed things up.' She reached for the Dijon mustard and put a good teaspoon into the yolks. 'We need an emulsion and the mustard will thicken it.'

'But won't it taste too mustardy?'

'Not if we incorporate the curdled mayonnaise too. You hadn't put any mustard in that, had you? '

37

Angelica shook her head.

'Right. Now, you whisk like the devil and I'll add the oil.'

In a few minutes Angelica had a thick yellow sauce, which enveloped the thin ribbon of oil as it hit the mixture.

'Why did he tell me to use a soup plate and fork?'

'Because he's a bastard. It's obviously easier with a whisk and bowl and he wants to make it hard. He made one of the girls in the other class whisk egg whites and sugar for meringue in a soup plate with a fork. It was impossible. She quit after twenty minutes.'

They'd just got all the oil in, when Nicole looked across the kitchen.

'Damn, he's back.' She took the bowl and rapidly scraped the mixture into the soup plate. 'Grab the fork and keep going,' she whispered. 'Add the curdled stuff in teaspoons, whisking them in one by one.'

When Berger got back to Angelica, whom he'd studiously ignored as he made his rounds through the nervous students, Nicole was back at her own workbench and Angelica was spooning the last blobs of separated mixture into the soup plate, and incorporating it with a fork.

'Well, I see you have succeeded this time,' he said. He stuck his finger into the mixture and then into his mouth. Angelica winced as the finger disappeared between moist red lips surrounded by a full moustache and beard. 'You need pepper, salt, a little vinegar,' he said. 'Otherwise it is not bad.'

It was all she could do to stop herself shouting that her success was no thanks to him: Nicole had shown her what to do. She also wanted to tell him that she thought cooking schools were supposed to care about hygiene, and chef-tutors to set a good example, not stick the same much-licked but unwashed finger into successive bowls of mayonnaise.

That evening she risked the irritation of her landlady and made a reverse-charge call to her mother. Laura was sympathetic, but said, 'Darling, it's a simple choice. Is it going to be worth it? Never mind the tutor. He sounds like a horrible man. But are you learning anything? New ingredients? New techniques? Classic French cooking? Is your French improving? Are you learning to manage on your own? To love Paris? All these would be reasons to stick it out.'

So she went back to school and from then on things got better. Berger, seeing that she wasn't going to burst into tears any more, stopped tormenting her. Nicole became a good friend and they spent weekends discovering the city, and evenings hanging out in the cafés and clubs.

Then, when they were six weeks into the term, Nicole had a telegram from her mother summoning her home to Montréal – her father was ill.

Almost at once, Angelica's homesickness returned. Nicole's friendship had kept it at bay but now she longed for her mother, for Aunt Carlotta's kitchen where everyone was nice to her, for her father's powerful tenor belting out Italian opera, even for her cousins' teasing. She wanted to be at home in Paddington, with her family.

And then, one day two months into the term, as she came out of school for her lunch break and set off down the Rue du Faubourg Saint-Honoré, she heard a voice behind her: 'Angelica, *cara mia, come stai?*'

She swung round. 'Mario!' He picked her up and whirled her about. Oh, it was wonderful to be hugged, to hear Italian, to see the affection in his eyes.

'Angelica, you're so grown-up!' He stepped back and held her away from him. 'Like a film star.'

Angelica realized that they were in the way of an elderly couple who were standing patiently on the pavement, waiting to get past.

'*Oh, pardon, Madame, Monsieur.*' She stepped back, pulling Mario with her.

'*Non, ça ne fait rien, Mademoiselle,*' said the man. 'At my age it is the greatest pleasure to see young people in love.'

Mario, smiling broadly, stepped back and gave a slight bow. 'She is beautiful, is she not?'

'She is. You are a lucky young man.'

The little incident was over in a flash, but it delighted Angelica. That the couple had thought they were lovers was funny, and their friendliness and goodwill, on top of the surprise arrival of Mario, had her laughing like an excited child.

Mario hugged her to his side as they walked on. They passed a café with pavement tables and he slid into a chair, pulling her down beside him. 'What shall we have? Champagne?'

'Champagne? You're mad, Mario. This is the Rue du Faubourg Saint-Honoré. It will cost the earth.'

But Mario was ordering two glasses. Angelica studied his profile as he looked up at the waiter: olive skin, unruly dark hair, wide smile. God, he's handsome, she thought.

Mario swivelled in his chair, looking left and right down the street, his face animated and joyful. Then he fixed his eyes on hers, saying nothing. It was intoxicating.

She shook her head, dispelling his hold on her. 'Why are you here, Mario? What are you doing? Why didn't you tell me you were coming?'

'Oh, it's a long story. You remember your mamma kicked me out of the house and sacked me after that night I brought you home so late? Well, your father was a bit more sympathetic and slipped me a bit of cash. But then I got a job for Nice Cream, selling their stuff from a van. Giovanni went through the roof. He says they're frauds, they don't make real ice cream, et cetera. He couldn't bear me to be working for a rival, I suppose. Anyway, it was OK until last week when I got done for not having a driving licence.'

'Oh, Mario, really! But surely . . .'

'No one ever asked, so I didn't tell them I'd never taken the test. And then the guys I shared a house with kicked me out because I was a few weeks late with the rent.' He grinned. 'So I thought I'd try my luck in France. Follow the girl of my dreams to Gay Paree. I knew I'd find you at the school.'

'That last bit's not true.'

'It is, *bella* Angelica. But better not tell your mamma. She'll kill us both. I think she sent you here to get away from me, don't you?'

'I wanted to come. I've been pleading with her and Papa for ages to let me learn French cooking in Paris.' But she knew that Mario was right too: her parents did want to separate them. 'Anyway, you must know that some of your troubles are your own fault. I mean, why couldn't you pay your rent? It's not as though you didn't have a job.'

'It's the same old story, Angelica. Mario the irresponsible one. Charming, but useless.'

'Irresponsible, yes,' Angelica was smiling, 'but who says you're charming?'

'I do. And you agree. I know you do. Now, *cara mia*, what are we going to do this afternoon?'

'I have to go back to school,' she said. 'Pastry class.'

'OK. But shall we have lunch? I'm starving.'

'I've had mine. We made navarin of lamb this morning – we eat what we cook so I had that, followed by ginger ice cream, which we made yesterday.'

'Were they good? Are you becoming a proper French cook? Forgetting about your Italian roots?'

He was teasing her, but she was enjoying it. As a child, she'd found his joking hurtful. When she'd begun working in the business, it had seemed comradely. But now it was different.

As his questions multiplied, she saw that he really was interested in her life in Paris, in her school, in her. Something had changed in his attitude towards her.

Between mouthfuls of *croque monsieur*, Mario continued his questions. Did she like her landlady? Who were her friends? Did she have a boyfriend?

She laughed at that. 'No, but I'm determined to find a French one. That's the quickest way to perfect the language. But I never meet any French people. Only the teachers and my landlady, and she barely speaks to me. All the students are foreign, and most of them are girls.'

She found herself telling him about the horrible tutor, Chef Berger, and about Nicole going back to Canada. Mario listened attentively, his brown eyes fixed steadily on hers. She talked on, telling him how homesick she was, but not wanting to give up. 'If it wasn't for Chef Berger, I'd really enjoy the cooking.'

'Poor darling,' he said. 'You must be so lonely.' He pushed Angelica's hair off her face, and his touch generated a charge down her cheek. She looked up at him in surprise, wondering if he'd felt it too.

He took her hand across the table. 'You can't go back to school,' he said. 'I can't bear to let you go.'

She couldn't look away – didn't want to. His whole face was alive with excitement, his eyes holding hers, his mouth smiling broadly, showing white, not-quite-perfect teeth. It crossed Angelica's mind that if they'd been even and straight, like a toothpaste advertisement, she'd have been able to resist him. But one of his front teeth was chipped, and its neighbour a little askew. Oh, God, she thought, he's my *cousin*. Practically my brother. I shouldn't feel like this about him.

She remembered when they'd sat in his friends' flat in Chelsea, smoking pot, a year ago now, and she'd wanted him to kiss her. But he'd gone out and bought hot dogs. And now: I think he'll kiss me today.

As he paid the waiter, Angelica had a moment to decide. Was she going to skip the afternoon's pastry class? Of course she was. How often does your handsome cousin come to Paris?

43

CHAPTER FOUR

A month later, Angelica was sure she was in love, and that she'd always been half in love with Mario. As a little girl her father had teased her for trailing around after Mario, who used to get irritated and try to shake her off. And there was a photograph of them, when she was about nine and he was perhaps fifteen. In it, they were sitting in a fork of a huge walnut tree at Chorlton and she was gazing up at him with total adoration. As a teenager, she'd gained kudos at school for having such a handsome older cousin. She remembered when he'd made pizzas for her friends: she'd been jealous of the attention he'd paid them. She'd been proud to show him off, but he was hers, not theirs.

Mario was everything and anything a girl could want: fun to be with, generous, exciting, endlessly interesting. Sometimes she told herself it was crazy. How can you fall in love with someone you've known all your life? Especially someone like Mario. Even his mother, Carlotta, said he was lazy, vain, and lived off his charm. And her own mother considered him an untrustworthy chancer.

But they were wrong. Mario was talented. He was full of

ideas and had drive, energy, confidence. Maybe all he needed was someone to believe in him. Since he'd arrived, he'd never been late for his new job, never borrowed a franc from her, always treated her like someone he admired and, yes, perhaps loved.

Maybe it had been irresponsible to jump on a ferry and come to Paris without a bean or a job. But it was admirable too. And he'd landed a job within hours of arriving, and even persuaded his new boss to give him a loan, which he'd paid back out of his first week's wages.

That first afternoon, when she'd decided to skip her pastry class, they'd been walking along the banks of the Seine in the spring sunshine, holding hands. Angelica could feel an under-current of excitement running through her. She suspected Mario felt it too.

'Have you been on one of those tourist boats?' he asked, indicating a red, white and blue barge ploughing slowly up the river.

'I meant to do it with Nicole, but we never got round to it. Also it's been miserable weather. You need a nice day.'

'Like today?'

'Yes!'

They had bought tickets and sat in a row of tourists listening to the commentary as they craned their necks to see the Eiffel Tower, Les Invalides, the Louvre, the bridges. At one point Mario got up to talk to one of the crew, and Angelica leaned her head against the window, letting the thrum of the engines and the drone of the commentary lull her. The April sun's weak warmth was magnified by the glass and made her a little sleepy.

Looking at the mighty buttresses of the cathedral as the boat rounded the end of the Île St Louis, she thought Paris must be the most fascinating and beautiful city in the world. And the most romantic. And here I am, with a handsome man.

When they stepped off the gangway, Mario said, 'Angelica, come, we're going to find me a job. Otherwise I won't be able to pay the youth hostel, and I won't be able to buy my lovely cousin a good dinner.'

'But where? And how are you going to get a job just like that?'

'You'll see.' He laughed. 'Come on.'

They walked up the *quai* to the Bateaux Mouches offices. Angelica watched as Mario responded to a grumpy receptionist with his full-on charm. Within minutes her refusal to let him see anyone without an appointment and a written application had melted. Soon she was laughing and helping him to fill in the form. Mario was flirting with her so outrageously that Angelica wondered how the woman could be unaware that he was playing her like a fish on a hook.

Soon the receptionist went off with his form to find someone more senior to interview him. It didn't take long. She returned and led Mario away while Angelica sat waiting for him, reading a discarded copy of *Le Monde*, pleased that, after two months, she could understand almost all of it.

Eventually Mario had reappeared with a smiling manager behind him. The man bowed them out as if Mario was a valued customer, not a job applicant. 'Tomorrow, then, Mario. And welcome aboard. We're very pleased to have you on the team.'

'How did you do that?' Angelica gasped, as soon as they were out of earshot.

'Oh, he's a nice guy. He gave me a loan. So we can celebrate, I have a job!' Grinning, he had hugged her to him. 'And, of course, he was impressed with my languages. He interviewed me in French and I struggled a bit, but my Italian and English were just what he needed, he said. And he thought I'd charm the passengers.'

'Well, so you would, if buttering up the receptionist is anything to go by!'

'Aha! Do I detect a hint of jealousy?' He pulled her round to face him, looked into her eyes and raised his hands to each side of her face. 'Can I kiss you, little Angelica?'

She didn't answer. She couldn't. Her heart was banging in her chest. He held her gaze and lowered his mouth to hers.

Her eyes fluttered shut. The kiss seem to radiate from her lips through her entire body. He tightened his arms round her and then she was returning his kiss. She wanted it to go on for ever.

Mario spent his days on the boats, ploughing up and down the Seine. At first he'd taken tickets and marshalled the passengers, flirting with the women and joking with the men. He was popular with passengers and crew, and was soon promoted to giving the commentary in English, occasionally in Italian, about the bridges they chugged under and the sights they passed.

Mario's arrival had changed everything for Angelica. Far from being homesick and lonely, she woke every day excited by the knowledge that they'd meet. And Chef Berger had changed his tune. She felt sorry for the poor girl he'd decided to pick on instead, but she was learning French cuisine now with real pleasure.

Mario and Angelica slipped into a routine. Unless Mario was on duty for an evening supper-cruise, which was rare so early in the season, he would meet her as she left school at six o'clock. Then they would explore Paris on foot, a different *arrondissement* every day, stopping for a *tasse du thé* or a glass of wine off the tourist track. They mostly ate dinner in the self-service restaurants catering for students, or they would buy street food: pancakes in the posher areas, couscous in the poorer ones. They sought out cinemas showing *avant garde* movies, like *Jules et Jim* and *À bout de souffle,* and sat at the back, holding hands and kissing. Once they bought tickets to see Juliette Gréco in a nightclub cellar in Saint-Germain-des-Prés. Her huge rich voice reverberated in the tiny space. She sang revolutionary torch songs and sad ballads that had the audience mesmerized, then on their feet yelling and clapping. Hidden at the back with all the attention of the audience on the little stage, Mario and Angelica were wrapped in each other's arms. She thought she might faint from the bliss of it: the freedom to behave badly in public was intoxicating, the mood of yearning engendered by the music somehow translated into longing for each other.

At weekends, if Mario had a day off, they mooched around the galleries, drifted through the second-hand bookstalls and bird market on the banks of the Seine, or trawled the flea markets for hippie clothes: sequinned waistcoats, stone-washed jeans and Day-Glo trousers for Mario, drifting Indian-cotton skirts and cheap beads for Angelica.

Angelica said nothing to her parents about Mario's presence. He had told his mother he was going to the South of France, to try busking on the beaches with his guitar. He'd said there was no point in her trying to write to him because he would be moving around. He'd ring her up sometimes, he said – don't worry.

Angelica didn't like deceiving her mother, but if she told her about Mario, she'd be summoned home at once. Laura wouldn't

48

see that Mario was showing her a better way to live, not worrying all the time about money, work and the future, but rather enjoying the present. Anyway, they hadn't done anything wrong. Of course Mamma would consider smoking a joint in a basement dive a major crime, but that generation was hopelessly out of date. They saw the freedom and generosity of spirit of the 'hippie generation' as selfish irresponsibility.

Sometimes Angelica daydreamed about Mario asking her to marry him: her parents would reconcile with him, and Carlotta would be delighted. But she also loved the notion of the two of them living in sin, like true Bohemians, in a garret on the Left Bank, happily ignoring all disapproval.

It was only lack of opportunity that prevented them sleeping together, she knew. Mario was in a hostel and her landlady had eyes like a hawk. They did a lot of kissing – in the Métro, in dark corners, on park benches if it was warm enough. He would turn her to face him, hold her head in his hands and slowly put his mouth to hers. He'd kiss her very gently, his lips barely touching hers, and she'd feel faint with desire. She'd try to press into his face, to make him kiss her harder, but he would prevent this, holding her head still and tormenting her with fluttery kisses.

Sometimes he'd unbutton her coat and slip his arms right round her, and kiss her hard and deeply, then press his face into her neck, run his strong hands up her body under her blouse, cup her breast and squeeze the breath out of her. She would feel him losing control and she'd want to join him, just let go. At those times, pulling apart was almost impossible. Once, in the Parc Monceau, when they were sitting side by side on their coats on the slightly damp grass, he stretched out on his back and closed his eyes. The sight of him lying there, laid out like an offering, was irresistible. She looked around the park but there was no one in sight so she snuggled down next to him, her head in the crook of his arm.

At first Mario lay still, as though unaware of her body along-side his. Then suddenly he rolled towards her and a second later he was on top of her, the weight of his chest taken by his arms at either side of her, his lower body and legs pressing into her belly and thighs. 'Angelica, we have to make love. I can't go on wanting you so badly. And you want it too. Don't you, my darling?'

'But I can't. You know I can't.'

He kissed her nose. 'Yes, you can. You can do anything you want.'

'But no one has any respect for girls who do it before marriage. You wouldn't think the same of me, have any respect for me afterwards, would you?'

He rolled off her. 'Oh, *cara*, that's such nonsense. Of course I would. I love you.'

'Do you? Really?' He'd never said it before.

'Yes, I do,' he said, 'and if it matters so much to you, we can get married. Let's get a room together. Then we can lie in bed, our bed, all day, and you needn't worry about your reputation!' Now he was laughing, and Angelica was suddenly angry.

'Don't laugh at me, Mario! It's not something to laugh about. It may not be serious to you, but it's very serious to me.' She felt tears coming, and blurted out, 'And don't pretend you want to marry me just because you want to sleep with me!'

'*Cara, cara!* Don't be silly.'

'I'm not being silly!' Angelica was shouting now. 'For men sleeping with a woman is nothing, you probably do it all the time, but for girls it's a huge step, one you could regret all your life.' She struggled to her feet and, half running, set off across the grass.

Mario caught up with her on the path before she got to the gate. He stopped her, held both her hands in his and dropped to his knees in front of her. 'Will you marry me, Angelica?'

Angelica looked wildly around, torn between embarrassment at the spectacle they were making and delight at what he'd said. Fifty yards away, a family was coming towards them. She hauled on his arms to make him stand up.

'No, my darling. I won't get up until you say yes. Not if the whole world comes past and gawps at us.'

Angelica forgot about the approaching people. She looked down at Mario, his eyes earnest and shining with excitement, his whole handsome face an urgent plea.

She bent over his face, her hair falling like a curtain around them. 'Of course I'll marry you.'

CHAPTER FIVE

Jane had run out of eggs so she'd taken the lift from her penthouse at the top of her parents' home in Eaton Square to their flat downstairs, and invited herself to breakfast. She looked up from her perfectly poached egg as the maid entered with the post.

'Oh, good, is that *Tatler*? Can you pass it to me, Daddy?'

Grace was pushing down the plunger in the new cafetière. She poured her husband a cup. 'This makes much nicer coffee than the old percolator, don't you think, darling?'

George smiled at his wife vaguely but, absorbed in the City pages, he didn't answer. Probably didn't listen, thought Jane. 'I certainly do,' she said, 'although a proper espresso machine like Laura has in the Calzones is even better.' She turned to George. 'Daddy, pass me *Tatler*. Please.'

George apologized and handed her the magazine. Then he quickly sorted the rest of the post, passing most of it to his wife and a couple of large square envelopes to his daughter. 'You're popular today. Those look like invitations to dances or balls.'

'Or weddings,' responded Jane, turning an envelope over and running her finger over the embossed crest on the back. 'Though they're tailing off a bit now I'm heading for thirty. Most of my friends are married with squalling offspring.' She'd meant this to be light-hearted but somehow it came out as a complaint.

'Oh, darling, you're only twenty-eight – you've got plenty of time.'

Jane didn't answer. She didn't want to get into a conversation they'd already had, many times. The bottom line was that her mother wanted a grandchild, which meant Jane getting married. Of course, if the right man came along, tall, dark, handsome and rich, then OK, but why should she tie herself to some gold-digging chinless wonder?

She flipped through *Tatler*, noting that the 'girls in pearls' were getting younger and more common with every issue. Once they had been aristocratic debutantes but now they could be a butcher's daughter, if he could afford a ball at Claridges.

Suddenly she said, 'Mummy, there's a review for Giovanni's here. Daddy, listen. It's by Humphrey Lyttelton.'

George frowned. 'I thought he was a jazz musician?'

'He is, but he also writes about restaurants,' said Grace. 'He's very good. And funny.'

Jane read the review aloud, ending, '*If you can beg, borrow, or rob a bank to afford the most expensive dinner in London, and risk being mugged by going to the seamy end of Notting Hill, then do. I guarantee it will be worth it.* Laura won't like that,' she said, passing the magazine to George. 'He's pointed out that the place is very expensive and he advises anyone who can afford it not to go there. And he's right. The area is awful. Full of foreigners and council houses.'

'Jane,' said George mildly, 'that's not very kind.' He took the magazine from her and peered at the article. 'He's not said a word about the people who live there. And if I was Laura I'd be pleased. It's full of praise, which she richly deserves.'

Jane went upstairs and sat grumpily at her dressing-table. She didn't like her father ticking her off. She was grown-up and entitled to her opinion. But she also felt somehow peeved at the rave review for Giovanni's. She knew she should be pleased, not least because her father was a part-owner of the restaurant. But those Angelottis were all so damn *successful*, with their cafés and ice-cream parlours and now this restaurant. Angelica, set to be a great pastry chef, was beautiful. Silvano was really clever, and everyone thought the world of him, while Mario was a bit of a rogue, but all the more attractive for it.

She sat for a few minutes, wishing she was energetic and entrepreneurial, then concluded philosophically that she was fine as she was. She was healthy, young, aristocratic and rich.

Laura stared, appalled, at *Tatler*. 'Oh, God, no one will come! It's not fair. We're not nearly the most expensive place in London. How can he say that? And—'

'Shush, darling.' Giovanni put a comforting arm around her shoulders. 'All publicity is good publicity, remember? Anyway, he goes on to say the food is wonderful. And I have to eat my words about your first course and pudding trolleys. He loved them. And so do the customers.'

'But that stuff about being mugged! And describing these beautiful houses as "the seamy end of Notting Hill". For goodness' sake, it's not as if we were down by Ladbroke Grove tube station.'

'Wait and see, darling. It's my guess that middle-class London will decide that coming to Notting Hill is an adventure and they'll want to do it. Think of all the people who go to the East End to

54

that Chinese restaurant – what's its name? The Old Friends. And to the Omar Khayyam. They like being pioneers.'

But Laura was not to be comforted – or not until the phone started to ring and Giovanni was proved right. Fashionable London streamed into the restaurant. Suddenly everyone wanted to eat simple Italian food in a sophisticated venue away from their Mayfair and Knightsbridge haunts.

Soon they were booked up weeks in advance and they took to keeping a few tables back just in case the Beatles, Stirling Moss or Sir Alec Guinness wanted a table. Laura, who had never taken any interest in the rich and famous, had to learn fast who was who. One day Mick Furst appeared without a booking.

Silvano called Laura from the office.

'Mick Furst wants a table and we haven't got one. He's asked to see you.'

'Mick Furst? Who's he?'

'Oh, Laura! He's famous. He used to be a film director and now writes a restaurant column. You'll have to come and talk to him.'

As she stepped into the bar, Furst turned, champagne glass in one hand. 'You must be Laura Angelotti, the brains behind this Italian revolution.'

'How do you do, Mr Furst? We're delighted to have you here, but rather embarrassed because we don't have a free table.'

'Never fear, my dear. Your excellent barman has presented me with a glass of very good champagne.' He indicated Giovanni behind the bar.

'That's Giovanni, my husband. He's helping out. He likes a stint in the bar, don't you, darling?'

Giovanni came out from behind the counter and extended his hand. 'This way I get to see the customers.'

'So you are Giovanni of Giovanni's? The chef-patron?'

'Well, we've used my name, but only because it's obviously Italian. I'm not the chef, the manager or, indeed, the barman. As you rightly said, my wife is the brains behind it. She manages it, and we have a great head chef, Dino. I just stand in on their nights off.'

Furst glanced round the bar. 'Nice room, but I see no famous customers. Where *are* the glitterati?' He looked put out.

'Well, I don't think there's anyone—'

Giovanni interrupted, 'My wife is too discreet, Mr Furst. We have Shirley MacLaine and Jack Nicholson in the private room. It's some sort of Hollywood party. And Muhammad Ali will be dining with his agent later.'

'Good. We famous people like to be in the company of other famous people.' He smiled broadly.

Laura knew that Giovanni had invented his illustrious guests. What if Furst went looking for them?

But the critic seemed satisfied to be in the same restaurant as the stars, and settled for another glass of champagne. Giovanni kept him talking until a table came free.

When Laura had settled him with the wine list and menu, she came back to the bar. 'God, darling, why did you say all that? It's not like you, boasting about guests we don't have!'

Giovanni laughed. 'But he swallowed it, didn't he? He's such a snob. I know the type. If I'd mentioned a famous couple dining on their own, he'd have insisted on going to say hello. But even he wouldn't crash a private Hollywood party.'

'But why invent anyone at all?'

'Because if he thinks there are no famous people here, he won't enjoy his food. He might even leave.'

Laura had to smile. 'You're behaving like Mario!' She shook her head. 'What will you do if he writes an article and mentions his fellow guests?'

'I'll be delighted at the publicity.'

'But what if they complain?'

'Oh Laura darling, that lot are far too famous to worry about an incorrect mention in a London gossip column.'

Sure enough, Furst's next column lauded the restaurant and mentioned the Hollywood party and Muhammed Ali. And Furst took such a shine to Laura and the restaurant that he began to turn up frequently. She dreaded his visits: he never booked, generally insisted on sitting at any table other than the one he was led to, and was rude to the staff, but Laura did her best to keep him happy. And he'd been right about the famous wanting to be with other famous people. His article had spread the word that Giovanni's was packed with celebrities, and now hardly an evening passed without well-known faces at several tables.

The only problem with a successful restaurant, Laura discovered, was that the work never ended. She didn't like opening up in the morning with the smell of stale cigarette smoke in the air. She didn't like dealing with the dustmen, who were increasingly hinting that they needed a bribe to take away the enormous quantity of rubbish. And after a long day, her feet ached so much that she had to lie on the floor with her bottom close to the skirting-board and her legs raised against the wall until the pain subsided.

She never complained to Giovanni, much as she'd have liked his sympathy. It was she who'd wanted a smart restaurant and insisted on running it herself. Giovanni had backed her loyally, despite his misgivings. And he'd been right: it was hard to make a profit. They needed to be full most nights just to break even. Which they were, but for how long?

Giovanni works as hard as I do, she thought, and carries a lot more responsibility. He manages the overall group, and has direct responsibility for the ice-cream business, fourteen Calzones and two Deli-Calzones. She felt a little guilty. Giovanni's attracted so much publicity that everyone thought she was the driving force behind the Angelotti empire when the truth was that Giovanni controlled it.

Giovanni missed his daughter. Laura spoke to Angelica more often than he did, and he was pleased to know she was no longer homesick and lonely. She'd made friends at the fancy French cookery school and got over her dislike of her tutor – or he'd got over his dislike of her – but Giovanni hadn't realized how wide a gap she'd leave at home. With only him, Laura, Carlotta and the studiously quiet Silvano in the mews, there was a lot less laughter, teasing and singing. And they all tended to eat at whichever restaurant they were working at, rather than cook at home. To Giovanni that felt wrong. When Mario and Angelica were living at home the two families almost always ate together in the big communal kitchen.

'Laura darling,' he said one night as they got ready for bed, 'let's try to spend at least a couple of evenings at home each week, shall we? A seven-day week is too much.'

'But how can we? One of us has to be at Giovanni's.'

'I don't think so. Dino's an excellent chef, and Paolo could manage.'

'No,' said Laura. 'He's a good head waiter, but not ready to be maître d'. He's efficient and pleasant, but he can't chat to the guests the way you and I can.'

'Maybe we were too hasty in sacking Mario. He's got the gift of the gab, all right.'

'Yes, but he's dangerous. That's why we took Angelica out of his range.'

She was right, of course. 'I'm not seriously suggesting we get him back. But we do need someone who can cover for us. With Giovanni's and the Deli-Calzones running seven days a week, and all the rest of it, I hardly see you.'

Laura was smoothing some cream onto her face and wiping it off with cotton wool. Giovanni, sitting in his pyjamas on the edge of the bed, watched her face in the dressing-table mirror. For a moment he was distracted by the thought that, although she looked tired, really tired, he still preferred her without make-up. She insisted on her 'warpaint', though. She said she needed it to face their famous customers.

She was obviously thinking, and he didn't interrupt the silence. Then she said, sounding a little hesitant, 'We could train someone up for front-of-house, I suppose.'

So far so good, thought Giovanni. But not good enough. He stood up and put his hands on her shoulders. 'Even if we share the shifts between us, so that neither of us does a sixteen-hour day, we still won't see each other, will we? I didn't marry you never to see you. Or for you to be exhausted every night. And we didn't build a successful business to take the pleasure out of life.'

She stood up and went into the bathroom, her face troubled. He could hear her brushing her teeth, splashing water on her face.

When she came back she didn't say anything. Which, thought

Giovanni, was a good sign. At least I've lodged the idea in her head.

The next morning he was at his desk, looking at the new menu designs for the summer ice-cream offer, when Carlotta knocked on his door. He stood up to embrace her. '*Ciao*, Carlotta. What's up? Nothing wrong, is there? You never come to my office.'

Carlotta eased her ample bottom into the chair opposite Giovanni's desk. 'Mario's disappeared.'

'Disappeared?'

'Giovanni, when he left he promised to write and telephone but of course he never did. I had two postcards from him with French stamps so I supposed he was in the South of France, which was where he said he was going.'

'What were the pictures of? Riviera scenes?'

'Cézanne and Van Gogh.'

Poor Carlotta looked so worried. 'Did he say why was he going there?'

'He wanted to find a job in the sun. St Tropez, maybe. Lots of rich tourists. He took his guitar with him. Said he might play on the beach and pass round a hat.'

'So? Maybe that's exactly what he's doing.'

'Maybe. But I've not heard from him in nearly six weeks. Nor has Silvano.'

'Do you know if he found a job, Carlotta? Did he tell you the name of any company he was working for? Or landlady? Friends?'

Carlotta shook her head. 'Nothing. When he wrote he hadn't got a job. Too early in the season. But it's April now, so there'll be work if he wants it.'

'Carlotta, you're worrying about nothing. He's young. He's in the South of France, probably hoping to meet Brigitte Bardot or someone just like her. The last thing he'll be thinking about is his mamma.'

Carlotta gave him a weak smile. 'True. He never tells me anything.' She stood up and touched Giovanni's shoulder. 'Thank you, *mio fratello*. I will try to stop worrying – but he's a grown man now. Twenty-six. He shouldn't be drifting round the beaches of Europe, waiting at tables and singing with a guitar. Busking, he calls it. I call it begging.'

CHAPTER SIX

Getting married was proving more difficult than they'd thought. They needed a whole clutch of certificates and documents to prove their residency in Paris, their single status, their compliance with English and French marriage law. Most difficult was the demand for new birth certificates, less than three years old, from the record office where each of the births had been registered. Angelica knew she'd been born in London, and Mario that he'd been born in Abruzzo, but in which parishes, they had no idea. And they could hardly ask their mothers.

'Let's forget the civil wedding,' said Mario. 'We can just be married in church, can't we?'

'No, we can't. Priests can't do the service unless you have a certificate of marriage from the *mairie*.'

So they gave up.

'We'll have to lie,' said Mario. 'Tell our parents we're married.'

'But why? Why not just say nothing?'

'Because sooner or later they'll find out we're together and then they'll never leave us alone. If they think we're married, they'll finally accept it.'

They longed for a place of their own where they could make

love. Mario spent all his free time looking at rooms and flats. Either they were too expensive, or out in the *banlieues*, or they came with dragon landladies or concierges.

After a couple of weeks, Mario had found a room at the top of a run-down house in Montmartre. 'It's terrific, just a garret, no mod cons – no heating, no hot water, no kitchen, no bathroom – but it's cheap.'

'Mario, I have to have a kitchen. I'm a cook.'

'But you cook all day at the school.'

'But how will we eat?'

'There's a gas ring. And we can do what we do now. Eat in the street or in cafés. And we can't afford anything better.' He kissed her cheek. 'You'll love it. I know you will.'

Angelica doubted it. The very top of Montmartre was one of the few parts of Paris she and Mario had not been to. They'd walked along the Boulevard de Clichy, where she'd found the loud bars and strip-joints intimidating, the cafés unfriendly and expensive, and hadn't wanted to venture further.

And she wanted a kitchen. She longed to cook for Mario, show off her new skills. She'd been planning romantic suppers she'd make for him once she had a kitchen. But she agreed to see the room and read her guidebook on Montmartre. It trumpeted the unchanged architecture and history of the *communards*, the subsequent libertine artists' quarter, the bars and bistros, and interest stirred.

Mario wanted to show her the area as well as the room, so he led her along the steep and busy Rue Lepic, which wound up the hill of Montmartre. Then they wove through narrow streets with little shops selling artists' materials, pictures and bric-à-brac, and dark restaurants reaching deep inside old buildings.

The apple-and-caramel smell of freshly baked *tarte maison* came from an open doorway where the chef was sharpening his knife on the stone step. Angelica's mouth watered, and her heart lifted. This was the real Paris, just as it had been when all those artists, Picasso and Modigliani, Toulouse Lautrec and Van Gogh, had lived there.

They stood outside a shop admiring a painting of a cardinal dressed all in red. Angelica stared at their reflections in the window. We belong here, she thought. Mario unshaven and rumpled but so handsome; me a skinny waif, long hair, miniskirt and high boots.

When they got to the Place du Tertre, they found half a dozen artists at their easels, some painting the scene or large-scale versions of Paris landmarks, two doing charcoal portraits of tourists. 'They aren't much good, are they?' said Angelica.

Mario laughed. 'Well, at least they look the part, don't they? Think of them as background scenery to our new life in the *quartier*.'

'Except we haven't agreed to take the room, have we?'

'Wait till you see it. It's great.'

The room was just off the square in a five-storey apartment building in obvious need of attention. Mario had been lent the keys by the agent. They were enormous, the one for the peeling front door seven or eight inches long, heavy and worn with age. It turned smoothly and they were in an ill-lit, damp-smelling corridor. The stairs were solid wood but so worn that each one dipped in the middle. There was no lift, and by the time they'd reached the top floor, the fifth, Angelica was out of breath. The ceilings there were not as high as those below and the corridor was narrower.

Mario walked ahead of her. At the last door, he turned to her. 'I should carry you over the threshold, shouldn't I?'

'Only when we're married. And if we take the flat.' She tried to sound indignant but his upbeat mood was catching. She stepped inside.

It was a large room, sparsely furnished. A high brass double bed stood under a sloping ceiling. Two skylights over the bed afforded the only light and the sun streamed in at a slant, adding interest and drama to the bare floorboards, the wooden table with two chairs and the long, low chest of drawers against the end wall.

Angelica looked at the bed, covered with a faded red damask quilt. That was where she would lose her virginity. She turned to Mario, wondering if he was thinking the same thing. He was scrambling onto the bed. No, not now, not just like that. He was standing on it, opening one of the skylights. 'Come here, darling. This is why we have to have this place.' He crossed the bed to the other skylight, propping it open at its widest. He pulled her up. 'Look.' He poked his head out and so, after a moment, did she. She gasped. The view was like one of the paintings they'd seen in the square, only a million times better. To the left were the white towers and domes of Sacré-Cœur; nearer, to its right, there was a red-tiled church or abbey roof; directly ahead was Paris, street after street flowing down the hill of Montmartre and beyond.

They must have stood there side by side for fifteen minutes, trying to identify Paris's hotspots and boulevards. Then they sank onto the bed and held each other close. Mario rolled over to kiss her, but she struggled up. 'Mario, stop. Let's wait until it's ours.'

They agreed to take the room. Angelica steeled herself to tell her landlady she was leaving and ask to be let off the rest of her tenancy, which was not due to end for another seven months. Of course the woman said no. Why should she agree? Angelica was contracted to rent her room until Christmas. And, no, she could not sublet it.

But then, by the sheerest good fortune, she heard that one of the students at the École Gastronomique was looking for a room. Angelica knew the girl was the daughter of a well-off businessman so she asked her if she'd pay 10 per cent more than she herself was paying. 'My landlady won't let me sublet, but if I tell her you'll pay more than me, she'll agree, I'm sure.'

The woman did, with a show of tired impatience, but a glint of satisfaction in her piggy eyes. Greedy bitch, thought Angelica, but she smiled and thanked her.

She spent the week in a fever of excitement and anxiety. Every afternoon after school, she'd buy things for her and Mario's new home. The landlady agreed to return her deposit so she felt she could spend it on the bare necessities: a few pans and tools, and a good chopping-board. Most importantly, she bought a tiny fridge, which with the help of an electrician, she installed next to the table. She also bought linen and towels, and a pottery jug, which she planned to fill with flowers on the day they moved in.

The day before they took possession of their garret, Angelica went to the shop where they had seen the picture of the cardinal in the window. It was no longer there. She went inside, the doorbell clanging as she crossed the threshold. She asked about the picture.

'I'm sorry, Mademoiselle, but it's sold. To another artist.'

Angelica felt sharp disappointment, but also relief – the picture had probably been expensive. 'Oh, well.' She sighed. 'I dare say I couldn't have afforded it, anyway.'

'I have some sketches by the same artist. They're cheaper than the oil painting.'

The shop's owner shuffled down the stairs to the basement and soon reappeared with two unframed drawings. One was a pencil sketch of an old man looking out of a window at trees and a church beyond a tangled garden. The other was obviously a sketch for the cardinal painting. It was in heavy charcoal, and the secondary figures were impressionistic, just a few strong lines. But the lowered head of the central figure had the same expression of benign peace that, Mario said, had attracted him.

Angelica's heart was racing. 'How much would it be if it was framed?' she asked, knowing she would buy it.

They agreed on a red lacquer frame and pale grey mount.

'Could I have it by tomorrow, do you think?'

For a moment she thought he was going to say no, but then his face softened. '*Eh, bien, Mademoiselle*. I will do it. Because you look so anxious. It is for a lover, I think?'

Angelica felt herself blushing. 'Yes. Or, rather, I hope so.'

Mario and Angelica had agreed to move in on the Saturday. There was no school for Angelica and she was up early to move her things into the garret and make her preparations for Mario's arrival – he was booked to work on the boats all day. He'd collect his things from the hostel as soon as he'd finished, and join her in Montmartre for supper.

Angelica swept and cleaned the room, made the bed with her brand new sheets – they were coarse linen, the cheapest she could find, but they felt wonderfully old-fashioned and French. Then she went round the corner to collect her picture, begging a nail and borrowing a hammer from the shopkeeper.

She banged the nail into the wall, knelt on the chest of drawers to hang the picture, then scrambled down and stood back to look at it. Perfect. The wide frame and mount made the sketch seem striking and important, the first thing you would notice as you entered the room.

Angelica returned the hammer, then set off for the market. It was a warm spring day and she was in love with the world, even the grumpy concierge of her new building who never said a word to anyone. She smiled broadly at him as she jumped down the steps. He didn't respond, but she didn't mind.

The fishmonger was telling a customer that his oysters were the best he'd had in years. He and the man (a chef, she knew: he wore clogs, checked trousers and a white jacket) were animatedly discussing their merits. He bought three trays.

'*Et pour vous, Mademoiselle?*' said the fishmonger, turning to Angelica.

'I've never eaten an oyster,' she said. 'Where are they from?'

'Never eaten one? Oh, Mademoiselle, you must start now. They're the best, from Brittany.'

The woman next to her joined in, laughing, 'And they're aphrodisiac, did you know that? Do you have a boyfriend? They're just the thing. And, if not, maybe they'll get you one!'

Angelica knew Mario liked oysters. He'd been ogling them displayed on ice outside an expensive restaurant, the man behind the counter shucking them expertly for the customers inside. She hesitated, 'I don't think . . .'

The fishmonger was expertly opening one with his stubby

little knife. He threw away the top shell and loosened the oyster from the other. 'Go on,' he said, offering it to her.

She took the oyster, which looked both intriguing and disgusting. But she couldn't refuse.

'Open your mouth wide,' said the man, 'and tip it in. Chew a little and swallow.'

I've got to do it, thought Angelica. By now a little crowd of shoppers was watching the exchange, offering encouragement.

She threw back her head, tipped in the oyster and shut her eyes. It tasted mild and salty, of the sea. She didn't dare chew it. What if it was disgusting and she had to spit it out? She swallowed, and it was gone. She opened her eyes, and a couple of the bystanders clapped. Someone said, in English, 'Well done. A lifetime of oyster-eating lies ahead of you!' Everyone laughed and, the show over, dispersed.

Angelica bought two dozen. 'But how do I open them?' she said.

'Are they for today?'

'Tonight.'

'I'll do them for you and put them on ice. Come back and collect them when you're ready to go home. Keep them in the refrigerator.'

'But my fridge is tiny. A tray, even a big plate, won't go in it.'

'Can you come back about five?'

So it was agreed. She'd come back when her hands were free to carry the opened oysters without spilling their precious seawater, and the crushed ice would keep them chilled till dinner.

She bought the wherewithal to make steak tartare and chips (Chef Berger said hot chips were delicious with the cold raw beef) and îles flottantes. She could poach the meringue islands in a frying pan on the single gas ring. Finally she bought two bottles of wine and a bunch of yellow tulips.

When she got back to the room, she put the tulips in the jug on the chest of drawers, she diced the fillet finely by hand, added chopped shallot, capers, parsley, Dijon mustard and a dash of anchovy sauce. She moulded the mix into two fat patties but she didn't add the egg yolks. She wanted to serve them with a yolk in a dip in the middle of each portion, like in a restaurant.

She made the chips and drained them on newspaper. She'd do the final fry when Mario was there.

She made the meringue islands. They puffed up most satisfactorily in the simmering milk. Everything was going like a dream.

She started on the custard. She'd made *crème anglaise* successfully at school and now she heated the mixture slowly, stirring constantly, repeatedly checking the back of the spoon for signs of thickening. After ten minutes it was hot but no thicker. She turned up the heat a little – and suddenly she'd curdled the lot. She pulled the pan off the heat and whisked frantically, which brought up flecks of burnt bits from the bottom of the pan and failed to smooth the sauce. Oh, hell, she thought, and I haven't enough milk to start again.

She ran down to the street. The dairy was closed but would open again at four. If she waited until then, the custard might not chill in time. And would it fit into the fridge with the meat and the white wine? No. She should have got some cheese and fruit.

Dispirited and now anxious that her perfect meal wouldn't be ready before Mario got home, she dithered.

Suddenly she was hungry. She crossed the road to the little delicatessen and bought a *sandwich jambon* and a bottle of Coca-

Cola. As she was queuing to pay she gazed absently at the display shelves behind the counter. Bird's custard powder. Just like at home. Thank you, God.

'Do you sell milk too?' she asked. Yes, they did.

When she got back to the flat , she sat at the little table to have her lunch. She drank the Coca-Cola and ate half the baguette but all the ham.

Right, she thought. Plan of action:

1. Make custard again.
2. Lay table.
3. Wash and dress.
4. Plate up the steak tartare.
5. Fetch the oysters and ice.
6. Chill the wine.
7. Fry the chips.

This time the custard worked a treat. The milk, sugar and custard powder came to simmering point and thickened, as smooth as silk. She poured it into a jug.

Then she laid the table – the cloth was too large and the edge lay on the floor. Too bad, she thought.

When she got to 'Wash and dress' she had to fill the kettle at the tap in the corridor, boil it on the gas ring and tip it into the washing up bowl. Then back to the tap for more water to mix with the hot so she could wash her hair. It was an awkward business and she got the whole area wet. Then she undressed, stuffed her wet hair under a shower cap and had what her grandmother, Maud, called a 'flannel bath'. She dried herself with her lovely new bath towel, then dusted herself with lavender talc.

Still naked, she mopped the floor. Then she combed the tangles out of her hair and rubbed it more or less dry. She put on a clean orange skirt, a white cotton top and white sandals. She found her stripy orange Alice band and used it to hold her hair off her face.

It was five o'clock by the time she got back to the fishmonger and she had to wait for him to open her oysters. 'How do I serve them? Just with lemon?' she asked.

'If you like. Some people eat them with a drop of Tabasco, but most eat them as they are, just with the seawater in the shell.'

Twenty-four oysters lay on a large tray filled with crushed ice. She needed both hands to carry them and had to make a second trip to fetch extra ice to chill the wine and custard.

By the time she'd got back again Angelica was hot and sweaty, exhausted and less in love with garret living. She had to put the oyster tray on the floor. She wiped out the tin wastepaper container and used it as an ice bucket.

Six thirty. She was ready. Or nearly. When Mario arrived she'd plate up the oysters, and put the fat on to heat for the chips. Meantime she'd make herself look good.

She stood at the mirror to do her make-up. She smoothed Touch and Glow onto her cheeks, powdered them lightly and applied mascara to her lashes. Her hair was a mess, still damp and curling in the wrong places. She couldn't find a peachy or orange lipstick and the pink one looked wrong. She was scowling at herself when she heard Mario's step outside.

'God, I'm glad I've only got a rucksack. I'd never have managed five flights with a trunk!' He eased it off his shoulders and let it fall with a thud onto the floor. He flung himself on his back onto the bed. 'You haven't got a beer, have you, darling?'

'No. Tea or coffee. Or wine.' She was slightly put out that he hadn't greeted her, let alone kissed her, or noticed the picture, the flowers or, indeed, anything.

'Have we any soda water? I could add it to the wine.'

'Only water from the tap in the corridor. Not sure it's safe to drink. But I expect the wine would kill any bugs. Shall I get you some?'

He sat up, clearly disgruntled. 'Don't bother. I'll go and buy a few bottles of beer. Maybe have one in the bar.'

He stood up and came across to her. 'You don't mind, do you, darling? I'm so thirsty and exhausted. I'll see you soon.' He didn't wait for an answer.

She decided she might as well get everything ready. Maybe it was a good thing he'd gone out. They could start the evening again. And this time it would go perfectly.

She put the chip pan on to heat and when it was ready she slid in the chips.

She put a dozen oysters on each plate and set them on the table.

Mario reappeared. 'Oh, darling, I'm sorry I was so grumpy before. Just tired. But a beer does wonders.' He kissed her. 'You smell wonderful.'

She thought he smelt good too. Of himself, and slightly beery. He turned to survey the room. 'What's for dinner?'

She indicated the oysters on the table, but he had already spotted them.

'Oysters!'

He took a couple of strides to the table and trod on the cloth, dragging it down. As the wastebucket-cum-wine cooler fell off the table, he dived to save it and tripped. With a yelp of dismay,

73

he fell, clutching the bucket and sending one of the oyster plates flying.

Angelica leaped to retrieve the now half-full jug of custard, which she'd forgotten was still chilling in the ice, and the bottle of wine. 'Oh, no! The oysters!'

Mario sat up and started to gather the oysters and their shells.

Suddenly Angelica became conscious of a strong, delicious smell. 'Oh, my God! The chips!' She rushed to the gas ring and turned it off, then looked about frantically for the sieve to fish out the chips. The fat was so hot she thought it might burst into flames.

Mario was beside her in an instant, dropping the baguette left over from her sandwich into the pan.

'What are you doing, Mario? I've just turned it off.'

'Frying something, especially a big hunk of bread, is the quickest way of cooling down fat. Mamma taught us.'

They watched the bread rapidly darken. Mario lifted it out, then the very dark chips. They dumped them on a sheet of newspaper and Angelica sprinkled them with salt.

Mario took one. 'Perfect!' He laughed. 'Just as I like them. Well browned.'

Suddenly Angelica was near to tears. 'Mario, you have no idea of the effort I put into this supper and it's all ruined.' As she said it, she started to cry. 'The oysters are meant to have their seawater still in them. The custard was for the *îles flottantes* and now there's hardly any, and the chips were to go with your favourite steak tartare.'

By now Mario had his arms round her. 'Darling, the oysters will be lovely as they are. I'm sure there's nothing on the floor that would kill us. And, as I told you, the chips are delicious.'

She sniffled into his chest, thinking how good it was to have his arms round her. 'And,' she said, with a little sob, 'you never noticed my present.'

He pulled away to look down at her. 'What present?'

So she showed him the picture and he loved it. He spent a full two minutes just looking at it closely, then said, 'It's the same artist who did the oil painting of the cardinal, isn't it?'

'Yes, I went to the shop. I wanted to buy the oil, but it was sold. And it would have been too expensive, I'm sure.'

'I love this one. And I love you, Angelica Angelotti.' He came back to her and kissed her. 'Let's go to bed.'

'What about our supper?'

'Afterwards. It will all keep.' He held her face in his hands to kiss her. 'Just stand there. I want to undress you.'

Her heart started to bang in her chest. This was it. Would it be all right? Would she do it right?

He kissed her mouth and neck, then slipped his hands under her top, ran his palms up her sides to lift it over her head. He held her away from him as he dropped his eyes to look at her body. 'God, you're lovely, Angelica,' he murmured.

He led her to the bed, picked her up and pushed her back on it. Then he undid her zip and pulled off her skirt, then her knickers.

'I'm scared,' she said.

'Don't be, Angel. I won't hurt you. Or do anything you don't want me to. I promise.'

He climbed onto the bed next to her and held her to him, stroking her and kissing her. Gradually she relaxed and that warm lovely feeling she'd had when they were cuddling in the park or the cinema returned and she began to respond to his kisses, pulling his head down to hers, wanting more of him. He stroked her all over, her breasts, her belly, her hips, her thighs.

He was breathing quickly. After a while, he looked into her face. 'I want you so badly, my darling.' He lifted himself on top of her and she could see he was doing all he could to hold back, not to rush her. 'Can I?'

Her eyes on his, she nodded. '*Caro mio.*'

CHAPTER SEVEN

Giovanni was sitting with his back to her as Laura came into the kitchen. Immediately she knew something was wrong. She hurried over to him. 'What's the matter?'

He sat back, his face pale and blank. He had a letter in his hand, which he gave to her without a word.

She slid into the chair next to him and read:

> Apartment 55,
> 12, rue de Mont Cenis,
> 18 arr, Paris.

> 5 May 1968

Darling Mamma and Papa,

I'm sorry to upset you but last week Mario and I were married.

I know that you don't approve of Mario but I love him and he loves me, and he is not what you think. I am still at cooking school and he is working on the Bateaux Mouches on the Seine.

We are living in Montmartre. It's wonderful. I have never

been so happy. I know I'm young, but you were young when you married, weren't you?

Please write and tell me you wish us well and that you will love Mario. Knowing that you might not is the only cloud in my sky.

Your loving daughter,
Angelica

Shock seemed to paralyse Laura but now Giovanni jumped to his feet. His pallor had been banished by a furious red flush. 'That bastard! I'll kill him. She's a child! How could he?'

He paced round the room, threatening to have the marriage annulled, fetch his daughter home and kill his new son-in-law. Laura sat with her head in her hands, crushed. Twenty years ago she'd lost her son and now she'd lost her daughter. It was too much. She could understand why Angelica had fallen for Mario – he was charm itself – but Giovanni was right: he was also unreliable and selfish. Angelica had thrown herself away on a man who would ultimately make her miserable.

Giovanni was unstoppable. 'How's he going to support her? He's never kept a job in his life! And that girl has ambition and talent. She could be the first top female chef in Britain. She could inherit the business. She has her whole life ahead of her, a brilliant career. Now all she'll have is that man's brats. I bet he's good at making them. Probably has half a dozen scattered around already. Oh, Laura, what are we going to do?'

At that moment Carlotta stepped into the room. Laura jumped up and ran to her.

'What's the matter? What's happened?' Carlotta's face was full of fear.

'Sit down, darling,' said Laura, pushing her into a chair. 'It's not good news . . .'

'Has something happened to Mario? Tell me!'

'No . . . or, rather, yes. He and Angelica—'

Giovanni interrupted, 'Your Mario has married my daughter, that's what's happened.'

An hour later Laura strode into Silvano's office and handed him Angelica's letter. He skimmed it: *Mario . . . married . . . Montmartre.* He could hardly take it in.

'Did you know about this?' There was accusation in her tone.

'Of course not. Oh, God . . .'

'Did you know *nothing*? You're so close to them both. Didn't either of them say?'

He stood up, went round to her and put his arm round her thin shoulders. 'Honestly, Laura, I'd have moved heaven and earth to prevent it. She's too good for Mario. Much too good.' Anger was replacing his initial confusion.

Laura's hands were over her face and she was trying not to cry. 'Carlotta and I are going to Paris the day after tomorrow. But the deed is done.'

'At least he has a job. And they're happy.' Why did it cost him so much to say that? *They're happy.* He should want them to be happy. But he didn't, and he wanted Angelica at home, safe with her family, not with his rogue of a brother.

'I'm sorry, Silvano. I just thought, as you were always such friends with Angelica . . . But you were duped like the rest of us.' She smiled and reached up to kiss his cheek. 'Look after Giovanni while we're away, won't you? He's beside himself.'

Of course Mario hadn't told his brother what he was up to.

He'd probably lied from the start that he was in the South of France and had been with Angelica all this time. Maybe her occasional affectionate postcards were part of their plot to keep everyone in the dark. Meanwhile they were tucked up together in Paris, the city of lovers.

Two days later Carlotta and Laura were on the ferry to France. For both of them to leave the business together was unheard of, but Giovanni would cover for Laura, and Carlotta's deputy welcomed the chance to prove herself as acting head pastry chef at Deli-Calzone.

Laura was secretly pleased that Giovanni wasn't with them. His fury would have alienated Angelica, who would be desperate for his approval. He's jealous, she thought, just as my father was when I ran off with Giovanni. The deed was done and they must make the best of it.

The crossing was smooth, and they were over the Channel by eleven that morning. Then they sat on the train in Calais for two hours before it left. There was no explanation for the delay.

At the Gare du Nord, they had a long wait for a taxi. When they finally got one, and the driver realized Carlotta spoke French, he burst into animated conversation, gabbling and throwing his hands into the air. 'What's he saying?' asked Laura.

'The students at Nanterre University have been making trouble, protesting and staging "sit-ins". The administrator has closed the university and called in the police. Yesterday there was a riot.'

'What? Where?'

Carlotta asked the driver, then said, 'It seems students, mostly from the Sorbonne, held a protest march yesterday, in sympathy with the first group, and the police tried to break it up. They charged the crowd with batons, and it turned into a riot. Hundreds of students were arrested. He says the police behaved like Nazis.'

'What are the students protesting about?' Laura wanted to know.

Carlotta asked the driver, then turned to Laura to translate. 'I don't think he knows. Capitalism mainly. And bureaucracy, and the authorities generally. He says the students are right, the government is too right-wing, and he thinks de Gaulle should go.'

As they drew up in the Rue du Mont-Cenis, the driver told them to stay away from the Left Bank where all the trouble was.

At number twelve, Carlotta pressed the bell marked 'Concierge'. Eventually the door opened to reveal an unsmiling bearded man. An upward jerk of the head and a grunt served as both greeting and question.

Carlotta explained that they had come to visit the young couple in apartment fifty-five.

'They're not here.'

'Do you know when they'll be back?' The man shrugged, and started to close the door. Carlotta held it open and said, 'Do you know where they are?'

'*Non.*' He closed the door.

'Charming chap. What do we do now?' asked Laura.

'I think we'd better look for a hotel.'

They walked down the street and found a café, whose cheerful proprietor directed them to a *pension* in a narrow alley. They took a double room with single beds, then went back to the café for some *thé à l'anglaise*.

'Ugh, boiled milk. We should have ordered coffee,' said Laura.

'You English! You should drink it black, like civilized Europeans.'

The women explored the streets of Montmartre, then braved the surly concierge again. This time they explained who they were and suggested he let them into the apartment. He refused.

Both women were getting tired. They agreed they'd give it another hour, and if the pair were still not home, they'd leave a note for them. Meanwhile they went to Sacré-Cœur. Inside, Laura dutifully examined the enormous mosaics, but could think of nothing except her daughter, married to the black sheep of the family.

The third time they arrived at the apartment house door, the concierge went into an angry tirade. No, he would not walk up five flights to put their note under the apartment door. He took it from them and tossed it onto a narrow shelf, already cluttered with post. Laura started to protest: the chance of Mario or Angelica riffling through that mess to find a note they didn't know existed was nil.

Carlotta grabbed the envelope off the shelf and said, 'Don't try to reason with him. Come on.' She set off as fast as she could, Laura at her heels. The concierge followed them to the foot of the stairs and shouted up to them. The words *interdit* and *absolument pas* and something about *autorisation* followed them up to the second floor. Then they heard a door slam downstairs, and there was silence. Carlotta, already out of breath, leaned against the wall and started to laugh. Laura joined in.

'*Absolument pas! Non, non, non!*' said Laura. 'What a caricature of a concierge! He's unbelievable.' Weak with laughing, they sat on the dusty stairs to recover.

A few minutes later, Laura stood up. 'You stay here. I'll go and deliver the note.' But Carlotta wasn't listening. She was holding her hand up for silence. She was peering past Laura and listening. Laura now heard footsteps coming up the stairs and turned, ready for another fight with the concierge. But it wasn't him. It was her daughter, carrying an armful of groceries.

Angelica stopped, and her mouth fell open. Then she bent swiftly to put her bags on the floor, leaped the few steps towards her mother and flung her arms round her. She was on the step below Laura, and when Laura returned the hug, she found she was pressing her daughter's head into her bosom, just as she had when Angelica was a child. A wave of pure love flooded her.

A few minutes later, the three women were sitting around the little table. Laura couldn't hide her delight at seeing Angelica and had to remind herself that her daughter was now a married woman, with some explaining to do. But she didn't want to listen to explanations. And she didn't want Mario to arrive. She just wanted to look at Angelica, hug and kiss her, maybe brush her hair back so she could really see her face. It had been months since she'd been able to do that.

But Carlotta wanted to know about Mario. When had he arrived in Paris?

'About six weeks ago,' Angelica answered, 'and, oh, Aunt Carlotta, it was so wonderful. I'd been really lonely, and he—'

'Didn't he go to the South of France at all?'

'He came straight here.'

Carlotta shook her head. 'Where did you get married?' she demanded. 'And why? Are you pregnant?'

Laura wanted to intervene but she knew Carlotta was angrier with Mario than she was with Angelica and, in any case, she had a right to know.

'Because we love each other, of course. And, no, I'm not pregnant.' Angelica's eyes were defiant. 'We *are* adults, you know.'

Laura was impressed by her daughter's courage. Angelica answered their questions with energy but no desperation. She seemed so confident and happy, keen to reassure her mother and her aunt. But Carlotta wanted more detail.

'But, Angelica, how are you living? What does this room cost?'

Laura thought the room a dump, and was already wondering if Giovanni would agree to increase Angelica's allowance. That concierge was horrible, the stairs were dark and unswept, and as for the sanitary arrangements . . . But she said nothing. Not yet. She'd have to persuade Giovanni.

But as Angelica replied to her aunt's question, with such pride and enthusiasm, Laura's heart softened.

'Mamma, Carlotta, I know it's not smart and you couldn't bear to live here, but we just love it. Come,' She jumped up and pulled her mother to the bed. She scrambled up onto it. 'Get onto the bed, Mamma. Come on, Aunt Carlotta, you too. You have to see how wonderful Paris is.' Laura managed it easily enough but Carlotta refused. Angelica opened one of the windows and insisted her mother stick her head out. Laura did as she was told and the sight silenced her. It was like a painting, roofs and chimneys, two churches, stone walls and trees stretching away down the hill. The light was fading and the street lights were coming on.

She turned round. 'Carlotta, you have to see this – it's extraordinary.'

So Carlotta, with a bit of pulling and steadying from Laura and Angelica, stood on the bed too and peered out. When they got down, her mood had changed. She'd caught Angelica's enthusiasm.

Angelica told them about buying the picture and how it was perfectly possible to cook with one gas ring. How they loved the *quartier* with its mix of locals, eccentrics, con artists and tourists. Especially she loved the shopkeepers and the markets. 'Oh, Mamma, you'll go mad. And Aunt Carlotta! It's magic. They have everything, so fresh and so good – I can't wait to show you.'

Angelica, her face earnest, held Laura's hand across the table. She told them excitedly how well she was doing at school: 'At first I thought Chef Berger hated me, but he's fine now. And Mario is working so hard on the boats. The passengers and the staff love him.'

Carlotta seemed gratified at this praise of her son but then her expression hardened. 'That's all very well, Angelica, but he's your first cousin. It's crazy to marry your first cousin. Don't you realize the dangers? You could have babies that are not right, deformed or half-witted.'

'Carlotta!' exclaimed Laura.

'Don't be feeble, Laura. The girl must know what she's done. They'd better not have children. That's all there is to it.'

Angelica's face showed she was stricken. 'Is that true, Mamma? It can't be. I thought it was only brothers and sisters marrying . . .'

Laura longed to reassure her. 'Darling, I just don't know. There's certainly more risk of problems with parents from the same family. In some countries the marriage of first cousins is banned.' She squeezed her daughter's hand. 'But, darling, it must be legal in France or you'd not have been allowed to marry.'

'That's not the point,' said Carlotta. 'Whether it's legal or not doesn't alter the risk.'

Later the women made supper. All Angelica had bought were two aubergines, some onions, garlic and a packet of dried pasta.

They fried the aubergines and onions, then set aside the pan while they boiled the pasta. When it was drained, they returned everything to the saucepan with a splash of olive oil.

Carlotta looked sceptical. 'Is that enough, do you think? Giovanni would regard that as a first course and expect fish and meat to follow.' They added a tin of tuna from Angelica's meagre store.

'What time does he get home?' Laura asked.

'Round about now. Oh, he'll be so amazed to see you.'

As she spoke, they heard heavy footsteps in the corridor outside, and Mario walked into the room. He stopped in his tracks. 'Mamma! What on earth? And Laura!' Angelica ran to him and hugged him.

Laura noticed that Mario looked apprehensive. Carlotta is the only person he respects, she thought. But Carlotta was thrilled to see her boy, and reached up to hold his face. 'Oh, Mario, what are we to do with you?'

When the greetings and exclamations were over, Mario ran downstairs to get a bottle of wine. Laura wanted to give him the money for it, but he smiled. 'No, Aunt Laura, the *rouge ordinaire* is cheaper than Coca-Cola. We have Coke for a treat on Saturdays.'

Over supper Mario had to endure a lecture from his mother on his irresponsibility and deceit, but Laura could see Carlotta's heart wasn't in it. She softened under his affection, and let her relief at finding him alive and well take hold. To Laura's surprise, the evening was convivial and loving.

Eventually the two women walked back to the *pension* arm in arm. 'What's done is done,' said Carlotta, 'but it won't be easy. How do you say? Leopards don't change their spots. Mario sounds responsible now, but there's nothing responsible about marrying your cousin.'

'But they do seem to love each other, don't they? I'd have moved heaven and earth to stop them marrying, as you would, but they were too clever to give us a chance.'

'If they come home when Angelica finishes her course, maybe they could both work in the business again, and we'll be able to keep an eye on them.'

'I don't want Mario in my restaurant. We're sure to fall out. And I doubt Giovanni will ever forgive him. He'll have to find another job.'

The next day Laura and Carlotta resolved to see more of the city while Mario was at work and Angelica at school. They thought they might take a Bateau Mouche trip and hope to see Mario at work. Outside the Métro they bought *Le Monde,* which Carlotta translated on the train. There were pages on the protests. The police had occupied both universities, at Nanterre and the Sorbonne, the press and the public seemed sympathetic to the students, and wildcat strikes were popping up everywhere.

When they came out of the Métro, they saw posters in support of the students pasted on walls and kiosks. Laura had enough French to translate and the words made her vaguely nervous. What did they mean it was 'forbidden to forbid'? And 'Let pleasure rule'? And 'Down with the bourgeoisie'?

They walked to the *quai,* where half a dozen gendarmes were milling around. At the Bateaux Mouches dock, they were met by a notice saying that today's excursions were cancelled.

They decided to walk up the Champs-Élysées and then to Angelica's school. They would window-shop along the Rue du Faubourg Saint-Honoré and maybe catch Angelica on a break from cooking.

On the pavement beside the Champs-Élysées, a small crowd listened to a young woman on a soapbox. She was wearing coloured beads in her hair and a long dress with a sort of smock over it. She spoke loudly and with great passion. Laura couldn't catch what she was saying but Carlotta told her she was attacking her teachers at art school, who wanted the students to learn to draw, and to copy the old masters. The students wanted to express themselves, draw what their imaginations sparked, make true art of the people. 'She says the government's dictatorial about everything, especially education. And the people want freedom.'

At all the kiosks little crowds queued for newspapers. Laura felt increasingly anxious but Carlotta was striding along, exclaiming at the elegance of the clothes in the shops, her face alive. She seemed unperturbed by the signs of unrest: some of the smaller jewellery shops had their security grilles over their windows and Cartier seemed to have more security guards than customers. When they got to the École Gastronomique, a couple of middle-aged women, secretaries perhaps, came out of the front door. One turned to lock the door behind her. The other said to Laura, '*Fermé. Les étudiants sont en grève.*'

'What did she say?' asked Laura.

'Closed. The students are on strike.'

'Oh, God, where will Angelica be? Let's go home, shall we?'

Parts of the Métro had closed and the buses were crammed. They had to walk the last leg, up the steep hill from the Place de Clichy. Carlotta became breathless and Laura felt exhausted.

That evening Mario and Angelica came home together. Carlotta pounced on them. 'Mario, we went to your work and to Angelica's school but they were both closed. What's going on?'

'We couldn't run the boats because the student workers didn't arrive. Then the rest of us came out in sympathy.'

'Same with us,' said Angelica. 'The American and Belgian students led the walk-out. Chef Berger was furious. He said we'd be lucky to be let back in.'

'But where have you been all day?' Laura asked.

'Oh, Mamma, it was great. We went with Mario's friends off the boats and a couple of the American students from school came too, and we had such a good day. We went to a warehouse on the Left Bank where art students from the Sorbonne were making posters. We helped them. It was—'

'So that's what Giovanni and Laura are paying for?' interrupted Carlotta. 'For you to refuse to learn?'

Laura didn't want to have that discussion. She was glad to see her daughter back and she was tired and hungry. 'Let's go out for supper,' she said. 'We're all too tired to cook.'

She took them out to eat at Le Trou Normand, a tiny hole-in-the-wall restaurant in Rue Lepic. She could see that Carlotta would soon snap at her son, who was full of the students' cause. Eventually she did: she couldn't understand his espousal of what seemed to her their half-baked ideals.

Angelica jumped to Mario's defence. 'You're forever telling Mario that he should think about the future, Aunt Carlotta. Well, he is and he's right. The future will depend on us caring about each other, working together, not on rivalry and doing people down.'

Laura put a hand on Angelica's arm. 'Carlotta, they have a point. And surely you should be idealistic when you're young. I think it's rather splendid.'

'Mamma, don't be so patronizing.' Angelica shook off her mother's hand.

The progression from discussion to shouting took no time.

Though the evening ended with a truce, Laura could feel the young people's resentment. It was all so very different from last night, she thought. Then she'd felt the marriage might work. Now it was clear that Mario and Angelica still needed to grow up.

The next day the Métro was working again and so were the Bateaux Mouches. Carlotta and Laura took a trip on Mario's boat and Carlotta, her quarrel with her son forgotten, glowed with pride at Mario's handling of the tourists and his commentary in Italian and English.

When they got back to Montmartre they telephoned Giovanni from the local café with the assistance of the proprietor. Laura watched her daughter's face as she spoke to her father.

'You've got to forgive me, Papa. I love Mario. Just like you loved Mamma when she was eighteen.' Angelica looked at her mother as she spoke, her eyes pleading. Laura prayed that Giovanni had calmed down.

Now Angelica was smiling into the telephone, answering her father's questions, then wiping her eyes. She handed the receiver to Laura.

'Darling,' she said, 'I think they might be happy. Mario is working and Angelica is still committed to the École Gastronomique. And they do love each other. I'm sure of that.'

Giovanni wanted to know when she was coming home. And what about the student uprising? The news had been full of it.

'It's calmer today and the strikes seem to be over. We'll stay another two days, if we can, but are you managing? Can you do without us?'

'We're fine, *cara*. Stay with Angelica as long as you like. She's an idiot, marrying Mario, but she's still our daughter. And you deserve some time off. I wish they hadn't done it but at least it's got you away from the restaurant for a few days.'

He sounded wistful, and a little bitter, she thought. We must try to spend more time together, non-business time.

On Friday, Mario and Angelica said they would be meeting some friends after work but would be back for supper. They'd meet them in the café. It was nine o'clock before Angelica, flushed and excited, found them there, already eating. 'I'm so sorry I'm late,' she said. 'I left Mario with our friends on the Left Bank – I couldn't drag him away.'

'We thought you might've had trouble with the Métro, or with the police closing roads. Did you have to walk miles?'

'I got a ride on a friend's motorbike and we just sailed past the traffic. Or, rather, wiggled and wove through it. He brought me to the Place du Tertre.'

'Why won't your husband join us?'

'He was so involved with the others that I didn't want to insist. I know you don't approve, Mamma, but the students have right on their side.'

'What students?' barked Carlotta. 'Mario is not a student. He's twenty-six and a worker.'

'Our friends. They're mostly students who work part-time on the boats to get them through university. No wonder they're angry if they feel they're not getting a proper education. And they're so brave, determined to do something about it. The young are showing the older generation it's possible to be free and non-violent. Did you see the pictures of officers beating students with batons? All they were doing was peacefully protesting about their universities being occupied by the police.'

What a child she is, thought Laura, all trust and idealism. How can she be a married woman, not just out of our control but out of our influence too?

Angelica had *steak-frites*, then went home. She'd see them tomorrow, she said. Her school was closing again for the day. Maybe they could have lunch together.

But early the next morning Angelica arrived at the *pension*, her eyes puffy and shadowed. 'I don't know what's happened to Mario. He didn't come home last night.'

Laura's heart sank. Surely he couldn't be reverting to type already.

'I left him at the café on the Boul' Mich,' said Angelica.

'Who were you with? Can't you ring one of them up?'

'They're friends of Mario's, students. I don't know where they live.'

'What time would the café close? Would they have gone on anywhere else?' asked Carlotta.

'They might have joined a protest march. They were singing and drinking and wanted us to join them later at the Arc de Triomphe. Oh, God, something must have happened to him.'

Carlotta said, 'Angelica, what did he say he'd do? Was he going on the march?'

Angelica shook her head. 'He didn't say anything. I thought he'd come home.'

'Maybe he decided to sleep at one of their houses,' said Laura. 'Especially if it was late and he was tired. Are you sure you don't know where any of them live?'

Angelica looked from her mother to her aunt, her eyes wide and despairing. 'No, I don't. Maybe at the Cité Universitaire.'

'You didn't quarrel, you and Mario?' Carlotta looked beadily at her daughter-in-law.

'Of course not. We never quarrel.' A smile lit her face, then faded. 'I can't go to the Cité Universitaire,' she said. 'It's vast. I'd have no idea where to look. I don't even know anyone's surname.'

Laura persuaded Angelica to go back to the flat. She ought to be there in case Mario came back. 'Besides, darling,' she said, 'you've been awake all night fretting about Mario. You should get some sleep. We'll come round later and hope to find you both there.'

Angelica was too anxious to go home and knew she wouldn't sleep anyway. She went to the *préfecture de police* and reported Mario as missing. They told her she should come back on Monday. There'd been a major riot last night and they'd been inundated with missing-person reports. They didn't register them unless the person had been missing for two days. The officer looked weary. 'Don't worry,' he said. 'They usually turn up in a day or so, with nothing worse than a few bruises and a hangover.' He smiled. 'Lots of people go missing on marches and in riots.'

Angelica walked outside and down the steps. Riots? Mario would probably love a riot. And last night he'd been so excited, his eyes alight, talking non-stop, the life and soul of the party. The students were obviously in awe of him and Angelica had been so proud of him.

She trudged up the stairs to their flat, hoping against hope she'd find him there, but of course she didn't. She lay on the bed and tried to sleep.

At eleven o'clock she gave up, rolled off the bed and put on her shoes. Cooking was soothing and it would take her mind off Mario. She went to the greengrocer and bought a celeriac, two leeks, four carrots and two big potatoes. She hesitated over a cabbage: it was the size of a melon and she wondered if she dared ask the shopkeeper to sell her half of it.

'What are you making, Mademoiselle?' he asked, his fat face kindly.

'I don't know. Some sort of soup. It has to be cheap. To serve as a main course for four people.'

'Ah, *soupe de garbure*,' he said. 'Any vegetables will do, and a bit of bacon.' He waddled to the corner and picked up a box from the floor. 'Take that cabbage and I'll give you these. They'd be fine for soup.' He dropped the box at her feet. 'Help yourself.'

'Really?'

'Yes. They're no longer fresh so I can't sell them. Take what you want.' He handed her a large paper bag.

Angelica sorted through the box and selected turnips, spinach, mushrooms, spring onions and parsley. Then she crossed the street to the butcher, who had been monosyllabic and apparently disgruntled when he'd served her before, but now became positively animated when she said she needed bacon for a *soupe de garbure*. 'Ah, my mother, she makes the best *garbure*. She's from Gascony, that's why. It's a Gascon dish.' He kissed his fingers.

He sold her a bacon knuckle and a chunk of pork belly. 'Have you got the beans?' he wanted to know.

'Beans? No, the greengrocer said—'

'Dried beans. My mother uses *haricots blancs*.'

'But they'll need soaking, and don't they take a long time to cook?'

'They need soaking overnight.' He looked disappointed. 'But

you can use green lentils. Or pasta. They cook faster. And you need stale bread and some grated cheese at the end.'

By the time she'd been to the grocer, she had three bags of ingredients, and had had cooking lessons from two shopkeepers. She looked at her watch and saw she'd been gone for fifty minutes and had temporarily forgotten about Mario. But as she climbed the stairs again she could feel the panic battalions massing in her stomach. She prayed Mario would be there, but the empty room mocked her hopes. The bed was still rumpled, just as she'd left it.

She looked up *soupe de garbure* in her treasured copy of Escoffier's *Guide Culinaire*. It seemed simple enough. She put the meat and knuckle bone to simmer with garlic and a few cloves, and was turning her attention to peeling and chopping, when suddenly she could maintain the pretence no longer.

She dropped onto a chair. What am I doing, making soup? Mario could be in hospital, lying in a gutter or even in the morgue. Panic mounting, she covered her face with her hands and started to cry.

A little later, she was still sobbing when she heard footsteps outside, then the door handle turning. Mario! Thank God!

But it was her mother. Angelica sank back into her chair. Laura's arms were round her in seconds. 'Come on, darling, it may be nothing. He's not been gone a full day yet, only twelve or fourteen hours. I know it's worrying, but he probably got drunk and is sleeping it off. Isn't that the most likely possibility? This is Mario we're talking about.'

'Don't you dare say anything against him.'

'Ssh, ssh, darling. I'm sorry.' Laura climbed onto the bed and lay down alongside her daughter. Angelica felt her mother's arms go round her again and breathed in her familiar smell. She felt herself slowly relax, her mind calming. Her mother was rhythmically stroking her back, as she used to when, as a child, Angelica had had a bad dream.

When she woke up, her mother was leafing through the *Guide Culinaire*. 'Darling, how are you feeling?' Laura looked at her watch. 'You've only slept for forty minutes.'

Angelica swung her legs off the bed and stood up. 'I feel better. Calmer anyway. Thanks, Mamma.'

They made the soup together, peeling, slicing and chopping. 'Soup is the most comforting food,' said Laura.

'Yes,' agreed Angelica. 'And if Mario turns up I'll run down to the shop and buy a tin of duck confit to turn this one into a celebration.'

Mario didn't appear, but in the middle of supper there was a knock on the door. Angelica ran to open it, her heart pounding. It was Hugo, one of their friends from the boats.

Angelica grabbed his forearms. 'Hugo, where's Mario?'

'In gaol. The *flics* dragged him off.'

'What happened?' She pulled him into the room. 'Is he hurt?'

'He's fine. But he's in the police station near the Eiffel Tower. In the morning he'll be charged with causing an affray or something but then they'll let him go until it comes to court if . . .

Carlotta interrupted. 'I'm his mother. And this is Angelica's mother.'

Hugo was looking at Angelica. 'We can get him out if we can raise the bail money, but none of us has any money, so—'

'We'll put up the bail money,' said Laura.

*

Mario bounced down the police station steps and kissed everyone extravagantly. He got into the front passenger seat of the taxi, the three women in the back, then swung round to talk to them. 'Last night was amazing,' he said. 'We were—'

Angelica touched his shoulder. She could tell from the speed at which he was talking and his glittering eyes that he wouldn't like being interrupted, but she hadn't any choice. 'Darling,' she said, 'tell the driver where we want to go.'

Once the car was moving, he was off again. 'We were so well prepared,' he said. 'We made our main barricade in advance. Some of the students had brought crowbars for prising up the paving stones and six of us would push a car into position, then roll it on its side – that's what made the best barricades. When the *flics* arrived, we torched the cars. It was like Bonfire Night. Fantastic.'

Angelica felt excluded, not just from last night's events but from Mario's thoughts. She wanted his attention, or some of it, but his focus was all on last night. Also, she could feel her mother's disapproval, Carlotta's too.

Mario was still talking. 'The police are fascists,' he said, 'so brutal. But we threw stones and bottles, anything we could lay our hands on, at them. We used planks to push them back and we got them on the run. Fascist pigs. You've no idea.'

Carlotta raised her voice to interrupt him. 'And you've no idea of the agony Angelica's been through, not knowing where you were, while you were behaving like a delinquent.'

'She should have come.' Angelica opened her mouth to protest, but Mario raised his voice. 'I told you, Angelica. You should have listened. You missed something that will change history.' He looked from one of them to another. 'I promise you, we'll

97

force this government out. There'll be a general strike any day now.'

When they got home Mario declared himself starving. He'd been, he said, too fired up to eat the prison supper and he'd only had coffee this morning. Angelica heated up the remains of last night's soup and Mario sat at the table and wolfed it down without comment. Then he leapt up to continue his tirade. He strode around the room, talking nineteen to the dozen, the words coming hot and fluent. Angelica knew that if their mothers weren't there, she'd admire his fervour, his shining eyes, his commitment.

He paused for a moment and looked at Angelica. 'Have we got anything to drink?' He answered his own question: 'Obviously not. *Merde*.'

Angelica sat back and closed her eyes. She just wanted to be alone with him, but there was no hope of that.

To Angelica's surprise it was Laura, not Carlotta, who stood up, grabbed Mario's arm and forced him to look at her. 'For the love of God, Mario, just shut up. You've frightened us to death, and all you can tell us is what a great time you're having, playing the revolutionary. You should be ashamed of yourself.'

Mario seemed taken aback, but he rallied quickly. 'Oh, Laura, Mamma, you're so bourgeois. There are people out there who've been beaten by the *flics*. They have bruised heads and broken legs but they don't complain.' His voice resumed its declamatory tone. 'And Angelica knows that what we're doing is important. Tomorrow I'm meeting with the others who work on the boats and I'll lead them on strike. I'll have them all out until the employers come to heel. You'll see.'

Angelica couldn't bear it. She could see Carlotta wanted to

join the fray but Mario had just got out of gaol and needed rest. She whispered to Laura, 'Mamma, please take her away.'

Her mother put a hand on Carlotta's shoulder. 'Carlotta, let's go. Leave these two alone for a bit.'

Once they'd gone Mario, to Angelica's relief, seemed less excitable, though still talking. She made them both tea – more calming than coffee – and he told her that the previous night, before they'd joined the crowds, they'd agreed he would lead a breakaway watermen's union, where the members, not the leaders, had the power. The current leaders were no better than the government. The new union would fight for democracy, freedom and civil rights.

Angelica didn't want to have this conversation now. She'd end up challenging him, asking what those grand words meant in practical terms at his work. She'd not heard him complain about the boats. He liked his boss, who was easy-going, with a sense of humour. The company had given him a loan and paid reasonably well, with extra for late-night shifts. She didn't think Mario had grounds for a quarrel.

She put her hand over his mouth gently, as much a loving gesture as to stop him talking. 'Darling, it's so good you're back.' She fluttered her fingers along his lips, then pushed between them. He opened his mouth and sucked them. She withdrew her hand and replaced it with her lips, open and eager, kissing his mouth, his unshaven cheeks, his eyes.

He held her, his grip tight on her upper arms. 'Get on the bed,' he said, his voice low and gravelly. She obeyed and he made love to her, very fast, almost violently. She tried to respond but he was too rushed, too brutal, and suddenly it was over. He rolled off her, panting, gave her a quick, hard kiss and jumped off the bed. She was baffled. Usually afterwards he was spent and dreamy, and they would drift off in each other's arms. But this was different: he was like an excited schoolboy.

'I must go,' he said. 'People to see.'

'But darling, it's only two-thirty . . .' She stopped, knowing she couldn't reason with him in this mood. She watched in silent dismay as he pulled on his jeans, shirt and jacket and shuffled into his shoes. 'Where are you going?'

'To meet the others, get on with the plan.'

'What about me? When will you be back?' She could hear the pathetic wail in her voice.

'You can come. But I can't wait for you. We'll be at the bar on the Boul' Mich. Come.'

'But Carlotta? And Mamma?'

A flash of exasperation crossed his face. 'They're so boring. Forget about them.'

'Mario, I can't do that. You've given them enough reason to be hostile already. We should have supper with them, try to make amends.'

'For what? Confronting their bourgeois prejudices?' He laughed and blew her a kiss. 'They'll be fine.' And he was gone.

CHAPTER EIGHT

Angelica was nearing the end of her first term in advanced French cuisine. The student uprising, though only a month ago, might never have happened. Paris was back to normal. Mario had failed to get his union off the ground and was still working on the boats. Her école had barely missed a beat and they'd now cooked their way through all the classics in the *Guide Culinaire*. She loved her course and was looking forward, albeit a little nervously, to the exam.

Her test piece was a stuffed sea trout in aspic, and she had to cook it for Chef Berger and his boss, the formidable Madame Plouvier. To earn a distinction in the final exam next term, she had to get one now too.

First she made the aspic. She filtered her good strong fish stock and felt a little buzz of satisfaction as it ran out clear as crystal.

Next, she made the stuffing, a quenelle mixture of pike beaten with cream and egg white. Poaching the sea trout would be easy, she thought, but preparing it wouldn't be. She cleaned and scaled the fish, trying to prevent the wretched scales flying everywhere. If Chef Berger found a single scale clinging to the table she'd lose marks. She filleted the fish, using her fingertips to locate the pin bones and extracting them with kitchen tweezers, then spread the fish with the quenelle mix, closed it and wrapped it in muslin. Then she put it into a fish kettle, brought it to a simmer and let it cool in the liquid.

She scrubbed down the table and made the béchamel sauce, adding four leaves of gelatine to make sure it would set. Now all she had to do was put together her work of art. She set her fish on a long white platter, peeled off the skin and gave it a deep ruff of fine cucumber slices round the neck. Then she carefully spooned the sauce over the body of the fish, exempting the head and the tail. When it had set she decorated it with tarragon leaves, arranged like fish bones. Now for the tricky bit, she thought as she spooned the aspic thinly over the sauce. It set immediately, giving the fish a delicate shine, rather than a clumsy PVC overcoat.

She didn't like the eye staring at her so she covered it with a tiny disc of cucumber skin. Then she cleaned round her fish, and covered almost the entire platter with a sea of paper-thin overlapping cucumber slices, which she painted with a mild French dressing.

She stepped back to examine it. That's good work, she said to herself. Chef won't be able to fault it.

Fifteen minutes to go before they had to present their dishes to the examiners. She put hers into the fridge, then went to shower and change. Once the judging was over they could leave, taking their exam dishes with them. She was anxious to get home as soon as she could. She hoped to cheer Mario up with her gastronomic creation. He'd been so depressed of late, not himself at all.

Beside her table once more, she waited for the judges to reach her. They were taking their time, examining each dish with great care. They tasted only a little of everything, making an effort not to spoil the look of the dishes. But they did not spare the students.

'Too much salt.'

'Not enough salt.'

'Overcooked.'

'Clumsy chopping.'

The occasional nod betrayed approval, but few compliments were dispensed. As they tasted a variety of dishes – a vol-au-vent filled with sweetbreads, a stuffed *ballon* of lamb, a *coq au vin*, a duck *ballotine* – they pronounced their verdict. It was a simple one-word judgement, which would go on the certificate: 'fail', 'pass' or 'distinction'.

When they got to her, Angelica's confidence waned. She knew she'd done well, but ever since those first difficult weeks, she'd been nervous of Chef Berger.

The examiners tasted the trout and the pike stuffing separately, then each took a composite mouthful with a slice of cucumber. Madame Plouvier was nodding with a satisfied expression, and Angelica almost relaxed, until she saw Chef Berger frown.

'You have made one big mistake here, Angelica. Look carefully.'

Angelica looked down and immediately saw what he meant. The cucumber juice had leaked onto the plate to dilute the French dressing. The slices were swimming in liquid.

'Well?'

'I forgot to *dégorge* the cucumbers, Chef.'

'Correct, and it has ruined your dish.'

Angelica stared at him. He couldn't fail her for forgetting to salt the cucumber slices, could he? The dish still looked great. She'd been surely heading for a distinction. Then she noticed that the cucumber slices round the neck of the fish were beginning to slide out of place. The salt in the aspic was drawing the juice out of the cucumber and they were going to slip off. In half an hour it would be a wreck. Angelica closed her eyes. Oh, please, let them not fail me, she prayed.

She kept her head down and her eyes closed as she heard them muttering together. Then there was silence and she looked up. Chef Berger said, 'Pass,' and turned away. Madame Plouvier gave her a weak smile, then followed him to the next table.

Angelica picked up her dish and went to cover it with cling film from the dispenser on the wall. The student next to her complimented her on the decoration but Angelica was so close to tears she couldn't answer. How could she have been such a fool? She knew salt drew the liquid out of anything. All it would have taken to get a distinction was to sprinkle the slices with salt, leave them for half an hour to lose their juice, then rinse and dry them.

She was still unhappy when she got home. She'd carried the dish on the Métro, and had spilled the oily cucumber juice on her skirt.

Mario didn't move as she came in. Lying flat on his back, he ignored her cheerful 'Hello, darling,' and addressed the ceiling: 'Where've you been? You're late.'

'I told you I'd be late. I had my exam today.'

He didn't respond, just curled on his side, his back to her. Her immediate reaction was anger. How could he be so insensitive? Didn't he know how important this was to her?

Normally she would have gone to kiss him, probably climbed

onto the bed to snuggle up to him and ask him what was wrong. But now she went to the kitchen corner, laid the table with two plates and the fish. On the Métro she'd hoped Mario might greet her with a bottle of wine to celebrate the halfway mark of her course, or her triumph in the exam. But there was no wine and she took the half-empty Coca-Cola bottle out of the fridge.

'Supper's ready,' she said, her voice carefully neutral.

'I'm not hungry.'

Angelica wasn't hungry now either. She sat at the table, staring at her fish, watching the last of the cucumber scales slipping off. Tears ran down her cheeks. I should feel sorry for Mario, she thought, but I'm so tired of him being like this. He won't go to a doctor, won't let me tell anyone about his misery and lethargy, won't make any effort at all.

She couldn't understand it. During the two weeks of the student uprising, Mario had been in his element. He'd led his colleagues in a strike, and spent his days manning barricades, making speeches and nailing posters to trees. And she had been at his side, in the thick of it all. She had been caught up in the extraordinary feeling of comradeship and purpose. A photographer had caught her with Mario and another girl. They were marching, arms linked, at the head of a crowd, striding through St Germain. Her head was thrown back as she sang 'La Marseillaise', and Mario's clenched fist was raised. She'd thought it was a great picture and summed up exactly how they had felt: liberated and drunk on excitement. She'd bought a copy of the paper and stuck the photograph to the wall.

She looked at it now, then at Mario's immobile back.

They were like two completely different men. Back then Mario had hardly slept. At night they'd met their comrades in cafés and talked of freedom and making love, not war. Angelica had been full of admiration as well as overwhelming love for Mario. The girls in their group of student friends were as fervent and free as the men. If she felt like kissing Mario passionately in the street, she could, and it didn't matter that they were in the middle of a crowd. Mario had adored her, and they had made love all the time. Now he was too depressed, or too tired, to notice her.

And yet, she thought bitterly, he can snap out of it if he tries. If friends come to see him, he bounces up, smiling. But for me he can't raise the flicker of a smile, let alone a kiss.

She undressed and climbed onto the bed behind Mario. He was still in his shirt and jeans but if she nagged him to undress he'd resent it and take no notice anyway. It was hot in their room, and they lay side by side on top of the quilt, not speaking, not touching. Eventually she rolled towards him and dipped her head to give his shoulder a perfunctory kiss. Immediately the smell of him ensnared her and she thought, It's not his fault he's so miserable. She snuggled against his back with her right arm round his chest and rocked him gently as though he were a child.

Mario's dejection lasted several weeks, He went to work, and presumably did a decent job, but at home he was miserable, eating little, just wanting to sleep. She felt helpless but tried again anyway: 'Darling Mario, there must be something we can do. You're not yourself. There must be a doctor who could help.'

He refused to discuss it, saying only, 'Don't worry about me. I'm not worth it.'

He usually answered when spoken to, but briefly, with no life in his voice. One day, she wouldn't let him turn away. She held onto his jacket lapels and looked into his face. 'Mario, you have to tell me what's wrong. Have I done something? Has something happened? I have to know. Talk to me, my darling.'

'You can't help, Angelica. And you don't want to know.'

'Yes, I do. I'm going mad. What's happened to us? We were so happy. For God's sake, Mario, tell me.'

So he did. He told her he'd always had these weeks of depression when he saw clearly what he was really like: worthless, someone who had achieved nothing. If only he had the energy, he'd kill himself. She listened in silent horror, until he said, 'There's nothing to live for.'

'How can you say that? What about me?' Her voice got stronger as she spoke. 'Am I not worth living for? You told me I was the light of your life, that I made everything a joy, even walking down the street or taking out the rubbish!'

'It's no use. We'd both be better off if I was dead.'

A few days later, she awoke to find him up and making coffee. For the first time in weeks he asked her what her day would hold, and within two more days he was his old self, happy, affectionate, alive.

Summer gave way to autumn. They saw friends, went to the cinema, took a bus out into the country to go foraging for *cèpes* in the woods, then fried them in butter with garlic and ate them on toast.

Angelica almost felt she had imagined the weeks of misery. It was like a nightmare, losing its power as you woke up.

Through October the weather was glorious. Changing into her whites in the school cloakroom, she studied her reflection. Her skin was pink and clear and she'd gained a little weight. She looked less like a skinny adolescent and more like a woman, with breasts and a slim waist.

In November, a few weeks before her final exam, in the middle of skinning kidneys for a vol-au-vent, she had to make a dash for the lavatory to throw up. Oh, God, she thought, excitement and apprehension making her heart beat faster. Maybe I'm pregnant. She sat on the loo seat, fished out her pocket diary and tried to work out when she'd had her last period. Eight weeks ago.

All day she thought about it, veering between worry about how Mario would take the news and uncontrollable waves of pure joy.

That night, at supper, she said, 'Darling, I've something to tell you.'

Mario looked up, eyebrows raised.

'I think I'm pregnant.'

His smile vanished, replaced by wide-eyed horror. 'You can't be. We've been so careful.'

'Well, I've not seen a doctor but I'm sure I am.'

'It's not my baby, though, is it?' His voice was suddenly harsh.

She looked at him in astonishment. 'Of course it's yours. What are you talking about?'

'It can't be mine. It can't be.'

Angelica stood up. 'Mario, are you telling me you think I've slept with someone else? Been unfaithful to you? Is that what you mean?'

Mario's eyes drilled into her, intense and angry. She'd thought he would feel as she did about the baby, worried but thrilled. She hadn't expected anger. And certainly not accusation.

Mario got to his feet and turned his back to her. When he faced her, he had one hand in his hair, clutching it. 'I'm so sorry, darling. Of course you weren't unfaithful. I don't know why I said that. It was crass . . . But you'll have to get rid of it. We can't have a baby. I don't want a baby.'

'But I want to keep it. It's ours.'

'That's just nonsense. You'll do as I tell you, Angelica. We are not having a baby.' He might have been a stranger.

She picked up her handbag, ran out of the door and clattered down the five flights of stairs. Breathless, she leaned against the wall in the vestibule and listened in case he was following her. No sound.

No longer shaking but still upset, she ordered a hot chocolate in the café-bar where her mother and Carlotta had often eaten while they'd been in Paris. Maybe Carlotta was right: Mario was too irresponsible and volatile for marriage.

Angelica stayed in the café for a good half-hour, drinking a second cup of chocolate and summoning the courage to return to the flat.

When she did go back she was relieved and a little ashamed to find it empty. She didn't want to see him and risk another argument about her pregnancy.

She went to bed and, exhausted by the day's emotions, fell asleep. She was woken by Mario's hand on her back, sliding round to her breast. Half asleep, she rolled over, her arms going round him as she arched her body into his.

Then her eyes shot open as she remembered what had happened last night.

She tried to sit up but Mario hugged her to him. 'Darling, I am so, so sorry. I behaved like a brute.' He kissed her forehead, then pulled back to look into her eyes. 'It's just that I love you, darling, and I want you to myself for a little while. We haven't had a year together yet. One day we'll have *bambini*, lots of them. But not this one. We didn't plan it. And you're too young. You haven't lived yet.'

Angelica tried to argue with him, but when she thought of the effect a baby would have on her career, and the damage it might do to their relationship, she weakened. Babies needed to be wanted by both parents. And she remembered Carlotta's dire warnings about cousins marrying. Maybe the baby would be mentally or physically deficient. Besides, an old-fashioned bit of her wanted to be married before she conceived.

So she agreed to an abortion, tears streaming. 'But you have to make all the arrangements. I just can't.'

'I'll find out about it. But you could go home. Abortion's legal now in England.'

'No. I couldn't face my mother knowing I was doing such a terrible thing.'

'They needn't know. All you have to do is go to your doctor and he and another doctor have to agree that you'll go mad if you have it, or something like that.'

'But even if I could bear to do it, stay in some boarding-house, how could I afford it? We don't have any money.'

Clearly Mario hadn't thought of that. 'Well, there's no big rush. I'll ask around. It can't cost much in Paris. It must happen all the time.'

A fortnight later, Angelica found herself tramping up three flights of stairs behind Mario in a gloomy house near Château Rouge Métro station. When they arrived at the flat, there was no name on the door, just a big knocker above a six-inch-square window with a grille. Mario knocked and soon a young man's face appeared. Mario repeated what he had said to the concierge downstairs. 'We have come to see Madame Grosport.'

'What is your name, please?'

'Smith. Mr and Mrs Smith. From England.'

The door opened and they followed the young man into a sitting room furnished with old-fashioned brown armchairs. A glass coffee table held several out-of-date women's magazines and a big ashtray containing cigarette butts. A wooden pipe was balanced on the edge. The two windows had floor-to-ceiling dark red curtains in shabby velvet.

Angelica shuddered. The desire to leave at once was almost overwhelming. I'm doing something wrong, she thought, something terrible. But she said nothing.

Soon the young man returned with a cashbox and sat down next to Mario. They had a whispered conversation, then a louder argument about the money. He'd had to get another loan from his boss and promise to work more hours and most nights to pay it back. Angelica half hoped he'd refuse to pay. But they came to a deal. She turned away so she couldn't see her lover paying to have their child killed.

After a while a stocky woman in her fifties, with her hair in a net, came in. 'Madame Smith? This way.'

Angelica followed her into a room with a table standing on stacks of books. On it, an oilcloth lay over a thin mattress. In a corner there was a basin. She tried not to look at the bucket under the sink or the window shelf of instruments and kidney-shaped dishes. At least, she thought, the place was clean and the equipment looked medical. She'd heard of this being done with knitting needles or wire coat hangers.

Madame Grosport indicated the curtained-off cubicle in the

corner and told her to take off her trousers and knickers. She could keep on the rest. Angelica removed her shoes and socks too, then regretted it. The carpet looked grubby and felt gritty.

There was no anaesthetic. She felt something cold being pushed into her, then an uncomfortable scraping followed by a sudden sharp pain. She gasped and instinctively brought her knees together. The woman slapped her thigh and barked, 'Open.'

Angelica tried to float above what was going on, to pretend it wasn't happening.

'*Bien. C'est fini.*' Madamme Grosport handed her a sanitary towel. 'Get dressed now. Your boyfriend has gone to get a taxi.'

Before they left, the young man gave them a paper bag containing two sanitary towels and a packet of penicillin. 'That should be enough. The bleeding will stop, and the pills will prevent infection. Keep quiet for two days. No running or jumping for a week.'

After two days she went back to school, but she was still bleeding, and she felt dreadful. On the Saturday, she stayed in bed while Mario, who seemed determined to believe there was nothing wrong, went to work. By midday the dull pain rose to prolonged cramps and she forced herself to get up, dress and travel by Métro to the hospital at St Ouen. By the time she arrived, the cramps had lessened but she was shivering and aching all over. She had no idea if they would admit her but they did, and almost at once, she was in surgery.

When she came round, she was in a ward, and it was dark outside. A nurse gave her a *tisane* and the surgeon who had operated on her came and sat by her bed. 'You're a lucky young woman,' he said. 'Whoever did your abortion failed to do it completely and has damaged the uterus. I'm afraid that in future you may not find getting pregnant again so easy.'

That might be a good thing, she thought but did not say. Mario was difficult enough now, but if he was competing with a baby for her attention?

The doctor was still talking. 'At least there's no infection, which is a miracle.'

'I was given a course of penicillin. I'm still taking it.'

'Well, thank God for that. Infection could have killed you. So could a major puncture of your uterus. It's scarred but is still intact.' He was looking at her sternly, like a schoolmaster, she thought. But then his expression softened. 'Well, I don't suppose you'll make that mistake again,' he said. 'But I'm afraid you will have to answer some questions from the police.'

Angelica shut her eyes. Now she'd be charged with a criminal offence. The doctor read her mind. 'Don't worry. They never charge the women. They go after the abortionists.'

Angelica said nothing. What could she say?

He stood up. 'I will prescribe a further course of antibiotics. You can go home tomorrow morning.'

'Thank you, Doctor.' Her eyes filled with tears. I wish I could just stay here, she thought. I don't want to be questioned by the police, and I haven't the money to pay the hospital.

The next morning she woke feeling more like her old self. She ate a croissant and drank the cup of *café-crème* the nurse had brought her with pleasure. She dressed, and was told to go to Reception where she could collect her antibiotics and pay the bill.

She wrote a cheque, knowing it would bounce. But she'd woken up clear-headed. She must telephone her mother and ask her to wire her the money. She wouldn't tell her about the abortion. She'd say she'd had a miscarriage.

The thought of her mother, who would be loving and sympathetic, made her long to be at home in Paddington with her parents. Not with Mario.

Her mother wired the money. She wanted to come to Paris and be with her. 'Oh, sweetheart, will you be all right? It's so terrible to lose a baby. Poor darling, and poor Mario. Would you like me to come over?'

Angelica wanted her mother desperately, but she couldn't have her here. How could she keep up the pretence about the miscarriage and that all was fine between her and Mario?

Sometimes it *was* fine. Even most of the time. Mario had been kind after her return from hospital, but incurious. He seemed glad it was all over and she sensed he didn't want tears or histrionics from her, so she bit her lip and didn't talk about it. Mario returned to his old hard-working self, loving and fun. He was proud of her excellent results at school, full of praise for the dishes she brought home, and optimistic about their future.

One day he told her he'd been taken on to the permanent staff at the boat company, and was now on a fixed salary as a manager. He had to cut his hair ('They said I looked like a hippie') and buy a business suit. The next evening he came home with a short-back-and-sides, wearing a striped suit with a waistcoat. He strutted round the flat, pretending to be a boss, giving orders and clicking his fingers. They laughed a lot, went out to supper and drank a couple of bottles of wine.

But something had changed for Angelica. She didn't trust him any longer, and lived in fear of him falling into another deep trough or flying so high that he talked too fast and wouldn't listen to anyone else. One weekend they hired a motorbike with a sidecar and drove to Champagne. Angelica had objected to the expense but Mario said, 'You deserve it, darling. You've worked so hard and we're only young once. Besides, I've had a rise.'

Angelica was beginning to learn about wine and the thought of visiting the great champagne houses was tempting so she gave in. They drove from château to château, tasting the wines, exploring the underground chalk *caves*, eating delicious food in wayside restaurants. Mario taught her to ride the bike, brushing aside her concern at having no licence. The weather was cold but clear, and the roads were almost empty. They were carefree, irresponsible and having fun.

On the second day, Angelica wanted to see Rheims Cathedral. 'It's one of the wonders of the world. We can't be here and not see it.'

'It'll be dark and boring, and some old fart of a priest will bend our ears about God, and try to extract maximum francs from us. I hate those places.'

Angelica was offended, not least because he seemed to leave no room for discussion. 'So that's that, is it?'

'Well, I'm not going, that's for sure.'

Angelica was driving. 'OK,' she said. 'Where do you want me to drop you? Or do you want to wait for me?'

He raised his voice. 'You'll take me to the hotel, and you'll come too. Neither of us is going to see a bloody cathedral.'

Angelica glanced at him. His face was flushed and his eyes alive with hostility. 'You can't order me to do anything. You're bossing me about as if you owned me.'

'You're my wife. If I say jump, you should jump.' He was almost shouting now.

'Mario, have you gone mad? First, let me remind you, I'm not your wife. We never got married, did we? And even if I was your wife I wouldn't jump to your command.'

That seemed to stop his flow, but as she slowed at a junction he barked, 'Turn left here.'

'It's a No Entry, stupid.' She drove on.

'If I tell you to turn left, you turn left, do you hear? Even if it's into a brick wall, you should do it!'

'And kill us both? You're insane, Mario.'

Suddenly he banged both hands hard on the sidecar. 'Stop the bike, damn you. I'm getting out.'

This time she did as she was told. As soon as Mario had climbed out and slammed the door, she shot off, all her pent-up rage released as she drove at breakneck speed out of Rheims.

She was on her way back to Paris before she calmed down enough to stop. She parked the bike in the shade beside the road and took herself for a walk. She sat on a tree stump, and tried to think: Mario was still the man she loved but he was a manic depressive. When she'd been in hospital, and weeping a lot, she'd found herself confiding in a nurse who'd opened her eyes to the condition. Mario, she'd said, sounded like he had what used to be called Melancholia. He had all the symptoms. The profligate spending for a start – ever since he'd been promoted he'd seemed to think he was as rich as Croesus, splashing money around as fast as he earned it, buying himself clothes he didn't need, once coming home with a suede handbag for her that must have cost two weeks' wages. If it wasn't for her allowance they'd have no money for rent or food. Then there were the delusions of grandeur: he sometimes referred to the Bateaux Mouches as 'my company', as if he owned it; he often treated waiters with contempt – and now he'd decided she should obey his every word. And he didn't sleep: he'd get up at two in the morning, plotting some hare-brained business venture that would make them millionaires.

She couldn't leave him in Rheims. If he went on a bender tonight he might not have the money for the hotel or the train fare home. She drove back, hoping to find him in the hotel.

As she walked in, she saw him sitting at the bar. She slipped into the seat beside him. '*Ciao.*' He smiled at her. 'Did you enjoy the cathedral?' No hint of what had gone before. No concern for her. But, thankfully, he wasn't angry.

'What are you drinking?' she said. 'I'd love a glass of white wine.'

A month later Mario had lost his job. He was nonchalant about it, saying the bosses were idiots. Angelica couldn't get to the bottom of what had happened because he brushed it off. 'Who cares? I can get another job whenever I want. Actually, it's lucky. I'm feeling really creative and I can concentrate on my other ideas.'

'But why did they sack you, darling? What did you do?'

'I lost my temper with some stuck-up old trout who came into the office to complain about something. She turned out to be a journalist deliberately being difficult to see how we coped.' He laughed. 'She was probably delighted since she got a story out of it. But my boss was livid when he read it. We had a shouting match, and he fired me.' He kissed her exuberantly. 'They'll want me back, you'll see. There isn't anyone else who can do my job. No one. But they won't get me.'

Angelica was appalled, but she held her tongue. This was the moment to tell him they should go home.

'Mario, let's go back to London. My course will be over in a couple of weeks, and we could be there for Christmas. I need to get a job too. You know I wanted to work in one of the top restaurants – Maxim's, the George Cinq, the Tour d'Argent. I've tried them all, but they won't let a woman through the door.' She paused, but Mario showed no interest. 'I guess I'll have to lower my sights until I have more experience. At least Mamma and Papa will take me on.'

CHAPTER NINE

Silvano was delighted that Angelica was back at Giovanni's, now making the *focaccia* and the desserts. He usually sat with her at staff lunch. He told himself this was perfectly OK. They were cousins, after all. Friends since childhood.

She was always ravenous. 'You've the appetite of a soldier on the march,' he said, as she heaped her plate for the second time with salad, topping it generously with fried chicken livers, bacon and mushrooms.

'I know, but I start at five and I've had no breakfast. Only lazy accountants get in at nine thirty, fortified with bacon and eggs.' She prodded his midriff. 'Look at that. Too much *gelati*,' she teased.

When she'd gone back to making walnut cake and panna cotta, Silvano stayed at the table, thinking. Sometimes he wanted to strangle Mario for treating Angelica so casually. At one moment he was charming to her and at the next insupportable. In short, he was being Mario. The worst thing was Silvano couldn't do anything about it. Sure, he could read his brother the Riot Act if he owed Carlotta money, or if he borrowed Giovanni's car and brought it back with the tank empty, but he couldn't shake the living daylights out of his brother when he promised Angelica a visit to the cinema, then changed his mind, or said they'd go for a walk in the park and then wouldn't get out of bed.

He should avoid their company, but he knew he wouldn't. Tonight, for example, they were all going to Giovanni and Laura's to watch the moon landing on television. He had a fleeting vision of Angelica sitting on the sofa between him and Mario. For a second he could almost feel the warmth of her shoulder against his, see her long legs stretched out before them. But he squashed the thought. He must avoid that, for all their sakes.

'That's one small step for man, one giant leap for mankind.'

'What did he say?' asked Giovanni, his eyes fixed on the small screen as Neil Armstrong, in a white space suit, stepped off the lunar module *Eagle* and onto the moon.

Laura repeated the astronaut's phrase, and added, 'We'll remember this moment for ever, don't you think?'

The black-and-white images were extraordinarily clear: the cumbersome little figures with their bouncing steps; *Eagle* looking like a cross between a giant insect and an unstable stack of rubbish; the fluttering flag.

When the live film had ended, and they had digested the enormity of seeing men land on the moon, and watching it as it happened, and the moon scenes were replaced by commentary and re-runs of the event, Laura looked round. 'What happened to Silvano? And where's Mario? You need to give your grown-up sons a clip round the ear, Carlotta. They said they were coming.'

'Oh, Laura. I forgot to tell you. Silvano said to tell you he was very sorry but he has to do something at Giovanni's.'

'And Mario, Angelica? I thought he was going to watch it with us.'

'I don't know, Mamma. He said he'd be home, but who knows?'

Laura saw the exhaustion and despair in her daughter's eyes but she couldn't talk about Mario with the others in the room. Giovanni's mistrust of his son-in-law had grown into positive dislike since he and Angelica had come back from Paris. That had been six months ago and Mario had yet to get a job. He was, Giovanni said, sponging off them, living upstairs.

Laura didn't want to start Giovanni and her daughter off. Giovanni was quick to criticize Mario and Angelica, just like her father, was combative if challenged. She'd fly to Mario's defence even if she knew he was right.

When they'd watched the moon landing again on the news, Laura went down to the kitchen to make supper and Angelica offered to help.

Laura split the Belgian endives into two and sweated them in butter, while Angelica made a cheese sauce. They wrapped the cooked endives in thin slices of ham, laid them side by side in a dish and covered them with the sauce, then scattered breadcrumbs and grated *parmigiano* over the top and put them under the grill to brown.

Carlotta put a foil box on the kitchen counter and removed the lid. Inside was some of her famous three-bean salad from the deli. 'Here you are, *cara*,' she said to Laura. 'This salad would still be good, and saleable, tomorrow but I dare not break your rules so I brought it home.' She tipped the beans into a dish.

Angelica picked out a couple of broad beans with her fingers, earning herself a half-serious slap on the hand from her aunt.

'The other Laura diktat is no fingers in the food, remember?' said Carlotta.

Angelica laughed. 'That doesn't apply at home, does it?' She reached for a spoon. 'This is good, Mamma. Carlotta's right, we shouldn't chuck it.'

'I know, darling. And at home I never would. But if you serve the public, and you have new staff who aren't cooks, you need rules they understand. Sure, cooked dried beans and pulses don't deteriorate fast, but green stuff does.'

They ate the endives with the bean salad, followed by sliced oranges with a dose of Amaretto.

Mario failed to turn up. Laura wasn't surprised: she'd suspected there was something seriously wrong with him ever since Paris. Sometimes he was so manic there was no talking to him, then a few weeks later he'd slide into depression. Once, when he was in bed for no apparent reason, she'd sat her daughter down and challenged her directly. 'Darling, I know you're worried about Mario. He needs help, doesn't he?'

'Oh, Mamma, if you only knew!' And then it had all come out. The times when he refused all help and only wanted her arms round him. He wanted physical comfort but nothing else – no food, no music, no newspapers, nothing. 'He won't let me tell anyone. He'd be furious if he knew I was talking to you. He's so ashamed of himself, as if it was his fault. He can't get up, he believes he's worthless, he talks about killing himself. He says he spends hours planning how, and despises himself for being too spineless to do it.'

Laura had been appalled. She knew Mario could be over-excitable or moody, but this was much worse. Poor Angelica. 'Oh darling, what have you saddled yourself with?'

There was more to come. Angelica told her of the periods when Mario felt wonderful, spending money like water, talking very fast and sometimes incoherently. Then he'd be furious with her for not keeping up and believed he was the best at everything. 'But, Mamma, some of the time, even most of the time, he's everything he was before – enterprising and happy, loving, fun to be with. I don't know what to do. I still love him, I really do, but the loving times are getting fewer. When he's high he thinks he doesn't need help, just says I'm exaggerating or making it up. When he's at the bottom, he hasn't the energy to talk at all.'

Laura didn't say anything to Giovanni about her conversation with Angelica. It would only worry him and make relations between him and his son-in-law even worse. Besides, that night in bed, Laura found herself listening to her husband's troubles.

'I'm a bit worried about the ice-cream business,' said Giovanni. 'That new chain, Nice Cream – remember Mario worked for them when they started up? – well, they can pay more for high-street sites than us, and they're taking a good bit of our business.'

'I can't believe it. If it was Marine Ices, I'd understand. They make proper Italian ice cream. But Nice Cream is rubbish. All cheap fat, sugar and fake vanilla. I know because one of their lads is working for us now. He couldn't stand the company.'

'They're very good at marketing. You'd think there was a mamma in every shop, churning the stuff by hand. They imply that the milk and eggs come from their own farm, which is rubbish. They're giving our vans in Hyde Park a desperate time.'

Laura frowned. 'But don't we have exclusive contracts for the parks?'

Giovanni gave a cynical smile. 'Not worth the paper they're

written on. Nice Cream send their vans into the park and when the police catch them, they act all innocent and leave.'

Angelica made a conscious decision not to let Mario's moods take over her life. She had to get on with her career. She was working full time at Giovanni's, making bread and desserts. She was out of the house by five, seldom home before nine, and welcomed the long hours. She had to be in the kitchens early to get the bread made before the other chefs needed the ovens, and often stayed on until the pudding trolley went out so she could supervise the look of the dishes and instruct the evening brigade on how to cook and serve the hot desserts.

She'd have loved a proper wood-fired bread oven to work with, so she could experiment with different, more interesting breads, sourdoughs, like *ciabatta* and Italian country breads, but she didn't have the oven, the space or the time. She had to knock out between eight and twelve loaves of *focaccia* a day. Customers and staff gobbled it like gannets.

But she was eager to get back to classic French cooking. She applied for a job as senior commis chef at the Savoy Hotel. The hotel boasted a reputation for *haute cuisine*. The chef of chefs, Escoffier, had reigned there once. She signed her application 'A. Angelotti', not Angelica. If she could just get an interview maybe she could persuade them that the sky would not fall in if they hired a woman.

She didn't tell her parents or Mario, just slipped out one afternoon at four o'clock for an interview. The Savoy was so huge she couldn't find the staff entrance, and had to pluck up courage to ask one of the commissionaires at the front. She was directed further down the Strand to a side alley.

The staff entrance gave onto a wide basement corridor with huge reels of fire hose on the walls. She passed a room full of round banqueting tables, stacked with legs folded, and towers of gilt chairs, then stores and staff cloakrooms. She finally came to the room she was looking for: *Interview Waiting Room.* She knocked and entered to find herself in a largish room lit by neon strip lights. It was sparsely furnished with a table and what looked like old restaurant chairs. Half a dozen young men in suits were sitting on them. Angelica smiled briefly and sat down.

They waited in silence, the only sound the rhythmic tapping of a nervous young man's foot on the linoleum floor. One by one they were called by a neat, bespectacled young woman, perhaps a secretary. Angelica was last, having waited over an hour. By then she had established that she and all the young men were after the same job.

She followed the woman through a vast, brightly lit kitchen with white-tiled walls, stainless-steel tables and enormous oven ranges. Thick metal pipes and ventilation tunnels ran overhead, and pot racks and shelves were suspended from the ceiling on iron poles. Huge mixing, slicing and mincing machines were interspersed with sinks standing on steel-grille floors for easy drainage.

Perhaps twenty cooks were at work, but the place was surprisingly quiet. They were prepping for the evening service in an atmosphere of unhurried efficiency. She passed a commis pulling the tails off live shrimps, giving them a little twist to extract the entrails. Another lad was scrubbing mussels and dropping the cleaned ones into a bucket. A tray of oysters, some with shreds of seaweed attached, lay on the table next to his sink. Beside him, an older chef was demonstrating the art of cleaning squid to an apprentice.

And that's just some of the seafood, thought Angelica. Somewhere there will be lobsters and crabs, not to mention the fish: huge turbot, halibut and salmon. The meat section, with steaks and roasts, poultry and game, would be over there in the distance. And somewhere else a bakery, a chocolate room or rooms, a pastry section, a larder section with terrines and pâtés, *ballotines* and *galantines*. Oh, to work in this kitchen . . .

The chef's office door was closed. On it was written in gold letters, Silvino Trompetto, *Maître Chef des Cuisines*. The woman knocked on the door and immediately opened it. 'Your last candidate, Monsieur le Chef,' she said. Angelica walked in and the door closed behind her. Monsieur Trompetto was sitting behind the desk with papers before him. He was youngish, slim, with a neat moustache. A tall chef's toque stood to attention on the desk. He didn't look up, or offer her the chair opposite him, obviously placed there for the candidates. Angelica, nervous, stood next to the chair, thinking this man was even scarier than Chef Berger. She saw that her application for the job was on the top of his pile.

He pushed his papers aside and looked up. She saw his eyes stretch in surprise. 'You're a girl,' he said. 'I don't employ women.'

Oh God, she thought, I've lost already. Then her courage returned, fuelled by a spark of indignation. That's ridiculous, she wanted to say. Unfair. 'Why not?'

Monsieur Trompetto leaned back in his chair, eyeing her speculatively. 'I don't need to, and I don't want to, miss.'

'But that isn't fair. I've skipped out of work and come halfway across London for this interview. And I really, really want to work for you.' Angelica's indignation was growing. 'How do you know I'm not the best-trained cook you've seen all day, or the hardest worker, or the most co-operative?'

Trompetto laughed, 'Fiery little thing, aren't you? You might be all those things – your application is certainly good, though borderline dishonest.' He looked down at her papers. 'A. Angelotti. You were trying to hide the fact that you're a woman, weren't you? Well, I admire your pluck, but I won't have women in my kitchen. Full stop.'

I'd better get out of here, thought Angelica, feeling the prick of tears. She turned to leave. But Trompetto said, 'You asked me why. Do you want the answer?' She turned back, expecting some nonsense about women being too weak to pick up a full stockpot. As if a man could! Or girls taking the boys' eyes off the job. Or females getting pregnant all the time.

'At a certain time of the month,' he said, in his almost stagey accent, 'they curdle the mayonnaise.'

Angelica was amazed. 'You're not serious? You can't believe that!'

'Of course I'm serious. And you are an extraordinary young woman to challenge me. I should just throw you out.' There was a brief silence in which Angelica considered apologizing but decided not to. She wasn't going to get the job – that was clear – so she might as well challenge him.

'But that's not true. That'd be witchcraft.'

Trompetto shook his head, confident in his power and amused at her impertinence. 'But I'm right. In France, on mushroom farms, women are not allowed to enter the sheds. They prevent the spores germinating.'

Angelica burst out laughing. 'I'm sorry, Chef, I shouldn't have laughed, but that's just medieval superstition. Myth.' He didn't answer but didn't seem angry. He looked thoughtful. She turned to go.

He said, 'Wait a minute, Angelica – it is Angelica, isn't it? I apologize for getting up your hopes. I should have told my secretary to filter out applications from females. But we never get any. Big hotels don't employ women, except perhaps a few in the pastry department where they're out of sight and gone before the evening service, when the real work is done.'

Angelica thought pastry work the most exacting task in the kitchen, but this time she kept her mouth shut.

He picked up her application. 'But I have an idea. Would you like to work in the pastry section? There are no women there either, but you have enough spirit, I think, to be the first.' He spoke into the intercom, in French. 'Monsieur Blanchard to Chef's office, please. Blanchard to see Monsieur Trompetto.'

Then he said, 'Wait here, young lady. Chef Blanchard will come and see if you are suitable for his department. He may not agree, of course, but at least you will have had your interview. Meanwhile I will get back to the kitchen.'

Angelica just managed to thank him before he'd gone. She watched him through the big window, peering into pots and at the tables, with a brief word to the cooks or an order to change something. As she followed his progress, he was joined by a portly chef with a round face. Trompetto put his arm round the man's stout shoulders and turned him towards the office. This must be Blanchard, thought Angelica. Their heads were close together so the other cooks couldn't hear. The conversation ended with Trompetto indicating the office and clapping Blanchard on the back.

Angelica got the job. It was for second commis in Pastry. Blanchard was polite, but unimpressed that she'd not done a specialist pastry course, had had only six months' patisserie experience and none in confectionery. Angelica was fairly sure he'd been told he had to hire her. Trompetto had liked her, and that was that.

She left the hotel elated. She'd be the first woman in the Savoy kitchens. And one day, she promised herself, she'd crack the hot kitchen too. All I have to do, she thought, is be good at the job and not do things girls are supposed to do, like cry, get pregnant, make eyes at the boss. No chance of the latter, anyway.

CHAPTER TEN

How good it was, thought Giovanni, to eat in someone else's restaurant once in a while. He and George Frampton were lunching together at the Savoy Grill. The conversation ranged widely: Angelica's marriage, Jane's inability to find a boyfriend. Giovanni even found himself confiding his worries about Laura, telling his old friend about her occasional lapses into misery and guilt about their long-lost child, adopted at birth, who must now be over twenty.

'The attacks of guilt are more frequent because she feels she's lost Angelica to that useless Mario. And we could do with a son. If only Angelica would come back to Giovanni's, maybe Laura would let up a bit. She keeps saying she'll do less, but she doesn't.'

'Any more than you do, my friend,' George said, with a smile. 'But why did Angelica leave Giovanni's?'

'She's mad about French food, silly girl. Says she needs more experience.'

They ordered pudding. 'We have to,' said Giovanni. 'Angelica won't forgive us if we don't. She says to order the *îles flottantes* or the *pêche aux fraises*. She says the peaches are perfect right now

130

and they get those beautiful white ones from Italy. You know, they smell like flowers.'

They ordered one of each. George's was a large peeled peach, its stone removed and filled with an almond cream. It sat in the middle of the plate, covered with a fresh strawberry sauce, the colour an electric pink and the consistency just thick enough to stay on the peach. Giovanni's floating island was served in a shallow bowl, literally floating on a little lake of creamy custard. He exclaimed with pride and pleasure. 'It just vanishes in your mouth,' he said, 'light as silk.'

Over coffee, they turned to business. Giovanni explained that he and Laura had been talking about another Italian restaurant, simpler than Giovanni's and less expensive. 'In South Kensington, perhaps, near Deli-Calzone. Or Knightsbridge. Or maybe even Islington, which is up and coming, I'm told.'

'We could have a chain,' said George. 'It would need to be replicable, not like Giovanni's, dependent on a brilliant cook. A posher alternative to Berni Inns. I think it could work.'

'If we get the menu right – somewhere between the Deli-Calzone dishes and Giovanni's, and if we spend some money on the décor. Laura wants it smart. You know, modern and colourful.'

'Well, the Calzone cafés taught us how to how to control a chain, establish consistency. And they've become a real alternative to fish and chips or Wimpy for ordinary folk. So why not Britain's first upmarket chain?'

Giovanni hadn't expected George to be negative – he never was – but his immediate enthusiasm was cheering. 'Whoa, George,' he said, smiling. 'Let's start with one, shall we?'

'How soon before we cover our investment?' George asked.

'Depends on whether we own the freehold or rent the site, and on all sorts of factors. But I'd expect to break even on the trading account in six months, and cover the investment in three years. If we don't feel fairly sure we can do that, we shouldn't risk it.'

'Sounds good to me. At that rate we could open two a year, once we've proved the formula works.'

Giovanni laughed. 'You've backed me for twenty years and I've never known you say no.'

'You've been a good investment. A dozen ice-cream parlours, fourteen Calzone cafés . . .'

'Fifteen. Plus the three Deli-Calzones and Giovanni's.' Giovanni felt a wave of satisfaction. 'I think we've earned lunch at the Savoy. Shall we have a cigar?'

When the cigars were chosen and lit, George returned to business. 'This new one won't have a deli. Is that right?'

'Yes, it will be more restaurant than café, and open at night as well as for lunch. We'll call it Laura's. Which is what Giovanni's should have been called but Laura said no one took women in the business seriously.'

'Well, they do now. She's seen to that. Giovanni's has been far and away our top earner.' George looked hard at his friend. 'But she can't run them both, Giovanni. If she goes to Laura's and you run Giovanni's you'll never see each other.'

'I'm trying to persuade Laura that Paolo could do it now. He knows Giovanni's backwards and he's much more relaxed and confident. It turns out he's quick on the business side too. Silvano's been teaching him accounting . . .'

Giovanni sat back in the taxi to finish his cigar. He looked at his watch. Nearly four. After such a good lunch, with the wine and brandy, he decided not to go back to the office. With George bankrolling him again, he felt pretty good. He'd go home, watch the cricket for an hour and enjoy having the house to himself. As an Italian he felt a little embarrassed by his enthusiasm for cricket, but George had taken him to Lords to watch the Eton–Harrow match soon after the war, and he'd somehow caught the English bug.

In plotting his afternoon off, though, he'd forgotten about Mario. His heart sank as he walked into the kitchen and saw the back of his nephew's head, with that ridiculous over-long hairstyle, sitting at the table. Mario jumped up, revealing orange trousers, tight at the top, flared over his shoes. He was grinning. 'Hi, Giovanni. Are you skiving? Gone AWOL?'

'Well, you'd know all about that, wouldn't you?' He walked past Mario to put the kettle on.

'I plead guilty,' said Mario. 'I've not done a lot since Paris, but you'll be pleased to hear that I got a job today.'

Giovanni was sceptical. He turned back to the kettle and took a cup and saucer from the shelf. 'What job?'

'I'm going back to work for Nice Cream. Area manager.'

Giovanni spun round. 'You're *what*?'

Mario looked nonplussed, but answered equably, 'I'm going to work for Nice Cream. They want me to manage West London. They have fifteen outlets now and about the same number of vans. Not bad pay and I get some wheels.'

'But I thought they'd sacked you?'

Mario chuckled. 'Yeah, well, they did, but only when they discovered I didn't have a driving licence. Once they knew that they could hardly go on employing me to drive an ice-cream van, could they?' He grinned. 'But I've got one now. One of the benefits of unemployment – there's plenty of time for driving lessons. Which your lovely daughter gave me for Christmas, remember?'

'But how could you work for that firm? Don't you know they're our rivals? And I've told you before that they're the worst. They make dreadful—'

'Hey, Uncle, don't flip your wig.' Mario frowned, his good humour disappearing. 'No, I don't know they're dreadful. You think everything's dreadful if it's not made by Angelotti. And, yes, I know they're your rivals, but you're always preaching that competition is good for business, keeps you on your toes. So I'll be doing Gelati Angelotti a favour, won't I? Stimulating your creativity.'

Giovanni was trying hard to control his temper. 'Mario, it's one thing for you to take a job driving one of their vans. A sort of student job. But management! Don't you see how disloyal it is? A member of my family working for an outfit like that? And how can I know you won't tell them our ice cream recipe? Knowing you, you won't be able to keep your mouth shut. You'll have no respect for trade secrets.'

Mario burst out laughing. 'Trade secrets? Uncle, everyone knows how you make ice cream. It's written on the tubs! Real cream, real eggs, real fruit. It's hardly a trade secret.' He picked up his jacket and swung out of the door, 'See you.'

Angelica was relieved that Mario had a job at all. She'd become so used to him being unemployed that she could hardly believe it. It paid reasonably well, and at the moment Mario's mood seemed stable. He was good-tempered, affectionate and, most important, behaving like a grown-up. It was he who suggested that they move into one of the remaining mews cottages, number six, and start paying rent.

'But you'd better ask your father, darling. He'd probably say no to me,' he said.

But would her father let her and Mario have number six? Her mother would be in favour, she was sure. Her ambition had always been for the family to occupy the whole row.

Angelica walked through the house to her father's study. She stood by his desk and he put his arm round her narrow waist in a tight hug. 'Hello, *cara mia,* and what can I do for you?'

She turned to push some papers to one side so she could sit on his desk. 'I wanted to ask you when the lease of number six will be up. Mario and I would love to take it if we can.'

She could almost read her father's thoughts as he frowned. He was weighing the joy of getting Mario out of the house against the unpredictability of their income. She earned a pittance at the Savoy and she knew, as her father certainly did, that Mario was unlikely to be in his job with Nice Cream for long.

'Papa, you have to let us. Please. Mario needs more space and I know he's getting on your nerves.' She put her small hand over his big one. 'And I would really love a proper place of our own, with a bathroom and a kitchen, not like the freezing garret in Paris. You've spoilt me, Papa.'

Giovanni sighed. 'Very well, my darling, you deserve a bit of comfort, even if Mario doesn't. Tell him if he's late with the rent, daughter or no daughter, you're out!'

Angelica kissed the thinning patch on the top of his head. The threat was empty, and she suspected he knew it too.

PART TWO

1972

CHAPTER ELEVEN

When her husband's fork clattered to the kitchen floor as she was serving their rhubarb crumble, Sophie thought nothing of it. But when David didn't reach down for it but left his mother, still spry at eighty-four, to make the attempt, Sophie got there first. She didn't want her mother-in-law straining or overbalancing.

'Butterfingers, David,' she said, putting the fork to one side. 'Do you want some custard?'

David gave a sort of grunt. Sophie looked at him sharply. He was trying to speak, and his face looked odd, lopsided and rigid. He was sitting at an awkward angle, half over the table. Oh, Christ, she thought. He's having a stroke.

'What's the matter?' cried Maud, as Sophie jumped up.

Sophie put her hands on each side of David's face, trying to hold his gaze. 'Darling, don't move. I'm calling an ambulance.'

She pulled a chair close up to David. 'Maud, can you sit here and look after him?' She ran to the telephone on the wall and dialled 999. 'Ambulance, please. I'm a doctor and my husband is having a stroke.' While she was talking, she watched David and Maud. Maud's cheek was against David's shoulder, but he seemed unaware of her. He wasn't distressed, but had slumped sideways, over the table and the arm of his chair. Thank God it's an armchair, thought Sophie. Otherwise he'd be on the floor.

Her mind was oddly clear, planning ahead. She must get Grace or George to come across from Frampton. She couldn't leave Maud alone, worrying about her son. She dialled the number and Marston the butler answered, then called Grace. A moment later a different voice said, 'Hello?'

'Grace, darling, David's had a stroke. I'm going with him to hospital. Could you or George come and sit with Maud? She'll be so worried on her own and I don't want to take her to the hospital. I don't know how long I'll be.'

She rang the hospital and spoke to the Casualty duty officer. She didn't know the woman but she did know many of the hospital doctors. She gave her name, explained that she was a local doctor, and warned her that David was on his way. She would accompany him and be there in forty minutes or so.

She put the phone down and hurried back to David. He tried again to speak but couldn't find the words. He looked confused, but not frightened. Maud was sitting upright, now holding her son's arm.

Fifteen minutes later Grace arrived with her daughter.

'Good of you to come too, Jane. Really kind,' said Sophie.

'Mum insisted.'

How can she be so ungracious at a time like this? Sophie wondered.

Relief flooded her as the headlamps of the ambulance swept the windows. She had already opened the kitchen door and left all the lights on, so within seconds the men were inside. They were professional, kind and authoritative. It was a relief to relinquish responsibility.

She watched as one of the men climbed into the back to sit next to David, talking to him quietly as he buckled the safety straps over David's prone body. His colleague closed the doors and pulled himself into the driver's seat.

She stood at his window. 'I'll follow you,' she said.

Sophie got back to Chorlton at two in the morning to find Grace asleep on the sofa. She woke her gently, then gave her a heartfelt hug and answered the unspoken question: 'No news until the morning, I'm afraid. But he's in good hands. Where's Jane? And how's Maud?'

'Jane's upstairs in Laura's old room, I'm afraid. She was falling asleep in that chair. I hope you don't mind.'

'Of course not. And Maud?'

'She's fine. What a remarkable old girl she is. Since Donald died she seems to have got younger. She was most indignant that you'd summoned me to babysit.'

'I thought she would be.'

'She said we shouldn't worry until we know for certain there's something to worry about. She offered me a whisky, had one herself to help her sleep and took herself upstairs.'

Sophie lay in bed, wide awake, her mind circling. Now she'd dealt with all the practical things – tidying the kitchen, giving David's dog a belated walk, shutting up the house – she had no option but to confront her situation.

David had had a serious stroke, but they'd saved his life. Of course there was hope for a full recovery, but she knew it was faint. They'd told her very little at the hospital, just that the next few days were crucial. And she'd seen enough patients of her own to know that some people got better miraculously fast from a stroke and others didn't improve at all.

How could she bear it if David didn't recover? If he could never again put his arms round her? Make love to her? Was she facing the rest of her life as his nurse? Or as a widow?

For the first time in years, Sophie reviewed their decision not to have children. The twins had been only two when they married and they had needed stability and undivided love. She'd looked after them since the fateful day when they had entered the world and their mother had left it. To her they *were* her children. Besides, she was so busy with her medical practice and with them, why would she want more children? She hadn't even considered it until, when she was approaching forty, she'd briefly hankered for a baby of her own.

'David, my love,' she'd said, one evening over supper, 'don't you think we should have another baby?'

He'd been appalled. 'Sophie darling, no, I don't. I'm just beginning to enjoy the freedom we have now, with the boys growing up. The last thing I'd want is to go back to worrying about a baby.' He'd also argued that if they had one they'd have to have two, the boys being too old to be much good as siblings. And they could barely afford the school fees for Richard and Hal as it was. And, he said, didn't she think there were enough children in the world?

He'd persuaded her, and she hadn't regretted it. She'd put her brief desire for a baby down to fear of the empty nest. The boys, then strapping teenagers, were becoming more independent by the day.

Now, as she mopped her face with a sodden Kleenex, she thought again that they should have had more children. The twins had pretty well left home, and if David died, she'd have no one to love and be loved by. If they'd delayed conception until the boys were at boarding school the house would still have young children in it. With two old women and David in a wheelchair, Chorlton wouldn't be a proper home.

Well, she told herself, it's too late now.

She squeezed her eyes shut, trying not to cry. With a deliberate effort she redirected her thoughts to the practical. It would be months before he was well enough to take charge of the estate again. How would they manage? They were in the middle of the harvest, and it wasn't just the Chorlton farms: they also managed the four Frampton farms for George and ran his two subsidiary businesses of cheese-making and country wines. Cheese production was only in its second year, and struggling to make a profit. Frampton Country Wines was twenty-five years old and going like a train. Next week David was due to host a launch party for their new damson and quince wines at Fortnum & Mason. Maybe George would be free to do that. Everyone loved an earl, especially the press.

She was just nodding off when she remembered the new milking parlour, half built and behind schedule. David was overseeing that too.

She had to tell their sons. Hal, newly down from agricultural college, was in Australia, getting experience on a cattle station. Richard was in his final year at Oxford, reading economics.

Suddenly she pushed herself into a sitting position. If she wanted to speak to Hal she couldn't wait till morning. If it was the middle of the night here, it would be the middle of the day there. She got up and pattered barefoot down to the study to find the telephone number of the cattle station. Mackenzie, that was it.

It took a while to get put through the various telephone operators, but eventually she heard the telephone ringing on the other side of the world. They took a long time to answer.

'G'day. Mackenzie Ranch.'

'I have an overseas call from England. Will you take the call?'

'England? Sure.'

When she asked if she could speak to Hal Oliver, there was a pause. Then: 'Oh, you mean the Pommie. Sure thing, I'll get him. Might take a while – he's in the shearing shed.'

Sophie's heart was racing as she waited. If only she could see him, she could somehow make it less of a shock.

'Hello?'

'Darling, it's your mum.'

'Gosh, Mum. What's up? Has something happened?'

'Hal, Dad's had a stroke. Last night. He's—'

'Oh, God, Mum. That's . . . Is it bad?'

'We got him into Casualty pretty quickly. But I don't know whether he'll make a full recovery.' Her voice broke.

'Oh, Mum . . .'

Sophie told herself to brace up. Her voice steadier, she went on, 'Stroke patients do recover completely sometimes, but this was a bad one. He can only move his right arm and leg and at the moment he can't talk – he can't find the words.'

'Jesus, Mum.'

There was a silence and Sophie could almost see the shock and worry on Hal's face. 'I'm sure he'll get his speech back,' she said, although she wasn't.

'I'll come home, Mum.'

'No, darling. This is probably the only year you'll ever have like this, when you can travel and learn from other farmers.'

'But I want to see him, Mum. What if he dies? I'm coming home.'

They argued a bit and then a disembodied voice interrupted to tell them they'd had three minutes and did they want another three?

Sophie said no, and told Hal to ring her in a day or two, reversing the charges, when she'd have more news. She hung up, biting her lip to stem the tears.

It had been good to hear Hal's voice. Even though he was so distressed, his concern and love for his father were obvious. Richard would be the same. Although the boys seldom showed emotion (she blamed their school for that: British public schools seemed to regard anything other than a stiff upper lip as weakness), at heart they were warm and loving. She went back to bed and this time she slept.

Early next morning, before Maud and Jane woke, she made a cup of tea, took it through to the study and rang the hospital. The ward sister said David had had a good night, seemed cheerful, and the consultant would be in to see him at ten. She added something about visiting times and Sophie didn't argue. As a doctor she could get in any time she liked, and she wanted to catch the consultant on his rounds.

She telephoned Dr Drummond, the senior partner at the Moreton practice. She'd long ago negotiated a deal by which she could work part-time, but now she needed to be in the farm office to fill in, as far as possible, for David. And when he came home, he'd need a lot of nursing. Could she, she asked, just cry off for the foreseeable future? They ought to be able to find a locum if she went on unpaid leave. Of course, Dr Drummond said. They'd miss her sorely but they'd manage. David must be her priority.

Next, she spoke to Richard, who abandoned his studies to catch the next train from Oxford.

Then she rang David's sister. Laura had been her best friend since childhood and Sophie knew how devoted she was to her brother.

'He's only fifty-five!' she exclaimed. 'Oh, my poor brother, he'll hate it. He's always been so active.'

'I know, and he was very fit. Always out on the farm, lots of exercise, slim and very strong. It does seem unfair.' Suddenly Sophie felt exhausted and close to tears.

'Darling, I'll come down this afternoon. Mum must be worried stiff. I can be company for her, and generally help. I'll bring a load of food from Deli-Calzone. Save you some cooking.'

'That would be wonderful. Richard's coming home too, so at least David will know we all love him.'

Her most urgent calls made, Sophie put down the telephone and stood up. She'd lay the breakfast things, get dressed and go to the hospital. When she entered the kitchen she was taken aback to see Jane sitting at the table wearing the white dressing-gown trimmed with lace David had given her on their one and only holiday abroad, in Madeira. He'd bought it for her birthday. A flash of annoyance shot through her, but she made an effort to be polite. 'Good morning, Jane. I see you've found my dressing-gown.'

'Well, yes. I hope you don't mind. It was hanging on your bathroom door.'

If I had more energy, Sophie thought, I'd ask her what she was doing in my bathroom when there's a perfectly good one next to her bedroom. Instead she said, 'But shouldn't you get dressed? Is Grace coming to fetch you?'

'I've no idea. But I came down because I was hungry. Breakfast first, I thought, then I'll dress.'

Sophie put the kettle on and made them both tea, porridge and toast, then laid a tray for Maud. 'I'm not up to frying bacon and eggs, I'm afraid. I have to be at the hospital.'

Jane made no effort to help, so Sophie waited on her, took Maud's breakfast upstairs, then washed up. The irritation of having a young woman so ill-mannered and idle distracted Sophie from more important worries. I bet she won't strip the bed and fold the sheets for the laundry, or put my dressing-gown back, she thought.

David was in a side ward by himself. Sophie sat beside him, as he drifted in and out of sleep all morning, and didn't truly wake until noon when they brought his lunch. She propped him up and fed him soup, followed by jelly and custard. He tried to do it himself with his good right hand, but the left side of his face was pulled down and he became upset at the dribbling. He couldn't speak and she begged him not to try.

'Don't worry, my darling. It will come right. Just let me help. The main thing is that you can swallow so they don't need to feed you with a tube. And don't worry about the talking. The speech therapist will be in later and your speech will come back. Darling, you're alive, and that's what matters. And you will get better.' She kissed his forehead and stroked his good arm.

She knew the consultant had seen David but she told him again that they wouldn't have a meaningful prognosis yet, and the main danger was of a second stroke. The first twenty-four hours were critical but they had given him anti-coagulants and she was sure the worst was over. She couldn't tell if she was comforting him, but she felt better for talking to him.

'The main thing about strokes is not to lose any time. You were in here within fifty minutes so it's looking good.'

When she got home, George rang for news. She told him what she knew and George promised to do anything she asked. 'And don't worry about Country Wines,' he said. 'I'll cope with the launch at Fortnum's and help the manager with anything he needs. He'll tell me what role David was playing and I'll try to stand in for him.'

Sophie then met David's right-hand man on the farms, Tony, who said he'd manage the harvest as long as the weather held. 'I'll see if I can hire someone to drive the combine or one of the tractors. But labour's scarce at harvest time, which is why David put the hours in.'

'I could drive a tractor, I think,' said Sophie, 'but certainly not a combine-harvester.'

Tony grinned. 'It may yet come to that, Sophie. But I'll ask around.'

The next day she went to David's office where young Holly worked three days a week, doubling as David's secretary and bookkeeper. She was confident that she could cope. 'But what about cheques?' she said. 'The feed and seed merchants will need paying next week. We've ordered all the seed for next year.'

'Don't worry, I can take them into the hospital. His right arm is fine.'

Sophie looked round the office. God, it was a mess. The little desk where Holly worked was orderly enough, but the rest! David was untidy at home but no one noticed because she and Maud tidied up after him. Here his desk was buried under papers, catalogues and farming magazines, all held down by small bits of metal, some of them distinctly greasy, extracted from some machine. Boxes were stacked at the back of the desk, under the window. One contained a large torch (not working), another seed samples, and a third, which should have been in the workshop, was full of miscellaneous nails and screws. Last year's calendar and a dog-eared insurance certificate were stuck to the window, which was far from clean.

She was tempted to sort it out. It would distract her. She didn't want to go to the hospital in case they had bad news for her. But she longed to see David, comfort him. Tell him he'd be fine. Oh, please, let that be true, she prayed. She climbed into her car and headed for the hospital.

Through the next weeks, driving a tractor and helping to run the businesses helped Sophie. She could tell David how the harvest was going, and it was a welcome antidote to the hours of sitting in the bleak hospital, and the twice-daily drive to and from it.

It was Maud who had quietly set about tidying David's office. When Sophie had protested, saying there was no hurry and she'd get round to it, she'd replied that it gave her something to do. 'Being old is so boring,' she said, 'and I like doing something for David. It's like sorting out his toybox when he was a boy.' She fished a handkerchief from under her cuff and blew her nose. 'I couldn't bear it if he dies before me. It's not right to outlive your children. I felt that so deeply when Hugh was killed.' She pushed the hanky back up her sleeve. 'But it was wartime.'

'I don't suppose that made it any less painful.' Sophie put an arm round Maud's bony shoulders and held her, her heart contracting at her mother-in-law's distress. She must feel as desperate as I do, she realized. She had been so worried about David, and anxious for the boys, that she'd not given poor Maud much thought at all.

They had stayed like that, not speaking, until Sophie felt the stiffness go out of Maud. Her shoulders came down a fraction and her arms relaxed. They drew apart, smiled at each other and Sophie had left the room, the scent of Yardley's lavender talc in her nostrils.

David had daily appointments with a speech therapist and a physiotherapist. Sometimes Sophie was with him when they fetched him for his sessions, and neither minded her being there. She could see that he liked the speech lady. She got him making extraordinary noises, pulling faces, clicking with his tongue (which he couldn't do at all), trying to sing.

'Physio is a bully and a torturer,' he wrote on his pad, after the first couple of sessions.

'But, darling, you must do the exercises. It's the only way to get the movement back,' said Sophie. And he did try. She could see his face straining, but his arm and leg wouldn't move of their own accord.

After three weeks, David's consultant had come into the ward when Sophie was there. She made to get up – she usually left them alone while David was examined – but the doctor said, 'No, stay, Dr Oliver, if you don't mind,' as he drew the curtains round the bed. 'I thought you'd want to know exactly where we are and what we can hope for.' He seated himself on the edge of the bed and looked steadily from one to the other, his expression neutral.

He's done this many times before, thought Sophie. He's steeling himself to tell us the worst.

He went on, 'I'm sorry to say, Mr Oliver, that the part of your brain that controls the movement of your left leg and arm is severely damaged. I fear the damage is irreversible. I know you won't believe this now, but I assure you many people go on to live a full and good life in spite of that.'

'You mean he won't walk again?' asked Sophie, her eyes going from the doctor to her husband.

'Yes. I'm sorry, but yes.'

David shut his eyes briefly, an expression of acute suffering transforming his lopsided face for a second. Then he nodded. 'What about the speech?' he said, correctly but haltingly.

The doctor's face lightened and he smiled. 'Well, there you are! Your progress has been excellent. You're speaking now and eventually I think you'll have no trouble with word retrieval or articulation. But you must keep up the exercises. Talk and sing all day. Don't slack, because now is the time to retrain your brain.'

By the time David came home he had no difficulty finding the words, but forming them was a struggle. Sophie could see the frustration, sometimes fury, in his eyes as he repeatedly tried to say the same word, knowing it was coming out wrong. But he could make himself understood, and as the weeks progressed, and he diligently did his exercises, his speech returned to normal.

But his paralysis was another story. It was as the consultant had predicted. No improvement. He went on with the exercises, but Sophie knew it was because she insisted. Fortunately, two years ago they'd replaced the mix of flagstones in the kitchen, vinyl in the passages and loo, fitted carpet in the study and uneven floorboards in the dining and living rooms with expensive Amtico flooring throughout. It looked exactly like stripped pine and once they'd taken the rugs away, it was the perfect surface for a wheelchair. Even Maud could push her son from room to room.

Maud, Sophie saw, enjoyed the time she could now spend with her son. It gave her a purpose and the satisfaction of being needed. She looked at them sitting side by side, he in his wheelchair, she in the straight-backed wing chair – the only one she could get out of unaided. Maud was reading the paper and David was turning the pages of the *Farmer's Weekly* expertly with his right hand. Occasionally one would make a comment, or share a snippet from their reading. It looked so companionable, and Sophie felt a little twinge of jealousy. She had no time to read anything. But she was grateful too. With Maud around, he wouldn't be stuck shouting uselessly in an empty house. I suppose, thought Sophie, it's like getting your boy back. He's yours as a child, then replaces you with a wife – in David's case, two wives. Then his family and work take all his attention and love. Now he's back with his mum.

Towards the end of October, Laura, Giovanni and Angelica were down for the weekend. Mario hadn't wanted to come and Angelica, sensing he was becoming depressed, hadn't insisted. But Richard came for Sunday lunch and they were all out on the terrace, enjoying the autumn sunshine.

'Shall we go for a walk?' Laura asked her brother.

Giovanni and Richard lifted the wheelchair down the steps, and Laura pushed it to the end of the garden so that they could look up through the yellowing leaves of the chestnut trees at the clear sky. She tipped the chair back so she was holding the handles at the level of her knees, and David was lying almost flat.

'When I was ten, this was the best tree for conkers,' he said. She set the front wheels back on the ground. 'I was the conker champion at school. And in the cricket and swimming teams. *And* captain of rugby. A regular athletic hero.'

There was something sardonic in his voice. 'You were always my hero, bro,' she said cheerfully, as if she hadn't heard the bitterness. 'Still are, in a way.' She squeezed his shoulder. 'I used to think I was so lucky to have two much older brothers. Hugh was so handsome in his RAF uniform, like a god, but far away. Twenty years is such a gap. He seemed part of Mum and Dad's generation rather than mine.'

'He was my hero too, though I didn't admit it. I wished I had his looks, of course, and that devil-may-care attitude to everything. He was always happy, wasn't he?'

'I don't know. I was only fifteen when he died and I was away at school most of the time. I remember him as laughing a lot, and teasing me, but I liked the attention rather than feeling picked on.'

David was looking through the gap in the trees to the fields beyond. 'He died in the prime of life. One minute grinning, probably, the next minute, bang, shot out of the sky.' He looked at her, an ocean of sadness in his eyes. 'Good way to go, really.'

They bumped back along the uneven path. Laura made a mental note to suggest Sophie get all the paths smoothly re-paved before winter set in. Suddenly there was a shout from the terrace. Giovanni had jumped up, and Angelica and Richard were hurrying into the house. They stopped just inside the

French windows and were laughing and talking, but to whom? Laura couldn't see. Soon Maud had joined the huddle of people by the open doors.

'What's happening?' David's eyesight had been mildly affected by the stroke.

'David, it's Hal!' she cried, as the huddle broke up and Hal stepped onto the terrace. She grabbed the wheelchair handles and took the rest of the path at a run. By the time they were at the bottom of the steps, Hal had jumped down them and was sitting lightly on his haunches to look into David's face.

He was grinning broadly. 'G'day, old man, how ya doin'?' he said, in a mock-Australian accent. 'Strewth, mate, you don't look so bad at all.'

Then Sophie was there, tears on her cheeks, kissing her boy. He wrapped his arms tightly around her. 'Mum,' he said, 'you need feeding up. You're so thin.'

David hadn't spoken beyond an astonished 'Hal!' but Laura saw the pleasure on his face. He was smiling as broadly as the paralysis would allow, one side of his face looking as it always had been, the other pulled down, like an image in a distorting mirror.

Richard came down the steps and David's two sons got him back onto the terrace, where Laura noticed a young woman standing diffidently in the French windows. Sophie saw her at the same time. 'Goodness,' she said, 'I'm so sorry, you must be a friend of Hal's?'

She was an astonishingly beautiful girl. Laura thought immediately of Botticelli's *Birth of Venus*. She had long red-blonde hair almost to her waist, held off her perfect oval face with a beaded band round her high forehead. Her eyes were large and dark;

she had a wide mouth and lovely skin – pale, with the lightest overlay of tan. She wore no make-up.

She was tall and slim, with long arms and delicate hands, and was dressed, Laura thought, like *Vogue*'s idea of a hippie: long skirt, sandals, soft flowered blouse and sleeveless suede jerkin. 'Yes,' she said, 'I'm Pippa. We flew from Sydney together.' Her smile revealed white teeth with a pronounced gap in the middle. I wonder how old she is, thought Laura. She doesn't look more than eighteen, twenty at the most. She seemed perfectly calm and relaxed in the middle of all the excitement of Hal's arrival.

Suddenly Hal was beside them. He put his hand round Pippa's waist and pulled her to him. 'I'm so sorry,' he said. 'I should introduce you. This is Pippa. We met, can you believe it, on Bondi Beach!' He took her round the family, explaining to her who they all were, who was married to whom.

That afternoon Sophie took Hal and Pippa round Home Farm and Angelica came too. Hal wanted to see everything, and Sophie noticed he was anxious that Pippa should approve. But as the conversation became more technical, Sophie bringing Hal up to date on the grain yield, the cost of labour, the new milking parlour, whether to plant Top Field with barley or oats, Hal became absorbed in Chorlton, so Angelica and Pippa dropped back behind them.

Conversation turned to the beef cattle. Sophie said, 'David's thinking of crossing the Herefords with French Charolais – using AI, of course – to improve the next generation's conformation and growth rate, also the killing-out percentage . . .'

Hal stopped in his tracks. 'Mum, I can't believe this. "AI"?

"Killing-out percentage"? Have you become a cattle farmer in six weeks?'

She laughed. 'No, but I've spent those six weeks either talking farming with your dad or actually farming with Tony. I like it.'

Hal shook his head, half in astonishment, half in admiration. 'And here was I thinking I'd be Dad's understudy and general manager. But my mum's got there before me.'

'Oh, darling, you're a proper farmer. But I'm good at organisation. We'll be a great double act with Dad pulling the strings.'

She felt a sudden warm wash of happiness. Hal was apparently home for good, David was cheerful and much better. And she'd be working with her son and husband. It could have been so miserable: David dead or completely incapacitated, their boys away, herself grief-stricken and trying to cope with Chorlton.

'Back to the Charolais, then,' said Hal. 'I know they're all the rage. Last year a bull went for ten thousand guineas, can you believe it? It even made the farming news in Australia.'

'Mmm. But I do worry about dystocia. Those Charolais are enormous and the Hereford cows are so small. Something like ninety per cent of difficult births are caused by the calf being too big for the cow. Our Herefords seldom have any trouble. It would be cruel, surely, to force them to bear huge calves.'

'I agree,' said Hal. 'But maybe we're sentimental. I'd like to see a little Hereford bull in the field. Can't get excited about a package of sperm delivered in a phial. And I like the idea of holding on to our old British breeds. We should talk to Dad.'

On the way back Hal turned to shout to Pippa and Angelica, 'Hey, you two, enough girly gossip. Come and join us. No more farming talk, I promise.'

They talked about Australia, and Sophie asked Pippa, 'You met Hal on Bondi Beach?'

Pippa started to answer but Angelica cut in, laughing. 'Pippa, Aunt Sophie's going to pump you dry. Why don't I just short-circuit it? Sophie, your boy Hal and Pippa are together, a couple. She's come to England to be with him. Isn't that wonderful?'

CHAPTER TWELVE

Giovanni was to spend the day at the not-yet-open Laura's, just off Kensington High Street. The decorators had finished so he was going to meet the staff, and ginger up the new chefs.

He couldn't believe how smoothly the preparations for Laura's had gone. Opening a new restaurant was nearly always a last-minute scramble. But this time the building had already been a restaurant so all the Angelottis had had to do was change the staid décor. And, amazingly, all had gone to plan. Now they had a fortnight to train the new staff and iron out any problems. Unheard of luxury.

Laura led him into the middle of the room with the blinds down so they could assess the night-time lighting and study their creation. She'd had the staff lay up a couple of tables to see the effect. The tablecloths were old-gold damask, but they and the crystal chandeliers that had come with the lease were the only traditional elements. The tub-shaped chairs and the sofas in the bar were upholstered in vibrant yellow and orange, and each side of the tall Georgian windows, curtains had been painted on the wall, orange-and-yellow-striped, elaborately draped and tied with tasselled ropes. It was a perfect *trompe l'oeil*, took up no space at all, and had cost a fraction of what real curtains would have set them back. And they made you smile.

'What do you think, darling?' asked Laura. Giovanni had agreed the design and approved the budget, but he hadn't seen the results until now.

'I like it. I didn't think I would. Sounded too *avant garde* for me. But you have better instincts, *cara*. And you were right. It's fresh and modern, but not cold. And the chandeliers are funny.'

The huge traditional chandeliers still shone in all their old-fashioned pomp. But a second glance revealed knives and forks, spoons and ladles glinting between the crystal drops of one, while the other was strung with antique cups, saucers and little jugs, brightly patterned and jaunty. In the smaller dining room there was only one chandelier, and it was hung with tiny copper sauté pans and saucepans.

Giovanni smiled, remembering Laura's objections to their keeping the chandeliers. He'd thought they spelled class and tradition; she'd thought they were boring and pompous. Angelica's idea had solved the problem.

'Angelica says we should make the festooned chandeliers Laura's signature,' said Laura.

Giovanni smiled. 'OK, but next time, if there is a next time, we'd have to buy the chandeliers, and I'll certainly veto that. These came free.'

The kitchen was a modern chef's dream, complete with separate cooled pastry section, walk-in fridge and freezer, eye-level salamanders and a charcoal grill. The ovens, the dry store and the refrigeration were all designed to take standard containers: lidded plastic for the stores, stainless steel for the ovens. The shelves for the dry store, fridge and freezer were of sturdy stainless steel racking, and had wheels.

Giovanni, now a businessman rather than a chef, knew he wouldn't have equipped the kitchen so well – you'd never get a return on the most expensive new French ranges, the best automatic pot washer, the self-defrosting under-counter fridges. But he was enough of a chef to appreciate what he saw. He felt lifting excitement as he tested the fiendish heat of the salamander grills, and admired the water tap and runnel at the back of the range so you could rinse a spoon or pot, or add water as you cooked.

The new manager assembled the staff and made a little speech about how honoured and privileged they felt to have the owners of the company with them today. Giovanni shifted on his clogs, not wanting to humiliate him by telling him to shut up, but wishing he'd do so all the same. He looked across at Laura for help.

'Thank, you, thank you,' she interjected, when the man paused for breath, 'but we'd both far rather be working with you here than sitting in an office.' She paused, then went on briskly, 'Today we're going to cook and serve everything on the menu, and everyone – front-of-house, porters and office staff – will get a chance to taste the dishes.'

Giovanni was enjoying himself. He just wished he had a restaurant full of eighty people and a dozen waiters queuing for orders. But, still, perfecting the dishes was satisfying too, getting a cook to understand that to sear scallops well the pan had to be blazing, the scallops dry; explaining that, on the plate, 'The food must look as if it just landed there, casually, perfectly. It must not provoke the thought that our fingers have handled every single mouthful, even if they have.'

As they worked, Giovanni found himself getting more and more enthusiastic. The cooks, three lads and a girl, were nervous, but keen, silent and concentrating. The head chef, who had been a sous-chef at Le Gavroche, knew what he was doing. He might be scared of me, thought Giovanni, but he's got the respect of the kitchen, and once he has a knife or spoon in his hands, he's all control and confidence.

But he was worried about the pastry chef. Her food tasted good, but it was too clumsy for Laura's. Her grilled peaches with Amaretto were either too burned at the edges or not done enough. Her flourless chocolate cake was too heavy. She overfilled her grapefruit and mint *granité* glass and served it with a veritable hedge of fresh mint on top.

It was not disastrous. All could be remedied if she was willing to learn. But was she? He looked at her polenta cake with poached plums. It smelt wonderful and tasted good. But the texture was almost gritty.

'Laura's will be expensive. You've seen the prices, haven't you? Not as expensive as Giovanni's, but way above a café. If I was serving this in one of our Calzones, I'd be happy with it. But Laura's? No.'

He made her start again, and immediately saw what the problem was. 'That's not polenta flour,' he said. 'It's polenta for the savoury dishes. What we need for the cake is polenta flour, very fine, almost the texture of cornflour. And you need ground almonds in a packet. Grinding your own is a big mistake – to get them fine enough risks over-grinding so they become oily and heavy.'

He sent the kitchen porter off to Deli-Calzone to get the right polenta and some ground almonds. Meanwhile he had the pastry chef lift the plums out of the syrup she'd cooked them in and boil down the syrup to a thick, electric purple. 'Make the cake again,' he told her, 'and call me before you cut it. Let it cool in the tin. It should be soft and fragile.'

On the way home in a taxi, he and Laura sat side by side. He reached for her hand. 'I loved today. So good to be back in the kitchen. But I'd forgotten how tough it is on the feet.'

'We ought to work on giving you a half-day kitchen fix. Just to keep you cheerful. Look at you, grinning all over your face.'

CHAPTER THIRTEEN

When Angelica and Mario had moved into their mews house, number six, Angelica had had high hopes that their new situation – a home of their own, both of them working – would help Mario relax, that his moods would be more even, with fewer manic highs and bottomless depressions. Sadly, this didn't happen.

Their rows when Mario was high, delusional or paranoid were worse than they'd been before they'd moved. At least when they'd lived with her parents, he had made an effort to control his temper and had mostly succeeded, though not always. On one occasion, they'd had a monumental argument that Angelica could still not forgive.

They'd been unable to agree on how the house should look. Angelica wanted it to be light, pretty and fairly conventional, with country pine furniture and Provençal or Laura Ashley prints. She was quite happy to accept a sofa from Chorlton that her grandmother, Maud, was throwing out, and buy second-hand furniture in the Old Kent Road or at World's End. But Mario, who had decided he was a master of design, wanted the latest 'far-out' look: dark fake fur on the ceiling, pierced by tiny lights and an orange 'conversation pit' in the middle of the sitting room.

'It's so cool,' he said. 'It's like a circular sofa. You step down into it and your feet are lower than the floor. You have a round coffee table in the middle. It's so intimate and casual. We'll be able to lie back and look at the furry star-studded sky. So much trendier than a boring old sofa.'

'But, Mario, if it's in the middle of the sitting room and has to be lowered into the floor, the kitchen ceiling would have to be lowered too. And then we'd have to lower the kitchen floor to get enough headroom. It's crazy.'

'You're so negative, that's your trouble, Angel.'

'I'm not negative. I'm just practical. But you never *think*. All those tiny light-bulbs in the fur ceiling will have to be replaced. Who's going to be up on a ladder doing that? It'll be me, won't it? And fake fur is disgusting. And on the ceiling? How do you clean it? It's like that horrible shag-pile carpet you like. It's a breeding ground for creepy-crawlies.' She was getting really worked up, and she knew perfectly well, from years of living with Mario, that she never won these arguments. He might say sorry later, but you couldn't reason with him.

In the end, for the sake of peace, Angelica proposed a compromise. 'Mario, you design the sitting room, and I'll furnish our bedroom and the kitchen. We'll agree a budget for every room and then we both have to stick to it. And accept each other's décor. It'll be fun.'

Angelica duly bought a good double divan from John Lewis that could be unzipped to make two beds. She told herself that was because it would be impossible to get a double mattress, never mind a bed frame, up the narrow stairs. In a corner of her mind, though, she thought that if things got really bad they could split the bed and put one in the tiny study, currently used as a box room.

She bought a blue Provençal-print quilt for the bed and had the bedhead and a small tub chair covered with the same material. The chest of drawers came from an auction house in Lots Road, and along the wall opposite the door, she installed a white Formica built-in cupboard. You hardly noticed it when you entered the room. Even the handles were concealed. I can always stick a poster or a picture, or a great piece of fabric on one of the doors if it looks too bleak, she thought. But she liked the room as it was: cool and blue and peaceful.

The kitchen was completely functional, even, she admitted, boring. It had a sturdy second-hand table and six chairs in the middle, and all round the walls were modern kitchen units, a double sink, a six-burner gas cooker, fridge and freezer. The only innovation was the smooth cork on the walls, which softened the laboratory look.

She'd done her kitting-out within six weeks, in spite of working full-time at the Savoy, and was pleased with herself for spending less than they'd agreed.

Mario's project had hardly begun. He was close to manic, going in a dozen directions, but his mood was more euphoric than impossible. She didn't like his ideas for swirly orange wallpaper, shag-pile carpet, G-plan teak wall fittings and uncomfortable trendy furniture. And she was deeply hurt by his suggestion that they get rid of the sketch of the cardinal she'd bought in Paris and which now held pride of place in the sitting room.

'What do you mean, get rid of it?'

'Oh, Angel, don't make a scene. It's a nice enough picture. Of course it is. But I don't want figurative paintings. I'll get abstract modern pictures. Like Rothko or Miró.'

Angelica closed her eyes. No use telling him that a Miró or a Rothko would cost hundreds of thousands. Even a good print would be way beyond them. And no use reminding him that the cardinal picture had been a true present of love. That she'd bought it on the day they moved into the Paris apartment, that they'd both adored it.

'All right,' she said, 'but don't throw it away, or sell it. I'll keep it even if I have to put it in the bathroom.'

She knew she had to stick to the agreement. At least he'd gone off the conversation-pit idea.

Then one day he produced an architectural magazine full of the grandest wares, fascinating and beautiful, but impossibly expensive.

'I hope this is just to get ideas, and then you'll go to Habitat for something similar?'

'No. We don't want cheap rip-offs. We should have the real thing.'

'For goodness' sake, Mario, we can't afford this stuff. Thousands of pounds for a single chair!'

'But they're works of art, baby. We should be buying paintings too. Today's art will be worth a fortune one day.'

'Or nothing.'

Suddenly he was shouting: 'Negative, negative. You're always so bloody negative.'

Angelica left the room, telling herself to walk away. Just walk away. At moments like that she almost wished he'd go into a depression. Then he'd have no energy for this mad idea of being an interior decorator.

By that evening, as always, she felt uneasy and a little guilty. Maybe she had been negative. Maybe they could afford one wonderful piece. When they went to bed, she took the magazine with her, studied the pictures and read about the artists and designers. She had to admit their products were original and somehow satisfyingly logical. There was an article about Charles Eames and how he'd designed a chair in the fifties, specifically to watch television from. But the prices were just ridiculous, way out of their league, even for a single piece. When Mario came to bed – he'd been out with some friends – she didn't mention it. She pushed the magazine under the bed. She'd just have to insist he give up this nonsense.

Angelica was owed a week's holiday. If she didn't take it, she'd lose it, so she decided to spend it at Chorlton. Mario couldn't come and, anyway, didn't want to. She couldn't really blame him. None of her family approved of him and, though they were polite enough, he knew it. He said he was going to get on with the sitting room.

Aunt Sophie was wonderful. She took one look at Angelica and said, holding her by the shoulders, 'I know what you need, young woman. You need sleep, lots and lots of it – no getting up for breakfast – and plenty of good food. You're skinny as a rake. Plenty of fresh air, too – you look as if you never see daylight, never mind the sun!'

Angelica laughed. 'Oh, Aunt Sophie, that sounds blissful. I'm so tired. And you're right. Mostly I arrive at work in the dark and leave in the dark and there's no daylight in the bowels of the Savoy, for sure . . .'

She went back to town refreshed and happy. She'd resolved to be more understanding of Mario. And she'd try, yet again, to get him to a doctor, any doctor, never mind a specialist. She and Sophie had discussed it and Sophie had confirmed that he needed the professional help of a psychiatrist, but a doctor would be a start.

'It's typical of manic depressives,' Sophie had told her, 'the resistance to treatment. They love the highs, the euphoria, the feeling of being a creative genius, with masterful control of everything. He'll be suspicious that medication will take all that away. And he'll be frightened of being clapped into some asylum and given electric-shock treatment.'

And who could blame him? thought Angelica, as she put her key in the lock of number six and opened the front door. 'Mario? Darling, are you home?'

'I'm here. Come up.' He sounded happy, normal. Good, she thought, dropping her bags and bounding up the stairs.

He met her at the top, his arms open, and hugged her.

Over his shoulder she saw, to her astonishment, that the sitting room was finished: carpet, furniture, even pictures. She took in the record-player with radio and cassette recorder on the wall shelves and the huge speakers at the end corners. Three of the walls were white and one was covered with a bright lime-green foil. In the opposite corner a glass lava lamp made slow psychedelic patterns that picked up the lime green and swirled it with orange. It was amazing.

'Good Lord, darling!' She eased herself out of his arms and walked slowly round the room. She was speechless. It wasn't her taste – it was very masculine – but it all went together beautifully. She couldn't believe it. After all the talk of shag-pile and fake fur, she was also relieved.

She sat in a black leather chair with a matching footstool and leaned back against the wide leather headrest. It was wonderfully comfy.

And then her mind went into overdrive. She'd seen this chair before. Oh, please, God, *no*.

She sat bolt upright. 'This is that famous Charles Eames chair, isn't it? We can't possibly afford it.' She looked round the room, recognizing the white 'egg chair' by the Danish fellow, the black leather and chrome stools, the glass coffee table. She couldn't remember the designers' names, but she'd seen all this furniture in the magazine, all priced at hundreds, sometimes thousands of pounds. She looked around the room. Was there nothing that hadn't cost an arm and a leg? Even the mirror on the wall, which looked like a giant amoeba-shaped pool of silver paint, and the hanging chandelier made of a cluster of multi-coloured oval shades hung at different heights, seemed familiar.

She couldn't stand it any longer. She couldn't have this fight over and over again with Mario. Anyway, it was too late. She'd said no a dozen times to this expenditure, but he'd just gone and bought it all.

She raced down the stairs, grabbed her bag at the door and ran out. She really, really didn't want him to follow her. She scrabbled in her bag, found the key to her parents' house and let herself in. She closed the door behind her and slid the bolt. Mario had keys to this house too.

Laura installed Angelica in the bedroom she'd vacated to move to number six. She lay, red-eyed, on the bed. 'Mamma, I do love him, but I can't go on all my life with him doing these mad things.'

Laura knew her daughter would never be happy with Mario.

The man wasn't well. And, of course, Giovanni believed that even if he got help, took the medication, went through electric-shock treatment, Mario would still be untrustworthy. But marriage was for life, for better, for worse, until death . . .

'Darling, you stay here for a few weeks. We'll keep Mario out. The thought of losing you may bring him to his senses.' She stroked her daughter's thigh through the coverlet.

Giovanni said he'd take care of the furniture fiasco. It turned out that Mario had gone into Chelsea Interiors, in the King's Road, and had simply ordered everything he liked from the magazine. He'd hired a designer too, who'd managed the decorative aspects, like wallpapers and lamps, and found a specialist decorator to hang the foil wallpaper. The fees alone were exorbitant.

'And it didn't stop there,' said Giovanni. 'All that music equipment is from Bang & Olufsen, top of the range, the sort of stuff musicians might order.'

'But what about the furniture, darling? Will they take it back?'

'Yes, but I had to agree to a thirty per cent penalty charge, to cover the designer's fee and the labour. I suppose it's lucky he bought everything through Chelsea Interiors. The owner has enough clout with the manufacturers to get them to take the furniture back. I suppose he thinks that if he's nice to me, maybe we'll use him for a restaurant design one day.'

Carlotta must have tackled her son. Laura had no idea what she'd said to him, but she knew the one person in the world Mario respected was his mother. One day he appeared at the door, all apologies. 'Honestly, Aunt Laura, I don't know what came over me. I know we can't afford that stuff. Angelica's right. Please can I see her? Just to say I'm sorry.'

'No, Mario. She's exhausted, she needs a rest. She'll come back when she's good and ready, not before. Meanwhile you owe Giovanni thirty per cent of your decorator's bill, and he won't let you off.' Mario had nodded, contrite. How extraordinary, thought Laura. He's just like Jekyll and Hyde.

When Angelica went back to number six, relations with Mario improved. But it wasn't like the old days. He could still be amusing and affectionate, and when they made love she sometimes believed, for an hour or so, that he was better, that all was well. But she was wary, watching him for signs of depression or mania, her heart sinking when they were confirmed, as they inevitably were. One day, when Mario had been melancholic for weeks, she realized that they'd not made love for over a month. Even more surprising, she hadn't minded.

Mario now freely admitted the depression, at least to her. In the past he'd hidden it, somehow forcing himself to get up, to smile, to pretend all was well. But now he'd tell her when he felt the black cloud descending and his energy evaporating. He liked her to be with him in the bed, to get undressed and snuggle up to his back, her arm over him, stroking him. Or hold him like a child, his head on her breast. At those times she'd feel the waves of love. But it was maternal love, not love as it used to be.

He'd never admit to mania, though.

'Nonsense,' he'd say. 'This is how I always am. You have to take me as I am, Angelica. This is me, the real me. Me at my best. I can't change and I don't want to. Besides, this is what you fell in love with.'

'No, I fell—'

'You told me, Angelica. You used to say, "I love your energy, your enthusiasm, your confidence."'

It was useless to protest that there was a difference between the sane, charismatic Mario and the man who'd snap his fingers at waiters, get furious with taxi drivers, believe he could sing professionally if he wanted to, that he would be a multi-millionaire one day.

Angelica concentrated on her career. When she'd been in the Savoy pastry department for two years, she was promoted to sous-chef, which meant, thank God, that she spent only half her time standing at a bench or range, tempering chocolate, spinning sugar, piping fine trellises on wedding cakes. Now she spent some of her time demonstrating cake-making at exhibitions and entering competitions. The Savoy liked to boast of their staff's skills.

She was also in charge of teaching the apprentices, which she loved. And, bliss, she could sometimes get off her aching feet and sit in the office with a cup of tea, planning menus, doing the buying, hiring new staff, evaluating their progress.

One day Monsieur Trompetto summoned her to his office. 'The BBC have requested permission to film in my kitchens for a television programme. They want to film me making Pêche Melba as Escoffier first made it, in an ice sculpture of a swan. I'll need an assistant. Since it's good publicity for the Savoy to show that we are liberal-minded and have women in the kitchen, I have decided that you will be the assistant.'

Angelica was astounded. She was too nervous to smile at 'liberal-minded', but as she digested his words, she felt a flutter of excitement. She'd be on television.

'Don't get any fancy ideas,' Trompetto went on. 'Our ice carvers will have made the swan in advance. I'll make the ice cream and arrange the spun sugar on top. You will barely be seen, but you'll spin the sugar in the background and help me as needed.'

'*Oui, Chef. Merci, Chef.*'

On the appointed day, Angelica was in the kitchen early. She needed to keep up with her usual tasks as well as this filming business so she planned to clear her paperwork and get everyone's job sheets organized before the film crew arrived. Chef Blanchard came into the office and sat on her desk. 'So, young lady, you are to be the star of the show!'

Angelica laughed. 'Hardly,' she said. 'Chef Trompetto is the star, as always. I'm just his skivvy.'

'Not any more you're not. Tromps is ill. He's got a throat infection and lost his voice. He'd sound like a frog, he says. You'll have to be his understudy and save the day.'

'I can't do that! He does radio and television all the time. I've no idea how to be on television.' She jumped up. 'You do it, Chef. You're the head of Pastry.'

'Ah, but the hotel bosses want you, not me. The public-relations chap is overexcited about the Savoy demonstrating its liberal attitude to women. I think he's secretly delighted that the famous *chef des cuisines* is indisposed.'

When the film crew arrived, the director decided the kitchen, with its hard artificial light, clanging pots and reflective stainless steel, wouldn't do so everything was moved into one of the private Oliver Messel rooms upstairs.

By the time the half-dozen members of the film crew had lugged in all their cameras, lights and sound equipment, there was little space for Angelica's equipment. Blanchard and a junior commis helped her assemble everything she needed. The activity kept her nerves about the actual filming at bay.

The ice swan would make a late entry. It sat on a massive silver salver and would remain in the freezer until the last moment. It was magnificent, nearly three feet high and carved with extraordinary precision. A large bowl had been cut into the bird's back, hidden by the slightly raised wings. The crew had already filmed the hotel's ice carver putting the finishing touches to it.

They placed an ice cream container filled with scoops of her best vanilla ice cream under Angelica's worktable. It wouldn't melt for hours, providing they resisted the temptation to open the drum to check. The ingredients and equipment she needed for demonstrating the dish were placed on the table and covered with a white cloth. On a trolley in the passage, there was a back-up load of equipment and measured ingredients in case they had to re-film something.

The spun sugar would be the biggest challenge. She'd be working with a saucepan and two forks over a portable gas ring, with strict instructions from the hotel's fire officer not to set off the alarms. What with all the lights and the people, the room was warming up, which worried Angelica. She needed cold conditions for the spun sugar and the ice cream.

She was ready long before the crew had set up, which gave her a good hour to get nervous. She went to her desk, wrote down what she knew about Pêche Melba, and learned it by heart.

Eventually Percy, the director, asked her to 'walk him through' what she needed to do. Then they had a rehearsal, Angelica miming her actions so the director could decide which camera would take the close-ups and which would be on her.

After that they had another rehearsal, a run-through they called it, when she was still miming, but this time the presenter, who was called Melvyn something, asked her questions and she answered as she went along.

After a little discussion and a few directions ('Can you tip the bowl a bit towards the camera so we can see into it?'), Percy clapped his hands and raised his voice: 'Right. Let's have a go. Angelica, we'll just do the first bit, when you explain the history of the dish to Melvyn. Just a conversation. No cooking, OK?'

She nodded, her throat tightening. Her voice would sound funny, she knew it. One of the assistants stood in front of a camera with a clapperboard, waiting until he got a nod from the cameraman, then clapped it shut. Percy checked the cameraman was ready. 'Quiet, please.'

Angelica swallowed. The room was deathly quiet. 'Action.'

Melvyn faced the camera. 'Here we are in the magnificent Savoy Hotel. We're here with Angelica Angelotti, one of the top chefs in the pastry department, who I hope will tell us about the hotel's most famous dish, Peach Melba.' He turned to Angelica and said, 'First the obvious question, Chef, why Melba?'

'Well, the most famous chef of the Savoy, even more famous than the present chef Silvino Trompetto, was Auguste Escoffier. He invented this dish for the opera diva Dame Nellie Melba. She was starring in *Lohengrin* at Covent Garden and staying here at the hotel. There's a swan on stage in the opera, so when a banquet was held in her honour, Escoffier used an ice swan to present a simple dish of vanilla ice cream and peaches.'

'Cut,' said Percy. 'That was fantastic, Angelica. Not an um, not an er, no waffling. Just perfect.' He seemed to mean it! Angelica was amazed. 'You're a natural.'

It was true. Her nerves had vanished as soon as she started talking about the dish. She found she was enjoying it, and she could hear the enthusiasm in her voice. That was what she felt, enthusiasm and pleasure, not fear. How very odd. She smiled. 'So I was OK?'

'OK? You were brilliant. One-take-Angelica, we'll call you.'

Angelica was determined to be as efficient at the demonstrations as she had been in the introduction. They only had one extra lot of ingredients, and if she messed it up, there'd be a long delay before more would arrive from the kitchen downstairs. She would not mess it up.

Most of Melvyn's questions were hardly a distraction. They were mainly of the 'So what are you doing now?' variety, and all she had to do was what she did every day with her apprentices – demonstrate the technique while describing her actions. It wasn't hard because the whole item had to fit into four minutes, so there was no point in filming her making the ice cream, skinning the peaches or sieving the raspberries for the sauce. It was an assembly job really, the sort of thing her team had to do during the service.

But they did want to film her making spun sugar, because it would look good and it wasn't the sort of thing people could do at home.

There was a longish gap in the filming when she was trying to get the temperature right for the sugar. She'd demonstrated stage one, heating the sugar until it turned to caramel then stopping it cooking but standing it in a bowl of cold water. But then it cooled too much before the next shot and she had to heat it again. Then something went wrong with the sound and there was another pause and again it cooled too much. The director wanted her to have a go anyway, but she refused: she knew it would make ribbons as thick as shoelaces and nasty blobs.

She was determined to stay calm, but she could feel her cheeks getting hot. Well, at least the camera's filming my hands, not my face, she thought.

Finally they got there. The caramel was pale as straw and just cool enough to produce whisper-thin threads when she dipped in two forks held side by side in one hand and waved them gently back and forth over an oiled wire cooling rack. The spun sugar piled up like gossamer. While it was still warm and malleable, she formed it into a sort of wreath to go round the top of the bowl and set it aside, hoping it would survive in the warm room until she was ready for it. She filled the glass bowl with ice cream balls and raw whole peaches, peeled and stoned. She coated the peaches with the raspberry sauce.

'I thought Escoffier didn't use raspberries?' said Melvyn.

She looked up at him. 'That's right. At the first banquet it was just ice cream, peaches and spun sugar. But the dish became a regular, and he added the raspberry sauce.'

'So that's it. Quite simple, really, isn't it?'

'Yes, if you skip the spun sugar,' she said, smiling. 'It's all in the quality of the ingredients. But Pêche Melba isn't always as it should be. It's often a disgusting mix of cheap ice cream, slimy peach slices out of a tin and over-sweet raspberry syrup that has probably never seen a raspberry. I really hate that.'

'You sound quite indignant, Angelica.'

She smiled. 'I'm sorry, but I am indignant. Escoffier only used the best ice cream, made with Jersey cream, fresh eggs and vanilla pods. He only did it when the best peaches were in

177

season. And fresh raspberries from Scotland. That's what good cooking's about. Good ingredients, not messed about.'

They'll cut all that out, for sure, she thought.

The final sequence was the *pièce de résistance*. They filmed two liveried waiters setting the swan on the table, and her placing the bowl of raspberry-coated ice cream and peaches between its wings, then putting the circlet of spun sugar on top.

'*Et voilà!*' she said, looking straight into camera.

Two days later, she found a letter on her desk at work. It was on BBC Education letterhead.

Dear Miss Angelotti,

My colleague Percy Thomas has shown me the footage of your filming in the Savoy. We are both impressed and would like to ask you to come in to see us to discuss the possibility of your presenting our new cookery series. We will be going into production next March and the series will be directed by Percy.

I look forward to hearing from you at your earliest convenience.

Yours sincerely,

Cedric Maples
Producer, BBC Education

PART THREE

1973

CHAPTER FOURTEEN

Laura was glad to see her brother looking well and cheerful. When he'd first come home after his stroke he'd been pale and morose. He'd developed a little paunch, perhaps because his body wasn't used to doing nothing – he'd always been so active on the farm.

Sophie had confided her anxiety about him to her. 'I wish I knew what to do. He's obviously unhappy, but he won't talk to me. Of course I understand he's got good reason to be miserable, but he's eating and drinking too much, and he seems to cast a veil of gloom over the whole house. Poor Hal. He told me he doesn't recognize the father he left when he went on his travels. He said, "He looks the same, but there's no joy in him."'

Laura had tried to jolly her brother out of his dark moods but it was Pippa, Hal's girlfriend, who shook him out of his lethargy. She'd been a sports trainer in Australia and was as fit as a flea, with not an ounce of fat on her. She was very keen on the new craze of jogging. Laura watched her from the bathroom window, running along the path between the fields. She'd run for at least half an hour every morning. One day she and David were sitting in the kitchen when Pippa had puffed in, dropped into a chair and buried her face in her towel. When she looked up, her cheeks were pink and her eyes shone. 'Oh, David, that's so good. Running. I don't know how you can bear being stuck in that chair. Don't you miss being able to run?'

She's nothing if not direct, thought Laura. No one else would ask that. It invites the response 'What do you bloody well think? Of course I miss it, stupid.'

But David said, 'Every day. But not as much as I miss walking.'

'It's not just the running or walking you're missing,' said Pippa. 'It's seeing the countryside, butterflies, rabbits scattering, And the sky, clouds, light. The light is different every morning.'

David nodded. 'I remember.'

The next morning Pippa took David with her. She said the wheelchair would be like weights, forcing her to work harder. And she'd only run on the smooth lane and the road with him. They were gone for half an hour and when they returned David's mood had lightened. 'Sophie,' he said, 'we went to the Frampton Gate. We should take that hedge down a bit. It only needs to be five feet high to keep the stock in, and somehow it's shot up to about eight.'

After that, Sophie told her, David had gone out with Pippa every day if the weather was dry. They'd pick up the morning paper from the box at the gate and set out at a run down the lane. They visited every inch of farmland that the wheelchair could get to, and when it couldn't go further, or if Pippa wanted to run really fast, he'd sit in his wheelchair and wait for her, reading the paper. 'It's extraordinary,' said Sophie. 'Neither Hal nor I could interest him in the farm. Now, because he sees what the men have done, sees the result of Hal's decisions, sees what's wrong, he's interested again.'

'Good for Pippa. She's not the dreamy hippie she looks.'

'She's great. Especially with David. I'm beginning to really love her. Hal says they want a baby. I'm trying to persuade them to get married first!'

'I don't suppose they believe in marriage, do they?'

'Hal would be willing enough, I think. But Pippa spouts a lot of hippie nonsense about free love and not needing a piece of paper. They're awfully young, of course, but I do think they'd make a good pair. Don't you?'

Three months later, when Laura was once again at Chorlton, this time to celebrate David's birthday, Pippa was still taking David with her on her morning runs.

'Isn't it uncomfortable, bouncing along in that chair?' Laura asked.

'Sometimes, not often. I can't feel the left side, of course, and the new chair is stronger, better sprung and has some padding. Pippa says it's good for me. Hanging on and bracing against the bumps makes my right arm stronger.'

Pippa had taken on the task of keeping David's body going – strengthening his good side with exercises, doing what she could for his paralysed left arm and leg, massaging him and making his unresponsive muscles move. She's a considerable woman, thought Laura, even if she looks like a seventeen-year-old waif.

Inspecting the wheat that afternoon, David was every bit the man in charge, like his old self. He made Laura fetch him a couple of ears so he could roll them in his fingers, flaking off the chaff to feel the size and the dryness of the corn. Scattering the grain and brushing the chaff from his fingers, he smiled at Sophie. 'Perfect. We should try to get it in early in the week.

We'll do it first, then do Longacre at Middle Barrow, then the rest of the wheat. The barley's nowhere near ready, is it, Soph?'

Laura was touched by the way he treated Sophie as a fellow farmer. It's almost like the early days, she thought, when he was married to Jill, who lived and breathed the Chorlton farms, and all the talk was of farming, new machines and meeting wartime production targets.

When they got back to the house, the telephone was ringing and Sophie ran ahead to catch it. She came out, dangling the car keys, her face alight with pleasure. 'It's Richard. He's at the station.'

'Good Lord! I thought he'd gone to Germany,' exclaimed David.

'He's back. Says he'll be home with us until the beginning of September.'

Laura hadn't seen her nephew for months, not since they'd all come to Chorlton when David had had his stroke. He didn't come home from Oxford every weekend and she'd missed him on her visits. She knew he spent odd days at his parents' flat in the mews, but she was at work before he surfaced and he naturally spent his time with friends, rather than his relations. She was surprised to see how he'd filled out. She still thought of him as young and slight, with a boyish litheness, but now he looked altogether adult. His hair was thick and curly, with sideburns down his cheeks. He was a handsome young man.

'Right, everyone,' he said at tea time. 'I'm cooking supper tonight. You ladies get a night off. I bought all the ingredients in the covered market.'

'Do you like cooking?' asked Laura, surprised.

'I love it. Since I moved out of college, I do all the cooking in our flat. None of the others can be bothered. Their idea of

184

gastronomy is a Vesta chow mein from a packet, or chop suey and chips from a van. So I cook.'

'Lucky other lads!' said Sophie.

'Yeah, well, they wolf it down, that's for sure. Doesn't mean it's gastronomy but I do make a tasty spaghetti bolognese.' He grinned confidently. 'And a pretty mean curry, a fact I intend to prove to you tonight.' He turned to Maud. 'Grandma, I hope you like curry.'

'I do, young man. And I can tell a good one from a bad one. I spent several years with your grandfather in India, when he was stationed in Delhi.'

Richard did make a good curry – although, thought Laura, it bore little relation to any genuine Indian dish. She volunteered to be his assistant, and watched him make a basic English stew, swimming in gravy thickened with flour, but flavoured with curry powder. While the curry was simmering he produced a packet of Uncle Ben's rice, a jar of mango chutney, and a packet of poppadums.

They fried the poppadums in shallow oil. Hal came in and watched in wonder as they turned from thin, flat discs to huge, crisp and curly shapes.

Richard put the curry casserole and the bowl of rice in the middle of the table and surrounded it with the poppadums, mango chutney, a little dish of mixed raw tomato and chopped onion, and another of banana slices tossed in desiccated coconut. He went out onto the terrace to pick a few sprigs of parsley, chopped the leaves and scattered them on top of the curry.

Everyone was hungry and the curry disappeared fast, even gaining the approval of Maud.

Over strawberries and cream, Hal asked Richard when he'd get the result of his finals. 'You took them in May, didn't you? It must be any minute now, surely.'

Richard looked uncomfortable, even embarrassed.

Surely he can't have done badly, Laura thought. He's so clever.

Everyone was staring at him. His face had gone bright red. He looked at his father. 'I got a first, Dad. And I won the Roxburgh Prize. I'm going to work for Goldman Sachs.'

CHAPTER FIFTEEN

Angelica was spending less and less time with Mario. They made love rarely and usually perfunctorily, as though they wanted to get it out of the way. She suspected he was having an affair: he was out a lot in the evenings. Work, he said, which hardly tallied with the ice cream business. I should be unhappy, thought Angelica, but I'm not. Somehow Mario doesn't matter to me any more and I'm having such a good time in the rest of my life.

Ever since she'd made the spun sugar at the Savoy for the BBC programme, her TV career had been flourishing. Her first series, *How to Make Cakes*, had surprised everyone with its above-average audience ratings, and had led to her current programme, which had her demonstrating different nations' versions of the same dish: French navarin of lamb compared with Lancashire hotpot, German *Bratwurst* and boiled potatoes beside English sausages and mash.

Her television profile had led to a job as food writer with a weekly column on the *Daily Mail*. She had the use of a desk at the Fleet Street office but mostly she wrote by hand in a lined foolscap book, working in her dressing room, on a train, at home, anywhere. She'd frequently go to the newspaper office to turn her scribbles into clean copy and hand her pieces to the editor. The atmosphere there, with everyone writing to deadlines, meant she, too, kept her head down and worked. She could write what she liked, providing she remembered her readers were not professional chefs and she included at least one recipe in every column.

One early morning, she had to be up before dawn to set off for Somerset: she was to make a Danish apple cake, a French *tarte Normande*, and a good old English apple pie. Half asleep, she blundered downstairs for the cup of tea that would force her awake.

As she turned on the kettle, she heard the unmistakable sound of the front door opening. She froze, then reached over to the block and pulled out the carving knife.

It was Mario, dishevelled but sober and on the defensive, babbling about being out with the boys, sleeping on a sofa, not wanting to wake her.

Anger replaced fear. She shoved the knife back into the block with a vicious thrust. She didn't believe a word of it. 'Oh, do shut up, Mario. I don't care where you've been.' She turned her back on him, made her tea and forced herself to let it brew. She heard the scrape of chair legs as he sat down. She poured her cup and carried it past him to the stairs. 'I didn't even notice you weren't here,' she said. 'What does that say about our relationship?'

Later, as she drove over the Robin Hood roundabout onto the A3, she thought how rapidly their love affair had given up the ghost. Once she'd have followed him to the ends of the earth. Now she was more interested in her career.

Neither her presenting nor her writing pleased Mario. Her being on television seemed especially to annoy him. Everyone else was thrilled for her, impressed that she was so good at it, enjoying the reflected glory of her little bit of fame. But he always had some criticism of the programme or unwelcome advice ('You shouldn't wear blue. It doesn't suit you' or 'When you chop things you shouldn't look straight down. It gives you a double chin').

But I don't want to leave him, do I? Or do I? When he's stable and happy, he's still lovely, isn't he? Yes, she responded sourly. But how often is that, these days? Then she thought how hard it must be for him, an Italian full of *machismo*, to have her earning more than three times what he brought in, and getting all the praise and attention.

She smiled wryly to herself, thinking of her mother. About the only thing Laura and Mario agreed on was that she should be having a baby. Sometimes, just to put a stop to her mother's hints, she was tempted to tell her that she hadn't married Mario. Or remind her of Carlotta's warnings about the risks of inbreeding. But if her mother knew she wasn't married to Mario she might urge her to find someone better, while she was still young.

There might be some sense in that, thought Angelica, but I no longer believe in happy-ever-after and, anyway, I'm too busy. It may yet all come right, but one thing is certain: I'm not going to have a baby. I don't want one, and that's that.

At the *Daily Mail*, she shared a little glassed-in office with two other writers on *Femail*, one a famous columnist who could write a provocative column in twenty minutes and without apparent effort, and the other a glamorous, exquisitely dressed fashion editor. They both typed their copy, clattering away at speed, oblivious to each other's noise or to that of the busy newsroom next door. Angelica wrote by hand. She'd never learned to type.

Her telephone rang. It was her boss. 'Christ, Angelica, what have you done? Come here, will you?'

Angelica had no idea what he was talking about. Heart banging, she hurried to the feature editor's office. He had yesterday's *Femail* on his desk, open at her column.

'What is it?'

He pushed the paper across to her, turning it so that she could read her column, one on making dark Seville marmalade. There was a big ink circle round one of the ingredients in the recipe.

She was so nervous she couldn't concentrate. It said, '2 tbs black treacle'. What was wrong with that?

He said, 'The telephone's been red hot all morning. Half the nation is ringing up to complain they have a lot of expensive gunk in their pans.'

She looked harder at the ingredients list. And then she saw it. 'Oh, God!' She hadn't crossed the T in '2 tbs'. It read '2 lbs'.

'Two fucking pounds of black treacle in a marmalade recipe for six oranges. We're going to have to compensate every bloody housewife who makes the stuff with the price of the ingredients. Eighty-five pence for every one of them. And there have been hundreds so far.'

'Oh, God,' she said again. 'I'm so sorry. I didn't notice.'

'No, and neither did the sub nor the proof-reader. But you are the most to blame, Angelica.'

It flashed into Angelica's mind that he'd missed it too. Wasn't he meant to read the stuff he edited? But she didn't dare say it. 'What can I do?' she said. 'What do you want me—'

'I want to wring your neck, that's what.' He stood up. 'You'll have to answer all the complaint letters and field the phone calls. Don't leave your desk, not for lunch, not for a pee, not at all. Meanwhile, Christ help me, I'm going to plead your cause with the editor. Much as you deserve the sack, I don't want to have to find a replacement in a hurry.'

When Angelica told Mario what had happened he laughed. 'Oh, Angelica, it's hardly the end of the world! It's very funny. So what if you get sacked? I might see a bit more of you, have you at home where you belong for a bit.' He patted her bottom as he walked out of the door. 'Forget it, *cara*. It's only a recipe, after all.'

Angelica was seething. Only a recipe! OK, but what about her reputation as a food writer? What about all those poor women who'd used two pounds of expensive treacle? If they'd followed the boiling instructions as literally as they'd followed the ingredients, they'd have burned toffee and a wrecked saucepan. How could he be so unsympathetic?

The following day Angelica was in the office, sorting the mail, most of which would be, she thought, complaint letters for her. But one of them made her stop, horrified.

'Oh, my God,' she said, 'It's a letter bomb.' They'd all been given bomb training because the IRA's letter bomb campaign was currently targeting newspaper offices. They'd been told anything squashy could be Semtex, and if you could feel wires through the envelope, well, that was very bad news.

She felt oddly calm. She called the post room. Both her colleagues found they needed to leave their office. She stayed, eyeing the package nervously. Within ten minutes she saw two policemen walking through the newsroom, ordering everyone out of the building. As she emerged a contingent of earnest-looking officers in flak jackets went in.

There must have been a hundred or more staff milling around

in Carmelite Street, wondering why they'd been evacuated. Some of the journalists repaired to the Wig and Pen or El Vino's and others went home.

After forty minutes they were allowed back into the building. The post boy flung the offending package, now slit open, onto her desk. He was grinning. The envelope contained a lump of marmalade toffee in which was embedded a dental brace with two teeth attached. It also contained a large orthodontist's bill.

Somehow Angelica survived this farce, and another time when she wrote a recipe for a ginger *brûlée* with 'One ounce of ginger' by which she'd meant an ounce of stem ginger. But readers understandably thought she'd meant ground ginger. An ounce was the whole jar.

Food writing, she realized, was a serious business. If you made a mistake in an opinion piece or a cricket score, you might feel a fool but you wouldn't be wasting your reader's time or money, or spoiling your reputation.

She didn't tell Mario about the *brûlée* fiasco, but a few weeks later, when she could see the funny side, she told her mother about both incidents, and how narrowly she'd escaped dismissal.

Laura was sympathetic, though she did laugh. 'Maybe you're not cut out for food writing,' she said. Her face grew serious. 'To be honest, darling, I rather hope you aren't. I need you back at Giovanni's. Your father would make you head chef now. With two Laura's already open, a third on the cards and Giovanni's now open seven days a week, we're desperate for good head chefs. And it would so please your father to have you back in the fold.'

'Oh, Mamma, I'd like that too, but I'm really enjoying my new life, half on TV, half on the paper. Even with both jobs I do fewer hours than I would at Giovanni's, and half as many as I did at the Savoy. And I want the time to write a cookbook. A simple guide to Italian cooking.'

'Italian cooking? I thought you were mad about French cuisine?'

'I am. Maybe I'm just greedy. I love everyone's food. Our next TV series is to be called *Angelica's World* and I'm to start with Chinese dishes, then Indian, then South American . . .'

'You don't know anything about any of those!'

'I know, but this is television!' She gave her horrified mother a hug. 'You'll see, Mamma, they'll make me into an absolute expert. And, anyway, I can mug it up. How hard can it be to make sweet and sour soup? Or chicken curry?'

Angelica watched her mother's face relax, reflecting affection and pride. 'You make everything look as easy as pie. It's a real gift to be so calm and yet convey enthusiasm the way you do. I'm so proud of you, darling.'

'The next series is to have a bigger budget.' Angelica went on. 'The plan is to knock Fanny Cradock off her throne and put me in her place as the queen of television cooking.'

'Well, don't get too big for your boots, madam,' said Laura. 'People fall in love with being famous, and it's horrible. Your father thinks you were born to be a restaurateur. That's why he let you go to Paris.'

'And he may be right. But now I want to do what I'm doing. Besides, I'm committed to the next series, so there's no giving up now.'

'OK, my darling. We'll ask you again in a year's time. Your father and I are both getting on, and we'll need a successor one day. Silvano's good, but he's not a cook. And, besides, we'd prefer our daughter.'

Both Laura and Giovanni were avid watchers of their daughter's weekly television series. That evening, after her conversation with Angelica, both she and Giovanni were at home early to watch her making an pineapple upside-down cake.

They had ten minutes until the start of the programme when Laura put two glasses of wine on the coffee table and snuggled up to her husband on the sofa. Aware that she might be about to provoke Giovanni's wrath, she nonetheless reported her conversation with their daughter.

But Giovanni was philosophical. He gave a shrug, sad but resigned.

'It's not unexpected,' he said, 'but I did hope she'd be back with us by now. I thought the television series would be a one-off.'

'The trouble is,' she said, 'Angelica is so good at everything. Cooking, writing, TV. It's natural she should want to enjoy her success.'

'I know, and I'm proud of her. But it's not unreasonable to expect your child to join the family business, is it? You could really do with her, *cara*. I can't understand why she doesn't jump at the chance. I'd planned to put her in charge of Giovanni's kitchen for a bit, and then in Silvano's office to learn more about the money side. Within a couple of years, we'd give her overall management of the Laura's chain.' Giovanni caught his wife's mildly raised eyebrow. 'With your agreement, of course.'

Laura smiled. 'It's our daughter's agreement we need, darling, and that's what we haven't got.'

'We'll manage,' he said. 'We've got a few more years in us.'

'I know, but she and Silvano would make such a good team. I could murder her.'

Laura wondered if he was thinking what she was thinking: that if only she hadn't given away their first baby at birth, they might have had a son in the business now. But he never mentioned it and neither did she. She wrenched her thoughts back.

At the end of the programme Angelica, in close-up, spoke directly to her invisible audience. 'So that's our pineapple upside-down cake. Next week we'll be making infallible Swiss meringues and a perfect Pavlova. Her smile was as wide as sunshine. 'Can't wait. Let's make a date.' Giovanni and Laura looked at each other in mutual pride. Then Giovanni voiced both their thoughts. 'That's our girl! I never cease to be amazed.'

Laura laughed. 'And she's worked a little miracle by getting you and me to spend time together other than fast asleep. I love our Tuesday evenings, it's like a secret tryst.' He kissed her cheek, and she put a hand up to the side of his face and pulled his head round to kiss his mouth. For a second, as she felt him responding, the thought of making love flashed into her head.

But Giovanni pulled away. 'OK, darling, tryst time is up. I've been talking to Silvano about cash flow and I need to talk to you about Laura's.'

Laura frowned, puzzled. 'But we're making good money, aren't we? They're all very profitable.'

'Yes, but I don't think we can go ahead with the Covent Garden proposal. It's the capital cost.'

'But we've done it before, haven't we?'

'Yes, but this is huge. We would be buying a long lease and the building needs a lot spent on it before we even start fitting it out as a Laura's. The difference this time is we'd have to borrow almost all the money and interest rates are now at fifteen per cent and rising.'

Laura felt the disappointment like a physical blow. She'd been so excited about the new restaurant. The building was an old banana store and the plan was to take it over when the market moved out the following year. It was perfect for a restaurant, with a huge ground floor and a lofty basement, like a crypt.

But Giovanni was the boss and she understood his argument. She nodded reluctantly. 'You're right,' she agreed, 'but it hurts, doesn't it?'

As she drove back to the office she told herself there must be a way. A shorter lease, but renewable, a less dilapidated building, one that didn't require so much up-front capital; maybe a partnership with the freeholder. There had to be a solution. The Laura's restaurants were absolutely what the public wanted right now. They couldn't just stop.

She went to see Silvano. 'I agree with you,' he said. 'We need to keep the Laura's bandwagon rolling. I'll make some calls, see what else we can find. Maybe a smart department store that wants a named restaurant. Or a hotel.'

A week later he telephoned her. 'Laura, the most extraordinary thing. This morning there was a call for you at Giovanni's, and I took it. I don't suppose it will come to anything, but the owners of the Mirador gambling club in Park Lane want to know if we'd be interested in tendering for the VIP rooms at their casino. Apparently they feed the gamblers right royally. I said we weren't caterers, but he wants to talk to you.'

'What's his name?'

'Ramón Danziger. Do you know him?'

'Yes, I do. Nice old guy. Customer of Giovanni's. Tips really well. The waiters love him.'

So Laura went to see Ramón at the Mirador. The entrance was just off Park Lane, and big double doors led into an old-fashioned but grand lobby full of chandeliers, gilt mouldings and red velvet plush. On the right there was an open door, through which she could see the entrance to a more modern-looking dining room full of laid, but empty tables.

Ramón had the old-world elegance of the aristocratic European. He bowed over her hand, ushered her to his office, and ordered tea. 'I dare say you're wondering why I insisted on seeing you when your nice Mr Silvano has told me you are not contract caterers. The truth is, I've followed your career closely for several years and I'm impressed. Frankly, I don't think there's a caterer in the country that could do what I want as well as you. All the Angelotti businesses are good, based on excellent ingredients and straightforward cooking. And Giovanni's is exceptional. You have shown the British just how good real Italian food can be.'

Laura was charmed. Of course you are, she told herself. Flattery laid on with a trowel is always charming. Just be careful. 'You're too kind,' she said, rather stiffly.

'I'm not at all kind. I can be very tetchy if things aren't right. But I'm genuinely impressed. I've eaten several times in all three of the Laura's and found them consistent, and very good. Which is what makes me think you're the right person, contract caterer or not, for the Mirador clients.'

Laura smiled. 'Perhaps you should tell me what you have in mind.'

'In essence I want you to put in a tender for providing all the food in the VIP rooms, which constitute a restaurant, bar and lounge, and the at-table service in the casino of drinks and canapés. If you're interested I'll get my general manager to show you round now.'

Laura felt her heart speed up. 'Is that the restaurant with the Park Lane frontage?' she asked.

Ramón shook his head. 'No, that is the members' restaurant and we'll be keeping its management ourselves. We're looking for a caterer for upstairs in the casino. There's a smaller, smarter restaurant up there, overlooking the park, as well as a big bar and lounge, all serving food and drinks while the gaming rooms are open.'

Laura said, 'Well, I'd certainly be fascinated to see the operation.' Even if they didn't win the tender, it would be interesting. 'Can I ask you who the competition is?'

'Oh, I don't know. It'll be all the big caterers. Lyons, Grand Met, the usual suspects. But I doubt if any will have your flair.'

CHAPTER SIXTEEN

Far from having free time to write her Italian cookbook, Angelica was so busy she took to getting up at five in the morning to put in a couple of hours before her day began.

Two things had grown to fill the space. In addition to her *Daily Mail* column she was now writing regularly on food for *Nova* magazine. Her brief was to keep *Nova's* readers – mostly bright career women – informed about the latest trends in food, the fashionable new restaurants like Lacy's, the Nouvelle Cuisine revolution filtering in from France, new kitchen machines, like the Robot Coupe, new ingredients like paw-paw and mango, new food writers like Claudia Roden, new chefs like the Capital Hotel's Richard Shepherd. She enjoyed it: she could mix opinion with recipes, cover people, places, markets – anything, as long as it had something to do with food. 'What I want,' said the editor, 'is intelligent, lively and well-written copy.' Angelica loved writing for *Nova*, even more than for the *Daily Mail*. But she needed the money from both, and the *Mail* paid better.

The other new venture was public speaking and demonstrating. She had an agent now, Lucy Rock, who managed her media work, negotiating the fees, collecting the money and doing the boring bits, like invoicing and tax. Angelica was in demand for women's clubs, catering exhibitions, and charities trying to raise money. She found herself travelling all over the country, often with ingredients and kit in the back of her car. She didn't charge for the charities, but Lucy insisted that commercial organisations should pay a proper fee.

Mario had been opposed to her having an agent. 'Why do you need one? You'll have to pay her a slice of everything you earn.'

'Yes, but she'll get me more money than I'd dare ask for, and I hate negotiating.'

'I could negotiate for you. I could be your agent.'

Angelica sighed. 'You might be good at talking up the money, Mario, but you don't have the contacts in publishing or television. Lucy knows everyone. The *Nova* job came through her. And the talks and cookery demonstrations. They pay a better day-rate than anything else.'

Mario had complained of Angelica's neglect of him for years. She'd stopped trying to cook for him because he'd never say when he'd be in. And she knew he could always pick up something from Deli-Calzone or, indeed, eat at a Calzone if there was nothing in the fridge. That was what she did, after all.

One evening she didn't get home until nine and she was so tired she'd decided to skip supper, watch the news and go to bed. She'd not reckoned on finding Mario at home. She could tell at once that he was grumpy. He was standing at the fridge with the door open, peering inside. He didn't turn to greet her. 'I suppose there's no supper for your husband again, is there?'

'Oh, darling, how can I cater when you don't tell me if you'll be in?'

'You're a cook, aren't you?' He met her eyes, his own cold. 'A famous cook who produces delicious meals for the enlightenment of the nation. You could whip up something, surely.'

She made an effort not to rise to his taunt. She joined him at the fridge and looked inside. 'Well, there are eggs and bacon. And tomatoes. I could do you a Spanish omelette. Or pasta. There's some tomato sauce. She kept her voice neutral, disguising her rising irritation. He made a face.

'Or sardines on toast. Or baked beans,' she added.

'No. I'll have an English fry-up. Eggs, *pancetta*, tomato and fried bread with baked beans,' he said. He plonked himself down at the kitchen table, confident she'd fall to and get cooking.

Suddenly she'd had enough. She turned towards the door. 'Fine. Cook it yourself. And don't forget to turn on the fan or the place will smell like a chip shop.' She walked upstairs and was relieved to hear the front door slam. With any luck he'd be gone all night.

But he wasn't. An hour later, as she was drifting off, she heard the door. She pretended to be asleep while she listened to him undressing, kicking off his shoes, dropping his loose change on the chest of drawers. He made no effort to be quiet. Why did it irritate her so much that he never shut the bathroom door when he was having a pee?

He climbed into bed and immediately put his arm round her, sliding his hand under her pyjama top to her breast. Oh, bloody hell, she thought. I really, really don't want this. She grunted and tried to roll over on her stomach, away from him.

He pulled her back. 'Don't pretend you're asleep, Angel. I know you're not.' She could smell beer on his breath. 'You're just cross with me,' he went on. 'And maybe I deserve it. I'm sorry.'

He was kneading her breast now and Angelica debated which

would be the quickest option: to persuade him to stop, or to give in and get it over with. 'No, Mario,' she said, 'I really don't want it. I'm exhausted.'

'C'mon, baby,' he said. 'You know you love it, and I won't get to sleep now you've got me all excited.'

She tried to slip out of the bed, but he held her. 'I could force you, you know. It's my right. My conjugal right.'

'Except, since we aren't married, you don't have any conjugal rights,' she snapped. She jerked herself free of him and stood up.

Mario sat up in bed, his face flushed. 'What's the matter with you?' he said. 'All you do is work. You're hardly ever here, and when you are you won't cook for me, talk to me, or fuck. What kind of a relationship is that?'

Angelica thought there was a tiny spark of justice in this, the bit about not talking to him. There was nothing she wanted to talk to him about. But she replied, with spirit, 'I can't have dinner on the table like a good little housewife because you don't tell me if you're coming home. And as for talking to you, you don't want to hear about my work. You make that abundantly clear.'

'And what about the no fucking? Is that my fault too?'

'Mario, you can't be surprised I'm sometimes reluctant to sleep with you. Have you not thought that I might be exhausted? I work hard, and you don't seem to have a problem with spending the money I make. Well, that money comes at a price. The price is that sometimes I'm too tired to make love.'

'It's not exhaustion, Angelica. It's because you don't want to get pregnant, isn't it? We should have had at least two *bambini* by now. You've become one of those frigid Englishwomen who don't want children. That's the truth, isn't it?' His voice was rising.

202

No, that wasn't it, and it was all Angelica could do to resist the temptation to tell him the truth, that there was no danger of her getting pregnant. She'd had a copper coil fitted as soon as they'd come back from France. She'd done it for good reason. Many good reasons, actually: he might have insisted on another abortion and she could never do that again; she wanted to get on with her career; Mario was her first cousin with the risk of a less-than-perfect baby; his moods would make him an unpredictable father and he drank too much. Finally, she didn't want Mario's baby. It would be like a wedding ring, chaining her to him for ever.

She didn't answer his taunts until he called her a sulky bitch and took himself off to the sitting-room sofa. But at four in the morning he was back, apologetic and loving, and he finally had his way. Angelica was too tired to respond with any ardour but also too tired to object. Half asleep, she endured it. What a travesty of love, she thought.

And then, thank God, she had a few hours' deep sleep before her alarm went off.

She could see the signs of Mario's mania growing. He wasn't sleeping for more than a few hours a night; he was talking a lot and very rapidly. He'd started expensive singing lessons and was thinking about making a record. He told some friends who came to supper that he had a recording contract to sing popular arias from Italian opera, which wasn't true. She didn't betray him, and he didn't seem worried that she might. He believes it, she thought.

One Saturday morning they were walking together through Berkeley Square. Mario was going to have his hair cut in Mayfair, and since it was a nice day and Angelica had slept well, she suggested they walk there together, then maybe have lunch in Shepherd Market. They stopped at the car showroom to look at the red Lamborghini in the window. 'Wow!' said Angelica. 'You'd have to shoehorn yourself in and lie on your back to drive it.'

Mario didn't reply. He was absolutely intent on the car, as if memorizing its every dimension. Suddenly he grabbed her hand and walked into the showroom. A smooth young man approached. 'Can I help you, sir? I see you're admiring the Lamborghini Espada.'

Mario nodded slowly. 'Yes. I've read about the improvements. Very impressive. Have you driven it yourself?'

'No, sir, but I've been in it when a customer was test-driving it.'

'So he didn't buy it, then?' Mario was walking round the bright red car, peering in at the dashboard. 'What was wrong with it?'

'He asked for all the technical information and went home to think about it. I'm sure he'll order it, though. He buys a lot of cars from us. The last was a Maserati.'

The young man opened the bonnet and Mario, entranced, peered at the enormous, immaculate engine. His eyes were glittering with excitement.

Angelica's heart sank. Mario was at his most charismatic and charming. She could see the young salesman being sucked into his orbit. He was smiling, too, but with a calf-like fixation. 'What a coincidence,' said Mario. 'I have a Maserati. The Ghibli. I was thinking of trading it in for a Quattroporte. More room for Madam here, and her shopping.' He indicated Angelica, smiling at her affectionately.

He's utterly confident I won't blow the whistle, she thought. Either that or he really believes what he's saying. And why don't I just tell this young man that my husband is mad? That he doesn't own a Maserati. Doesn't own a car at all and is lucky if I lend him my Morris Oxford.

But, of course, she didn't. She didn't want an embarrassing row, and she couldn't humiliate him. Instead she said, 'Darling, you can't buy a car right now. We're late for Lord and Lady Donaldson. You know what they're like. You can come back later.' There was no Lord and Lady anything, but if she joined his *folie de grandeur* fantasy she might get him out of there.

The young man, sensing a lost sale, said, 'Perhaps you'd like to book a test drive, sir? I could get the Maserati Quattroporte in then too.'

'Good idea,' said Mario, and Angelica watched in horror as he took out his diary and made a show of trying to find a suitable date. They agreed on Monday.

At last they were out in the square. Angelica felt relief, swiftly followed by anxiety. She had two days to persuade Mario to rejoin reality and cancel the appointment. He was laughing, delighted. Angelica gripped his arm and shook it angrily. 'You idiot, Mario. Why did you do that? You know you can't begin to afford those cars.'

To her surprise, Mario said, 'Of course I know that, darling. But wasn't it fun? He really believed I was rich as Croesus. You shouldn't have said that Lord and Lady stuff. I was about to get a test drive. But, still, now I'll get to drive the Maserati too.'

'You can't go through with it, Mario! It's madness!'

Suddenly Mario stopped laughing and turned on her. 'Will you bloody well stop calling me mad? I'm perfectly sane. What is so crazy about wanting to drive the best Italian cars in the world?' He was shouting now. 'Every man in the world wants that. I just know how to swing it, that's all. So get off my back, will you?'

Not for the first time, Angelica left him in the street. She looked round, saw a cruising taxi and put her hand out. She directed the driver to Paddington and leaned back, her eyes closed.

So much for trying to spend time with him. This is never going to work. I'm becoming indifferent. Even a year ago I'd have been in floods of tears if he'd shouted at me like that. Now I just want to get away. And what am I doing trying to cover for him? Lord and Lady Donaldson indeed!

She decided to do nothing about the test drives. If she managed to persuade him to cancel them he'd never forgive her, and he'd use it endlessly as an example of her bossy nature. And what might happen if he did drive the cars? Presumably if he crashed one, it would be covered by the dealer's insurance. If he agreed to buy one, they'd find out soon enough that he couldn't pay for it and he'd never take delivery. His problem. Not hers.

On Monday, Mario went to work as usual. He didn't mention the test drives. Maybe he's come to his senses, she thought, as she drove up Edgware Road. She was on her way to Birmingham to film a piece about curry for her new TV series.

They filmed her and the owner of the restaurant discussing Bangladeshi cuisine over dinner, and next day she and the chef made curries and accompaniments in the restaurant kitchen. Filming went slowly. The chef was nervous and talked too fast. They had to do multiple takes for almost everything and she didn't get back to London until after dark. As she drove into the mews she felt mild annoyance that someone had parked in the space outside number six that she regarded as hers. But as she drove past the car, she jammed on her brakes. It was the red Lamborghini.

Rage filled her. She wanted to kill Mario. She yanked her keys from her car's ignition, got out, locked it and fumbled wildly to get the right key into the front door. The delay calmed her a little, but she rushed into the house, saw no one in the kitchen and ran up the stairs. Mario was lying on the sofa, watching television. Angelica marched across the room and punched the TV on-button. As the screen flickered and died, Mario jumped up. 'Hey, how dare—'

'How dare I? How dare I turn off the television?' she shouted back. 'More to the point, how dare you buy that car? What the hell do you think you're doing, Mario?'

'Angelica, calm down.' He tried to take her shoulders but she twisted away. 'I know what I'm doing and we can afford it. It's on the never-never. We pay by the month over three years. It's fine.'

'Don't be such an idiot, Mario. You won't even be able to afford the petrol or the insurance. You have to take it back. Tomorrow. Do you hear?'

This time he succeeded in catching her by the arm, and pulled her towards him. 'It's all right . . .'

Suddenly the energy went out of her to be replaced by a sensation of utter bleakness. For a second she was tempted to drop her head onto his chest, let him pull her in, comfort her, tell her lies.

But she raised her head to look at him, 'No, it's not. Nothing's right. You aren't right, our relationship isn't right. And I'm through.'

He dropped her arm. 'Are you telling me you don't love me? Really? Because of a car?' He smiled at her, the apologetic smile that had won her back a hundred times before. No longer.

'Right now, Mario, I positively hate you. I don't want anything more to do with you. I'm sick of your moods, of your refusal to get help and treatment, of your selfishness, of your ridiculous behaviour.'

She walked to the top of the stairs. 'I'm going to Papa's. When I come back from work tomorrow you'd better be out of this house. And you can take that ridiculous car with you.'

The next morning she woke up in her parents' spare room, feeling like a failure. Here she was, back with Mamma and Papa again. She felt very sad, but calm.

She wasn't due at the TV studios until noon, so she sat at her mother's desk – Laura had gone to work – and wrote Mario a letter.

Mario (I wish I could put Darling Mario, but I'm still too raw to do that)

When you're in the mood you're in, you can't listen and you don't want to. But I hope you will at least read this letter, or keep it to read when you're less high. I really do want you to understand some things.

First, you are right that I've been refusing to have a baby. In fact I had a coil inserted to prevent conception. At first it was because I couldn't bear to go through another abortion, and nothing had changed to make me think you would want a child now any more than you did the first time. Also, I wanted to get on with my career, something you have never understood or supported. And we are first cousins, Mario. There is a real risk of a baby of ours not being normal. And your moods would make you an unreliable father. And since our relationship is falling apart, I don't want your baby anyway.

The whole problem with our relationship, I believe, boils down to your manic depression. I used to think that if only you would get help and treatment you would be restored to the Mario I loved – bright, charismatic, fun and loving. I would happily stay with you for ever. But you would not agree to treatment, even for the depressions, which are so horrible for you and so tedious for me. So now I've given up.

I'm very glad we never married and can just walk away from each other without some lawyer making things even worse than they are. I'll never forget how much I loved you, Mario. That time in Paris before I was pregnant was the happiest of my life. But it's over. Finally and absolutely over.

Angelica

Silvano was sitting at his desk, thinking about his brother. Giovanni had just told him about the Lamborghini fiasco and he had promised to sort it out.

Silvano listened to the tale, his mood sombre. But when Giovanni said, 'She's through with him this time, I'm certain,' he felt relief and, he had to admit, pleasure. He tried to reason with himself. This changes nothing, you idiot – she's not going to jump from one brother to the next, is she?

Mario's getting worse, he thought. He'd had to rescue his younger brother so many times from scrapes, even as a little boy. He'd once stolen liquorice strings from the sweet shop and Silvano had had to spend his own pocket money to pay for them, then persuade the assistant not to tell their mother. They'd had to sweep the yard behind the shop and wash out the rubbish bins to buy the woman's silence.

Then there was the time Mario had stolen an English exam paper, and was threatened with expulsion. Silvano had had to summon up his courage and go to see the headmaster. By then the academic star of the school, he'd pleaded that Mario wasn't evil but a terrible show-off. When a teacher had forgotten to lock the cupboard, he had been unable to resist having a look. 'Honestly, sir, distributing that exam paper to the class was too good an opportunity to miss. Mario is actually very good at English. He didn't need to cheat. But he regarded it as an adventure, something Desperate Dan or Superman might have done.'

'Nonsense,' the head had said.

But Silvano had a more subtle card to play. 'Sir, I'm really saying all this not just for Mario but for me. If Mario has to leave and go to another school, I'll have to leave too. My mother would never let us go to different schools. I have to be with him. You know what he's like, sir, always in trouble, and I often manage to stop him doing something daft. And I really, really don't want to leave.'

Silvano knew that the head wouldn't want to lose him, and he'd watched him rapidly calculating that he'd be better off with the pair of them than with neither. So Mario wasn't expelled, but he had to stay late every day for the rest of the term, weeding the grounds, sweeping the tennis courts, cleaning the art-room windows. The class completed a different exam paper. Mario got an A.

Silvano stood up, squared his shoulders and set off to see Mario, still in the mews cottage. Mario is my albatross, he thought. All our lives, I'll be bailing him out. Partly because he can't help his condition, partly for Mamma's sake, but mostly because I don't want to leave Angelica to cope on her own.

Accepting Mario and Angelica as a couple hadn't been easy. When they'd first got back from Paris and he'd heard Angelica call Mario '*caro*' or 'darling', it had been pretty painful. But he'd got over it. Thank the Lord for the swinging sixties! They'd allowed him to lose himself in loud music, to play the field and make love to a succession of young women. One or two casual affairs had turned into long-term relationships. He smiled as he remembered jolly, easy-going Julia, almost always smiling, never complaining. And there had been straight-as-a-die Anthea, intense and intelligent. At the start of both affairs he'd thought he'd found a woman he could stay with. But, no, when it came to the inevitable choice between commitment and separation, he had ended the affair.

Mario came to the door, looking sleepy. He saw his brother and walked back upstairs, leaving Silvano to follow, and to shut the door behind him.

Silvano dispensed with any polite niceties. 'What have you done now, Mario? Angelica won't come back this time, you idiot. You've just lost the best thing that ever happened to you. That girl is a perfect saint to have stuck with you so long.'

Mario laughed. 'That's women for you!' he said. 'Silly bitch. She'll come back. She's just having a tantrum. Take no notice.'

Silvano tried to reason with him, but it was impossible. When Mario went into the bathroom, Silvano picked up the Lamborghini key from the dresser and walked out. He drove the car straight to Berkeley Square and parked outside the show-room window.

He asked for the salesman who had sold Mario the car. 'Do you think you could get the car parked in your garage?' he said. 'Then perhaps we can sit somewhere private for a conversation.'

Bemused, the man did as he was asked, then led Silvano into the office, asking the secretary to cover for him in the showroom. They sat down on the padded leather sofa.

'Now, what can I do for you, sir? I hope Mr Angelotti is happy with the car? Nothing wrong, is there?'

'Well, the car is fabulous. But I'm afraid my brother Mario, the purchaser, is delusional. The cheque he gave you is going to bounce. He sometimes thinks he's a multi-millionaire, but in fact he's a junior manager at an ice cream company. I'm afraid you're just going to have to take the car back.'

'Oh, God,' said the young man, clearly stricken.

'He's ill,' said Silvano, 'with manic depression. Sometimes he gets so depressed he wants to commit suicide. Other times he thinks he's a music star, or rich as Croesus.'

'Oh, God,' said the lad again. 'He told me his father was the catering tycoon Angelotti and he would guarantee the money.'

'Well, firstly, Mr Angelotti is our uncle, not our father, and secondly he wouldn't have dreamed of guaranteeing anything. He dislikes Mario.'

'But I can't take the car back. I've already entered it as a sale.'

'You'll have to un-enter it, then.'

'But I can't—'

'Look, I'm sorry to be tough with you. But you must admit you are partly to blame. How could you have handed over the car without checking the buyer's financial situation? What if he had been a real con man? That car could be in Germany by now, resold and the buyer long gone. Then you'd be in real trouble.'

The young man put his head in his hands. 'I've only been here a week. I'll lose my job.'

Silvano shifted a fraction closer to him. Poor boy, he couldn't be more than nineteen. 'My advice would be to tell the truth,' he said gently. 'Go to your boss today, before he's even seen the sales figures, and tell him exactly what happened. And apologize for being an idiot.'

Silvano walked back to Paddington from Berkeley Square. It was a long way but he needed time to think. Somehow he'd have to get Mario into a clinic. His brother was more malleable when he was depressed so he'd wait until the next black period, then take him to the Friern Barnet Hospital and have him admitted.

Meanwhile, today, he must get him out of number six. He'd rent a room for him somewhere, move him and his things into it and take the cottage's key from him. It was the least he could do for Angelica, saddled with his madman brother. He was more concerned for Angelica than he was for Mario, who loved being high as a kite, without a thought for anyone else. Meanwhile Angelica was resolutely getting on with her career, trying to help Mario, never complaining that she was, in effect, the breadwinner.

It was lucky they'd not had children. He wondered if she wanted any, and smiled at the thought. She'd make a wonderful mother, but Mario would be a dreadful father, one minute indulgent, the next angry, then oblivious. *I'll help her get him right out of her life.*

CHAPTER SEVENTEEN

When Ramón's manager showed Laura over the Mirador casino, she saw at once the missed opportunity for the restaurant. 'I know it's none of my business,' she said, 'but may I ask why you don't have the front door to the restaurant on the Park Lane side instead of through the casino?'

'What would be the point? People would have to go out of the building to get to the restaurant.'

'I'm not suggesting you block the members' entrance from the club, but if you used the Park Lane entrance as well, you could let the public in.'

'We don't want the public in. It's a members' only club.'

'Is the restaurant profitable?'

'That is, as you said, none of your business. The restaurant is not part of the proposed catering contract for the rooms.'

Put in her place, Laura asked no more questions.

The VIP rooms scared her. It would be the first time the Angelottis had worked for someone else or taken a fixed-price contract. The terms seemed extraordinary. For a price agreed at the start, they would have to provide unlimited food for unknown numbers of guests to eat as much and as expensively as they liked. For free. She was assured it was common in the gambling world for serious players to be wined and dined at the club's expense. Gambling bosses just wanted their clubs to offer the best food in town.

They looked over the kitchens (more than adequate) and the rooms (not to her taste, but certainly luxurious), then sat down with a cup of coffee.

'Our high-rollers come in from all over the world to gamble,' the manager explained. 'They're going to lose a great deal of money. And the only thing that makes losing at the tables palatable is being treated like royalty. Our aim is to make the whole thing so painless that they keep coming back to lose a bit more.'

It made sense.

'Which means,' he went on, 'a truly groaning board. Caviar, lobster, the best Aberdeen Angus beef, and every nation catered for. Our big spenders come from all over Europe, Asia, the Far East and, of course, the Americas.' He smiled. 'And some of our clients, I'm afraid, are less than gourmets. So, apart from the buffet, your chefs need to be able to produce a perfect hamburger, bowl of spaghetti, fried rice or jam doughnut. On demand. Do you understand?'

Laura heard his words, but couldn't believe what he was saying. 'So we just have to take it on the chin if we're losing money, and carry on providing the best?'

'Exactly. You've got it. Which is why you need to propose a budget that will cover your costs, profit, and a contingency for the risk you're taking. Obviously, if you ask for the moon, you won't get the contract. If you quote too little you might land the contract and lose your boots.' He stood up, handing her the tender document. 'Good luck.'

*

Laura, Giovanni and Angelica agonized long and hard over how to price for the unknown. In the end, Giovanni said, 'Let's just reckon on the majority of people eating sensibly but fifteen per cent of them eating nothing but caviar. Just lay it on thick. Put in a bid that will cover us comfortably. If we make too much money, it'll be a nice problem to have.'

'They'll never swallow that,' said Laura.

'My guess is that they will. They admit they're not restaurateurs. They just want to hand over the lot to someone who knows what they're doing and will leave them free to do what they do best – parting their customers from their money.'

'OK, but I want them to give us a lease on the ground floor for another Laura's. Their restaurant is losing money hand over fist. If we took it over they'd cut those losses and get a decent rent.'

'Only if they allowed us to let the public in,' said Angelica.

Giovanni frowned. 'I doubt they'd do that. And anyway, is this the right time for us? With high interest rates and rocketing inflation?'

Laura tried to seem interested while her husband complained of industrial unrest, balance-of-payments difficulties and a possible currency crisis. Angelica tried unsuccessfully to stop his flow, gave up and sat resigned to defeat. But suddenly her mother threw her arms round her father's neck and burst out laughing. 'Stop, darling, stop! We're cooks, aren't we? And people have to eat. We should just keep making great food, and let the politicians worry about the economy.'

Angelica chipped in, 'And, besides, Papa, the existing Laura's are making good money and we won't have to borrow at all for the Park Lane fit-out. It's a chance in a lifetime.'

Laura and Angelica were too much for Giovanni. They delivered two proposals to Ramón, for the ground-floor lease, and for the VIP rooms' catering contract. Laura wanted to make the offers contingent on each other, an all-or-nothing bid, but Giovanni put his foot down. 'No, *cara*,' he said. 'If they agree to our terms for the VIP rooms we'll be in the money. And it smacks of arrogance to demand both.'

Two weeks later Laura was in her office, sitting on the sofa with a cup of tea, planning next month's weekly menus. She was immensely proud of her growing chain of Laura's. The food was not exclusively Italian, like Giovanni's: they served classic dishes from France, *lapin à la moutarde* and *soupe à l'oignon*, alongside English steak and kidney pudding, and the American hamburger. It was autumn, which meant more hearty dishes, and she was scribbling '*borscht*' and '*vichyssoise*' when the telephone rang.

It was Ramón. 'Well, Laura, I look forward to your namesake restaurant in my front window!'

For a second she couldn't breathe. A Laura's in Park Lane! 'I . . .Oh, Ramón . . . thank you . . .'

'Don't you want to know about the catering contract for upstairs?'

Maybe we haven't got it. That might be good, less to worry about. No, it would be terrible. We must have it. Would they have given us the restaurant without the VIP rooms? Why not? Her thoughts flew about like paper in a storm. 'Yes, I do. Of course I do.'

'You've got that too.'

Within six weeks they had refitted the restaurant, persuaded Dino to move from Giovanni's to be Executive Head Chef at the Mirador, hired the staff and opened the third Laura's.

CHAPTER EIGHTEEN

Laura was at her desk when her nephew Richard telephoned. 'Aunt Laura,' he said, 'can I come and see you about something?' He sounded strained.

'What's up? Is something wrong?'

'No, I don't think so, but I do need some advice. Can I come tonight? Or tomorrow?'

'Tonight's fine. Sixish? I'll be at home.'

Richard arrived, looking rather sheepish in a navy pinstripe three-piece suit that was slightly too big for him. 'Sorry,' he said, taking his jacket and waistcoat off and yanking up his too-loose trousers to try to tuck in his shirt. 'I hate wearing this stuff but I've come straight from the office.'

'You look very nice.'

'So Mum says, but that's what I wanted to see you about. Mum and Dad are so pleased that I've got this supposedly terrific job. They've spent a fortune on my education, and bought me a couple of posh suits. The thing is . . .'

He hesitated, so Laura finished for him: 'You hate the job.'

An expression of relief washed across his face. 'I do. I loathe it. I hate the pompous idiots I share an office with. All testosterone and booze, talking about the birds they've shot and the girls they fancy. And the work is deadly. I just sit all day working out answers to economic questions I can't believe anyone seriously needs to know. I'm not going to be able to stick it, Aunt Laura.'

'Didn't you know what you were in for?'

'I think I did and I certainly dreaded it, but my tutor was so excited at the job offer, and Mum and Dad were so proud – apparently, getting into Goldman Sachs is like scooping the pools – that I thought I ought to give it a go. But I hate it. It's banal stuff, like working out the actual growth rate versus what some poor blighter predicted, or some investment trust's performance against the average over the last five years. Who cares?'

'Be fair, Richard. Someone, presumably a Goldman Sachs client, will be paying good money for those answers. They care.'

'I suppose so. But I'll never be able to make myself care.'

'Poor you,' said Laura. He looked woebegone. He was twenty-three, but with his clean-shaven baby face, he seemed much younger. She wanted to hug him but that would embarrass him and it wouldn't help.

'Does your boss know how unhappy you are?'

'I shouldn't think so. He loves all this stuff and thinks I must too.'

'Well, what do you want to do instead of accountancy or whatever it is you're doing?'

He was clearly astonished. 'Can't you guess? I really, really want to be a chef. I want to cook.'

Richard seemed much happier when he left than he had when he'd arrived, though a lot more dishevelled. He'd pushed his fingers through his hair so often during their conversation (Laura had resisted telling him he couldn't do that as a cook) that it stuck straight up. He looked like a junior boffin, all high fore-head, wide eyes and out-of-control limbs. 'I'm going to hand in my notice this afternoon,' he said, his eyes shining. Laura opened her mouth to object, but then thought better of it. Goldman Sachs had never made him smile like that.

At the beginning of December Laura offered him a trial month in the Mirador kitchens. It would be up to him to prove his worth to the head chef. Junior commis was his title, but right now everyone was on cleaning duty.

One day she came upon him in the yard. He was wearing an old Barbour jacket over his chef's whites, wellington boots and industrial-weight rubber gloves. He was using a pressure hose to clean out the enormous refuse containers. 'You poor boy. You didn't think that would be your first job as a cook, did you?'

'No, but I'd rather be doing this than sitting in City comfort.'

'Good. How are you getting on? Is the brigade being nice to you?'

Laura saw the hesitation in his eyes, but he nodded. 'Sure. They're OK,' he said. 'They rib me for being the boss's nephew, but that's fine. Like at school, really. Initiation ritual.'

Damn, Laura thought. I should have made it clear when we took this lot over from Mirador that their jobs depended on them behaving like civilized adults. Teasing was one thing, and all teams of workers teased one another, but bullying was another. The industry was rife with it. She hoped the atmosphere in her own restaurants was different. She employed almost as many women in the kitchens as men, which, she thought, had a moderating effect. But you never knew for certain. Playground rules applied in kitchens: however much someone was victimized, they never complained.

Laura had told Kurt, her newly enlisted manager, that today she'd spend longer with him than usual. Could they take a quick look at Laura's and the casino kitchens, then go through the figures for both operations? Though she'd come in almost daily since they'd taken over, she hadn't seen any financial results for the VIP rooms yet. Now that they were three weeks in, she felt they should have enough information and results to see if they'd got their bid right.

She met him at five o'clock in the bar at Laura's. The room was ready for the evening, with immaculate white linen, heavy silver cutlery, her trademark hexagonal jam-jars of mixed herbs and country flowers on each table. She picked one up to examine it. Flowering hyssop and marjoram, dark-leafed sage, tiny white Michaelmas daisies and pink geraniums. All looking good. She tipped the jar a fraction. Then she frowned and held it out for him to see that the water was murky and came only halfway up the jar.

He met her eye and shook his head, irritated. 'I'll see to it.' Poor Kurt. He'd soon learn that she always checked the flower water. It had to be sparkling clear if seen through glass. And full to the top. If a customer put his nose into a neglected jar of flowers, he'd smell nothing but rotting stems.

'How are we doing here, Kurt? What's the average spend? Is it holding up?'

'Pretty good. About four pounds for lunch and at least five for dinner, both without drinks. The bar takings, per person, are averaging two pounds seventy. That's eight per cent up on what we'd budgeted, so it's satisfactory.'

'Very well done.' She meant it. To be ahead of budget in the first few weeks of a restaurant's life was almost unheard of. And so was a manager who was on top of his figures. 'What about the VIP rooms?' she asked.

He smiled. 'I hardly dare say it, but I think we're going to make a lot of money. So far the casino management is delighted with what we're offering – we really are buying the best. The punters aren't eating as much as we'd estimated – they mostly get stuck into the free bar. Thank God you pushed the drinks budget so high. The bar needs a staff of four to keep up with demand.'

'Shall we have a look?'

Laura's heart was beating a little faster than usual as they rode in the lift to the VIP rooms and bar above the gaming floor. Financial success gave her a real thrill. Maybe Giovanni's right that I'm a born businesswoman, she thought.

'Of course,' Kurt said, 'we're helped by the fact that we don't have to pay rent or bills for electricity, gas, maintenance, or even heavy cleaning. It's a bit of a dream, really.'

'We'll have to be careful we don't become complacent. Just because they pay for everything doesn't mean we shouldn't watch the costs like hawks.'

'I've got a close eye on them. But thieving's going to be a problem. Especially with the old-timers we kept on. They regard the stores as a kind of help-yourself outlet. I need to catch one soon and make an example of him or her to deter the rest.'

Ever since Richard had been working in London, he'd been living in his family's flat in the Paddington mews. But since he was alone, except on rare nights when Hal and Pippa came to London, he mostly ate with the Angelottis on his nights off. He'd always got on well with his aunt and it was good to relax. He was still sure he'd made the right decision in leaving the City, but his new job was tough.

He was in the fish section, which meant, since he was the most junior member of the team, that he cleaned lobsters and crabs, cracked their claws, or scrubbed and opened oysters all day, every day, with an occasional turn at the deep-fryer. He didn't mind, and after a while he got more proficient and speedy, but his hands were raw and scratched.

One Monday, he had the night off and was regaling Giovanni and Laura with tales from the VIP rooms' kitchen. 'I'm still so clumsy, though. I stabbed my hand today. Look.' He turned it over to show them a scruffy bandage, stained with blood, now brown.

His aunt's face became serious. And anxious. 'Who did the bandage?'

'One of the boys.'

'Did he disinfect it?'

Richard shook his head. 'I don't know. Don't think so.'

Laura got up and came round the table. She took his hand and carefully undid the bandage. Richard protested that it was fine but Laura snapped, 'Richard, keep still.' The reprimand made him feel like a schoolboy. Laura turned to the drawer behind her and found the scissors. 'The blood has stuck it all together, but we have to get it off. We need to disinfect it. Come.' She pulled him to the sink.

She made him stick his hand into a bowl of warm water to soften the dried blood so that she could peel off the bandage. The wound started to bleed again and she made him run the cold tap over it, which hurt. The cut was an inch long and quite deep. 'They should have sent you to have it stitched,' she said. She turned to Giovanni. 'Darling, have we any peroxide? We should sterilize it.'

Giovanni went to look and came back with a bottle of whisky. 'This is what we used in the war, if we were lucky enough to have any.' He spooned a tablespoon into and over the cut and Richard hopped from foot to foot, determined not to swear in front of his aunt and uncle.

Giovanni drove him to the hospital. It was only a few blocks away and they could have walked, but it was very cold, with frost on the pavements.

The next day, Richard was told to fry the cod *goujons*. He was relieved, because he could wield the huge open sieve with a long handle (he'd learned to call it the 'spider') with one hand. If he'd been on fish prep, he'd have needed to use his injured hand all the time.

He was about halfway through when Laura came in, said, 'Morning, chefs,' to everyone, then walked over to him. 'Oh, they smell delicious,' she said. 'Can I taste one?'

'You're the boss, Aunt Laura.'

She picked one up from the doubled kitchen paper on which they were draining, waved it in the air briefly to cool it, then nibbled it cautiously. 'Delicious,' she said, and popped the rest of it into her mouth.

He was aware that the other cooks were watching the exchange from where they were prepping the *goujons* for him to fry. Damn, he thought. I shouldn't have called her 'Aunt Laura'.

Maybe she realized she had been too friendly with him in front of the others because suddenly she was brisk and business-like. 'Here,' she said, producing a packet from her bag. 'The glove is for whoever is opening oysters. You wear it on your left hand so you don't repeat the foolishness of yesterday. The goggles are to stop you getting flying pieces of shell in your eyes when you're cracking crabs and lobsters. Don't let me catch you not wearing them.' She turned away, then looked back. 'And, Richard, look after the glove. They cost a fortune.'

As soon as she'd gone, Bobby, the Scots commis, sniggered. 'Oh, has kind Auntie Laura brought her bonny bairn a wee present? Gi' us a look-see then.' He walked over, opened the package and pulled out the chain-mail glove. 'Oooh, nice.' He put it on, and reached for the goggles. 'And a pretty pair of goggles too! So, lads,' he said, turning to the others, 'that's what you get if you're the boss-lady's ickle boy.'

Richard yanked the goggles out of Bobby's grip. But he couldn't get the glove off him. He gave up and went back to work. He'd find it later if the idiot didn't return it.

That afternoon, the sous-chef in charge of the fish section put Bobby on opening oysters. He didn't wear the glove so Richard went up to him. 'You should wear that mitt, Bobby. You heard what she said. Where is it?'

'Wouldn't you like to know?'

'Bobby, don't be stupid. It makes sense to wear it when you're doing that.'

'I don't need it, pal. I'm not a little toff with delicate hands and no ken about nowt. You wear it if you want to – keep your little handies in perfect shape for takin' tea wi' the Queen.'

'Where is it?'

'Ah, that'd be tellin'.'

Richard turned away. He had to fillet and skin two salmon,

which was wet work. He went to the pot wash and borrowed a rubber glove from the kitchen porter to keep his bandage dry.

In mid-afternoon he returned his descaled, boned and filleted salmon sides to the large cold room. He'd stretched a sheet of plastic wrap over the fish, remembering that his mother wouldn't use the stuff. Sophie still covered sandwiches with damp tea-towels and put beaded doilies or net cloches, inherited from Maud, over milk jugs or bowls of leftovers.

He turned to leave the cold room when the door suddenly slammed shut. He caught a glimpse of Bobby and heard his laugh. Then all was quiet. Whether they were deliberately silent, or the fridge door was so thick it blocked all sound, he couldn't tell. A second later the light was switched off.

Richard pushed against the door, but it was locked. He told himself not to panic. It was only the fridge, after all, not the freezer. But it wouldn't be much above freezing. *I won't call out. They probably can't hear, and if they can, they'll just laugh.*

He couldn't stop his heart banging, though, and a feeling of deep injustice assailed him. Why were they so beastly to him?

He stood in the pitch dark, not wanting to sit on the floor or lean against the shelves or door because they were so cold. And he did feel very, very cold now. Thank God for his watch, which had luminous hands and numbers. He wondered how long you had to be in there before you died of hypothermia. He tried to smile in the dark. Stupid, it would be days before that happened and someone would need something out of this fridge within an hour, at most two.

And then another thought made him panic. Was there any ventilation in here? It would be logical not to have any. Any exchange of air would raise the temperature and increase the electricity costs. But, again, even if there was none, he'd last a couple of hours, wouldn't he?

His thoughts veered between rage at his colleagues and rising fear. He kept having to tell himself that even such oafs as Bobby wouldn't murder him just for a laugh.

He tried not to look at his watch but he couldn't help it. The time went so slowly he put it to his ear and was reassured by its steady tick.

He'd been standing in the dark for just over fifteen minutes when suddenly, with relief, he remembered. He almost laughed. The fridge and freezer rooms were both fitted with escape catches. There was a big green knob beside the door. If you punched it the door clicked open. He felt around the door, found the knob and banged it home with the heel of his hand. There was a click, and the door loosened. Straightening his face so that he didn't appear frightened as he walked out, Richard pushed the door. It rattled and moved, but wouldn't open. The bastards had used the padlock. It was massive. It went through a heavy-duty metal hasp and staple fitted to the door frame and door. It was used to prevent pilfering and it was kept in the chef's office. But how had they got hold of it? Surely Chef Dino wasn't in on the game.

Unable to control himself any longer, he banged on the door and yelled at the top of his voice, 'You bastards, let me out. Open the bloody door, d'you hear?'

Suddenly it opened and Richard had to put his hand over his eyes. The light was blinding. When he looked up, Bobby stood there grinning. Richard made a lunge for him, but he dodged aside and one of the others restrained Richard. 'Whoa, laddie,' said Bobby. 'You only had to ask. It was just a little game, a wee intelligence test to see how long it would take ye to find the door release. Twenty minutes! That's the worst score we've ever had. Aye, you must be very, very thick.'

Richard felt close to tears. *God! You're twenty-three, you idiot!* As he walked away, he saw that it hadn't been the padlock that had held the door: a wooden spoon had been dropped through the hasp. One decent shove would have snapped it.

The following day his oyster glove was back at his station. He didn't say anything and neither did Bobby. In spite of his 'intelligence test' score, he'd obviously gone through some sort of initiation ritual, because the bullying stopped. They still teased him about being related to Laura, but it was water off a duck's back.

CHAPTER NINETEEN

One day in mid-December, Laura was in the new restaurant, discussing Christmas menus with the chefs, when Ramón came searching for her. He looked anxious, not his usual suave self, she thought, as she excused herself and led him to the empty bar. 'What's wrong, Ramón? You look worried.'

'I am. Have you heard the news?'

'What news?' She was catching his anxiety. What could have gone wrong?

'The prime minister has just announced something called the Three-Day Work Order. It means we can only open three days a week.'

'What? He can't do that!'

'I'm afraid he just did.'

'I don't understand. I knew things were bad, but . . .'

'He doesn't have much option. The economy's at breaking point, with oil prices and inflation at record levels, and low coal stocks on account of the miners working to rule. The idea is to save electricity and limit pay. Heaven knows if it will work, but it could certainly ruin our business.'

But Laura was thinking of all their other businesses. How

could they survive? 'I'm sorry, Ramón,' she said, 'I must ring Giovanni.'

'I'm so sorry, Laura.' He put a hand on her arm. 'Restaurants are exempt so it won't affect your other businesses. But the casino, and obviously the VIP rooms . . .'

'Hang on. Let's think.' She sat on a sofa and Ramón took a chair opposite her. 'Are you sure about the exemption?'

'Restaurants, food shops and newspapers.'

'Right. Can we choose the days we work?'

'I should hope so. It would bankrupt us if we had to work Monday to Wednesday, wouldn't it?'

'The VIP rooms take two thirds of their money on Friday and Saturday. I imagine it must be similar at the gaming tables in the casino?' He nodded and Laura went on, 'We're closed on Sunday anyway. So, if we do Thursday to Saturday, we'll ride the storm, I'm sure. How long do they think it will last?'

Ramón said, 'They haven't said. A "temporary measure", Mr Heath called it.'

'If it's more than a few weeks, we'll have to lay off staff.' It would be the first time in sixteen years that the Angelotti business had gone backwards.

Ramón stood up. 'I'll call a meeting for this afternoon with our senior managers and before then we'll get the full details. Can you and Giovanni come?'

The relaunch party of the VIP rooms and Laura's restaurant in the Mirador was due to be held on New Year's Eve, to welcome the new year of 1974. The invitations had gone out in November, and almost everyone invited had agreed to come. But after Edward

Heath's bombshell, several Middle Eastern guests, nervous of even more cold and dark than there was in a normal English winter, decided not to attend the party. Ramón suggested they delay the celebration. 'It does seem rather crass to be holding a party on the day the country closes half its doors,' he said. 'We could get a lot of adverse publicity.'

'I don't think so,' said Laura. 'The press will see it as an example of the Dunkirk spirit, carrying on regardless, not allowing the forces of darkness to extinguish the light, and so on.' She smiled with a confidence she only half felt. 'Especially if we help them see it that way.'

New Year's Eve fell on a Monday, and the three-day week would start at midnight. As the Tuesday would be a non-working day for the casino, the gambling would have to stop at midnight.

'OK,' said Laura, 'but as long as no one is paid after midnight, and the party becomes a private affair, held in candlelight, we need not shoo anyone out of the door. Don't worry, Ramón. I'll get enough unpaid volunteers to do the serving, and it'll be fun. A kind of New Year statement that life goes on.'

Angelica spent the week between Christmas and New Year working in the VIP rooms kitchens. There was no filming going on and her *Daily Mail* copy, about how to be clever with Christmas leftovers, and the New Year piece about New Year resolutions, to cook small portions of fresh and healthy food, *à la* nouvelle cuisine, were both done.

At first the rest of the brigade treated her with suspicion. Not only was she the Angelottis' daughter but she was on television, a food writer, and beautiful to boot. It was this last attribute that seemed to throw the young male cooks. Either they gawped silently or they became loud and foul-mouthed, showing off like children.

But Angelica, now twenty-five, had learned a lot in the last few years. Television had taught her patience and given her poise and confidence. And Mario had taught her that life was not a bed of roses. As a temporary sous-chef, she soon established a reputation for efficiency, toughness and fairness. Chef Dino put her in charge of the food for the party.

At eight o'clock on New Year's Eve, Angelica took her mother on a tour of her buffet. Most of the dishes came from the VIP rooms' menu and the cooks knew what they were doing, but tonight Angelica was determined that it would be especially magnificent, and it was.

For the middle of the room, she had commissioned a huge ice sculpture of all the symbols of celebration: champagne bottles in buckets, flags, presents and flowers. The centrepiece of the dessert table was a great platter of fruit, made with blown sugar. It looked entirely realistic, almost too perfect: red apples streaked with green, fat yellow pears, a half watermelon complete with black seeds, a cascade of apricots, bunches of red and green grapes spilling off the edges.

'This is astonishing, darling,' said Laura. 'Who made them?'

'Chef Huber, from the Ealing confectionery department. Wonderful, aren't they?'

The entire buffet was spectacular. The tablecloth was of gold damask, and the food was all on silver platters. At the back, on a raised shelf, silver and gold candelabra had been fitted with gold candles and interspersed with low arrangements of holly and ivy, some of the leaves gilded and silvered. A huge gilt mirror behind the buffet doubled the effect of sparkling opulence.

'Wait till you see what it will look like at midnight, Mamma,' said Angelica. She walked to the door and switched off the ceiling candelabra.

The candles glittered and the ice sculptures, lit from inside a central well by battery-powered lanterns, glowed mysteriously. In a second, opulence became romance. The candles on the tables had been barely noticeable when the lights were on, but now the room took on a magical intimacy.

'It's staggering, darling. Well done! Are you sure you don't want a job?'

Angelica laughed. 'I've so enjoyed this week that I almost think I should give up television and be an outside caterer. I've really loved the logistics of it all: pulling together decoration and good food, thinking about the atmosphere and the event. Something you can't do as a cook.'

Laura smiled in the way Angelica remembered from her childhood: indulgent and proud. 'Darling, you always love what you're doing at that moment, whatever it is! It's a great gift. You should hang on to it.'

They switched the lights on again and continued their tour. The hot section had six domed copper warmers, inside which were various sauced dishes, each with its attendant accompaniments around it. An Indian chicken korma, made, Laura was glad to see, with boned thighs and the birds' 'oysters', rather than the potentially dry breasts, was surrounded by silver bowls of relishes (fresh mango and onion, tomato with mint, cucumber with yogurt) the ingredients cut into perfect tiny dice. There was hot naan bread, puffy and aromatic, alongside steamed white rice. Several kinds of chilli were on offer, for those who wanted something hotter than a classic korma, alongside mango chutney, toasted coconut flakes, and pickled lemon slices.

Laura lifted the lid of the *coq au vin*. 'Lovely,' she said. 'Look at that rich shiny sauce coating the chicken. So often it's not properly reduced and tastes thin and winy.'

They asked for a dozen teaspoons and tasted their way down the dishes: the curry, the almost black *boeuf bourguignon*, the lamb tagine, fragrant with apricots and spices, the velvety fish chowder and the Swedish meatballs.

'I learned how to make these from that Swedish chef I interviewed on my programme,' said Angelica. 'Veal, with lots of dill. But what I like is the mash. Look.' She lifted the lid and in one of the compartments were the meatballs in a creamy sauce, speckled with dill, and in the other boiled potato put through a ricer so that it lay in soft airy strands, light as a feather. Angelica took half a teaspoon of mash, and another of the sauce. She poured the sauce onto the mash and said, 'Mamma!'

Laura opened her mouth and closed her eyes. 'Mmm.'

The attention to detail seemed to please her mother most. It was the same with the cold sliced sirloin, which was displayed both American style in thick slices, and English style, carved thinly and curled to make the slices easy to lift. There was mayonnaise, horseradish sauce and three kinds of mustard.

The stuffed boned duck had an accompanying orange sauce, Morello cherry chutney or gooseberry pickle. The *foie gras* had its own dedicated waiter to cut careful slices and offer freshly toasted brioche and a glass of Sauternes.

On and on it went. A good kilo of Beluga caviar and another of

Sevruga, each piled high in cut-glass bowls, buried in crushed ice in an elaborate silver tureen decorated with carvings of entwined fish – sturgeon, Laura supposed. The usual accompaniments of sour cream, chopped egg, shallot and parsley were presented in a line-up of silver bowls.

By nine o'clock bar and buffet were surrounded by guests, happy, laughing, exquisitely dressed. Angelica thought they looked like a poster for a cruise ship or a grand hotel, and she was proud of the smartly dressed waiters, admirably combining charm with efficiency. Soon the gaming tables resounded to the click of chips and the calls of the croupiers. Waitresses carried trays of champagne coupes to the players and a waiter offered a selection of Davidoff cigars from a compartmented wooden box.

Angelica had hired a dance floor and a stage, and had them set up in the mostly cleared lounge area of the gaming room.

At five minutes to midnight Ramón stood on the stage in front of a jazz band and a piano. The band gave him a drum roll ending in a cymbals clash. '*Rien va plus*' could be heard all over the room as gaming stopped. Everyone hushed as he lifted the microphone.

'Welcome, everyone. In a few minutes we will sing "Auld Lang Syne" and wish each other the best of everything for the New Year. And we at the Mirador wish you, our customers and friends, the same. You will know, too, that midnight brings us the unwelcome start of the three-day week. But we will be open on Thursdays, Fridays and Saturdays as usual. Tomorrow is the day the law comes into effect. But please don't worry. It's true we have to stop gambling, but we can go on with the party. We aren't allowed to operate as a business but this is now a private

235

function and the wonderful comedian and pianist Victor Borge will, I know, distract you from the lack of gambling. The buffet will remain and the wine will continue to flow. After Mr Borge's entertainment, the band will play for you and we expect you to dance till dawn. So, please, be my guests, eat, drink and be merry. Happy New Year.'

He stepped off the stage and Angelica's well-rehearsed team turned on the wireless. The sound of Big Ben's sonorous chimes heralded 1974 and everyone cheered, then kissed friends and strangers. A minute after midnight they turned off the lights, the band struck up and a procession of waiters marched into the room, bearing silver soup tureens of flaming brandy cup. More waiters brought up the rear of the procession with glasses and ladles. They dispensed the drink from tables in every corner of the room.

The last guests left at four thirty and the staff put the club back to rights by candlelight. Just as well the next two days were non-working ones, thought Angelica. They'd probably spend them asleep. In the yard behind the club, with a big apron over her evening dress, her shoes changed for cook's clogs, she helped the porters heave the rubbish into the containers and stack the last of the empty bottles into the crates. She waved goodbye to the porters, then made a final inspection. She checked the entire club by torchlight, making sure there were no burning candles or paraffin lamps and that everything was as it should be. She left at six forty-five, not a bit tired and really, really happy. This is why I should be in catering, to produce perfect food, magnificently displayed, and hear guest after guest raving about it, she thought. It had been a whale of a party. And she'd made it so.

*

Broadcasting had to stop at 10.30 p.m. under the three-day week regulations but Angelica's programme, which went out at 7 p.m. on Tuesdays, wasn't affected. In the middle of January when she started filming again, she found she had a new director. He'd been a schoolteacher in his pre-television life and he obviously believed in learning by rote. So far, Angelica had relied on her natural confidence to present unscripted programmes. Of course she learned a few opening lines, of the 'Welcome to another edition of *Angelica's Kitchen*. We will be bringing you X, Y and Z' variety, but she had never had a script. But William O'Neill did not believe in spontaneity. He had a script for every moment of the programme.

'But that's absurd,' protested Angelica. 'How can you script an interview? If I ask a question and the interviewee's answer cries out for a further question, am I supposed to go on to your next question regardless? And leave the audience thinking I'm not listening? Or that I'm an idiot?'

'Don't worry your pretty little head about it. That's not your problem. It's mine. We'll sort out any anomalies in the edit,' he said, 'and, never fear, my dear, we won't let you look an idiot.'

She had to restrain a shudder. 'Pretty little head' indeed. And she hated the way he called her 'my dear'. I must get a grip, she told herself. It's only television. And he doesn't mean to be condescending.

It got worse. One of the items on every programme was a four-minute cookery spot, where Angelica demonstrated a dish she recommended for the weekend. During William's first filming day, she was making cheese soufflé. She had to mime her way through the actions twice for the director to decide which camera should do what.

The crew had filmed her doing similar dishes – cakes, meringues, puddings – many times before and they were all confident they knew what they were doing.

The first run-through was going well, but Angelica found talking to camera and reading from the autocue below it difficult so she decided to use the script as a prompt, but to say what she wanted in her own words.

'The trick is to grip the bowl in one hand and a really big spoon, like this one, in the other, then lift and fold the mixture, in a kind of figure-of-eight movement. You can swing the bowl round and back with your left hand as you go. Three or four movements is enough. Don't worry about getting all the bubbles and froth out of the mixture—'

'Cut,' barked William.

Everyone waited for him to appear on the floor. Angelica looked at the nearest cameraman, raising her eyebrows to ask, 'What's up?' He shrugged.

William stepped through the control-room door, frowning. 'Angelica, please will you stick to the script? It's best if you learn it by heart between takes.'

'Didn't you like what I said? I thought I covered it, but in my own words.'

'They are your own words, dear. We took them straight from the recipe we're using for the book.'

'But that ignores what's happening in the bowl. Just saying "Fold in the egg whites," is shorthand for cooks who know what they're doing. But if there are foamy bubbles still there, I need to explain—'

'I would still prefer you to stick to the script, dear. Word for word, if you don't mind.'

Angelica's irritation was swelling into anger. Patronizing old sod, she thought. Who's the cook around here? Him or me? But she swallowed her mutinous urges and did as she was told.

It was torture. Angelica was sure she'd come over as wooden and anxious, because that was how she felt. And it wasn't just the script. William found fault in her every movement. 'Angelica,' he said, 'in the first rehearsal you put the spoon down on camera right. This time it was camera left. Which is it to be? I need to know.'

At the break – the television unions insisted on fifteen-minute breaks during which the crew could do nothing that might possibly be interpreted as work – Angelica asked the lead cameraman, 'Does it really matter where I put the spoon?'

'Not to us, no.' He smiled. 'We can follow you fine. But I'm afraid what the director says goes.'

As the weeks went by, Angelica found it more and more difficult to be obedient. She wasn't enjoying the filming as she had done. Because of the frequent retakes (mostly because she was hopeless at sticking to the script) the filming took much longer than before. A sixteen-hour day (which the crew rather liked as they were on double time after eight hours, but which she hated) was not uncommon.

One day Silvano came to see the filming. He'd never been in a film studio and said he'd love to see behind the scenes. She'd asked William and been surprised at his agreement. 'Just so long as he stays behind the cameras in the studio, I have no objection,' he said.

Luckily, filming stopped that day at about 8 p.m., early enough for them to go to the pub. It was bliss – filming over, blazing fire, gin and tonic.

'Silvano, you don't know what a treat this is. Lately I've just been scurrying home, eating a Ski yogurt out of the fridge, falling into bed and getting up, either for more filming or writing. It feels like a treadmill.'

'You should try working on accounts all day. Your jobs sound heaven to me. And, by the way, I know you don't like the director, but the crew thinks you're the bee's knees. They told me that "the talent" – by which I gather they mean the presenters – are usually full of themselves and a pain, but that you're a pleasure to work with. So there!'

'I like them too. It's the director none of us can stand but, equally, we can't complain.'

'I'd have thought you could, Angelica. You're quite the star now. And the BBC won't want to lose you. You should talk to the guy who hired you in the first place. That fellow who discovered you in the Savoy.'

'Mmm. Cedric Maples. Yes, I could, I suppose. But it's not just the frightful William. I think I'm falling out of love with television. We spend so much time waiting for someone or other –' she ticked them off on her fingers '– the sound man, the cameraman, the director, the union rep, the props department, my make-up lady, the wardrobe mistress. And they sometimes all have to wait for me, often have to wait for me, to get the wretched words right.'

Silvano went to the bar to get them another drink. When he came back he told her about Mario, who was still living in the rented room Giovanni had found for him. 'He's much better. Your kicking him out was the shock he needed. That, and the thought of losing his brother and mother as well, which, as you know, we threatened him with, finally made him agree to see a psychiatrist. He's on lithium now and it seems to be working.'

Silvano said Mario wanted to see her, but he'd advised him to stay away.

'Good. I don't mind meeting him with the family or with other people, but I don't want to see him alone. We're bound to get into a fight.'

Silvano nodded. 'I understand. He's impossible.'

'We were never married,' said Angelica suddenly. 'We tried to get married in Paris, but the bureaucracy defeated us. So we just pretended.'

Silvano's mouth dropped open. For a long moment he was speechless. 'No! Y-you were . . .' He was stuttering, then grinned. 'Really? That's amazing.'

Angelica was puzzled by his reaction. 'It's not such a big deal, Silvano. I was still committed to him. Marriage isn't—'

'So you could have walked away at any time?'

'I suppose so, but I loved him. And I knew if I told Mamma and Papa we weren't married, they'd pressurize me to leave him. They only accepted him because they thought I'd tied the knot. And you know my parents. Marriage is sacred to them.'

'Do they know now?'

'No. I could tell them, but I haven't the energy or the time for all the recriminations and celebrations. I guess there would be both. And then Mamma would start badgering me to find another man, and I couldn't stand that.'

'Couldn't stand the badgering, or couldn't stand another man?'

'The badgering. I don't want another man anyway. I may not have been married but I've had enough of a taste of it to know I don't want it.'

She expected him to laugh with her, but his face was solemn, even pained. 'What is it, Silvano? Don't feel sorry for me. I've got you for a confidant and best friend. What more could I want?'

PART FOUR

1975

CHAPTER TWENTY

Giovanni was home unusually early. He'd been to see the bank manager and it hadn't seemed worth going back to his office. Now he had the house to himself and was lying on the sofa with Maria Callas in full voice on the stereo. He closed his eyes. For twenty minutes he lay there, letting the sound pour into him and fill his brain. When La Callas's voice died away, Giovanni didn't get up to turn the record over. He felt too content to move.

Life was pretty good. Ever since the Mirador party, Angelica had been working Wednesday to Saturday for the family firm, taking some of the pressure off her mother. His daughter was now executive head chef for the Laura's restaurants, which, since the Park Lane opening a year ago, had spawned two more.

Angelica's presence meant he and Laura had had time to get close to each other again. Laura would be home soon, he thought, and we'll make supper together, then snuggle up to watch the news, maybe go to bed early and make love. He wondered how many other couples still made love after nearly thirty years.

Some of his satisfaction related to that afternoon's meeting. The bank manager had been positively fawning, wanting to lend him money he didn't need. That his darling Angelica had come back to him, in every way, accounted for the rest. She was once again the lively, enthusiastic girl she'd been before Mario had dragged her down. She was her father's daughter, all right. Giovanni amended this thought to 'her parents' daughter': she had Laura's stamina and determination, and she was a real cook, like him. Sometimes he envied her. These days he spent most of his time in the office, but in his heart he was still a cook. If anyone asked what he did for a living, he'd say he was a chef.

Angelica had done wonders with the Laura's menus and the quality of the cooking. Giovanni smiled, remembering how, at a Laura's board meeting, she'd pressed her case for investing more in education for the cooks. 'We have to pay for them to eat in good restaurants, and see what the competition's up to. Most of them aren't trained to love food, only to cook it.'

'But they should eat out on their days off,' protested Giovanni. 'Why should we pay for them and their girl- or boyfriends to eat expensive meals? It's unheard of.'

'If this was Italy I'd agree because there's a tradition of eating out. And the home cooking is mostly good. You Italians know about food and love it. But the English don't. Our young chefs probably go for fish and chips.'

'Well, that's their problem.'

'It's ours too. If they never go to restaurants they'll get stale and unimaginative.'

'But you do the menus and recipes. They just have to follow orders. We don't want them having ideas of their own.'

'Oh, Papa, of course we do. We want them to love food, love cooking, love their jobs. If they have no interest in any of it, they'll never be great cooks and, anyway, they'll get bored and leave.'

He knew she wouldn't give in, so in the end he did. Anyhow, how could he resist her? He'd give her the moon if he could.

She's the son I never had, he said to himself. It occurred to him that this was the first time he'd thought of his lost son without a cloud descending, without the puzzled resentment that Laura had done such a thing filling his mind. It was nearly thirty years ago now that she'd given up their first-born for adoption. He'd never even seen the baby, and she'd only glimpsed a bundle as it was swept out of the labour room to be claimed by its adoptive parents.

The wound, he thought, had finally healed. For years he'd pushed all thoughts of the baby boy to an inaccessible part of his mind. And, after all, who was to know how things would have been? The boy might have caused them endless grief – he might have died as a child, which would have been even worse. And, unthinkable, they might not have had Angelica.

You foolish idiot, why did you blame Laura for all those years? She had her reasons and they were perfectly understandable, even noble ones. He'd not wanted to listen when she'd said they had no money, he didn't have a job, they had nowhere to live, and the child would have a better home with other people. At the time she'd been as low as a woman could get, but unselfish enough to part with her baby for its own sake. He'd never thought of it like that: if he'd been an impartial judge back then, would he have given a baby to them, unmarried and near-destitute, or to a prosperous middle-class couple who were longing for a child?

When Laura got home, she told him Angelica was joining them for supper. As always, Giovanni's heart lifted.

'What about Carlotta and Silvano?'

'They're both working.'

'Just us then.' He gave her bottom a gentle pinch. 'So what'll we eat?'

Laura slapped his hand away, 'Angelica's bringing mussels. We could do them *à la marinière.* And I couldn't resist some veal chops. We could grill them and have them with lemon and butter. And some spinach.'

They were having coffee, after supper, when Giovanni saw that his wife was looking steadily at him. 'Is something the matter?' he asked, suddenly uneasy.

'Darling, I've got some bad news. I didn't want to spoil our dinner, but I can't put it off any longer.'

Giovanni's heart skipped a beat. *She's going to tell us she's ill.*

She must have caught his look, because she said, 'No, darling, it's nothing tragic. It's just that Silvano's going to leave us. He's going to work for George at Frampton.'

'What? No! Why?' Giovanni's voice was loud with outrage. 'How dare he?'

'He wants to do something new. And George wants to turn the pub into a restaurant. Silvano has been the accountant in the background for ever, he says. He wants to get away from the books. And be the boss, I suppose.'

'I can't believe it! George stealing my finance director! I thought he was my friend. Wait till I see him, the underhand—'

'Papa, it's not George's fault if Silvano wants to leave.'

'Silvano would never leave of his own acc—' He stopped in mid-sentence and looked hard at his daughter. 'You knew about this, did you?'

Angelica's chin came up. 'Silvano consulted me. He knew you'd be furious.'

'Of course I'm bloody furious. That boy has lived in my house and we've looked after him and trained him since he was a kid. It's treachery, that's what it is.'

He saw Laura signal to Angelica not to take her father on. *Bloody women.* Was there no loyalty around here? 'So he's got you all on his side, has he? It's a fine thing when my wife and daughter—'

Laura's voice was steady, but crisp. 'Darling, do calm down. There are no sides in this. Silvano is going to be here . . .' she looked at her watch '. . . in fifteen minutes. He wants to talk to you.'

Giovanni's anger was turning to desolation. More quietly he said, 'Silvano works directly for me. I'd have thought he'd tell me first. Getting the women to do his dirty work is lily-livered—'

Angelica laid a hand on his arm. 'It's a good thing he didn't go to you first. Better you vent your rage on us rather than Silvano. You'd have called him a traitor and a turncoat and lots worse, and probably caused a family rift. Carlotta knows, too, and, of course, supports her son. You don't want to lose her, too, do you?'

Under Silvano's leadership, the financial control of the business had always been tight. He expected the individual managers of the restaurants and cafés and the ice cream factory to be responsible for their unit's books, filling in every sale and every expense. The thirty-two-column double-entry account books, covering food, drink, cleaning materials, fuel, rent and so forth, showed running totals so that the managers would know at any time how they were doing. Silvano would have the group results ready for Giovanni a week into the following month, and he saw every manager monthly to review results, sometimes to congratulate, sometimes to sharpen them up.

Giovanni had to admit that Silvano handled his departure most honourably. He didn't leave for six months, and in that time he handed over responsibility for financial control to his second-in-command, Aziz, who had been with him for ten years. The transition was seamless, and Giovanni slowly became reconciled to the loss of his nephew.

One day, Giovanni and Carlotta were driving together to the original Deli-Calzone in the King's Road.

'Giovanni,' said Carlotta, 'I'd like to give up some of my responsibilities. I love it all, of course, but standing all day in the kitchen is getting a bit too much for my fat legs. I'm fifty-five and wouldn't mind taking it a bit easier.'

'You aren't old! You've got more energy than the rest of us put together. I've never heard you complaining.'

'I'm complaining now.'

'Maybe you just need a holiday. Get a bit of Italian sun. When did you last go back to Abruzzo?'

'Not for years, brother. Too busy working. That's the problem.'

Giovanni backed the car into a parking space. 'OK, let's think about it. I'll come back to you.'

He meant to think about it and talk to her again, but somehow, with the restaurants all so busy, he kept putting it off.

*

Silvano handed Angelica his draft menu for the Frampton Arms. 'What do you think?'

They were sitting in the pub near her television studio, and she took her time, her heart sinking as she read. Oh dear, she thought, I'm going to throw cold water over his dream. 'Well,' she said, 'if you can produce all this, and do it well, it would be amazing. But it would take a miracle to pull it off. It's far too ambitious, Silvano.'

'Really? The dishes aren't that difficult, surely?'

'No, but it's far too long. How will you keep stocks fresh with this much choice?'

'Well, we'd need the turnover, of course, but—'

'It's a little country pub. It'll take ages to build the clientele. Most people expect a pint and a pickled onion in a pub. Have you got a chef yet?'

'No. But I don't think we'll have too much trouble. Except that all these dishes are traditional English – fish and chips, pies and whatnot – and all the good chefs are French or German.'

'I don't think that'll matter. A decent chef will learn fast. But do you really need an expensive foreign chef? If you're clever, and just have a few recipes, all excellent, you might be able to hire someone local. And save yourself a lot of headaches.'

'Really?' Silvano looked rather downcast. 'But I do want it to be a smart pub. Not a local café serving baked potatoes.'

Angelica laughed. 'Yes, I'm with you. But could I have a go?' She reached for the menu. 'I could give you some suggestions, and make sure the recipes are clear.' She felt the familiar excitement, which rose with every new challenge. That evening she produced a menu that she thought even an organized non-cook could manage, and the customers would love:

Coupe Caprice
Italian tomato soup

Cod and salmon fishcakes
Chicken and ham pie
Lamb steaks with garlic and rosemary

Main courses served with chips and a choice of
petits pois à la française, or salad

Treacle tart and custard
Pears poached in spiced red wine, served with vanilla ice cream

Coupe Caprice was a Robert Carrier recipe, basically a prawn cocktail with melon balls and a little chopped green pepper on top. Easy to do and very fresh. The soup, made with tinned tomatoes, the fishcakes with fresh cod and tinned salmon, and the pie were all straightforward. The lamb steaks depended on a good butcher, who would be prepared to cut a leg in even slices through the bone. There was nothing special about the puds, but they'd be delicious if the cook followed the recipes. Almost everything could be prepared in advance, with the actual cooking done to order.

Now enthusiastic about how it could work, she wrote step-by-step instructions for all of the recipes, then costed each dish and calculated its selling price.

Finally she specified the kitchen and serving equipment necessary to produce the menu, the staffing needed to execute it, and a draft profit and loss sheet, assuming an average of twenty-five covers a night. At that level, she knew, Silvano would lose money on the food, but probably break even if the customers all had a couple of drinks. If they ever got up to fifty covers, they'd be making a decent profit.

By midnight she'd finished. As she put a neat version of her scribbles into an envelope for Silvano, she found herself longing to be the one to train the currently mythical country cooks. She thought how refreshing it would be to spend a month or two in the country, getting the menu up and running, and staying at Chorlton. Maybe, she thought, if Silvano goes for my easy-peasy menu, I could suggest doing that.

Two days later Silvano was on the phone. 'Angelica, you're a genius. It's so simple, but mouth-watering. Can I come and see you to go through it blow by blow?'

He came that night. He looked by turns nervous and oddly embarrassed. How strange, she thought. He'd sounded so enthusiastic on the telephone.

Silvano sat down. 'Look,' he said, 'I'd better come straight to the point.' He took a breath, then went on in a rush, 'The thing is, Angelica, I need to ask you . . . You wouldn't like to join me? Be a partner. I'd give you some shares and pay you a salary. Not what you're getting now, I'm afraid, but if you were living in the country, life would be cheaper, and if the business works and you're a partner, one day you could make lots more money.'

Angelica was astounded. How extraordinary! Two days ago she'd dreamed of doing exactly that. Only she'd not thought about the money. She heard herself say, 'I think I'd love to. Why not?' She burst out laughing, excitement filling her. 'Yes, Silvano. Let's have a go.'

She stood up and hugged him. He was laughing too now. Then the same thought struck them both. 'Oh, God, Uncle Giovanni,' he said, stepping back.

And she said, 'Papa's going to kill me.'

CHAPTER TWENTY-ONE

Angelica and Silvano agreed to say nothing to anyone until the Frampton Arms was much nearer completion. 'It was bad enough your leaving, Silvano, but if he knows that I'm going too, he'll fight the decision for the next five months and we'll all have a miserable time.'

Poor Papa, she thought. Any member of the family who works anywhere other than for the Angelotti company he sees as a traitor. Even Mario. He still hasn't forgiven him for going to Nice Cream, even though Mamma sacked him and the poor guy has to have a job. And look at his reaction to Silvano's idea that his mother should retire and come to live with him in the Cotswolds.

Angelica had been sitting with Giovanni in the kitchen when Carlotta came down and announced she'd be leaving after Christmas.

'You can't, Carlotta,' he'd shouted. 'Who'll make the pasta? Run the deli kitchen? Oversee the ice cream business?'

'Giovanni, I've been telling you for months that it's too much for me. I'm tired. My legs ache. My back aches. How many times have I told you to get someone to do at least some of my job?

Well, you took no notice, so now I'm taking matters into my own hands.'

'You'll go mad in the country. You're a worker. You can't just pick flowers and take the dog for walks.'

'I don't have a dog. And I will work a little. I'll help Silvano with his new business. But I won't be the head chef and I won't have three other businesses to supervise.'

Giovanni had stamped out of the kitchen and up the stairs. Carlotta had shrugged and gone out of the other door, up to her flat.

Since then Giovanni had persuaded his sister to rethink her decision. He'd agreed to her relinquishing her job as head chef to Deli-Calzone. They would replace her with a new chef and someone who would come in for a few hours each day to make the pasta. From now on her job would be to oversee the range and quality of the deli foods until they were confident that the new chef knew what he was doing. She would continue to oversee ice cream production. Angelica smiled, remembering how her father had got his way. One day, the poor woman might be allowed to leave and live with her son in the country, but not yet. And by then, she thought, with a sudden clutch of anxiety, I'll be there too, with my father's recriminations echoing in my ears.

Angelica knew that, for the past two years, Sophie had been hoping that Hal would marry Pippa, while Pippa had been clear in her conviction that love would keep them together, not a formal document. She wasn't going to tie Hal down with a contract. Hal himself seemed easy either way. If Pippa didn't believe in marriage, he said, that was fine, just so long as she believed in him.

But then, one Sunday teatime when Angelica and her parents

were at Chorlton for the weekend, Pippa announced she was pregnant. After the kisses and congratulations, Giovanni said, 'Are you sure you don't want to get married, Pippa? I thought all girls wanted a wedding day. Especially now there's a *bambino* on the way. '

Pippa laughed. 'Well, I do like a party! But, no, I don't care about marriage, babies or no.'

'Well, you ought to, Pips,' said David. 'It'll be easier for the child, or children. And if Hal goes under a bus, you won't have a battle with probate.'

To everyone's surprise, Pippa said, 'Oh, OK, since the consensus seems to be in favour of a wedding, what do you think, Hal? Shall we do it?'

Hal came over and kissed her cheek. 'Is that a proposal? If so, I accept.'

Everyone gathered at Chorlton for the wedding celebrations. At three o'clock Hal and Pippa went to the register office at Moreton-in-Marsh with Pippa's parents, who had come from Australia, Maud, David and Sophie to witness the marriage. Then they came home for a giant tea party. The rest of the family, some London friends and all the neighbours, milled about on the lawn drinking champagne or Frampton's best scrumpy, waiting for the bridal couple.

Watching Pippa and Hal come down the steps, Angelica felt an unexpected pang of envy. Pippa had found the kindest, most solid man in Hal. She was going to have a baby, she was at the centre of an adoring family, and she was five years younger than herself. Angelica had wrecked her own chances, she thought, by falling for Mario.

She made an effort to switch her thoughts. She didn't need a loving husband or a baby. She had a great career as a chef, and another as a food journalist and television presenter. A family would slow her down. She was perfectly happy as she was.

She turned away from the sight of the happy couple to find Jane beside her. She was exquisitely dressed in a lemon silk suit by some London designer. She was undoubtedly elegant, her outfit a far cry from the Sunday best of the farming folk or the Biba look of the young. The two women exchanged polite smiles and looked across at Pippa and Hal.

'What *does* she think she's wearing?' said Jane.

'Oh, I think she looks lovely. Unusual and so romantic. Don't you think?'

Jane shrugged. 'If you like that sort of thing.' Unsmiling, she wandered away.

Jane was her own worst enemy, Angelica thought. What would it cost her to be nice? She might even find that smiling did her good. She was the complete opposite of Pippa, who was as unconcerned about fashion as Jane was devoted to it. Not for Pippa the streaked and layered 'big hair' and structured suits of the women's magazines or the wide trousers with tight tank tops or smart little miniskirt suits worn by the younger guests. She looked much as she always did, with no make-up, a long, drifting dress, hair down her back, some loose and the rest in thin plaits. Her only concession to the occasion was a homemade circlet of wild flowers and wheat stalks on her hair, and a pair of incongruously smart high-heels Sophie had bought her. She radiated health and happiness.

Angelica joined the crowd round Hal and Pippa and kissed the bride. 'You look like a Greek goddess with your swollen tum and the fruits of the harvest in your hair,' she said.

Pippa gave her a huge grin. 'Oh, good,' she said. 'Greek goddesses went barefoot, didn't they? I've got to take these things off.' She pulled the smart white heels off her bare feet and pushed them under the buffet table.

'I think they wore sandals,' said Angelica. 'Shall I get you your flip-flops?'

Pippa shook her head. 'No, thanks. At anyone else's wedding I wouldn't have dared, but I guess at my own I can go barefoot if I like.'

Angelica was pleased to find herself sitting next to Richard. She'd always been fond of him and had been impressed that he'd quit the City and taken a massive salary drop to join a kitchen. She asked him how he was getting on. 'It's great,' he said. 'I'm learning so much – Dino's a brilliant head chef. I'm a million times happier than I was in the City.'

'I thought you looked a bit stressed at first, but you seem better now.'

'Stressed? God, Angelica. Stressed doesn't begin to describe it. It was terrifying. The rest of the kitchen really had it in for me. They just didn't like me at all.'

'But everyone likes you!'

'I was teased rotten about being Laura's nephew.'

'What sort of teasing?' Angelica made an effort to sound casual. She knew her mother's attitude to bullying in the catering trade. As long as Richard didn't clam up, she could find out what had been going on.

'Oh, you know, the usual thing: hiding your kit, ribbing you.

On my first week, they pulled my clothes off and threw curry powder, spices and treacle all over me.'

'My tutor in Paris used to force us to make mayonnaise in a soup plate with a fork. But once you've weathered the first weeks, it's fine. '

'One day they locked me in the walk-in fridge. They didn't mean any harm, but I didn't know that at the time. It was pretty frightening. Pitch dark and freezing cold with the fridge locked from the outside.'

Angelica had had no idea any of this was going on. And neither, of course, had Laura. What if they'd locked him in the freezer? 'Is every newcomer treated like that? Or was it just because Mamma's your aunt?'

Richard laughed. 'It's everyone. A kind of initiation. If you survive it, you're one of them. I really like those guys now, and it seems so strange that I was once frightened of them.'

On the train back to London, Giovanni went to find a seat where he could get away, he said, from chattering women and go to sleep.

Angelica told Laura what she'd learned from Richard. 'We have to put a stop to it, don't we?'

Laura was appalled. 'Of course we do. It would never happen in a Laura's or a Calzone. I don't think so anyway. And we can't have horrible practices imported via the old VIP rooms staff.'

'Being nasty to newcomers, foreigners, women, anyone it's easy to bully, is so common. At the Savoy I saw the grill chef deliberately hand a blazing grill tray to a new commis. "Here, grab this," he said. Of course he was holding it with an oven cloth, but the poor boy automatically took what was thrust at him. He lost the skin of his fingers.'

Laura winced. 'But why? That's a horrible thing to do.'

They were both silent for a moment. Then Laura said, 'Unless we get Dino to really stamp on the teasing, it'll grow into serious bullying. He has to put a stop to it.'

'But how, Mamma? Dino's a first-class chef, and we don't want to give him an excuse to leave. You know he could get more money and a free hand in someone else's kitchen.'

'I'm more worried about Richard. They'll think he broke ranks and told on them. That brigade could make his life a misery.'

Angelica had an easy answer to that. Giovanni's restaurant had a vacancy for a senior commis in the larder section. Would Richard be up to that? Then he'd be out of the casino kitchen.

Her mother's eyes lit up. 'Excellent, darling. And we'll put it about that all the restaurants are getting training about intimi-dation, how to get the best out of new staff, and so on.'

'Good idea, and it wouldn't hurt actually to do that. Every-where. We could just add it to our training-day sessions,' said Angelica, 'like the food tastings and safety issues. No one will think Richard tipped us off.'

Laura decided Angelica should lead on the issue at their next head chefs' meeting. 'I think they'll open up better with you,' she said. 'Maybe I'll just introduce the subject and leave.'

Angelica took the job very seriously. At the Savoy they'd had a kitchen staff meeting once at which a doctor had talked to them about the dangers of drink. It wasn't a moral lecture on the evils of alcohol, more a revealing tour of a problem rife in the industry. After his talk they had broken up into little groups to discuss different aspects: the effect on the family, on relations with other staff and on performance. Then they'd all got together again to suggest ways of dealing with the problem. Angelica decided to do much the same now.

The meeting was attended by all the Laura's head chefs, the senior chefs from Giovanni's and the casino, the manager of the ice cream factory and the executive head chef and quality controller from the Calzone chain. And Carlotta. Everyone knew that the deli kitchens were domestic affairs staffed mostly by women cooks and dominated by a forceful mamma who didn't tolerate the mildest swearing, but Laura agreed that if Carlotta didn't come it wouldn't look good.

It was the last item on the agenda, and Laura started the session in a conversational tone, clear but determined. 'Today's main topic is all about the atmosphere of a kitchen. I hope that in our kitchens it's one of enjoyment, hard work, achievement and comradeship. Almost all of us will have been in kitchens where the exact opposite is true, with a background of intimidation and fear.

'I'm aware that some old customs seem like rites of passage, or ancient initiation traditions, harmless and fun. But they're not harmless, and the victims are not having fun. We don't allow staff to be rude or aggressive to customers and we shouldn't be cruel to each other. Of course I don't know how much, if any, bullying goes on in your kitchens. I'd be the last person to know. But you senior chefs will know and I'm asking you to keep your kitchens free of it.'

There were some lively nods, and the odd sceptical shake of the head. Then Laura left the meeting and Angelica took over. She gave her colleagues bullet points to consider, each one written out on a page of a flip chart. She turned the pages as she read out each statement, keeping her voice neutral and letting the statements speak for themselves.

- When someone is frightened, the brain closes down, leaving just the fight or flight instinct. No one can learn by being shouted at.
- Children who are beaten often grow up unable to love and with a propensity to become bullies themselves.
- Throughout industry, the catering trade has the highest acceptance rate of teasing, intimidation and bullying practices.
- More than half the senior chefs in a recent survey by the *Caterer and Hotelkeeper* thought there was 'nothing wrong with a bit of bullying'.

Then she chaired a lively discussion, with a few chefs expressing disbelief that a bit of teasing could be harmful, but the majority agreeing that intimidation did not contribute to productive learning or a happy kitchen.

She was pleased with the day's outcome. The break-out groups had come back with a clutch of good ideas, not least that staff should be told on joining that it was their right to be treated politely, and their duty to report any unkind teasing or outright bullying directly to Laura or Angelica.

At the end of the afternoon, Dino came up to Angelica. 'I assume this whole bullying exercise is aimed at the VIP rooms. Isn't that so?'

'Should it be?'

'Well, probably, yes. I've inherited almost a dozen staff from the previous operators and casino kitchens are very macho places.'

'But do you think the team's behaviour is right?' asked Angelica.

'Actually, no, I don't. But I've enough on my plate teaching the guys to cook, and stopping them stealing, without having to mollycoddle the apprentices.'

'Dino, if the cap fits, *il mio amico*, you must wear it, no?'

Dino's face screwed into a puzzled frown. 'What does that mean?'

'It means you have to do something about it. Make them see sense, or sack them.'

CHAPTER TWENTY-TWO

Giovanni seldom walked anywhere, but the thought of having his daughter to himself had persuaded him to accompany her. Carlotta and Mario would be coming to Sunday lunch and Laura had stayed at home to roast a leg of lamb and make blackberry and apple crumble.

The late October air was clear and perfectly still. Leaves lay thick under the trees in Hyde Park. Angelica kicked through them, sending up flying drifts. A sudden memory of his three-year-old daughter kicking leaves came to Giovanni. 'You used to do that as a toddler in this very park – maybe under this very tree.'

'I remember. I know every inch of Hyde Park and Kensington Gardens. I wonder how many hours we've spent in them.'

They walked along the northern side of the Serpentine, past the boathouse to the Dell Restaurant.

'Shall we have some coffee, *cara mia*?'

'Yes, let's. I like this place,' said Angelica. 'The building's lovely, like a tent nestling by the waterside.'

'The food's dreadful, though. Look at that!' He pointed to the hot dish in the cafeteria wells: soggy chips, battered fish that had been sitting there too long, peas and carrots kept warm in hot water, some sort of brown stew. A couple of pies and a single sausage roll sat in a steamy warming cupboard.

'You should bid for the catering contract, Papa. A Calzone would do well here, don't you think?'

'Maybe I will.'

They took their cups of coffee to a table outside. 'Will you be warm enough, darling?'

'I'm fine. And even if it's chilly, it's nicer outside.' They watched the ducks and geese on the water. A family were feeding the pigeons. The birds strutted round their feet and landed on their table. Giovanni shuddered. 'The English! Those birds are vermin.'

'Papa,' said Angelica, 'I need to tell you something. And I'm afraid you won't be pleased.'

'Please don't say you're going back to that scoundrel!'

'Mario? No.' She smiled. 'Certainly not.'

'Well, what, then?'

'I'm going to leave Laura's after Christmas and help Silvano with his pub in Frampton.'

Giovanni's heart contracted. Not again. She couldn't. 'What? But why?'

Angelica leaned across the table and gripped his wrist. 'Papa, please try to understand . . .'

Giovanni's shock lifted into anger. 'I thought you were happy with the job at Laura's. You're doing so well with it. And your mother has at last been able to have a little time off.' He heard his voice rising. 'I was looking forward to you taking over the whole business. But, no, you're going to give it all up for a tin-pot pub in the country. It's that bloody George! First he steals Silvano, now—'

'No, Papa.' Angelica's face was stern, her voice rising to counteract his. 'It's nothing to do with George. He doesn't even know.'

'But why? How could you?'

'Papa, if you'll just let me try to explain?'

He didn't really want explanations. He understood all too well. You bust a gut to give your children everything and they repaid you with a kick in the teeth. That was the long and the short of it. He'd sent her to France to learn cooking, and she'd married the wretched Mario. He'd given her a good job at Giovanni's, and she'd taken a junior job at the Savoy. When she'd left the Savoy, you'd have thought with all that training she'd come back to the family firm. But, no, she'd become a television cook and food writer. And then finally, finally, she'd seen sense, and proved herself to be, as they'd always known she was, a great chef and manager. Now this.

'Papa, I want to do my own thing. If it works out with Silvano, I'll get thirty per cent of the business. And what attracts me most is that we'll start an outside catering division, doing parties and weddings from the barn behind the pub.' He couldn't take it in, but the central fact that she was leaving settled on him, like a dark cloud. She was saying something about loving being in charge of Mirador's New Year's Eve party, about being in her element. He tried to concentrate.

'Yes, I love cooking and I want the food to be delicious and the service to be perfect, but it's bringing everything together – music, entertainment, hired staff, transport – that grabs me.' She smiled. 'Maybe I should have been in the army. In logistics.'

'Does your mother know about this?'

'Yes. She was only worried that you'd feel betrayed.'

'Well, she was right there.'

The coffee had been grey and weak. Neither of them had drunk much and now it was cold. They left their cups and walked home in near silence.

'Don't sulk, Papa.' She twisted round to look into his face. 'Do you remember that, when I was little, you'd say if the wind changed I'd be left with a sulky expression for ever?' He didn't respond, although he felt a tiny splinter of amusement.

'It'll be fine,' she went on. 'Mamma says she wants to slow down, but the truth is you both love working. She's not fifty yet and has more energy than anyone I know. And my going won't make all that much difference. There are lots of people out there who could do my job.'

Giovanni didn't agree, but what was the point of arguing?

Angelica was still speaking. 'You thought it'd be the end of the world if Silvano left, and then if Carlotta stopped making the pasta. But it's all going beautifully.'

They were in Kensington Gardens before Giovanni had recovered his composure. He found himself saying, 'Did your mother ever tell you about the child we lost?'

Angelica met his look, puzzled. 'Yes, I think so. Or, rather, Granny did. That Mamma had been pregnant before I came along, but the baby was stillborn.'

He nodded. 'It wasn't quite like that. Maybe it's time you knew about it.' He looked into her eyes, saw the concern and pleading in them. They were on the path to the Italian Gardens. Queen Anne's Alcove was empty and he took her arm to lead her to the covered bench. They sat down and he continued, 'We weren't married then, and your grandfather was implacably hostile to me, not wanting his darling daughter to be wasted on a penniless Italian. I understand that now – only too well after your experience with Mario. But at the time I saw it as blind prejudice. We ran away to London and she had the baby.'

Angelica took his hand.

'It was soon after the war. I didn't have a proper job, we weren't married, we had nowhere to live, it was the coldest winter on record and we had no money. So your mother gave the baby up for adoption. It was a boy.'

How strange to be saying this after so many years. 'I want you to understand why I'm sulking, as you put it.'

Angelica was looking at him, her eyes filling with tears. 'Do you know where he is now? My brother?'

'No. A prosperous couple adopted him. He could be anywhere.'

'He'd be about thirty, wouldn't he?'

'Not quite. He'd be twenty-nine in January. Old enough to take over the business.'

Angelica bit her lip. 'But, Papa, he might not have wanted to. You can't make your children follow your path if they don't want to.'

'So I'm discovering.' He could hear the bitterness in his voice and went on, in a more neutral tone. 'Both your mother and I think about that baby a lot, though we never speak of him. You see, she didn't tell me she was giving him away because she knew I'd have stopped her. I tried to get him back. The irony was that within days of his birth I'd found a job and a flat.'

'Poor Mamma. Imagine the courage you need to give away your own baby.'

Giovanni stared in silence at a moorhen trampling over the waterlilies. Angelica had immediately seen it from Laura's point of view, not his. But mother and daughter had always understood each other better than he understood either of them.

Well, he'd started on this tale, so he'd better finish it. 'So I've had to make do with other people's sons. Mario turned out useless, Silvano upped and left. I'd just begun to realize *you* were the son I'd never had – and better than any son I might have had.'

'Oh, Papa!' She dropped her head onto his shoulder. He felt a little shaft of satisfaction as he twisted the screw. I'm being unkind, he thought, but I can't help it. 'I suppose now I must pin my hopes on young Richard – who doesn't have a drop of Italian blood in him. And we run an Italian business.'

Angelica tried to smile. 'Papa, the business is teeming with Italians! They're not relatives, true, but they're great cooks and waiters, managers and ice cream makers. There's no danger of losing the Italian flavour.'

When they got home, they walked into a comforting wall of Sunday lunch aroma. Roasting lamb, scented with garlic and rosemary, took precedence, but the crumble, cooling by the side of the Aga, also released its heady smell of hot apple and blackberries with a hint of spice.

Laura's face was flushed from cooking. Angelica looked at her mother with new respect. Imagine going through what she'd had to. 'Mamma, leave that. I'll lay the table,' she said, taking the plates from her.

'I'm nearly there,' said Laura, 'but I'd love a cup of coffee.'

'Me too. The stuff in the park was disgusting.' Angelica laid the table and made the coffee while Laura finished the gravy and put the water on to steam the cabbage and carrots.

Giovanni had gone upstairs and Angelica chose her moment. 'Mamma, I told Papa about going with Silvano and he was so upset. Now I'm not sure I should go. He's done so much for me, all with the hope that I'd one day take over the business. And it's not as if I'm unhappy working at Laura's. I love it. It wouldn't kill me to stay.'

'No, darling. You were so excited about the Frampton opportunity. I think if you don't take it you may regret it, and end up angry with your father.'

'He told me about your giving up your baby son, my elder brother.' Angelica watched her mother's face cloud.

Laura shut her eyes for a fraction, then said, 'I'm not sure he's ever forgiven me. I've certainly never forgiven myself.'

'Oh, Mamma, couldn't we find him? Or would that be worse for you?'

Laura shook her head. 'I couldn't face him. Imagine him knowing his own mother had given him away. Even if he understood it was for his sake, he'd hate me.'

'I'm sure he wouldn't,' said Angelica.

'Your father had this fantasy of a son following in his footsteps,' said Laura. 'When you came back to do the Laura's job, he realized he had a daughter every bit as good as a largely imaginary son.'

'He told me that. And now I'm abandoning him.'

'He'll get over it, sweetheart. He loves you dearly and it's not as if you're going to Peru or Australia. You can always come back one day. You aren't even thirty yet. There's lots of time.'

When Mario came in, all bounce and *joie de vivre*, kissing everyone, chattering, Angelica couldn't help smiling. This was the Mario she'd known since childhood, the exuberant, charming man she'd fallen in love with. She felt a little frisson of desire. Oh, no, she told herself. No going back. He's dangerous.

They had a very merry lunch and even Giovanni was drawn

into a discussion about Nice Cream. 'Uncle Giovanni,' said Mario, 'you should make a bid. The company's so badly run we're losing money. But the sales are terrific. If you ran it, it'd make a fortune.'

Carlotta said proudly, 'Mario is the second in command now. Aren't you, Mario?'

'Really?' asked Giovanni.

Mario laughed. 'I find it unbelievable too. But, yes, I'm now the deputy managing director. But it's meaningless, really, because the MD is an idiot and will bankrupt the company in no time. Not least because he helps himself to the cash.'

'Who owns the company?' asked Angelica.

'The Grisetta family. The MD's the heir. His father is semi-retired but is still the chairman. There are some other family members, aunts and sisters, who turn up to board meetings, if and when we hold them, which is erratic to say the least. The only half-decent chap is the finance director and he's given notice. He saw the writing on the wall.'

CHAPTER TWENTY-THREE

Angelica felt only relief that the secret of her deal with Silvano was finally out. Released from filming until the following Monday, she went down to stay with Grace and George at Frampton and check up on progress with Silvano.

They had breakfast in the new Frampton kitchen, which Grace had recently built in the old morning room. When she'd married George, the kitchen had been in the basement, along with the silver room, walk-in silver safe, flower room, butler's pantry, larders and coal holes – a whole warren of antiquated domestic service. But the new kitchen was a dream, looking out over the park, which was stocked with deer once more. During the war, Grace said, it had been dug up to grow potatoes.

The kitchen was enormous, with a big dining table in the window bay and modern built-in walnut-faced units along the two side walls above gleaming white Formica work surfaces. The walls were painted blue and the four-oven Aga took centre stage, dividing eating from cooking.

At breakfast Angelica remarked on the enormous antique dresser on the end wall, which Grace used to display all the Frampton country wines: gleaming reds and yellows, tawny orange and pale green. 'They look stunning, so polished and shiny, like an art exhibition.'

'Frightful waste of space,' said George. 'I'd have thought Grace would use the shelves for jars of rice and sugar, but she's an artist, more concerned with colour and light.' He looked affectionately at his wife. 'Aren't you, darling?'

Grace laughed. 'The reason George objects to the wines is because he's so unsentimental. He's embarrassed that I'll tell people it's a monument not just to his wine business but to us. After the war he took me cowslip picking and that was the beginning of our romance as well as his country wines business.'

Angelica looked from one to the other. They were so different. Grace was an arty scatter-brain, and could giggle like a girl. Her blonde hair was streaked with grey now and tended to fall untidily out of its chignon, scattering hairpins. She never seemed quite in control, except in her studio at the top of the house, where Angelica remembered watching her as a child: Grace would stand stock still in front of the easel, then suddenly step forward and make confident charcoal or brush strokes. She could work for hours up there, oblivious of everyone.

She'd never had an exhibition, or tried to sell her work. There were portraits of all Angelica's extended family, Angelottis, Olivers and Framptons, as well as stacks of landscapes and sketches of horses and cows, chickens and dogs. She had no vanity, neither for herself nor her painting.

George was modest, too, but confident. He still had the bearing of the soldier he'd once been, elegant and upright, but he wore his expensive clothes like a second skin, not an adornment. He was conventional, but admired enterprise and imagination in others. He was clever, often serious and very generous.

A shaft of envy went through Angelica. That's what marriage should be, she thought. Grace and George were obviously still in love with each other, after . . . what? Twenty-five or thirty years of marriage.

Oh, to have a domestic kitchen like this: big enough and equipped to be efficient, but not the stainless-steel professional kitchen she was used to. This would be such a wonderful kitchen for children to grow up in, for friends to eat in, for experimenting with new dishes. A little like the family kitchen in Paddington, only with her in charge, not her mother.

'I'd love a kitchen like this, Grace! Does Jane cook?'

''Fraid not. She knows about food but rather expects other people to produce it.'

Angelica didn't much like her. Jane was bossy and spoilt, very sure of her position as heir to the Frampton acres. But she was aware that she had to get on with her. A few years older than Angelica, Jane was nominally in charge of relations with the tenants on the estate and Silvano was one of them.

Soon Jane appeared and the three of them set off to walk to the pub.

'Tell me how Frampton works, Jane,' Angelica asked. 'Is George grooming you to take over? To run the whole estate, even the wine business, or what? It must be a huge job.'

'Yes. But we have staff. There's Rupert, the estate manager, and the wine factory has its own managing director. They're pretty useless, but since I'm in London a lot of the time, I have to put up with them.'

She really believes she knows it all, thought Angelica. Silvano had told her that Rupert was supposed to be teaching Jane the ropes so that when she inherited she'd know the difference between a Welsh Black and an Aberdeen Angus. Poor Rupert, she thought. Jane can't be an easy pupil, especially as she prefers her London life of Bond Street shopping and smart clubs.

Silvano greeted them outside what was more of a building site than a hostelry. He took them to see how the cleaning and restoration of the bar and dining room were going. The chimney sweep was standing in the huge fireplace, his head and shoulders invisible as he hoovered out the soot of ages. The hunting prints that had adorned the walls were stacked in the corner, cleaned and some of them reframed. A middle-aged woman sat at a table, polishing the horse-brasses that had hung from the timbers. She smiled. 'Good mornin', Mr Silvano. These brasses, they're coming up a treat.'

Silvano picked one up and turned it in his hand. 'You're doing a great job.' He turned to Angelica, Grace and Jane. 'This is Molly, best cleaner of brass in the county!' Blushing, the woman scrambled to her feet. Jane barely acknowledged her but Silvano patted Molly's arm as he helped settle her on her bench again. 'And this is our head chef and my business partner, the wonderful Angelica Angelotti.'

Not for the first time, Angelica was struck by Silvano's kindness. What a catch he'll be for some lucky woman, she thought. He's handsome, too, not with Mario's rogue-hero looks, but tall and athletic, with such gentle eyes.

Silvano was talking to them, pointing to walls and ceiling beams. 'The plan is to put it all back much as it was but without the film of grease and smoke.'

The tables and chairs were odd sizes and nothing matched, but they were solid and comfortable and the stone-flagged floor, now sandblasted to its original colour, was beautiful.

'Can you imagine,' Angelica said, gesturing to the worn beige upholstery on the window seat and banquette, 'how welcoming it will be with warm red velvet instead of this awful stuff, and with a great log fire over there?'

The so-called public bar was still operational. Silvano hadn't dared close it for fear of offending the locals. He might be going upmarket with the food in the dining room but he didn't want to frighten away the old chaps who came in for their pints and occasionally bought a packet of crisps or a pickled egg. They sat on stools at the bar, mostly in silence, or chatting quietly, maybe watching the younger men play darts.

One or two still played shove-ha'penny on tables with a brass edge and sewing-machine legs. There were no hunting prints this side, just a large Ronald Searle cartoon of a hunt in full cry, with foxes riding the horses and the huntsmen running for their lives, and photographs of the estate cricket team, and of the winning marrow at the Frampton Show.

Angelica loved the atmosphere here too. The locals, she thought, looked like farmhands shipped in from Central Casting with their weatherworn faces. 'If they left,' she whispered to Silvano, 'we'd lose something. And we'd not be able to replace it.'

They walked out through the new kitchen and into the yard behind.

'Well, I don't think much of your renovation, Silvano,' said Jane. 'I'd have thought you'd show a bit more imagination.'

Angelica was irritated. Did the woman never have anything nice to say of anyone?

'Really?' said Silvano. 'I'm sorry to hear that. Anything in particular you didn't like?'

'Well, all of it, really. You'd have thought that public bar could

277

be better used than to keep it as a boozer. None of those old men spend any real money, do they? And keeping the private bar looking the same is hardly going to attract attention, is it? You should have redone the interior completely. Got some modern furniture, brighter colours. Decent lights.'

'That's a bit harsh, darling,' said Grace. 'I like the traditional country pub look.'

'Well, Jane, you may be right,' Silvano said equably. 'We shall see.' He smiled. 'If you are, I shall have to go back to being a boring accountant.'

Angelica watched this exchange in wonder. How could the woman be so rude and Silvano so unperturbed and polite? 'You know the people round here,' she said hotly. 'Trendy décor is the last thing they want. I'm with Silvano.'

'Of course you are,' said Jane, tartly. 'He pays your wages.'

Angelica flushed with sudden fury, and opened her mouth to rip into Jane, but Silvano took her arm and turned her away. He said, very quietly, 'Leave it, Angelica.'

She was seething. She went over to George, who hadn't heard the unfortunate exchange. He was talking to the decorator, who was working in the stable at the back of the yard, filling the gaps between a cross-beam and the wall. 'Look, Angelica,' he said, 'Jones here is using a mixture of . . . What is it, Jones? Straw, cowpat, horsehair?'

'Aye, and there's a bit o' clay and sand in there too,' said Jones, in a thick Gloucestershire accent. 'We be doin' the same as my father and grandfather.'

'And the same as their forebears too,' said George. 'This building is over four hundred years old, the walls made of wattle-and-daub. I bet modern breeze blocks won't last that long.'

The conversation calmed Angelica. There was something satis-fying in the old pub sitting so comfortably beside the road with its stable yard behind. The farmhouse and its outbuildings, now empty, stood a little higher up the slope, with the huge tithe barn at the very top of the hill behind. Four hundred years! It had been built as a coaching inn and had been a hostelry of some kind ever since. George had told her Frampton had been a real village then, but the plague had emptied it, and the stones from the houses had been used for farmhouses. Only the inn, Frampton Chapel and the home-farm buildings remained. She loved it.

In the week between Christmas and New Year, Angelica moved down to Chorlton. Sophie put her in Laura's old room, overlook-ing the vegetable garden. Most mornings, unless it was tipping down, she walked the couple of miles to the pub. She spent her time chasing supplies and hiring staff. She put advertise-ments for cooks and waiters in all the post-office windows in the surrounding villages and towns. She was looking for the right attitude rather than skills. She could teach a young enthusiast, and she wouldn't have to undo the bad habits of a lifetime in the trade.

The plan was to open the restaurant at the beginning of February and the catering business in the barn at Easter, in time for the summer party and wedding season. She needed to start marketing the party business now and had some brochures printed.

Frampton Feasts can offer you an unforgettable party in our mag-nificent medieval barn in the rolling Cotswolds. It will seat 250 comfortably for a dinner or hold 400 for a cocktail party. Or we can cater at your own home, and arrange everything you need, not just the food and drinks, but marquees, flowers, live music or disco, cabaret acts, children's entertainers, photographers, printing. Anything you would like, we would love to provide.

There followed four sample menus (a wedding tea, a dinner dance, a cheese and wine reception and a children's birthday party) interspersed with photographs.

Angelica set about training the two cooks she'd hired, Simon and Penny, while Silvano and the front-of-house boys cleaned and stocked the bar. Silvano determined to be disciplined from the start. Stocktaking would be done first thing every Monday. The stock, both for the cooks and the bar, would be arranged on storeroom or cellar shelves so that it would be easy to see what had been used and what should be ordered.

Angelica listened, amused that Silvano, who had been drilling staff in his stock-control methods for years, had never lost enthusiasm for it.

Penny was already a good home cook and learned fast. Simon had never cooked but was a good-natured farm lad, who was keen, he said, to learn a new trade. 'I used to work in the dairy, see, but that's all gone. We don't make cheese nor butter nor nothing. We just sell the milk to the Milk Marketing Board.'

Angelica and the trainees cooked their way through all the dishes on the menu, and for a week, the builders and the new pub staff sat down to lunch with Silvano and her. The next week, on the evening before opening to the public, they had a rehearsal with George, Grace and Jane at one table, Silvano and Angelica at another and David, Sophie, Hal and Maud at a third.

Pippa was at home with baby Jake, who was fractious.

Angelica looked around the restaurant. Even three tables made it seem a buzzing success. Soon it really will be, she thought.

Maud adjusted her spectacles to peer at the menu 'Well, thank the Lord for that!' she exclaimed.

David looked up, startled. 'What, Mother?'

'Two things, dear. For a start you can read the menu because the print is a decent size, and second, it's in English. I feared that all this smart décor meant a huge menu in incomprehensible French, like they have at the Feathers.'

Good for Gran, thought Angelica. Half the customers in restaurants are over fifty and wear glasses. And a menu is there to be read, not to be admired for its design. At the start of the meal she wanted to jump up to check the kitchen every few minutes and she noticed Silvano's eyes constantly following the bar staff, but all was going well and they gradually relaxed.

Until Jane sent back her lamb steak, complaining that it was raw. As the waiter passed Angelica with the rejected plate, she stopped him. 'What's the problem?' she asked.

Before he could reply Jane called, 'It's raw.'

Angelica looked at the lamb. Perfectly cooked. Pink, as she'd instructed it to be. 'Just ask Penny to put it back on the grill for another two minutes on each side,' she said.

Wanting to reassure Penny, Angelica slipped into the kitchen. Penny's face was flushed and she was close to tears. 'I'm so sorry. I thought I'd done it right.'

'You did it perfectly, just pink, as it should be. But not all customers know what they're talking about. That steak was medium, not even rare, never mind raw.' She gave Penny a brief hug and went over to the grill. 'Penny, feel it now.' She pressed the meat with her finger. 'It's firm so it's well done. Better get it off.'

They sent the steak back on a clean, warm plate with a fresh bunch of watercress disguising the cut Jane had made in it. 'There, no harm done.' Angelica sighed. 'What a pity, though. That steak is bound to be tougher and dryer. But, since the customers are always right, in future we'll get the waiters to ask how they like it.'

The next day, Thursday, the *Cotswold Echo* carried an article with a picture of Angelica wearing a chef's hat, stirring a huge saucepan: *TV Star takes on earl's country pub*. There was a quote from George: 'I've never been so proud of the Frampton Arms. It's such a pretty place, but the food tended to be standard pub fare. Now we've persuaded Silvano and Angelica to take it on, we hope to have the best inn in the county.'

Angelica was disappointed that only fifteen customers came that evening. 'You'd have thought there'd be more,' she said. 'It was such a nice article.'

'Maybe tomorrow,' said Silvano. 'You're doing such a great job, Angelica. What would I do without you?' He put an arm round her shoulders. 'C'mon, darling, cheer up.'

She looked up at him sharply. He never called her 'darling'. His eyes held hers briefly, then he dropped his arm and walked quickly out of the kitchen.

Silvano was right. The next day they did twenty-seven covers and took plenty of money in the bar. Angelica was pleased with the cooks, who'd managed with only a bit of help from her. A steady build-up is what we want, she thought. Maybe thirty-five or forty tomorrow. Then I can hire another cook and we can build up to sixty.

But on Saturday they were full, not just with diners packing the tables, but with local people from miles around coming for a drink at the bar.

At eight, when the orders were coming thick and fast into the kitchen, and Angelica was about to lug in another box of melons for Coupe Caprice, a man's hands reached down for it. 'I'll do that, Chef,' he said.

It was Mario. 'You're in a bit of a mess out there, aren't you, Angel?'

'Hell, yes. We're completely overrun. Can you get those inside and I'll get more prawns.' She ran to the freezer, grabbed a kilo pack of frozen prawns and followed him into the kitchen. She sliced one of the melons in half, scooped out the seeds and picked up the baller. 'Press it deeply into the flesh before you turn it to scoop out the ball. OK?' She showed him, then left him to it while she pushed the packet of prawns into a saucepan of tepid water and sat a weight from the scales on top to keep the packet under water. Then she went back to Mario, and worked beside him, chopping green peppers and shredding lettuce. Finally, she doctored some bottled mayonnaise with tomato paste, lemon juice, Tabasco and white pepper.

'Well, well,' teased Mario. 'I never dreamed I'd see you using bought mayonnaise.'

'And I hope you won't again. But we're up a creek here. We only had thirty bookings but half the people who just came for a drink are staying on for supper.'

'It's a good problem to have,' said Mario.

They knocked out another eight Caprices, then Angelica dispatched Mario to help load the dishwasher and wash the pots. Angelica worked beside Simon, slamming pies into the oven, grilling steaks, frying fishcakes and tossing ready-blanched vegetables in butter.

At nine thirty the washing-up was under control but the kitchen had run out of prawns, chicken pie and steak. At least it made things easier to manage, thought Angelica. Everyone had to have tomato soup followed by fishcakes, then treacle tart or pears in red wine.

Penny kept up with the salad, vegetables and puddings. Mario and Simon stood side by side, frying fishcakes and chips. Angelica stood at the pass calling the orders: 'One treacle tart, one pear. Three soups, four fishcakes with veg, one fishcake with salad.'

When the last pudding order had gone in, Silvano appeared, followed by a waiter with a tray of glasses, bottles of beer and a couple of bottles of wine. They put them down on the pass. 'Bravo, team, we've done it!' Silvano shouted. 'All the tables fed and happy. No complaints, not even about us running out of pie and steak. Huge compliments on the food. Many, many thanks to Angelica and her brilliant kitchen.'

Silvano and the waiter poured the drinks. Silvano raised his glass. 'Here's to the Frampton Arms. And to each other.' He looked round, meeting everyone's eyes, then held Angelica's as he sipped his wine.

When the kitchen was clean, the chairs on the tables, and the front door closed, Mario, Silvano and Angelica sat in the bar drinking champagne.

'Don't you feel terrific, Silvano?' Angelica said. 'I feel as high as a kite and I've had only half a glass with the staff and a sip of this.'

'It's the adrenalin,' said Mario. 'Makes you look good too. All pink with sparkling eyes.'

Angelica promptly stood up. 'You must be mad, Mario. I'm bright red and dripping with sweat.' She took the apron off and dropped it in the corner. 'How can you look so cool and collected, Silvano?'

'I've not been in a hot kitchen, like you two,' he said. 'But actually, Angelica, you look great. If you ever have your portrait painted, it should be like this. Chef's whites, pink face, hair all over the place.' She'd better remember this moment, Angelica thought, both Angelotti brothers telling her she was beautiful.

Silvano topped up their glasses. 'What a week! From rehearsal with the family to an overflowing restaurant in four days! Bit of a roller-coaster,' he said. 'Thank God for you, Mario.'

'Yes, indeed,' Angelica agreed. 'I didn't even know you were coming down.'

'It was meant to be a surprise. I thought I'd just come for a quiet little dinner and have a look. But my beloved brother here,' he said, punching Silvano's arm, 'caught me walking through the door and hauled me behind the bar. I pulled beers for the locals and made pink gins for the toffs for an hour. Then Silvano decided your need was greater than his and shoved me into the kitchen.'

Angelica downed two glasses of champagne in swift succession. She felt on top of the world.

They talked on, reviewing the evening.

'Oh Silvano, I'm so happy,' Angelica said. 'I know we're onto a great thing here. We'll have a lovely pub, and Frampton Feasts is going to be fantastic.'

'What's Frampton Feasts?' asked Mario.

Angelica started to tell him, but Silvano put a hand up to stop her. 'Mario, she'll keep you up all night if you get into her plans for Frampton Feasts. I'll leave you to it. I'm off to bed.' He stood up and went to the bar for the keys. He threw them to Mario. 'Lock the door with both keys, and drop them back through the letterbox, OK?'

'Where are you staying, Mario?' she asked.

'Chorlton, like you. I rang Sophie this morning. You could give me a lift home, couldn't you? I came down by train and had to walk from Moreton station.'

'Let's not go quite yet,' said Angelica. 'I'm absolutely starving. How about you? Did you get anything to eat at all?'

'No.'

They raided the kitchen stores for cheese and biscuits and some sliced ham left over from staff lunch. Angelica made two big plates of Cheddar, ham, a handful of salad, butter, a spoonful of pickle and a pile of oatcakes. She was conscious of Mario watching her.

When she'd finished, he picked up the plates and carried them through to the bar. She lifted the bottle of champagne out of the bucket and held it up. 'Maybe one glass left. Shall we share it?'

'You have it. I'd rather have a beer.' He went behind the bar and pulled himself a pint of Whitbread Tankard.

She told him about the Frampton Feasts ambitions while they ate their supper. Mario was everything she remembered from their early relationship: interested, impressed, encouraging, with no hint of rivalry or jealousy. 'Isn't it amazing that we can sit here like this,' she said, 'when only two years ago we couldn't speak to each other without shouting?'

'Yes. And, *cara mia*, I've been meaning to tell you that I know

286

the bust-up was all my fault, and I'm really sorry I caused you such misery. I don't know how you stuck it for so long. When I think of all that ridiculous designer furniture, and the Lamborghini . . .'

'Oh, don't, Mario! It's behind us now. And you're well. Are you happy? You look it.'

'I am, yes, not least because I'm with you. And I'm well too, thanks to Silvano. He forced me into treatment and I now take the bloody lithium. Which of course I don't like, but I know better than to stop.' He sat down close to her and put his beer on the table. He took her hands in his and lifted one to kiss it. She looked at his thick curly hair as his head dipped and remembered how it felt to put her hands through it – how she used to force her fingers into its thickness and gently pull the curls. He was still kissing her hand, then turning it over and kissing the palm.

She didn't resist. Why should she? She felt so relaxed and in control, so happy and confident. He kept her palm to his mouth, and then she felt his tongue, and a bolt of desire shot through her. She freed her hand and put one on each side of his head, pulled him towards her and kissed his mouth, hard.

Oh, God, he smelt delicious, just as he used to. How had she lived without him all these months? He drew away from her, just enough to speak, 'No, no, darling, like this,' then put his mouth to hers again, but lightly, kissing her gently, gently.

Angelica was frantic. She'd never felt anything like this torrent of desire. Why wouldn't he let her kiss him properly? These butterfly kisses were driving her mad. Her mouth felt swollen and hot. Like the rest of her.

Suddenly Mario stopped kissing her and stood up. He yanked

her to her feet in a violent jerk and a shaft of satisfaction went through her. He wanted her as much as she wanted him.

Desire pumped through her body as he held her close against him, then twisted her round slightly so he could put his hands all over her, squeezing her breasts, down her belly, over her thighs, between her legs. She could hear herself moaning, gasping and desperate.

He pushed her onto the banquette and yanked her chef's jacket open. The buttons came undone and she heard a couple ping off and hit the floor. He undid her trousers and pulled them off. Then her knickers. She arched her back to undo her bra, and then she was naked.

The fact that he was still fully dressed somehow excited her more. Lying on the banquette she tried to reach up and undo his belt, but he turned away. 'Stay there,' he said.

She did as she was told. She watched him step out of his clothes, the tiny interlude allowing her to think, for a second, *What the hell am I doing?* But then he stood over her, looking down at her. 'Are you sure, Angelica?' he asked. She nodded.

'Say it, then. Say you want it.'

'Please, Mario. I want it. I do.'

Then he was on top of her, inside her, and it was glorious, better than it had ever been. She put her legs around him, pulling his body into her, demanding he go deeper . . .

They came together, which they'd never managed before, and she cried out.

'Sssh, darling. Silvano will hear us,' he said.

But she didn't care. She couldn't stop yelling any more than she could stop what was happening.

CHAPTER TWENTY-FOUR

The next morning Angelica was woken by Sophie putting a cup of tea on the bedside table. 'It's nine o'clock,' she said, 'and Mario wants to see you. He was all for waking you himself, but I didn't know if you'd want to have him barging in.'

Angelica stirred. Then she remembered. Her eyes shot open and she stared at Sophie.

'What's the matter?' Sophie sat down on the bed.

Angelica met her gaze for a second then shut her eyes and slithered back under the bedclothes.

'What is it? Angelica?'

Her thoughts were flying about. She mustn't see Mario. Oh, God, what had she done? But last night it had been so wonderful. *I need time to think.*

'Sophie, I feel terrible. Can you tell him . . .?'

'What sort of terrible?'

The concern in Sophie's voice reminded her that Sophie was a doctor. 'It's nothing,' she said, 'just an almighty hangover. Headache. And I feel sick.'

Both complaints were true. But the sick feeling, she suspected, related more to what she'd done than to whatever she'd drunk.

'OK. I'll tell Mario you'll ring him, shall I? He can't wait because he's got to be in Stratford about an ice cream concession or something.' At the door she turned. 'And, Angelica, drink plenty of water.'

A few moments later Angelica was standing under the shower. *I must have been mad.* Two years without sex, the excitement of the restaurant opening and champagne on an empty stomach – all good excuses – but did she want to go back to Mario?

She closed her eyes and leaned her forehead against the shower wall, letting the hot water run over the back of her head and down her body. He was well now, taking the lithium, but he was still Mario. He'd drive her mad with his macho egotism, his lack of interest in her career, his instinct that women should be at home having babies. And if Nice Cream went bust, which looked likely, what kind of a job would he get?

She straightened up, turned the shower to cold and lifted her face to get the full blast of it. She hopped about, gasping, but when she stood shivering on the mat, rubbing herself vigorously with a big towel, her thick head and nausea had gone and she felt better. And resolute. She knew she didn't want to go back to Mario. Of course she didn't. It had been a one-night stand. That was all.

Silvano was in the dining room laying up for Sunday lunch when she arrived. She went up behind him and gave him a hug. 'Hi, partner. I'm so sorry I'm late. I forgot to set my alarm.'

He turned, unsmiling.

'What's the matter, Silvano? Last night was such a tremendous triumph. Why aren't you grinning from ear to ear?'

He smiled, but Angelica could see it was forced. 'Something's wrong – what's up?'

'I'm fine, Angelica. But we need to get on. There are thirty booked for lunch. Is it all prepped?'

Angelica saw that he was determined to be brisk and business-like. 'Yes, as much as could be done yesterday. It's just Sunday lunch: roast pork followed by rice pud. We'll be fine. Are Penny and Simon in?'

'Of course. They start at nine.'

Which I failed to do, thought Angelica. Maybe that's why he's grumpy.

The pork was two seven-rib loin joints, on the bone but chined. They came from a Frampton Estate pig, which the village butcher had slaughtered behind his shop in the high street. Angelica had been to see him to ensure he scored the rind himself for crackling. It drove her mad when butchers' apprentices were trusted with the job. A few careless slashes that went so deep the juices bubbled up would ruin in seconds something that a dedicated farmer had taken months to produce.

The butcher had listened. The narrow parallel cuts into the skin were just right. She turned the joints over and saw that he had chined them perfectly, the ribs sawn through where they sprouted from the backbone without slicing into the meat. As she rubbed salt into the skin she thought that maybe she should have trusted him in the first place, not told him how to do his job.

Silvano came in to tell her there were four more bookings. 'Good,' she said. 'We should do well today. Pork is cheap, and so is rice. The gross profit will be seventy-five per cent, I reckon.'

Silvano nodded and left the kitchen without a smile. Angelica again felt anxiety stir. What was up with him?

The lunch service went well, and as no drink could be sold

after two o'clock, the customers were gone by three. The restaurant would be closed on Sunday nights and all day Monday, but Angelica thought the pub should at least provide sandwiches as well as the traditional pickled onions or eggs. She sliced pork and stuffing left over from lunch, and put it with some ham, Cheddar, tomatoes and cucumber (all sliced and ready) in the fridge. Silvano or the barman could manage the sandwiches.

Maybe we should buy a toaster, she thought. Toasted sandwiches might not be as good as the Calzone deep-fried *mozzarella in carrozza*, but they were an improvement on straight ones.

The pub would be closed until seven o'clock and, once the clearing up and the minimal preparations for the evening were done, everyone went home. They would have all tomorrow to prep the food for Tuesday when the restaurant would open again at lunchtime. Before she left, Angelica stood for a moment looking at the still-wet kitchen floor, the shining stainless-steel tables, the brand new fridges and sinks, the electric sockets suspended on poles from the ceiling so that machines could be used without cables trailing across tables. This is a dream, she thought. A dream come true. Silvano was the perfect business partner, and if last night and today were anything to go by, they would have a success on their hands. She steered her mind away from the scene with Mario.

Silvano was nowhere to be seen. Angelica walked to her car, carrying her dirty whites in a basket. She opened a back door and dropped her basket and handbag onto the back seat. She was about to drive off when she thought, No, I must find out what's upsetting Silvano. She locked the car, put her keys into her pocket and went round to the front of the pub, to the second, smaller, door beside the main entrance. She rang the bell marked 'Flat'.

'Yes?' Silvano's voice.

'It's me, Angelica. Can I come up?'

He didn't answer but the door buzzed and she pushed it open. She walked up the stairs. Silvano stood at the top. 'Would you like anything?' he asked. 'Drink? Cup of tea?'

'I'm fine, thanks.'

'Well, what can I do for you?'

Angelica couldn't believe it. He was talking to her as if she was a stranger. 'For God's sake, Silvano,' she said, 'what's the matter with you? We're supposed to be partners. Why don't you tell me what's bothering you?'

He looked at her, expressionless, at once making her feeling guilty for her outburst. 'I'm sorry,' she said. 'It's just that we've worked so well together for all the months up until the opening, and now you're barely speaking to me. Something's happened.'

He was obviously considering whether to say something or not. Then, 'OK,' he said. 'I'll tell you.' He led her into his little sitting room, which doubled as an office. 'Do you know where we are now?'

Angelica was baffled. 'Of course I do. We're in your sitting room, in your flat, above the pub.'

'Exactly. To be precise, we're above the bar. And last night, sitting here, I had the pleasure of listening to my partner and my brother fucking their lights out in my pub.' His eyes drilled into her.

Angelica's whole body cringed. She shut her eyes against Silvano's icy stare. The thought of him hearing them, the shame of it, the embarrassment, made her face burn. She shook her head, trying to reject the knowledge that Silvano had heard it all.

'You'll tell me it's none of my business,' said Silvano, 'and maybe that's true. If you want to behave like a slut, or a teenager high on dope, then of course you're entitled to.' He was speaking perfectly calmly. 'But I've been trying hard to help Mario get out of his cycles of depression and euphoria, and if there is one thing I've learned, it's that your leaving him was the single trigger for him getting help and trying to stand on his own two feet for the first time in his life. It doesn't take a professor of psychiatry to know that you picking him up again won't do him any good.'

Angelica opened her mouth, but she had nothing to say. She couldn't deny any of what he'd said and, worse, she'd never given Mario's mental state a thought. And it hadn't occurred to her that making love to Mario in the bar of a business of which she was a director was vulgar and crass. Last night, she thought, I'd have made love to him on Wimbledon Centre Court or in Trafalgar Square. And the worst thing is that I don't even love him.

She stood up. 'I'll go now,' she said, her voice barely above a whisper. Silvano stood too, and reached for something on the mantelpiece. He scooped it up and handed it to her. 'These are yours, I believe.'

They were the two stud buttons that had pinged off her chef's jacket when Mario had ripped it open. 'I found them on the floor this morning.'

Angelica drove straight to London, and to Mario's flat. She'd never been there, but she knew where it was. It was above a greengrocer's in Praed Street.

He wasn't in. So she went home and wrote him a note.

Dear Mario,

I'm so very sorry about last night. I was so high on the success of the evening, and pretty drunk. I guess I just didn't think.

Can we go back to being civil cousins? I expect that's what you'd want too.

It was all my fault.

Angelica

She walked the couple of blocks from the mews to his flat and rang the doorbell again. There was still no answer so she pushed the note through the letterbox.

The next day she drove back to Chorlton. She dreaded Mario ringing her, berating her, furious at her dismissal of him after what they'd done that night. But she heard nothing. And then, three days later, she had a message on her office answerphone. She could tell at once he was drunk. 'Hi. Just realized I didn't reply to your note. So just to say that's fine by me, baby. You were always a terrific fuck and it's good to know I can have you whenever I want. But go back to living with you? No. Not for me. See you.'

Its crudeness was hateful. Angelica listened to it again. Well, she deserved it. She'd behaved like a slut, and if it made him feel better to think of her like that, how could she object?

But it hurt. She'd thought of that night as amazing. Unwise, yes. Stupid, probably. But not demeaning and gross. She deleted the message.

Over the next few weeks Silvano thawed a little, but he was still cool, and when she thought of their past closeness, the easy laughter and their mutual pleasure in working together, Angelica wanted to cry. She tried to apologize and to explain, but Silvano wouldn't discuss it.

'It's none of my business,' he said, 'and I'm sure next time you'll choose somewhere other than my bar.'

'There won't be a next time.'

He gave a slight shrug and left the room.

That was downright rude, she thought, anger for once replacing hurt. How dare he be so standoffish? Hasn't he ever had a night he's ashamed of? He's behaving like a Victorian father.

But she missed him. Working with him wasn't the same.

Giovanni was still smarting at the loss of Silvano and Angelica to Frampton, and was inclined to refuse George's invitation to lunch at his club.

But Laura insisted he go. 'Darling,' she said, 'he's been your friend and backer for twenty years. He still is. The fact that he could offer both Silvano and Angelica what they really want and we couldn't, or didn't, is no reason to blame him.'

'What do you mean? We offered them everything. Between them they'd have taken over the whole business eventually.'

'But Silvano wanted to get out of the accounts office and Angelica wanted to get into events and catering.'

Sometimes his wife's unrelenting reasonableness drove Giovanni mad. 'And,' she went on, 'I expect both of them wanted to show they could run a business on their own. Not in your shadow. It's admirable, really.'

'OK, but I still think George shouldn't have stolen them. He's a partner in our business. It's a conflict of interests.'

'Darling, just think about it! They would have left anyway.

Which would you rather, that they went off and worked for a London rival or for a friend in the country?'

Giovanni knew when he was beaten. He couldn't counter her logic. Much as he'd rather have gone on comfortably blaming George, he gave in and went to lunch.

They ate in the members' dining room at the Athenaeum and, though Giovanni tried to retain his annoyance with his old friend, the combination of good wine and George's easy friendliness undid it. They talked a little about politics and about the food (spring sea-trout and Jersey new potatoes followed by bread-and-butter pudding), but mostly of cricket.

After lunch they ordered coffee and cigars in the drawing room. Deep in a leather wing chair Giovanni felt expansive and mellow.

'So, Giovanni, we're friends again, I hope?' said George.

Giovanni smiled. 'We're too old to make new ones, George. We'll have to put up with each other, I suppose.' He sucked on his cigar and leaned forward to balance it carefully in the dip of the ashtray. 'I'm sorry I was angry.'

'Think no more about it. Perfectly understandable.' George took a folded piece of paper out of his inside breast pocket. 'Now, I want to discuss something with you, which I'm not sure about.'

He went on to explain that Mario had brought his boss, the owner of Nice Cream, to see him. 'He'd like us to make an offer for the business.'

'Good Lord. I knew they were in trouble – the Inland Revenue's chasing them for unpaid tax. They're a dodgy lot, you know.' He thought for a moment. 'What are they asking for it?'

'They're hoping for the equivalent of one year's turnover. But let's leave that aside for the minute. Would there be any point in buying them?'

'Not for their business. I'd never stoop to making ice cream like that, but I'd love to get my hands on their shops and production unit. Mario says it's a small modern factory.' Giovanni frowned suddenly. 'I wonder why Mario came to you rather than me?'

'He did come to you, he said. But you didn't show any great interest and he thought, as I'm supposed to be the money man, he'd bring his boss to see me.'

Giovanni felt slightly put out. 'Well, I've no interest in their going concern. But if we could get the central production unit and the shop premises I'd be very interested indeed. But it'd have to be at a knock-down price.'

'I thought you'd say that. The trouble is they want to sell the business as a going concern. Mario says the turnover is in fact twice what they tell the taxman. His boss pays the family, half of whom are on the books but don't actually work for the company, with the cash. All the profits disappear like that so they report a loss and avoid tax.'

Giovanni shook his head, smiling. 'Well, if we have to buy the business they must clean it up first, get rid of all the family members.'

'OK, I'll take a closer look, shall I?' suggested George. 'Maybe make an offer based on the value of the properties only. It'll save them from bankruptcy or prosecution so they might have to take it.'

They walked out of the club into the sunshine. Giovanni was feeling the old excitement rising at the prospect of a good business deal. He looked forward to telling Laura.

*

He was pleased to find his wife at home, sitting in the drawing room, reading their daughter's column in the *Daily Mail*. He joined her on the sofa and peered over her shoulder to study Angelica's instructions on making brioche.

'She's good, isn't she?' said Giovanni. 'She writes so well, so clearly. But then she does most things well – cooking, managing, demonstrating, TV.'

Laura shook her head. 'I've no idea how she keeps so many balls in the air. Especially with the new series on TV. The pub must be a full-time job on its own.'

'She's her mother's daughter.'

'I think it's more that she has a failed marriage and no children. I'd rather see her happy with a family, wouldn't you?'

He gave her a rueful smile. 'Well, yes. And working in the family business, here, with us.'

Giovanni told her about the Nice Cream approach. 'The thing that would worry me,' he said, 'is Mario. The owner obviously will be out, the finance director is leaving, and the managing director wants to retire. That leaves Mario running the show.'

'Well,' said Laura, 'it would kill the deal for me. Imagine him running a company. He'll be no better than the current lot. Is Mario above putting his hand in the till? I doubt it.'

'Darling, that's a bit harsh! Mario's dodgy but he's not evil. And he's sane now. Maybe if he takes his tablets and I have him reporting directly to me he'll be OK. He'll be a great salesman, that's for sure. He has the charm of a magician.'

Laura smiled. 'On your head be it, then. You're the one who'll have to sack him next time.'

Giovanni gave her a hug. 'Let's hope there won't be a next time. Carlotta will be pleased too. She has no illusions about her son, but she's a good Italian mamma and she'd love to have him back in the firm.'

'Mm. I suppose that's true, but I remember that when he was a teenager she wouldn't have him in her kitchen.'

Eventually the deal was done. The name Nice Cream was replaced by Gelati Angelotti and Mario was employed not as managing director but as chief salesman, charged with persuading the cinemas and cafés that currently took Nice Cream to switch to their more expensive but infinitely better product. Giovanni was confident he'd made the right decision in rehiring his nephew.

Mario had come to see him for a semi-formal interview. They'd discussed his duties and salary and Mario had been enthusiastic. As they rose to leave, he said, 'I must thank you, Uncle. And I'll do my best this time, I promise. I intend to keep taking the medicine and make a success of this job.'

'Well, Mario, you'd better. I hope you do, for all our sakes. Especially mine. I had a hard time persuading my wife and daughter that having you back in the fold was a good idea. If you're a disaster I'll never hear the end of it. And, of course, you'll be out on your ear.'

'I know. I'm really sorry for all the rough times I've given you.'

'It's Angelica you should apologize to.'

'I have. I saw her at Frampton. We're friends. Separate, but friends.'

CHAPTER TWENTY-FIVE

Jane was out riding. It was a beautiful sunny October day, the air still, the leaves just turning. She'd been up on the hill, cantering steadily along the bridle path, then trotting down through the woods. Maybe, she thought, she should ride more. As a child she'd spent her holidays and weekends on horseback and term-time dreaming of horses. But, though they still kept horses, and George and she occasionally went out for a hack, she no longer rode regularly. The lure of London had proved irresistible, and somehow she'd lacked the energy to ride by herself. That morning's golden weather had lured her out and she'd enjoyed it.

On the spur of the moment, she turned into the Frampton Arms yard. She'd have a cup of coffee. She could see Angelica and several cooks moving about through the kitchen window. She swung off her horse and stopped a passing lad dressed in a butcher's apron. She handed him her reins. 'Could you just look after my horse? I need to talk to the chef.' She didn't wait for an answer but strode towards the back door of the pub. She stopped in the scullery where Angelica was at the sink, about to scale a huge salmon with a knife the size and shape of a machete.

Angelica let go of the salmon's tail and the fish bounced into the sink. She rinsed her knife, then stuck it, blade down, behind a narrow plank screwed to the wall behind the draining-board. She wiped her hands on her apron. 'Hi, Jane. What can I do for you?'

'Well, I've come for a cup of coffee, and I've given my horse to one of your lads to hold, if that's OK.'

Jane followed Angelica through the kitchen, which was bustling with purposeful cooks, to the restaurant. 'I'm afraid the coffee machine isn't switched on yet and it takes a while to warm up. But we can make you a filter coffee.' Angelica pulled a chair out for her, saying, 'Would you mind if I put your horse in the stable? That boy has probably never held a horse in his life – he arrived from London yesterday – and I really need him in the kitchen.'

Jane felt irritation rising. Typical Angelica! She always had to know best. I bet the espresso machine *is* on, she thought. She just wants to make me feel a nuisance, arriving before opening time. And that stuff about the boy and the horse. Really, I'm not going to be here for hours, am I?

In the split second when she had decided to turn into the yard, Jane had imagined that Silvano or Angelica would be pleased to see her, would sit her down, offer her coffee, make a fuss of her. After all, she was their landlord. But no: the successful chef, the darling of the Cotswolds and the well-known television presenter was much too busy messing with fish to spare her the time of day.

The coffee wasn't up to much either.

Angelica was still based at Chorlton, although she was seldom there other than to sleep. The pub and the catering business were filling her waking hours. When she wasn't organizing or supervising the cooks in the kitchen, she'd find a quiet corner somewhere to write her cookery columns. She went by train to London on Sundays for a few hours with her parents then a blissful night in her own bed in her own house. On Mondays filming sometimes ran on until the evening and she'd have to take the last train, arriving at Moreton station at midnight to pick up her car, usually the only one in the unlit car park.

One day she was desperate to get an article for the *Daily Mail* done, but couldn't find anywhere to sit and write it. There were florists and wedding decorators all over the barn, the restaurant and the bar were packed, and the office was occupied by Silvano and his bookkeeper. She considered asking Silvano if she could use his flat upstairs but dismissed the idea. Relations with him had not returned to the comfortable familiarity they'd had before the Mario episode. He was polite, professional and very contained. It worried her intermittently, but she didn't know what she could do about it.

She thought of going back to Chorlton, but with dear old Granny Maud, Hal and Pippa, new baby Oberon and Jake, now crawling, she knew she'd be drawn into helping with lunch or something. In the end she sat on a lavatory seat in the hired Portaloos set up for a wedding, scribbling a piece about the nouvelle cuisine revolution going on in restaurants, if not in homes.

She wanted to explain to her readers that the movement was not a rip-off so that chefs could get rich and diners go hungry. She wanted them to feel what she felt: the excitement of genuine culinary creativity. The combinations of unlikely ingredients didn't always work, but they could be fabulous. She liked the pared-down simplicity. Food was cooked lightly at the last minute so the flavour and colour weren't lost; only the freshest ingredients were used; no reheated pieces of meat with heavy brown sauces on top; no rich, creamy white sauces. Rather, food was seasoned with the natural juices in the pan, fresh herbs, a touch of lemon or with light butter sauces.

And food looked so good, arranged with precision and an artist's eye, the accompaniments enhancing the main ingredient. Extraneous decoration was out – no radishes carved into roses, twisted slices of orange, spring onions cut into bottle-brushes. Instead garnishes were relevant and edible: a sprig of fresh tarragon, a couple of crossed chives, a strip of spring onion or leek tying together a bunch of carrot sticks or French beans.

How to say all this in an 800-word article, which must include at least one recipe? She settled on two: a new lighter and more composed take on a classic salade Niçoise, and mango sorbet, served with a thin syrup flavoured with lime, fresh mint and coarsely ground black pepper. Black pepper, she thought, goes with almost anything. She'd dreamed up this idea a couple of weeks ago when her mother had served Angelotti's mango sorbet at supper, adding chopped mint and black pepper as an experiment. It qualified as nouvelle cuisine, she thought, for its simplicity, lightness, innovation and flavour.

She emerged from the Ladies just as the cleaners arrived to give it a final wash-and-brush-up. She went back to the office, mercifully now empty, and rang the *Daily Mail*. It had taken a while for her to get used to dictating copy down the telephone, especially as she needed to dictate all punctuation. Some of the sub-editors were difficult and pretended not to understand French words like 'nouvelle' or 'crème'. Angelica had a shrewd idea they understood perfectly well, but resented her. Today, thank God, she got Jim, who just took it all down, no fuss.

She left the office and went to the dining room, where she found Jane and Silvano sitting at one of the tables, which were laid for the evening service. Jane had a glass of wine in front of her and Silvano some water.

'But it's ridiculous, Silvano. She's writing about all these Michelin-starred chefs doing astonishing food, and what do we serve? Steak and kidney pie and rice pudding. We should be trying for a Michelin star.'

Silvano caught Angelica's eye. 'Angelica, we're talking about you. Why don't you join us?'

He looked, she thought, even sterner than usual. 'OK,' she said, 'but can I just check on the kitchen? We have a couple of specials on that they haven't made on their own until today.'

In the kitchen Simon had already folded and rolled a round of pastry into a bag shape and was gently easing it into one of four pudding basins. They were doing a variation of steak and kidney pudding, using mutton from Frampton and lamb's kidneys. Angelica felt the pastry between finger and thumb. 'Lovely, Simon,' she said, 'soft and light and not too thick.' She helped him put the cubes of lamb, sliced mushrooms, chopped onion and diced kidney into a big sieve and sprinkle the mixture with flour. 'Shake it well, you want everything floured, but nothing too thickly.' They added plenty of chopped parsley, ground pepper and salt, and gave it a final shake, then filled the pastry-lined basin with it.

'Did you make this?' Angelica said, tasting the jellied stock with a teaspoon. 'It's good. It's not lamb, though, is it?'

'No, the butcher didn't send us the lamb bones. The recipe says water. Should we use water?'

'No, veal stock is fine. I've used chicken stock before now. I always think stock, even vegetable stock, is better than water if you have it. But warm it only enough for it to liquefy and don't fill the puddings until you're ready to steam them.'

When she got back to the table, she was smiling. 'I'm so pleased with Simon. He's confidently making lamb puddings. Getting the suet crust right is really difficult.'

'There you are,' said Jane, looking at Silvano. 'Lamb puddings, for goodness' sake. You'll be serving fish and chips next.'

'We frequently do,' responded Silvano, pleasantly. 'On Friday nights. Probably our bestseller.'

'What's the matter with lamb pudding and fish and chips?' asked Angelica, trying to keep cool. Jane was such a pompous idiot. She thought she knew everything about everything and, really, what they served was none of her business.

'I was just suggesting that as you're so knowledgeable about haute cuisine and can cook, apparently, like Escoffier, it's a pity to be serving boring old boarding-house food. Why can't we have nouvelle cuisine? You've worked in the Savoy, after all.'

Angelica wanted to laugh. 'That's a bit confusing, Jane. Do you want classic haute cuisine or do you want nouvelle cuisine? It's as far away from Escoffier as you could get. It was started by a bunch of French chefs precisely to get away from classic cuisine. And as for the Savoy, nouvelle cuisine hasn't even begun to penetrate that temple of tradition.'

Jane drew herself up. Like a duchess in a pantomime, thought Angelica. 'Well, thank you for the lecture, Angelica,' she said, 'but I'd like to remind you that we own this place – not the business, of course, but the building – and I would have thought that entitles me to an opinion. I have as much at stake in the Frampton Arms's success as you do.'

'Oh, Jane, for heaven's sake.' Angelica sighed. 'Couldn't you get off your high horse for once? I'm sorry about the nouvelle cuisine lecture, but you do talk a lot of rot sometimes.' As she spoke, Angelica's irritation was turning to anger, her voice getting louder. 'And, yes, of course you have a stake in the success of the pub,' she went on, 'but it's our business, not yours, that will make it one. If you don't like my food, then fine. Good. Just stay away, collect your rent and be glad.'

'Whoa,' said Silvano, mildly.

He put his hand on her arm but she shook it off. She couldn't stop now. 'I'm sure the staff will be delighted not to have to serve you. You scare the socks off them. And Silvano and I pussy-foot around you, trying to please you. It's ridiculous. Why can't you just be pleasant?'

Jane stared at her, her mouth open. Good, thought Angelica, that's shut her up. She resisted the temptation to stand up and flounce out. If she did that Silvano would probably tell Jane to take no notice of her.

'Well,' said Silvano, calm as usual, 'I know nothing, and frankly don't care, about fashions in the chef world. But I do know that Angelica's lamb pudding is one of the most delicious dishes I've ever tasted and her battered fish is made with fresh haddock or cod and served with chips fried in beef dripping. Amazing. Come to lunch, Jane and I'll treat you.'

'Well,' said Jane, her chin up, 'I see I'm outnumbered.' She stood up. 'And I can't spare any more time now. I have to check on the blacksmith at Barrow End. We have a new tenant there and he seems to think he can put a great big sign on his wall, sticking out. It's dreadful. You can see it from miles away.' She didn't look at Angelica as Silvano ushered her to the door.

Angelica stayed at the table. Why had she got so cross? She'd probably embarrassed Silvano as well as making a fool of herself.

But Silvano came back, laughing. 'I expect that's the point of a sign. To be seen. Poor smithy. He won't know what he's in for.'

Angelica tried to laugh too, but suddenly she dropped her face into her hands. 'I'm sorry,' she said, grabbing a table napkin and burying her face in it. 'Take no notice. I always blub after losing my temper.'

She stood up, intending to make for the door, but almost immediately she felt Silvano's hands on her shoulders and stopped. His thumbs massaged her back. 'Come on, Angelica, this isn't like you. What's happened to the fearless woman giving the lady of the manor a good dressing-down? That was terrific. I wanted to cheer.' He turned her round, still laughing. She looked up to see admiration and affection in his eyes.

Now she was laughing too. It felt so good. Like the old days. It flashed across her mind that any second now Silvano would remember to be frosty and formal with her. She couldn't bear that. 'Please, Silvano,' she said, 'can we be friends now? I've missed you so.'

'Not as much as I've missed you.' His smile was warm and welcoming. It felt like coming home.

Then he looked away. 'Where were we?' he said, pulling out her chair and seating her back in it. 'Oh, yes, Jane. She's a pain in the neck, I agree, but I feel sorry for the poor woman. George and Grace have spoiled her so much, and she's never been trained for the position she has.'

'Maybe.' Angelica wasn't ready to be conciliatory. 'They should have sent her off to work for a land agent where she'd have learned what she can legitimately interfere with and what she can't.'

'I think her problem is that she doesn't like to see us succeeding. We're both younger than her, and have done something with our lives. She's never really had a career.'

'But if she'd only apply herself and learn from Rupert and the other estate staff, and stop running off to London all the time, she'd have a proper job. A terrific one. Grace and George are in their fifties and not about to produce a male heir, so Jane will inherit the lot – London properties, Frampton estate and a well-run, highly profitable bunch of businesses.'

'I thought the English aristocracy had to leave everything to their closest male relative,' said Silvano. 'George can't leave everything to his adopted daughter, can he?'

'Yes, he can. She explained it to me once. Apparently in some trusts, and the Frampton Trust is one, there's a provision for the trustees to alter the terms once every hundred years, and since it was set up in 1760, George got his chance in 1960. He persuaded the trustees to break the male-heir rule so he could leave everything to Jane. She won't get his title, but she'll get all the assets. She must be the luckiest woman in England.'

Silvano was alone in the bar, polishing wine-glasses and hanging them upside down in the overhead rack. He was thinking about Angelica. He couldn't imagine a better business partnership. She was endlessly creative, always aware of what was going on in the restaurant world and how they could improve the menu. She brought energy and intelligence to the business, with a dash of boldness. But, most of all, she had enthusiasm. She so patently loved the business, the staff, the customers, everything. And she was such fun. When she was in London, the whole place seemed duller without her.

He'd adored her ever since they were children and he'd had to protect her from his too-boisterous, teasing brother. Fat lot of good that had done, though. As soon as she was away from home, she'd gone and fallen in love with her childhood tormenter. At the time he hadn't blamed Angelica, though he was furious with Mario. She was so young she hadn't had a hope: of course she'd fallen for him, the handsome brother, the fun one, the carefree one. And, of course, Mario had failed her, as he failed in most things. But damn his eyes, he'd still managed to woo her back on that night.

When she'd finally thrown Mario out of her house and out of her life, Silvano had been so pleased. She'd done the only sensible thing. She'd escaped, he thought, like a medieval princess from her captor. Mario would never be a good husband. Or a good anything. He loved Mario – he'd been watching out for him ever since they were children – but his brother was unreliable, selfish, not to be trusted.

He smiled to himself. Angelica didn't need his protection any more. She was so confident now, so much the businesswoman. Most people thought it was her business and he was just the backroom boy. Which was fine by him. He'd loved seeing Angelica blossom, and since he was good with money, tax, investment, and all the boring bits – he never found them boring – they made a perfect pair.

I wonder . . . He shied away from the thought. A business partnership: that was what they had, and he mustn't jeopardize it.

But then, inevitably, his thoughts turned to opening night at the pub and the scene in the bar below his flat. He'd not seen them, of course, but he'd heard their cries of passion . . .

He shook his head. He'd thought he'd managed to get the thing into perspective: Angelica was a young woman; she was emotional and romantic; she'd had a great sexual relationship with his brother; she'd been celibate for months; she'd been drunk on success as well as champagne. But still . . .

Don't be such a prig, Silvano, he told himself. You're just jealous.

CHAPTER TWENTY-SIX

Jane liked Mario. He was fun and, unlike his uptight brother and the oh-so-famous Angelica, he seemed to approve of her. At thirty-six, she was two years older than him, and he teased her a bit about being lady-of-the-manor-in-waiting, but at least he knew she was the *de facto* boss of Frampton. Angelica must have been mad to leave him. He was good-looking, energetic, and had a dash of Italian *machismo*, which made him slightly dangerous.

The Angelottis were coming down to see how their daughter and Silvano's ventures were going, and to hunt for mushrooms. The Frampton woods were famous for ceps, which her grandmother called penny buns and the Italians called porcini. They picked baskets and baskets of them for the restaurants. Jane couldn't help a little stab of pleasure when her father told her that Mario was coming too and that he'd be staying with them for the weekend, not at Chorlton, which was full. She thought she might even go on the foraging jaunt.

Her mother was laying the table for Sunday lunch. 'Why are you doing this, Mummy? Honestly, what's the point of a butler when you have a dozen people for lunch and don't ask him to do it?'

'He's got the weekend off, darling, and I didn't like to ask him to change it. Besides, it's only family and I like laying the table. Cook's here, so it's not as if I'm overworked.'

If I were in charge of the house as well as the estate, Jane thought, I'd have no qualms about asking the man to change his days off. But that's Mummy all over. Soft as butter.

The table did look good, set with the family silver down the centre – strutting pheasants and baroque candlesticks, and a central silver rose bowl full of deep purple Michaelmas daisies and late red roses. She felt a little glow of pride. All this would be hers one day.

Her mother was pushing the antique high chair up to the table. 'Good God, Pippa's not bringing the wretched Jake, is she? That brat never stops whining.'

'Yes, of course she is, darling. And Oberon, too, though I expect he'll be fast asleep in his basket. It's a family lunch, not a smart dinner party. And we're all going mushrooming afterwards, so no one will be dressed up.'

Jane made a face. Jake could be quite sweet, but when he screamed she wanted to smack him. One day, when Pippa wasn't looking, she might.

Grace had seated her daughter at the end of the table, opposite George. Jane looked down the table, enjoying the feeling of being the hostess. On her right her uncle David was in his wheelchair. He was in good spirits. 'One day you must teach Jake to ride, Jane. Do you remember, when you were little, teaching Mario and Silvano?'

She had young Richard on the other side, who was complimentary about the raised game pie and the figs from the south-facing wall of the kitchen garden. Mostly, though, he sang the praises of his multi-talented cousin Angelica: her television work, her writing, her cooking and catering. 'She's a born chef,' he said, 'and a great teacher.'

Jane looked at Angelica. She was good-looking, too, with her mass of hair swept off her face with a band, her full mouth smiling, her eyes clear and shining. Some people had all the luck.

It was a perfect autumn afternoon, the air still and clear, the sun still warm but lower in the sky, casting long shadows.

Maud hadn't come. She'd said she was too unsteady on her pins for mushrooming, but she'd come over to Frampton at tea-time to inspect their haul. Everyone else was there. Giovanni, Laura and Carlotta had gone ahead and were already in the woods, Jake was riding in the other end of Oberon's pram and Pippa, Angelica and Richard took it in turns to push them and David's wheelchair along the footpath. Grace, Hal, Sophie and Silvano strode directly across the field.

Jane was walking with Mario. They'd got left behind because they kept stopping to gather large white horse mushrooms as they crossed the field on the way to the woods. When they got to the gate they found David in his wheelchair, with tiny Oberon, swaddled tightly and fast asleep, in the crook of his arm.

'So Pippa's saddled you with her newborn,' said Jane. 'What will you do if he wakes up and yells?'

'Well, I'll try jiggling him. I've got him in my good arm so that's OK. And if he doesn't stop I'll blow this very loudly.' He opened his right hand to show her a dog whistle.

'And where's Jake?' asked Mario.

'They've taken him with them. Poor mite, he can barely stand, but he wants to run. He spends more time on his bottom than on his feet.'

They left their basket of mushrooms next to the wheelchair. 'We'll collect them on the way back. But first we need to get some porcini,' said Mario. 'Do you know which way they went?'

'I assume they're near the bend in the stream. You know, Jane, under the pines?'

They set off in the direction that David indicated but Jane didn't want to join the others. She was enjoying Mario's undivided attention.

'Let's go this way,' she said, waving her arm to the left. 'It's so lovely not being in a chattering mob. The noise at lunch was deafening.'

In the woods, the sun lit the yellowing trees and there was a rich smell of damp earth and rotting leaves.

'You're so lucky to live here, Jane. I hear you're in charge of everything at Frampton now. Is that right?'

'Except the house, yes.'

'Wow, what a great job. No wonder we see so little of you in London.'

Was he flirting with her? she wondered. Ridiculous! As if I'd have Angelica's rejects. But, still, the admiration was nice. 'Oh, I still go to London. I couldn't stay stuck in the country all the time.'

'Do you still stay in your parents' house?'

'Yes, but I have my own flat there. At the top. You must come and see it. I've just had it decorated by Nina Campbell. Have you heard of her?'

'Who hasn't? Trendy new decorator to the rich. How exciting. I'd have loved to be an interior decorator. I once had a go at our

London flat, but got myself into serious trouble with Madam. It was all modern designer furniture, but Angelica and Giovanni sent it back.' He laughed. 'Not my finest hour.'

They soon found porcini and chanterelles growing together under pine trees and between rhododendrons. Once they'd filled their basket, Jane suggested a different path to go home, mainly to avoid David and the baby and having to push them.

'But what about the mushroom basket we left there?'

'Oh, someone else can bring it. David knows it's there.'

When they got back to the house, Mario put the mushroom basket in the larder, and Jane ordered tea. The others turned up half an hour later to find her and Mario reading the Sunday papers.

'Hey, you lazybones,' her mother called, 'didn't you find any mushrooms?'

Mario got to his feet. 'We certainly did. Two baskets full. We left one with David.'

'Which we brought back,' said David.

Maud volunteered to check the fungi against the book. 'It's hardly necessary, I know,' she said, 'but I'd feel anxious if we didn't go through the routine.'

Jane was fond of her grandmother, who never changed. Not her hairstyle, her opinions, her affection, her habits. 'You're nuts, Grandma,' she said. 'You've been picking ceps from that wood ever since I can remember.'

'And longer. Well over fifty years. I used to love it. But I'd be a liability now. Too wobbly.'

The pickers had used a separate basket for anything that wasn't a cep, and Maud went through the mushrooms in it, then through Mario and Jane's basket of horse mushrooms. She used

316

a little knife to cut the bulb off the stems, each time inspecting the cut surface.

'You didn't do that to the others, Gran. What are you looking for?' said Jane.

'I'm checking they don't go bright yellow. If they do, they're the poisonous yellow stainer, not horse mushrooms at all.'

She put the last mushroom back in the basket and told Jane to pass her the half-dozen baskets of porcini, one by one. She took her time checking through them. Ah, well, thought Jane, it gave her something to do.

At last Maud snapped the book shut. 'All edible and delicious.'

She picked up the few mushrooms she'd put aside in a big china ashtray. 'All except these, which aren't poisonous. They're just past it. Look, they're full of maggot holes, and under the lamp the flies are hatching. Take them out of the warm, Jane, dear.'

Why me? thought Jane. There're plenty of young men to order about. But she picked up the ashtray and took it through to the kitchen compost bin.

Laura and Giovanni packed the porcini into their car. With greedy, indecent pleasure, thought Jane. 'I'm not leaving them here,' joked Laura. 'My daughter would probably nick them for the Frampton Arms.'

Hal picked up the two non-cep baskets. 'What do you say to the Chorlton pickers claiming these as our fee for finding all those porcini for the Angelotti empire?'

'Good idea,' said Grace.

Richard chimed in: 'You're all coming to supper at Chorlton tonight anyway and we can have them then. I'll make mushroom omelettes. Would that be OK, Mum?'

'Fine by me.' Sophie turned to Pippa. 'You hadn't made any supper plans, had you?'

Of course she hasn't, thought Jane. Pippa's the original hippie, about as organized as a toddler in a toyshop.

At seven o'clock Mario and Jane were in the Frampton drawing room, waiting for Grace and George to come down. When they heard them on the stairs they went out onto the landing.

'Mario, Jane darling,' said Grace, 'I don't think we'll come. I find all of us together lovely, but totally exhausting. We'd both rather just put our feet up and watch *Kojak*. Will you make our apologies to Maud?'

As Mario politely held the car door open for her, Jane thought, Good. I'll have him to myself for a bit longer. It wasn't that she fancied Mario or anything but it was very nice to be squired about by a handsome man.

Three days later, Jane was in her flat at the top of her parents' house in London, trying on a dress she'd bought that morning at Fenwick's, when Angelica telephoned.

'Jane, I'm sorry, but you must come home at once. Both your parents are in hospital. They're seriously ill.'

'Ill? They can't be. They were fine—'

'They only became ill this morning. First your mother. George called the doctor who told him to take her to the Churchill Hospital in Oxford and then, while he was there with her, he became ill too.'

'But what happened? What kind of ill?'

'The symptoms are like flu, only worse: high temperature,

shivering, headaches, nausea. Grace is only semi-conscious now. Because they're both ill, they think it might be food poisoning.'

'Oh, how awful.'

'Jane, you need to be with them. There's a train at five twenty-two. I'll meet you at Oxford station.'

Jane didn't really believe it. Her parents were seldom ill and when they were it was just a cold and they'd shake it off quickly. It must be the drama queen in Angelica. But she could hardly not go. What if it was really serious?

It was Sophie, not Angelica, who met her at the station and drove her to the hospital. 'I know the staff there,' she explained. 'They may give a fellow doctor more honest answers than they'd give you, so I thought I'd come. Is that all right?'

On the five-minute drive, Sophie would only say that both Grace and George were being well looked after, in the best place for them to be. Both were now in an emergency ward, being monitored closely. They'd given blood and urine tests but it would take a while to get the results.

'But if it's food poisoning, what could they have eaten?'

'They think it could be mushroom poisoning. George told them about the mushroom hunt.'

'But that was last Sunday.'

'Yes. The truth is they don't know yet what the problem is. But they will soon, and then the doctors will know what treatment to give.'

'It can't be the mushrooms or we'd all be ill,' said Jane. 'Anyway, Granny checked every mushroom against the book, didn't she?' She was silent for a few seconds, then suddenly jerked her head up. 'But they didn't have any,' she cried. 'They didn't go to Chorlton, remember? They stayed at home to watch *Kojak*.'

'You're right. They must have been poisoned somewhere else.'

At the ward, the matron told them to wait while she fetched the doctor. He wanted to have a word with them.

Jane's heart was banging in her chest. Surely it couldn't be all that bad. People got over food poisoning.

The doctor was a youngish man, with a round face, pale and tired-looking. He looked surprised to see Sophie. 'Dr Oliver! Are you the patients' GP?'

'No, I'm a kind of relation. My husband's brother was married to the countess. We're all very close. This is Miss Jane Maxwell-Calder, the countess's daughter.'

He shook Jane's hand, then led them into a small waiting room with four chairs and a coffee table with a single magazine on it. They sat in silence. This must be a room they use to tell people their relatives have died, thought Jane. Maybe he's going to tell us Mummy has died. No! It can't be.

'Well,' he said, 'let me tell you where we've got to. We've had the blood and urine tests back and the news is not good. Both the earl and the countess have almost total renal failure, which means their kidneys have ceased to function.' He looked into Jane's face. 'We need to filter your parents' blood artificially as the kidneys can no longer do it.'

'Are they on dialysis?' asked Sophie.

'The countess has been on a machine for two hours. She will stay on it for another ten. At that point we can put the earl on it.'

'Won't the delay be dangerous for him? Another ten hours?' asked Sophie.

'Well, it's not ideal, obviously. But we only have nine machines and they're in use night and day.'

'But this is an emergency,' said Jane. 'Surely you can take someone off a machine and put him on it.'

'I'm afraid not. Being denied a treatment could have very serious consequences for any dialysis patient. Your father is going to need two twelve-hour treatments every week.'

'But he's the Earl of Frampton!' cried Jane.

'Dear Jane,' Sophie said gently, 'George would be the last man to want to jump a queue.'

'And I'm afraid we couldn't do it anyway,' said the doctor. 'As it is, I'm bending the rules a bit because normally dialysis is reserved for patients under fifty who are better able to take it. But your parents are obviously in good physical shape, and as we had the capacity, we put your mother on a machine. And we'll do the same for your father.'

'How long does the treatment take? How many weeks?'

'Their kidneys will not recover, I'm afraid. They will eventually need transplants. In the meantime they will have to stay on dialysis.'

'For ever? That's monstrous!'

Sophie put a calming hand on Jane's thigh. 'Have you established the cause?' she asked the doctor.

He looked at Jane. 'Your father said they had mushrooms on toast on Sunday night in front of the television. He had no idea what they were, and the countess was too ill to tell us. We'd like to get hold of a sample of the mushrooms if there are any left. He doesn't know if they ate all they had.'

A sudden terrible thought cramped Jane's abdomen. The basket of porcini she and Mario had picked. They'd got home before the others and put it in the larder. Maud wouldn't have checked it. She closed her eyes.

Sophie's hand was still on her thigh, and she felt her increase the pressure. She opened her eyes as Sophie slid off her chair and knelt next to her, examining her face. 'What is it, Jane? You look—'

Jane made an effort to focus. 'No, I'm fine, just felt faint. It's gone now.' She wouldn't say anything about those mushrooms. Not yet. She needed time to think.

The doctor said, 'You don't feel sick? No headache?'

Jane had pulled herself together. She forced a smile. 'Never had two doctors worrying about me before,' she said. 'But no, I'm fine, really.'

'The thing is,' said Sophie, returning to the question of poisoning, 'we picked porcini on Sunday, but no one ate any. The rest of us ate the other mushrooms, field mushrooms or chanterelles. I can't remember. And I think something else . . .'

'Blewits,' said Jane. 'Gran showed me when she was checking them against the book.'

'What happened to the porcini?' asked the doctor.

'Oh, my God.' Sophie had gone ghost-white. She looked at Jane, her eyes wide. 'They went to London, to a restaurant . . . There were pounds and pounds of them. They could have poisoned—'

Panic clutched at Jane. 'Sophie, I was at Giovanni's last night. We were all eating risotto with porcini. How long does it take to get sick?'

'It can be a few hours, or anything up to three weeks,' said the doctor. 'It depends on the mushroom.'

322

'Can I see my mother and father?' Jane's voice was uncharacteristically small. She cleared her throat and said, louder, 'I want to see my parents.'

'I'm sorry,' he said kindly, 'but not yet. As soon as your mother comes off the machine and is back in the ward, you can. But she's very weak, and I think it would be better to keep her calm and still for the moment.'

'And my father?' She felt bewildered and close to tears.

'Not yet. He's in a lot of pain and is vomiting. I don't want to add to his distress. Having his daughter see him like that might be more worrying than comforting.'

Jane didn't like the rebuff but a part of her was relieved. She didn't handle other people's pain well. She wouldn't know what to do or say.

'But we must find out the cause,' he said. He looked at Jane. 'Are you really all right now?'

Jane didn't feel all right. She was very frightened. She nodded.

'When you go home, could you see if you can find any remains of that Sunday-night supper? Cooked mushrooms in the bin, leftovers in the fridge, raw mushrooms in the larder or fridge? Will you have a good look?'

The doctor took them into his office, and Sophie telephoned Giovanni's.

Laura came on the line. 'Hello, Sophie. This is a surprise. What's up?'

'Laura darling, listen carefully. Have any of your customers been ill? Complained of food poisoning?' Sophie looked at the doctor, shaking her head. 'She says no.

'And have you any of the porcini left?' She listened for a second. 'OK, don't serve any more and don't throw them away. They have to be analysed. Grace and George have kidney failure and are on dialysis. The hospital thinks it's mushroom poisoning.'

Laura's voice rose, asking questions. Jane could hear her urgency.

'All of us down here who ate the mushrooms at Chorlton are fine,' said Sophie, 'but are you and Giovanni OK? . . . And Carlotta, Mario, Richard? . . . OK, that's good. None of us ate any porcini . . . No . . . We ate the mixed collection, remember . . . Grace and George weren't there, and we don't know what mushrooms they ate . . . Yes . . . They had them on toast at home.'

They all watched Sophie. She put her hand over the mouthpiece for a second to say, 'No one's sick, as far as she knows.'

Laura was talking again, and Sophie interrupted. 'Laura, I can't talk now, but I'll ring you again tonight when we've seen Grace and George. I'm at the hospital with Jane. Just don't serve any more porcini. And could you check round with everyone who ate them? . . . I know, you'll have to be tactful, darling. The first symptoms are flu-like: nausea, headache, stomach ache, general pain.' She looked up for confirmation from the doctor. He was nodding. 'If they have anything like that they should go at once to Casualty and say they might have mushroom poisoning.'

At nine o'clock that night, after failing to eat the thin soup or tasteless sandwich in the hospital refectory, Jane and Sophie were allowed, after all, to visit Grace briefly. Still on dialysis, she'd improved slightly and was awake. She was lying propped up on a reclining chair, with two pipes into her ankle taking her blood to and from the machine. She was very pale, her eyes shut and her mouth open. The nurse explained that once she was stabilized, they would move the shunt from her ankle to her arm.

Sophie said, 'Grace, Jane's here to see you.' Grace's eyes fluttered open and she gave a weak smile. She made no attempt to speak.

They stayed just a few minutes. Jane didn't want to look at her mother. She knew she should say something, but she couldn't do that either. She kissed Grace's forehead and turned away.

'We'll come back tomorrow afternoon, Grace, when George's dialysis is over. Then we'll see you both. They're putting you in the same ward,' said Sophie.

When they left the hospital, Jane insisted on going home to Frampton. Sophie had suggested she come to Chorlton, but Jane wanted to be alone. As soon as she was at home, she went straight to the larder. And there it was, the basket she and Mario had filled and placed there, so avoiding Maud's scrutiny.

Half a dozen mushrooms were left, drier than when they'd picked them, but still fairly plump. Orange-brown, not all the same shape. But they were obviously all the same species. She took them into the sitting room and looked for Maud's mushroom book, but she must have taken it home with her. She went up to her father's study and went through the farming and gardening section. She looked up fungi in the *Encyclopaedia Britannica*, but the entry went on for pages and there were only tiny line drawings, no colour pictures. Besides, since she didn't know what she was looking for beyond 'poisonous fungi' it was hopeless. Close to despair, she forced herself to keep looking. She went to the shelf with books on nature like *Wild Animals of Burma* and *Birds of the Andes*. Finally she found what she needed:

a little book called *Poisonous Fungi of Europe*. It consisted of ten pages of large coloured drawings of mushrooms.

Sitting at her father's desk, her heart thumping, she slowly turned the pages, each time feeling a tiny flicker of relief. The mushrooms on her lap were not *Amanita phalloides*, the death cap, or *Amanita virosus*, destroying angel. They weren't *Inocybe patouillardi* either.

And then there it was. Absolutely. No hope of being mistaken. *Cortinarius speciosissimus;* deadly webcap. The rounded top, reddish brown, a little raised in the middle. Some mushrooms rather misshapen, some taller and thinner, just like the ones in the basket. One picture was of an upturned mushroom, showing its pale gills.

She gasped. It had gills. She turned over a couple of the mushrooms in the basket. Unmistakable gills. Even she knew ceps didn't have gills. They had undersides with little holes in them, not slits. She sat absolutely motionless while the full horror sank in.

She'd poisoned her parents. She and Mario had picked webcaps, not ceps. Why hadn't she looked at them properly before pouncing on them so eagerly?

She knew the answer. She had been trying to impress Mario. She was keen to find porcini but not to take him to where everyone else was, where porcini grew.

She sat still for a moment, then bent her head and forced herself to read the text.

Cortinarius Speciosissimus *(deadly webcap) is the most dangerous of mushrooms. It contains the toxin orellanin for which there is no antidote. The poison is remarkable for its long latency, with symptoms seldom appearing until two or three days after ingestion, and sometimes not for three weeks. The time before the effects of poisoning becoming apparent and the quantity of mushrooms eaten will greatly affect the recovery, or failure to recover, of the patient. The effect of the toxin is to damage the kidneys, causing them to fail or partially fail, producing little and eventually no urine. Without dialysis or a kidney transplant the patient will die.*

Habitat: Grows on acidic soil frequently under pine trees. Common in mainland Europe, less common in Scotland, and rare in the south of England. Books published before the middle of the 1950s did not always include the webcaps as poisonous, since it was only in the early 1950s that Cortinarius Speciosissimus *was definitely identified as the cause of a mass poisoning in Poland.*

Jane lifted her head, gulping for air. She hadn't realized she'd been holding her breath.

But what to do? All her self-preservation instincts cried out for her to hide the mushrooms, bury them, pretend she knew nothing.

Then sense crashed in. What am I thinking? My mother and father are dying and the doctors want to know what they ate. I'll have to admit I picked them and that we didn't get them checked.

She couldn't bear it. She didn't want anyone to know that. Most of the family didn't like her much as it was. Now everyone would hate her. Except Mario. Mario was as guilty as her. He might not want them to know either. He's like me – not popular. He's the black sheep of that family. Should she phone him? No, not until she'd decided what to do.

She walked around the room, her thoughts flying in all directions. If I just got rid of them, and Mario doesn't mention taking the basket into the larder, no one will blame us. They'll just think Grandma made a mistake identifying something. Of course, it's a bit mean putting the blame on her, but everyone adores her and they'll be sympathetic, not nasty.

Jane bolstered her courage with the knowledge that telling the doctors about the webcab would make no difference to her parents: they've eaten deadly webcap, she told herself, and there's no antidote. The only treatment is dialysis or a kidney transplant and both her parents were now getting dialysis.

She tried to get a grip on her circling, desperate thoughts. Who, besides Mario, knew they'd put a basket in the larder?

Suddenly she jumped up and almost ran out of the back door, the basket of mushrooms in her hand. It was dark, and she had to return for a torch. Her heart thumping, she hurried to the compost heap and emptied the basket onto it.

Jane slept badly. She hadn't buried the mushrooms. And what about the basket? Where had she put it? There might be traces of mushrooms in it.

She was tempted to go out with the torch again and dispose of the evidence more carefully. But then she thought it would be better to wait for daylight.

When she woke up it was past eight o'clock. She dressed hurriedly, and went down to the larder, sneaking past the cook in the kitchen. There it was. The empty basket. Grabbing it, she hurried outside and quickly gathered the scattered mushrooms together. She used the pitchfork to heave clods of recent debris – dead flowers, vegetable peelings, rotting windfall apples – out of the way, then dug into the heap, to make a deep dip. She raked in the mushrooms and covered them.

On the way back to the house, she noticed a plume of smoke from a bonfire burning autumn leaves. I could have just burned them, she thought. That would have been better. She walked to the bonfire, took a quick look round to make sure the gardener couldn't see her, and threw the basket on the fire. It went up with a satisfying crackle and burst of flame.

She watched, breathing the lovely smell of burning leaves, her thighs pleasantly warm from the fire. I wish I could just stay here and do nothing. Not think, not worry about Mummy and Daddy, not get entangled in my web of lies.

And then, later, lying on her bed, she couldn't think why she'd got rid of the webcaps. The right thing to do would be to confess. Then everyone could stop worrying about themselves because no one else had eaten any webcaps. And Giovanni's could tell their customers it had been a false alarm.

Oh, God, I'm going mad, she thought.

Jane went back to the hospital in the late morning with Sophie. At the matron's desk they asked if they could see the Framptons, and were directed to a side ward. The curtains were closed.

'You go in. I'll wait,' said Sophie.

I can't, thought Jane, I don't have the guts. 'No, you come too, Sophie.' She wanted it to sound like a command, but it came out as a plea.

Her father was asleep. Jane was relieved, and also cheered that he looked peaceful, his handsome face a wan yellowish-grey. She realized she hadn't looked closely at him for a long time. His day-old stubble was grey and his hair was receding. His breathing was laboured and his ankles, protruding from the bedclothes, were very swollen. One was bandaged where the dialysis tubes had been.

Her mother was awake, and seemed something of her old self. Jane kissed her forehead and held her hand. Grace squeezed her fingers gently. 'Oh, darling,' she said, 'I'm glad you came. I was so worried about you. And, Sophie, thank you. Did you talk to the doctors?'

Sophie could only tell her what she already knew, that they had mushroom poisoning and dialysis was doing their kidneys' job.

They talked sporadically, Grace slipping in and out of sleep. She asked who else had been poisoned, and if Giovanni's customers would sue, but drifted off before she'd heard Sophie's answer.

Once when she woke, she asked for water. 'I'm so thirsty,' she said, 'I've been dreaming of water.' Jane wanted to ask the nurses for some but Sophie told them they wouldn't allow it. The dialysis was not yet extracting enough water from her body, she said, and Grace was restricted to a pint of liquid a day.

CHAPTER TWENTY-SEVEN

The next day Jane telephoned Mario and tried to explain their predicament. He didn't understand and she could hear herself becoming incoherent and slightly hysterical on the telephone.

'Whoa, Jane,' he said. 'Listen, as I understand it, no one is concerned who picked the mushrooms, so don't worry about it. The main thing is that Grace and George get better.'

She felt the reproof. He's right, she thought. I'm being selfish and not concentrating on what matters. But of course I'm worrying about being responsible.

'Just relax,' he said. 'Neither of us will mention the basket in the larder. You keep going to the hospital, and at the weekend I'll come down and we can talk about it, if it's still worrying you. OK?'

She was so grateful that tears sprang to her eyes. Thank God.

But on Friday morning a plain-clothes policeman was at her door, accompanied by a uniformed sergeant. She knew the bobbies at Moreton-in-Marsh police station, but these men were strangers.

He introduced himself as Inspector Fuller and explained that the hospital had to report all poisonings to the police. It was just routine. But they had to investigate. He'd like to ask her a few questions.

Her heart quaking, she led them into the study. The inspector took the chair she offered him, but the sergeant said he'd prefer to stand. She felt slightly intimidated by his looming frame, close to her shoulder as she sat in the corner of the chesterfield.

'I've spoken to your mother in the hospital so I know that there was a mushroom-picking expedition. In the evening she and the earl ate mushrooms on toast and were poisoned. I would like to start by asking who was on that mushroom hunt.'

She told him. It took a while but he wrote down the names of them all. Even David in his wheelchair. Surely, she thought, but didn't ask, he's not going to interview everyone.

'Did anyone check the mushrooms to identify them before you ate any?'

'Yes, my grandmother, Maud, went through the baskets. She always does. She has a big book. She did it in the drawing room.' She was gabbling.

'Did she check them all?'

'Yes.' *I've just told my first absolute lie.*

'Where did the countess get the mushrooms she cooked for their supper?'

'I – I don't know. There were baskets and baskets of mushrooms. It must have been one of them.'

'After your parents became ill, did you check to see if there were any mushrooms uneaten?'

'Yes.'

'Were there any?'

'No.'

'Do you still have the basket?'

Why had she burned it? 'I – I don't know. It was in the larder.'

'I thought you said you didn't know where your mother got her mushrooms from.'

She looked at him, trying to conceal her panic. 'Did I? Well, the truth is that I don't know, but there are always baskets in the larder. I must have seen one there.'

'Is it still there?'

'I don't know.' It was something of a relief to stand up. 'I'll go and look, shall—'

'No, don't worry, we can look later. Let's get the questions over and done with, shall we?' His voice was calming and she sat down again.

On and on it went. The worst bit was when he asked her about what each of them had picked. And where, and who with.

'Why did you and Mario go off on your own if the known place for getting the . . . er . . .' he looked at his notes '. . . the ceps, was by the river, where the others went?'

'I don't know. Mario's sort of my cousin. We don't see each other very often. We . . . I don't know. We just did. Just for fun, I suppose.' She was gabbling again.

'Are you and Mario in a relationship?'

Indignation overtook fear for a second. 'What on earth has that got to do with anything? As it happens, the answer is no. But, frankly, it's none of your business.'

Unperturbed at her outburst, the detective went on with his endless questions. 'What sort of mushrooms did you find?'

'We picked a smallish basket of horse mushrooms in the field before we separated from the others. We left them with David, who was looking after the baby at the edge of the wood.'

'And when you went off on your own, did you find any ceps?'

'Yes, and some chanterelles, I think.'

'And what did you do with this basket?'

'I don't remember. I think all the baskets ended up in the drawing room so that my grandmother could check them.'

'Would you say your grandmother is an authority on fungi?'

'No, but she's very careful and always checks mushrooms.'

The questions came thick and fast and got more personal: 'Do you get on well with your grandmother?' 'Do you get on well with your mother?' 'And your stepfather?' 'Was everything between you all harmonious, would you say?'

Will he never stop? Really, this is crazy. He obviously thinks I poisoned my parents. Suddenly she burst out, 'Why are you asking me all these questions? Do you think I poisoned them? Is that it?'

'Did you?'

She couldn't stop the tears now. 'Of course I didn't – how dare you! You will leave my house. At once.' As she shouted, unable to control her contorted face and with tears streaming down it, she knew she was acting like a character in a bad play and that her behaviour wouldn't help her. But she couldn't stop. She was beside herself. 'You think you can just come into my house and accuse me—'

'No one is accusing anyone, Miss Maxwell-Calder. This is a routine inquiry. It probably won't lead anywhere. I apologize for upsetting you and I'll go now. I'll just leave my sergeant to have a look round the premises, if you don't mind. In a case of potentially fatal poisoning, it's routine, I'm afraid. I'm sure you understand.'

Jane went into the kitchen and made herself a cup of tea. The cook, busy bottling greengages, asked if she'd like a tray with some scones in the drawing room. Jane shook her head. Her hand, as she poured water into the mug, was still shaking, whether from rage or fear she wasn't sure. Out of the window she saw the sergeant walking across the lawn. Should she follow him, try to deflect him from the compost heaps? That might raise his suspicions. Better do nothing. He'd probably not find the mushrooms anyway.

That evening Mario appeared, cheerful and confident. It was good to have him there. She told him about the police, and though she'd decided not to tell him about identifying the webcaps, she did. She told him everything, including her stupid attempt to bury the evidence and even stupider burning of the basket.

'Oh dear, Jane, that wasn't very wise. But don't worry about it. I'm sure they won't pursue it, and if they do, you'll just have to come clean and tell them you were deranged with worry and acting a bit oddly.'

'But they will pursue it! After all, I've a great motive, haven't I? I'd inherit a pile of money twenty or thirty years earlier than I would have.'

She noticed Mario's eyes light up. That got your attention, didn't it? she thought.

'Except you're already the richest young woman any of us knows. Another pile of money is hardly going to change your lifestyle, is it?' He stood up to pour himself some more whisky. 'You don't mind, do you? It's been a hard week and this Macallan is irresistible. You should have one, Jane. You've had a tougher week than anyone. It'll relax you.' He didn't wait for an answer, but poured her a glass while talking. He brought it to her, and sat beside her.

Jane watched him. She had no illusions. Mario had taken little notice of her for twenty years. It was the riches of Frampton that had changed his tune. He'd been there as a child when she'd taught him to ride, but since then, if he came to the Cotswolds at all, he stayed at Chorlton. She could almost see him working out how he could wriggle his way into her affections and scoop the pools. She smiled to herself. Even if his motivation was mercenary he was amusing to have around. He was totally unsuitable, of course, miles beneath her socially. Besides, she had no intention of marrying anyone. She might end up watching some spendthrift squander her fortune. But Mario was handsome. His deep eyes could fix yours so you couldn't look away.

Then Jane remembered that her parents were gravely ill. Speculating about Mario right now was vulgar.

On Saturday, and again on Sunday morning, Mario drove Jane to Oxford to visit her parents. He couldn't come in – only Jane and Sophie were allowed to visit because George was still so ill – but he was solicitous, opening the car door, kissing her cheek and giving her an encouraging hug. He said he'd collect her in an hour.

By Sunday morning her mother, though still pale, was slowly improving. She had no pain and responded well to the dialysis, peeing comfortably now and no longer so thirsty. But George looked worse. He was due for his second twelve-hour session of dialysis and he had a lot of pain around his kidneys, excruciating headaches, and swollen feet and hands. He was desperately thirsty. He looked grey and was hardly speaking.

'Can't they do something for his pain?' she asked her mother.

'He has tablets every four hours, sometimes more. But they don't always work.'

Poor Mummy, thought Jane, lying in the next bed, listening to him groaning and retching. The doctor had said she could be discharged if she liked, but she'd elected to stay with George.

Mario left for London on Sunday afternoon after tea, and Jane drove herself to the hospital. Her father's bed was empty and her mother was sitting with a book on her lap, but she wasn't reading.

'Darling,' she said, as soon as she saw her daughter, 'they've taken him back into the emergency ward. He's in so much pain. And vomiting again.'

Jane kissed her mother's cheek and took her hand. 'Is he . . . is he in danger?'

Grace looked directly at her and swallowed. 'I think he is, darling. They haven't said anything, of course. The doctor is due any minute and I expect he'll tell us.'

Her mother was still beautiful in spite of her pallor and the dark shadows under her eyes, but she looked so forlorn. Oh, God, thought Jane, poor Mummy. If Daddy dies what will she do? And what will I do? She'd have to run the Frampton estate then, not just play at it. But could she? The tenants didn't like her, and they loved her father.

Did she love her father? Of course she did. She was his daughter. Adopted, but still his legal daughter. And heir.

The doctor didn't arrive until six forty-five. He was the same one who had spoken to her and Sophie when they'd first come in.

Jane was sitting on her father's bed. The doctor drew the curtains to shut out the main ward, and sat beside her. She looked at his solemn face and knew it was bad news. In an effort not to hear it, or to delay it, she said, 'You look exhausted, Doctor.'

He nodded and gave her a bleak smile. 'I'm fine,' he said.

He turned to Grace. 'I'm afraid your husband has passed away, Lady Frampton. He died twenty minutes ago.'

Jane didn't move a muscle. Oh, Jesus . . . No – it can't be. Then immediately, like a sledgehammer, came the realisation: I've killed my father. She looked at her mother.

Grace, who'd been so composed, almost resigned, a few minutes ago, cried out, 'But he was on dialysis. He was supposed . . .'

'Yes, he was, Lady Frampton, but I'm afraid it was too late. Nearly three days passed before he got onto a machine. No one's fault, of course, you didn't have any symptoms for over forty-eight hours, but the damage was done. He was retaining too much fluid in his body, and that affects the other organs. He had a heart attack and, though we tried, we couldn't revive him.'

'Then why aren't I dead too?' whispered Grace, her shoulders shaking.

'Your husband told us that he ate a lot more mushrooms than you. Two large pieces of toast piled high, and you had one.'

'I'd prefer to be dead.'

Angelica arrived at Frampton as Inspector Fuller was getting out of his car with the uniformed sergeant. She recognized him because he'd taken statements from them all. She hurried over. 'Inspector,' she called, 'stop, please. I'm Angelica Angelotti, remember? From the Frampton Arms?'

'Yes. Good morning, ma'am.'

'I just wanted to say, if you need to see Jane, this is not a good time. Her father has just died. Yesterday afternoon.'

'I'm aware of that. My condolences,' he said politely.

'So could you come another time, do you think?'

'I'm afraid not. There have been, er, developments, and I need to ask her a few more questions.'

'But she'll be so distressed! Surely—'

'Miss Angelotti, the death of the earl makes the poisoning even more serious, and I do need to see his daughter.'

Angelica looked at his stern face and realized what he was saying: that for him this might be a murder inquiry. 'Well, can I be with her? Poor girl, I've come to try to comfort—'

'No, I regret not. But if you'd like to go in first and tell her I have a few more questions for her and that I won't keep her long, my sergeant and I could wait here a few minutes.'

So Angelica went in through the side door, used by the family except on grand occasions, leaving the detective at the front.

Angelica found Jane in her mother's beautiful kitchen, looking exhausted. 'The policemen are back, Jane.'

Jane closed her eyes. She shook her head slightly and sighed in resignation.

'I'll make some tea,' said Angelica. 'You let them in – they're waiting outside the front door. I'll bring you a tray and leave you to it.'

'Do we have to give them tea? I didn't last time.'

'No, we don't have to, but you could do with a cup and so could I. Where will you see them?'

'I'll get Marston to show them into the study,' said Jane, walking to the door.

Angelica made the tea and took a tray with three cups into the study. The inspector stopped talking as she came in. Jane, she thought, looked desperate. Poor girl, it's really too much having to answer more questions when everyone has already told the man all they know.

When the policemen emerged from the study she showed them out, then hurried back to Jane. She was sitting, pressing her eyes with a bunch of Kleenex.

Angelica sat next to her. 'Jane, what's the matter? What did he say?'

'I've been such an idiot. I can't bear it.' She was crying now. 'I must telephone Mario.' She jumped up and ran upstairs.

Angelica hesitated, unsure what to do. Jane was obviously frightened as well as distressed. What had the inspector said to her? And why did she have to speak to Mario? Angelica stayed where she was, and waited.

After ten minutes she heard Jane coming slowly down the stairs. She'd stopped crying. 'Mario says I must tell you everything and ask you to help me.'

Angelica listened in silence as Jane told her tale, of the basket of mushrooms she and Mario had picked, of Mario putting it in the larder, of neither of them thinking to include it in Maud's scrutiny, of Jane subsequently identifying the webcaps, panicking and burying them. And burning the basket. And now lying to the police. 'Now they think I murdered my father, I know they do.'

Recalling the tale had made her cry again. Angelica put her arm round her. 'Did they say they think you poisoned them on purpose?'

'No, but the sergeant found the mushrooms in the compost heap, and they had them identified.'

'What did you say to that? Did you tell them what had happened?'

'No, I couldn't. I just kept saying I didn't know anything about the mushrooms, or what had poisoned them, or how those ones got on the compost heap. I could tell they knew I was lying, but they didn't say so.'

'Jane, darling. You have to tell them. More lies will only make it worse.'

'That's what Mario said. He's going to come down tomorrow and we're going to the police.'

Good Lord! Mario's being responsible, thought Angelica. Wonders will never cease. 'He's right. Now, listen, I'll stay with you tonight, if that's OK?' Jane nodded. 'When all this is over, I want to ask you to help me with something. Is there anything for supper or shall we go to the pub?'

'Cook left a fish pie,' she said, 'and some stewed damsons.'

'Lovely. Why don't you have a bath or a rest or something and I'll get my stuff from Chorlton.'

Angelica didn't really need Jane's help, but she wanted to do something for her. Maybe if she worked a couple of days a week on the Frampton Feast parties, it would take her mind off her parents. Of course she would have to stay at Frampton with Grace – she couldn't just run off to London – but she'd have little to do. The Frampton staff would drive Grace to the hospital for her dialysis, and Maud would be with her as much as she could.

'Mum will look after Grace,' David said. 'She saw her through her first widowhood when Hugh was killed and she'll do it again. Mum is extraordinary, and she adores Grace.'

On the way back from Chorlton with her overnight bag, Angelica, on impulse, swung into the pub yard. She couldn't offer Jane a job without talking to Silvano. He was unfailingly polite to Jane but Angelica knew he didn't like her.

She found him up a ladder, unhooking a summer flowering basket, now looking distinctly over. She stood below him, took the basket, holding it with both hands under the bedraggled petunias, and put it on the ground.

'Thanks, Angelica. You wouldn't like to stick around while I get the rest down?'

'Sure. I'm just glad you didn't water them. That one was heavy enough.'

'Maybe if we'd watered them a bit more, they wouldn't be looking quite so *fin-de-saison*.'

As he moved the ladder along the wall, unhooking the rest of the baskets, Angelica stood below and told him of her plan for Jane. 'Would you mind, Silvano? I could do with some help in the office, and I just think she shouldn't be on her own, seeing no one but tenants and workers who don't like her.'

'No, I don't mind. Go ahead. And, you never know, the experience might make her a more understanding landlord.' He smiled. 'Unlikely, but possible.'

'You're an angel. Thank you.'

'You're the angel, Angelica. You're aptly named. You'll be the one who has to deal with her. But I admire you for it. You're truly kind.' He jumped off the ladder and took the last basket from her. 'Let's put these into the big barrow, and then can I offer you a cuppa? Or a drink?'

She'd have liked to accept the drink but Jane was expecting her, so she kissed Silvano's cheek, and turned back to her car. She was conscious of him watching her as she drove out of the yard.

Silvano's right, she thought, as she headed for the big house. Maybe working together would improve relations between them.

If she could get Jane to feel part of the business, she might be more reasonable.

The next day, Angelica and Jane met Mario at the station. Angelica had made an appointment for them with Inspector Fuller, saying she, Mario and Jane had something they'd like to tell him.

Mario did the talking, and Angelica was impressed. He really was an extraordinary man. Devil and angel by turns. Now he was serious, polite and apologetic. He explained that the mix-up with the mushrooms was his fault, and that Jane had panicked, having identified the webcaps. It was irrational, and stupid, and they were both extremely sorry.

Inspector Fuller looked at Jane. 'Is that the truth?'

'Yes. I feel such a fool. I didn't want everyone to blame us.'

Angelica said, 'Inspector, our poor grandmother has had the most terrible time. She believes she must have misidentified a whole lot of mushrooms, although she can't understand how, since she had no doubts about any of them at the time. She has no idea she missed a whole basket. Which she did but it wasn't her fault.'

The inspector thanked them for coming in and said he was grateful for the information. He would be in touch.

As soon as they were back in the car, Jane swung round to Mario in the back seat. 'He still thinks I did it on purpose, doesn't he?'

'I don't think so. We'd have had to do it together for that to be true. And I have nothing to gain from George's death, do I?'

You would if you were wooing Jane, Angelica thought, with

a little shaft of malice. He'd been all over her that weekend, knocked out by the glories of Frampton. Everyone had noticed it. Then she saw how mean she was being. Jealousy? Surely not.

CHAPTER TWENTY-EIGHT

George's funeral took place at Frampton chapel, which was full to overflowing. The bell tolled for a good twenty minutes before the service, and Angelica found the mournful sound somehow beautiful. Her extended family – the Olivers, Angelottis and Framptons – were there, of course, plus neighbours, friends from London and George's City colleagues. The entire village came – shopkeepers, tenants, estate workers, everyone.

Angelica watched Grace and Jane walking, controlled and dignified, behind the coffin. Her father was perhaps the only person Jane properly respected, who was capable of challenging her while still loving her, and now he was gone. How would she bear it? Angelica was rummaging in her handbag for a tissue, when Silvano, beside her, passed her a folded handkerchief.

She looked up at him in thanks, and he gave her forearm a little squeeze.

Giovanni gave the most touching eulogy. He spoke quietly but clearly. 'George has been one of the best things that happened to a lot of people in this chapel. His wife Grace, as a young war widow, and her baby daughter Jane found in him not just husband and father but a whole new life, secure, happy and loving.

'And then George's tenants and farmworkers have cause to be grateful that, unlike many landowners after the war, George worked hard to turn the estate into a good and growing business, giving jobs and security to many families.

'As a countryman George was ever ready to help a neighbour in trouble or put his fortune to good use. Although he did not hunt himself, the North Oxfordshire Hounds have been housed and supported at Frampton since long before the war. The village hall, the cricket pitch, the nursery school, this very chapel – they all owe their financial good health to George. Cottages and other buildings on the estate are in good repair. George was always sure that in any business the workers would be the most important asset. They needed to be happy. I'm sure you'll agree he did his best to keep his tenants and employees happy.

'But we're here to mourn a friend, not a grandee. Of course George was proud of his lineage and he counted some of the grandest in the land as his friends and relatives. You need only look around you to see that. But he was as much at home in the Frampton Arms – generally having a pint in the public bar – as he was in his London club or at the Ritz.

'I do not exaggerate when I say that George and Grace have been central to my family's happiness and success. They have been wise advisers, great friends, our principal backers and partners. If we ever tried to thank George he would tell us that it was a good investment, nothing to do with friendship. Which probably wasn't true, but it made my wife and me feel better.

'That's what George always did. He made one feel better.

'Today we're remembering a man who didn't have an enemy in the world. I've never heard anyone say a harsh thing about him. But, then, I never heard George say a harsh thing about anyone. He was living proof that being honest, loyal and generous is a recipe for a contented life, as a soldier, husband, son, father, landlord, employer and businessman. We will all miss him, and so we should. He was the best of men.'

Giovanni stopped for a moment. Angelica felt her throat swell and tears prick her eyes. With a break in his voice, Giovanni ended, '*Arrivederci, mio amico*. Goodbye, my friend.'

After the service, family and friends stood round the grave, taking turns to heap spadefuls of earth onto the coffin. Laura took her turn, her hand shaking a little so the earth rained down in uneven showers, then handed Angelica the spade. She dug it into the crumbly soil, and sprinkled it slowly on the coffin, unable to believe that George was lying inside it, dead.

As Angelica passed the spade to her uncle, David, she looked beyond the line of family and friends, and her heart sank.

That bloody detective was hovering, obviously wanting to speak to Jane. She strode up to him. 'Inspector Fuller, what are you doing here?' Before he could reply she felt her temper rising and she went on, struggling to keep her voice down, 'For pity's sake, can you not stop hounding the poor woman until her father is buried? Have you no humanity at all?'

'I was looking for you, actually.' As ever, he was unperturbed. 'I have to go back to London in an hour, and I just wanted to ask you to give Miss Maxwell-Calder a message. I wanted her to know now, rather than by post in the morning, that we're quite satisfied with her explanation, and our file on the earl's tragic death is now closed. I thought she'd feel easier, today of all days, to know that.'

PART FIVE

1977

CHAPTER TWENTY-NINE

By January, Angelica was feeling a lot less protective and under-standing of Jane. The woman was driving her mad. She'd accepted Angelica's offer to get involved in the catering business and had proved efficient in the office, doing the hire lists, getting the supplies in at the right time for a wedding, checking stocks.

But no one could stand her.

The fishmonger was a lone Italian trader who bought his fish from Billingsgate or Birmingham markets at dawn and drove it straight to the pubs and restaurants of the Cotswolds under chipped ice in the back of his van. 'She no say "hello". No "Good morning"! She just look the fish, and count it, and say to put on the scale again so she can see I no cheating. If no turbot in the market she look in the van to see I no give it another customer. I say, "No turbot in the market, madam." She say, "Humph". Like that. It ees no nice.'

It wasn't just the suppliers. The outside catering staff com-plained of her clicking her fingers, or poking them in the chest with a sharp 'Just do as I say,' or demanding icily, 'Are you ques-tioning me?'

The fact that she was their landlord made the situation trickier. Since her father's death, her sense of her own importance had grown, if that were possible. When she demanded they repaint the woodwork of the pub buildings to a lighter shade of Cotswold grey there was no sensible George to appeal to.

Silvano tried to reason with her. 'Jane, we discussed this with George. I accept that somehow between us we ordered the wrong shade, but it's such a waste of money to repaint now. We agreed to leave it for five years. It will fade anyway.'

'If you read your contract, Silvano, you'll see that you're obliged to use the standard Cotswold pale grey. The estate pays for the exterior decoration and we did pay for it. But you chose the paint. It is for you to rectify the mistake, not us.'

'I've no idea if it was George or me who OK'd the colour with the painter. It's in the building contract, and that was signed by George. But whoever did it, it's a waste of money to repaint now. No one has ever, apart from you, noticed the difference.'

'It's my job to notice the difference,' snapped Jane, 'and I consider it in very poor taste to blame my dead father for your mistake. It may cost money to put it right, but that's your problem.'

Angelica cut in firmly. 'Let's discuss it in the spring. We can't repaint until the dry weather returns anyway. And, you never know, it may have faded to Cotswold pale grey by then.' She tried to laugh, to lighten the atmosphere, but Silvano got up quietly, gathered his papers and left the room.

The tenants complained of her high-handedness too. One evening Angelica was filling in for a sick barman and was pulling pints in the public bar. One of the tables was occupied by the village shopkeeper, the baker, the blacksmith and two of the tenant farmers. They were talking in low, earnest tones. When the blacksmith came up to the bar to order another round, she joked, 'What's this then? You chaps organizing the village fête? I thought that was women's work.'

He smiled, but only briefly. 'No, but if Silvano wants to join us, he'd be welcome.'

'So it's boys' night out, then, is it? I'll tell him, but I think he'll be too busy in the restaurant. We're really full tonight.'

When Silvano came back to the bar from the dining room, she muttered into his ear, 'There's a bunch of tenants this side, and they want you to join them.'

Silvano peered into the public bar. 'I'm not joining that lot. I know what they're up to. They want to go to Jane's trustees and complain about her treatment of them. But it's no use. She's not doing anything illegal or unfair.'

'Still, maybe the trustees could rein her in a bit.'

'Not their job. She's just a very tough, by-the-book administrator, and she doesn't give an inch. They can do nothing about the fact that she's so unpleasant with it.'

'Perhaps you should join them, just to tell them that. Tell them not to waste their time.'

'Mm. Maybe, but not now.'

Angelica was delighted with the progress of her catering division. They'd started last year with a few dinners and cocktail parties for the local landowners and rich City men who were beginning to buy houses in the Cotswolds, and they'd held the harvest festival dance in the barn. Guests who came to the events quickly told their friends of the classy new caterers operating out of the Frampton Arms and the big barn. Before Christmas she did a twenty-first birthday ball, complete with dinner, marquee and kedgeree at two in the morning, which led to the first wedding booking, for early spring. That led to more bookings, including two weddings, for the summer. Soon Frampton Feasts was catching up with the pub and restaurant, not just in turnover, but in profit too.

'It makes sense,' Angelica said. 'Only one menu and a fixed number of guests means little waste. And we don't have empty nights with staff hanging around and no money coming in.'

'True,' Silvano agreed, 'but none of it would have happened without you. I'd never have thought of party catering, other than a boozy birthday in a corner of the pub. And you don't just have ideas. You're good at making them happen.'

Angelica couldn't help basking in Silvano's approval. He thinks I'm a genius, she thought. 'It's all of us,' she said. 'Even the maddening Jane. And we're lucky there's so little competition round here.'

By midsummer Frampton Feasts was bursting at the seams, and making life difficult for the pub. In June and July, Angelica ran three shifts because the kitchen couldn't hold all the cooks needed for the catering company and the restaurant. The early shift began at four in the morning with bread- and cake-making for the restaurant and the catering business. At noon the first lot of cooks left and in came the restaurant chefs, who did the lunch service, then spent the afternoon, when the pub was closed, preparing for the evening service and for the following day's lunch. Then they had a couple of hours' break and came back to do the evening service, leaving at nine when the last orders had gone into the dining room. The night shift came on then and worked until four making party food for the catering business.

No one liked the multi-shift system. Every shift blamed the previous one for lost or broken equipment, muddled stores and badly washed pans. Angelica couldn't supervise every shift. Because the restaurant cooks, led by Simon and Penny, knew what they were doing and the catering staff often didn't because every party was different, she tended to work the night or morning shift, sometimes both.

She was still doing her television programme and cookery writing, both of which she enjoyed, and they certainly enhanced her reputation. But it wasn't all roses. By Sunday afternoon, after several fourteen-hour shifts in the week, she was generally exhausted.

One Sunday night, at supper in London, her mother put her fork down and stared hard at her daughter. 'You look dreadful, darling. Too thin, exhausted, pale.'

'Thanks a lot, Mamma. That makes me feel just great.'

'Well, it's true. You're working far too hard. Not having any time off is ridiculous.'

'Mm. And you and Papa didn't work hard when you were my age?'

Giovanni chipped in. 'We did, of course. But that's no reason for you to kill yourself. Why don't you come with us to Abruzzo? Just lie by a pool, read a book, eat good pasta.'

'Oh, wouldn't that be wonderful!' She had a fleeting memory of picking figs in Carlotta's old garden, the sun so bright she could barely see the fruit through her squinting eyes. And lying on the rusty old seat, which squeaked as it swung, the pergola vines above her, bunches of grapes not quite in reach. And the lavender smell of the cool linen in her thick-walled dark bedroom, her book falling onto her chest as she drifted off to sleep.

'Oh, Papa, I'd simply love to. But I can't leave Silvano running the whole show, and—'

'Of course you can. You said yourself the catering side would take a dip between the summer season and the Christmas parties. And, anyway, isn't Jane there?'

'But what about the *Daily Mail*?'

Her mother put a hand on her arm. 'Darling, are you saying you can never take a week off? Find a way. Write your articles before you leave, or write about Italian cooking when you're there.'

'Think about it, sweetheart,' said Giovanni.

She consulted Silvano. 'Angelica, your mother is absolutely right. You need some sun, and a rest. Go. It will be fine.'

He was looking at her with such sympathy. He's the best of men, thought Angelica. 'Silvano, are you sure?' She saw nothing but affection and concern in his eyes. 'How will you manage with Jane?'

'It'll be fine. Don't you worry.' His smile was confident and reassuring. 'And when you get back, why don't we get you a good PA? Jane can't stay for ever – she ought to start working full time for the estate. You need someone pleasant and efficient, who'll realize how lucky she is to work for a boss like you.'

So, Angelica joined her parents in Italy. After a week of sun and heat, eating and sleeping, and a few pleasurable hours planning her Italian cookbook, she came home, feeling fit and energized. She was longing to get back to work, and eager to see Silvano. But he wasn't in the office.

Jane was. She was sitting at Angelica's desk. She didn't get up and barely smiled. Well, what did you expect? thought Angelica. That's just how she is.

'So, you're back. You're very brown.'

'Yes, it was heavenly, thank you. And how did you get on? Is there anything I should know?'

'No, not really. Except that I'm leaving. I've too much to do on the estate, which I'm sure you'll understand is more important than working with you.'

Angelica, as ever, marvelled at Jane's rudeness. Even Jane herself seemed to sense it, and said, 'But I'll work on until the middle of next month if you like. Give you six weeks to find a replacement.'

Even as Angelica was saying she'd be missed, she was thinking that Jane's departure would be a relief to them all. I bet Silvano put the idea into her head, she thought. They'd only employed Jane to help her through the difficult months after the death of her father and the guilt she must feel. Of course, Jane would never admit to any guilt or thank them, but that was just Jane.

Angelica hired Rosemary, an energetic young woman from Little Compton, who clattered into the yard each morning on her horse. She'd see her dismounting, her right leg making a swift but graceful arc over her horse's back, her feet landing neatly together as her arms lifted the reins over his head to lead him into the stable, all in one movement. That sort of sums her up, thought Angelica – graceful and efficient.

Rosemary had a degree from Bristol University, was outgoing, bright, and she could type. For her first month, she shadowed Jane.

'You'll find her rather unfriendly,' Angelica warned her. 'But it's only a month and she'll teach you a lot.'

One morning as she watched Rosemary swing off her horse, Silvano came into the yard. He went up to her and must have said something friendly, because Rosemary was laughing, looking up at him. As he turned away, giving Rosemary's horse a pat on the rump, she could see that he was smiling broadly. They made a handsome couple, the tall, dark, grown-up Silvano, now regularly wearing spectacles, and the willowy blonde Rosemary, all youth and openness. Angelica dismissed the thought. It made her somehow uneasy.

A fortnight later Angelica went to see Jane. She wanted to press her about letting them have more space for the businesses, a suggestion Jane hadn't welcomed when Silvano had first made it. Jane had a suite of rooms in the Frampton estate office, worthy, Angelica thought, of the chairman of Unilever. George had made do with a single room with a desk and a couple of chairs.

Angelica sat down rather self-consciously on a leather chesterfield, looking round at the shelves of old leather-bound ledgers, and the sepia photographs of estate workers carrying scythes and pitchforks, serving a stirrup cup at a meet, packing bottles of cowslip wine into wooden boxes, a land girl driving a tractor during the war, old Lady Frampton with two kennelmaids and a swarm of hounds. It was a picture of the past. Nothing of today, no plans for the future. How different from her father she was.

'This is very nice,' she said, looking around. 'I'd no idea you'd been doing it up.'

'Well, it needed it. Daddy never noticed if he was comfortable or not, but I do.'

Angelica smiled. Jane had probably never been uncomfortable in her life. 'It's good of you to teach Rosemary the ropes, Jane. You've done a great job with her.'

'She's very young but I think she'll do. She's keen, at least.'

In anyone else, that would have been grudging, thought

Angelica. From Jane it was a generous compliment. 'Yes, she's good, thanks largely to you. You could have just quit and I'd not have had time to hire her, never mind train her. We're getting busy again, with Christmas looming and the party season hotting up.'

Jane looked at her watch. 'What did you want to see me about? I've another meeting in half an hour.'

'OK. It's this. Since George got rid of the pig man in the farm behind the pub, the farm buildings, as you know, have been empty. Apart from the barn, of course, which we already rent. We thought, since the buildings are redundant, you might let them to us.'

Angelica produced her plans for the conversion of the old piggery into a second kitchen and the disused granary into two large walk-in fridges, one for the restaurant and pub, one for Frampton Feasts, and comfortable staff changing rooms for both businesses.

Jane shook her head. 'Don't bother with those, Angelica. I don't want to let those buildings.'

'But, Jane, why on earth not? We're not asking you to pay for the conversion, just allow us to do it. It's good business for you. We'd pay a decent rent, and if you don't do anything, in the end the roofs will fall in.'

'Angelica, you already have the pub and the barn. And, frankly, I wish my father hadn't let the barn to you. When the lease is up – you have the pub for twenty years but the barn only for three – I'll want it back.'

Angelica couldn't believe what she was hearing. She stared at Jane. Finally she said, 'Why? What's happened? Aren't we good tenants?'

'Yes, I'm happy enough with the pub. It's been a success, I admit. But my understanding is that the catering business was to be an adjunct to the pub, and the reason you took a short lease on the barn was because you weren't sure it would work. But now it has worked you want to expand and I'd be left with a farmhouse with no outbuildings. I have other plans for those buildings.'

'What plans?'

Jane stood up. 'Is that any of your business?'

Angelica stood too, trying to stay calm. 'Well, I'd have thought you could tell me why you're refusing a perfectly reasonable request.'

'I have my reasons, and if I don't wish to share them with you, I don't have to.'

'For God's sake, Jane,' Angelica cried, 'don't get all snooty with me. I'm Angelica, remember, not one of your minions. You've known me since I was born. Just tell me what the hell is going on!'

Jane's voice was cool. 'No. I don't need to tell you anything. Not yet anyway.'

Angelica wanted to shake her. 'You know as well as I do that George gave us a short lease on the barn so that we wouldn't be overcommitted. He wanted to help us. As you also know, we have a rental agreement that gives the estate a base rent and a percentage of profits. It's in Frampton's financial interest that we do well. The intention was always to extend the lease if Frampton Feasts took off.'

'I don't know what his intentions were. But the contract says three years, and three years is what it will be.'

Angelica was tempted to walk out and slam the door. But she

made an effort and said, in a reasonable tone, 'Jane, our immediate need is to have more space for the catering company. But
if it's the splitting up of the farmhouse and outbuildings that
worries you, I'd be happy to rent the farmhouse too – I can't
live at Chorlton for ever. It's a lovely little house and I would
look after it, as you know. Then you'd have one tenant for the
farmhouse and all the buildings. They would be occupied and
their value would increase.'

'Angelica,' said Jane, 'will you stop trying to tell me how to
run my business? I'm not interested in your proposal and that's
all there is to it.'

'Will you at least put the idea to your trustees?'

'No need. The trustees will do as I tell them.'

Angelica stood up. She couldn't keep the anger out of her
voice. 'Right. Well, the sooner we find somewhere else for our
business, the better.'

When she got to the bottom of the steps, she was shaking. She
leaned against the wall, taking deep breaths. Then she walked
fast back to the pub. She must find Silvano.

Silvano was checking the bookings and putting reserved signs on
the window tables, ready laid for lunch, when he saw Angelica
hurrying across the front paving, her thick hair catching the
late-summer sun, her bare arms still tanned from her Italian
holiday. Oh, good, he thought. She's coming here, not going up
to the office.

When she walked through the door, he saw at once that she
was upset. He wove his way through the tables and took her by
the shoulders. 'What's happened?'

'Bloody Jane. She won't tell me why but she's not going to

361

let us have the granary or the pig sties,' she said. 'I offered to take the farmhouse too, but no. She wouldn't even let me show her the plans.' She looked up at him, her eyes filling with tears. 'And she won't renew the barn lease. She wants the farm and all its buildings back.'

He released her shoulders and watched her wipe her eyes on the back of her fists, like a child. He handed her his handkerchief. 'I'm no good at negotiation, Silvano. I'm sure if you'd been there . . .'

Silvano hugged her close. 'No, no, darling.' It was the second time 'darling' had slipped out but he didn't regret it. He felt the old desire to protect Angelica. Didn't Jane understand how much Angelica had done for her? How dare she reduce her to tears? He dropped his head onto hers and immediately the clean smell of her hair filled his nostrils and he felt a rush of desire. He wanted to hold her close like this for ever, kiss her better, lick the tears from her cheeks.

Oh, God, what am I doing? He pushed her gently away, holding her gaze, wondering if she felt as he did. He watched her swallow and again brush the tears from her eyes. No, she doesn't, he told himself. She's determined to be business-like.

'What do you think she wants the buildings for?' he asked.

'She told me it was none of my business. But I had the feeling she just wanted to thwart us. That she doesn't really have a plan for them. Just that she hates our success.'

Rosemary came through the door, a piece of paper in her hand. 'I need to send off the hire list for the Paulton-Jones wedding. Do you want to check it, Angelica?'

Silvano watched Angelica with admiration. No sign of tears or distress in front of her assistant. 'No,' she said. 'I'm sure you'll have got it right, Rosemary. Do you feel confident about it? Anything you're not sure about?'

'Don't think so. The standard form helps because it forces you to think of everything: flowers, photographer, ice, musicians, paper or linen napkins, et cetera, et cetera.'

'And have you got the delivery times right? So the refrigerated trailer arrives before the wine, and linen before the florists and the florists immediately the tent is up?'

'Yes, I think so.'

'Good. Time to get rid of the leading rein, Rosemary.' Angelica gave her a little clap on the shoulder.

CHAPTER THIRTY

Angelica had insisted everyone went down to Chorlton after Christmas for Maud's ninetieth birthday party, to be held on the evening of the twenty-seventh. The restaurants were closed until New Year's Eve, when Giovanni and Richard would return to London to manage the New Year's Eve festivities so the women could stay longer in the country.

The last time they'd been in the Cotswolds together, Laura remembered, with a shudder, had been for the disastrous mushroom-foraging expedition, then for George's funeral. She wanted to shroud those memories with happier ones. She'd seen too little of her godson, Oberon, and of young Jake, and since David's stroke, he and Sophie had come less frequently to London. She was looking forward to spending some time with her brother and, of course, her mother.

Laura never arrived at Moreton-in-Marsh station without a mix of emotions: she remembered, aged six, the excitement of waiting on the platform for her father to arrive, and the pride she had felt at thirteen, waving him off in his RAF air commodore's uniform. And the mix of fear and rebellion when, at eighteen, she'd run away with Giovanni – in love, pregnant, and no longer welcome at home. Then there was the time she'd arrived with Giovanni for Grace and George's wedding and been unsure if her father would speak to her, or acknowledge baby Angelica in her arms. He'd been awful, but the train ride home had been so comforting: Giovanni had told her they'd won her mother round and one day they'd win her father. Eventually they had. Later there'd been her father's funeral, then Hal and Pippa's wedding, and so much more. She hadn't lived at Chorlton for over thirty years, but she still thought of it as home.

This time she didn't go straight there. She went instead to Frampton. She felt she had neglected Grace, who'd been such a great friend in the worst time of her life, when she was estranged from her father and homesick for Chorlton. She knew that in the crush of the big family party tomorrow she wouldn't have time to talk to her.

Frampton no longer had the busy atmosphere it had had with George in charge. He had done a lot of his work from his father's old study, and only spent odd days at the estate office. His manager, Rupert, came and went, as did the local Master of Foxhounds, and the dozen or so local people whose causes or businesses George supported, so there had always been an atmosphere of busy purpose. But Jane did all her work in the estate office, and Laura doubted if she supported local enterprises in the way her father had.

Looking for Grace, she popped her head into the old study and could see at once it was never used. It seemed soulless now, very tidy and conventional, nothing on the desk, bookcases locked shut, no newspapers lying around.

She found Grace in the morning room, sitting still, looking blankly out of the window. Angelica bent to kiss her and Grace looked up and smiled, life returning to her features. Jane came in and they made small talk until Marston announced lunch. Jane now rules the roost, thought Laura. Grace is just existing.

When a rather sorry lunch of tasteless soup and cold ham was over, and Jane had gone to her office, Grace and Laura went into the drawing room for coffee.

'Grace, darling,' said Laura, sitting down next to her on the sofa, 'why don't you come back with me to London? You're so sad here. Maybe a change of scene? We'd love to have you.'

'But what about Jane? I can't leave her by herself.'

'She'd be fine, surely. She's so absorbed in the estate. Which is good, isn't it? George would be proud of her. He used to worry that she preferred London and took no interest in Frampton.'

'I suppose so. But I'm not sure she has George's wisdom. And she won't listen to Rupert. Not that my being here makes her any wiser. I'm no use to anyone.'

Laura saw the bleak despair behind the attempt to smile, and put a hand on Grace's leg. It felt thin and bony under her dress. 'I think all widows feel that. Certainly Mummy did when my father died. If you've spent all those years primarily concerned with loving and looking after one person, how can you not feel bereft? But you're vital to Jane. She couldn't run both the house and the estate. You're doing the same job you always did. And one day it will be a pleasure again.'

Grace didn't reply, except with the faintest shake of her head, and Laura went on, 'I'm only suggesting a visit, a short break away from Frampton, where every object, every room, every field must remind you of George. Come up to town and bring your paints. We'll go to a few exhibitions.'

Grace was eventually persuaded. Laura suspected she'd agreed because she hadn't the will to argue. She said, 'Good, that's settled, then,' and changed the subject. 'So, tell me, what's happening at Frampton? Is Jane making many changes? Or sticking with her father's methods?'

'She's tougher with the tenants than George was, but maybe that's a good thing. Even I used to think some of them took advantage of him. But she's a good businesswoman, I think, and ambitious. She obviously wants to prove she's up to the job.'

'I'm sure she is, and even if she makes a few mistakes, she'll learn fast,' responded Laura. 'She's very bright.' And insensitive, she thought, but couldn't say.

'She's got some hare-brained idea of taking over Frampton Feasts from Angelica. Did you know about that?'

'No.' Laura shook her head. 'I didn't.' She smiled. 'But it might be a good idea. Angelica has such a lot on her plate with TV, writing and the pub. But she hasn't said anything to me. Except that Jane has refused permission for them to expand into the farm buildings and the old piggery and so on.'

'It's possible Jane hasn't talked to her yet. But the whole idea makes me nervous: Jane is very efficient but she won't have the loyalty of either customers or staff that your daughter has.'

Laura frowned. 'But what exactly is she planning? Maybe buying the business off Angelica and Silvano? But they wouldn't sell, would they? It's more profitable than the pub.' She thought for a moment. 'Perhaps a partnership. That might work, with Jane providing the premises and working on the admin, Angelica at the coalface.'

Grace sighed, closing her eyes for a second. 'I don't know. All she's said to me is that Frampton Feasts makes much more money than the pub. And that she'd like to get into party catering again. She got a taste for it, I suppose, when Angelica employed her.'

'But she must have discussed it with Angelica? Surely those two are never going to fall out. They've known each other since Angelica was born.' Laura smiled at Grace with a confidence she didn't feel. 'Don't fret, darling. Silvano's the one to sort it out and I'm sure he will. I'll tip him the wink.'

Maud had been outraged at the suggestion of a tea party for her birthday. 'I don't want a tea party! I may be ninety, but this is not an old-age home. You'll be suggesting a sing-song next, with Vera Lynn on the gramophone. No, thank you. I want a three-course dinner, then modern dancing, with a band. I may not be agile enough for the Charleston any more, but Richard or Hal can help me shuffle round the room with the rest of you.'

All the family were there and, of course, the Framptons, plus another fifteen or so neighbours and friends. The Christmas decorations of ivy swags and garlands were augmented with silver-paper stars and red carnations that Sophie had made out of crêpe paper. Candles glowed everywhere, well out of reach of little hands.

They had champagne and oysters in the hall and dining room to start, then dinner and speeches at a big U-shaped table set up in the drawing room. Frampton Feasts did the catering, and Laura was impressed and proud of her daughter's operation. The waitresses and barmen were smart in their white shirts, black mess jackets and green cravats held in place with an FF pin. They served Maud's favourite: roast beef and Yorkshire pudding, followed by jelly and custard. The beef was medium-rare and the Yorkshire pudding was as she remembered from her childhood, the batter risen in crisp brown hills and sunken in slightly soggy dales. Just like Yorkshire, her mother used to say.

The blackcurrant and port jelly was sensational. Laura had taught Angelica that recipe as a child. You kept the summer's blackcurrants frozen but raw, then stewed them and strained them though a jelly cloth. You added sugar to the juice, plenty of ruby port and enough gelatine to give a delicate, wobbly set. And the custard was made with Frampton eggs, Frampton cream and Frampton milk.

When coffee and the speeches were over, the waiters removed the tables, arranged the chairs in groups in the corners and cleared the centre for dancing. Music was provided by a piano, a guitar and a saxophone, played with gusto by a local trio. Laura felt her eyes prick when Richard led his grandmother onto the floor for the first dance. Maud moved with energy and grace, like a much younger woman. She sang along, knowing all the words of 'Smoke Gets In Your Eyes', laughing at Richard, who didn't know any.

When the band changed from mood music to thump out 'Satisfaction' and 'Lucy In The Sky With Diamonds' at full force, Maud, Laura and Carlotta retired to the dining room for a gossip.

'There's one problem with this family,' said Maud. 'There aren't enough children in it. What's the matter with the younger generation? Silvano and Mario are Italians. They should have wives and half a dozen *bambini* each by now! And Jane? Angelica? Richard? What's the matter with them all?'

'I agree,' said Laura. 'There's still lots of time for Richard. And I don't think Jane has any intention of having a husband, let alone children. But Silvano would be a wonderful husband and father, wouldn't he, Carlotta?'

'He would. Much better than Mario. Angelica chose the wrong brother, that's for sure.'

'But there'd be the same problem with children,' said Laura. 'It's just not a good idea for cousins to marry. They should both marry other people. And get on with it. Angelica is thirty now.'

'Have either of you said anything to them?' asked Maud. 'Carlotta, do you talk to Silvano about such things?'

'I used to. He used to beg me to stop trying to marry him off to every girl in the office! But since he's moved down here, I don't know what he's up to. I don't even know if he has a girlfriend.'

'Angelica says there's a girl called Rosemary,' said Laura. 'Rather horsey, but pretty and very nice. She's Angelica's assistant.'

'Oh, I know her,' said Maud. 'She's very beautiful, blonde and tall. Is she seeing Silvano?'

'I don't know. Angelica just mentioned her. I can't remember in what context.'

'I shall ask him,' declared Carlotta, stoutly. 'If we don't give them a shove, it will be too late. I can just see Silvano settling into being a self-sufficient bachelor, everyone's best friend or favourite uncle, but no family of his own. It would be a crime.'

'And what about Angelica?' said Maud, turning to Laura. 'Has Angelica had anyone since Mario? Should you give her a prod, my darling?'

'She's married to Mario, that's the problem. Perhaps she should go back to him but I don't trust him, even though he's been fine for ages now. Poor girl, I don't think there's a happy answer for her.'

On New Year's Day most of the family went for a walk over Chastleton Hill, Pippa, as usual, pushing David in his wheelchair.

But Angelica stayed with her mother, grandmother and Carlotta. They were engaged on a thousand-piece jigsaw puzzle that now took up most of the dining-table, forcing the family to eat in the kitchen.

After a while, Maud said she was chilly and went to sit by the fire in the drawing room, and Carlotta declared she'd come too: a jigsaw of a field of lavender was much too hard – every piece looked like every other. I know what she's up to, Laura thought. She's leaving me with Angelica so I can pump her about Silvano.

'Darling, a little bird told me there's a new woman in Silvano's life. Rosemary? Is that so?' Laura knew this was at best wild speculation, but she thought it would start the conversation. But she wasn't prepared for her daughter's reaction. Angelica's face drained of colour and her mouth opened but no sound came out of it.

'Rosemary?' she said eventually.

'Yes. I wondered if Silvano had a girlfriend?' Laura forced a laugh. 'Carlotta is desperate for a grandchild.'

Some colour had returned to Angelica's face. 'I don't know if they're together. She's very nice. They'd make a – a great couple.' Angelica stood up. 'Sorry, Mamma, I have to go.' And she was gone.

Laura sat for a while, thinking. So that's how it is. My poor darling Angelica. She's in love with Silvano.

She went through to Carlotta in the drawing room. 'Carlotta, I think Angelica is in love with Silvano.'

'*What?* Are you sure?'

'No, but when I suggested he might be interested in this Rosemary, she seemed shocked. And upset. She left the room.'

Laura sat down heavily. Dear Lord, she thought, either way it's a disaster. Which is worse? Unrequited love or no babies? Her darling daughter seemed to be doomed to both. And stuck in a marriage with no possibility of divorce.

CHAPTER THIRTY-ONE

Angelica was upstairs in her room, trying unsuccessfully to sort her stack of recipes and ideas for her as-yet-not-started Italian cookery book. But she couldn't concentrate. If she went downstairs she'd have to talk to people – she couldn't be rude. If she stayed upstairs much longer her mother would come and quiz her. She just needed time to get used to the idea of Silvano and Rosemary. Eventually she sneaked downstairs, got into the car and drove slowly to the pub.

How had she not noticed? She'd seen them together occasionally, of course, but that was natural when you worked together. And it had occurred to her that they made a handsome pair. But Silvano hadn't said a word. Neither had Rosemary, which must mean it was a secret. The sort of early-romance secret, when you didn't want anyone else to know.

But why was she so upset? She had to admit she was. She couldn't bear the thought of Silvano falling in love with Rosemary. Or anyone else, for that matter. She wanted things as they were now. Or as they had been until a few minutes ago. Just the two of them running the businesses, being together and helping each other. It wouldn't be the same with someone else in the mix.

She pulled up outside the pub, parking between two other cars, unsure of what she would do beyond going to the office and finding something to occupy herself. Then, as she stretched over to the back seat to grab her handbag, she saw, through the rear window, Silvano's front door open and Rosemary step outside, followed by Silvano.

She watched Rosemary turn towards Silvano, put one hand on his upper arm and stretch up to kiss his cheek. The gesture was, Angelica saw, intimate and casual, the behaviour of people who know each other well. He smiled down into her face and said something. She nodded and laughed, and he patted her shoulder. He stood on the step and watched her as she walked round to the pub entrance, which she went through. Only then did he turn and go back inside.

Angelica thought she would be sick. But then a steely resolve toughened her heart. This is ridiculous, she told herself. He's not yours. He can do as he likes. It's nothing to do with you. We're business partners. Not married to each other. Just partners.

She pretended to do a few things in the office, sorting through files without reading them. Rosemary popped her head round the door. 'Oh, hello, Angelica. I thought you were off today.'

'Yes, I was. I just came in to see to a few things.'

'Can I help? Is there something—'

'No. Thank you. I'm fine.' Only I'm not. Not fine at all. My voice is stiff and unfriendly. No wonder Rosemary nodded uncertainly and retreated.

Thank God her mother and Carlotta were leaving tomorrow. She dreaded any more conversation about Silvano's girlfriends and her domestic future. She knew her mother wanted a grand-child as much as Carlotta did. What stopped her nagging was the worry about consanguinity and her understanding that Mario was impossible. I should tell her and Papa that I never married him, Angelica thought. But she'd left it so long now, they'd be more hurt by her long deception than by the living-in-sin bit. At first she hadn't told them because they'd have pressurized her relentlessly to give him up. It would have been unbearable. And now she *had* given him up, their belief that they were still married prevented their nagging her to find someone else, get married and have babies.

Only Silvano knew that she wasn't married to Mario. She'd told him, but no one else, because Silvano was her best friend. They told each other everything.

Except, she thought, they didn't. She'd never tried to explain the mad love scene he'd overheard through his floorboards. Neither of them had mentioned it since Silvano had told her what had upset him, then handed her the buttons from her chef's jacket. Since then they'd both pretended it had never happened.

And now he hadn't told her about Rosemary. And she couldn't tell him how his relationship with the girl affected her. Maybe they weren't best friends at all.

Angelica was still brooding when Jane walked in. 'Angelica! Glad you're here. Where's Silvano?' She tossed her coat over a chair.

'Good morning, Jane.' Angelica knew her voice was frosty. She couldn't help it. Jane hadn't knocked, hadn't said hello. 'What can I do for you?'

'Is Silvano not here?'

'He's in his flat.' She wasn't going to offer to fetch him, or ask Rosemary to summon him.

Jane sat down opposite her. 'Well, you can tell him, I suppose. I just came to say that when your lease is up, I'm going to run the catering business from the barn. I came to offer you the job of managing it for me.'

Angelica wasn't sure she'd heard correctly. She didn't say anything for a second as the words sank in. She stared at Jane. 'You're *what*?'

'I'm going to take over the catering side. Silvano can keep the pub, of course, but Frampton will own Frampton Feasts. But I'll need someone to manage it.'

'Let me get this clear. You are proposing to take over my business – not offer to buy it, or even suggesting a partnership. You think you can just take Frampton Feasts off me. Is that right?'

'Yes, but you're making it sound like stealing, Angelica! You cannot go on without a lease on the barn, and I'm perfectly capable of running a small catering company. Frampton Feasts should belong to Frampton.'

Angelica couldn't believe what she was hearing. 'Are you mad?' She was having difficulty keeping her voice down. 'Are you actually saying you propose to employ me to run my own business?'

'It wouldn't be your business. It would be mine. But you're a good businesswoman so I'm offering you the job of running it for me.'

Angelica felt fury swell, then explode. She jumped up and leaned over the desk, shouting into Jane's face. It was all she could do not to lift her hands and strangle the woman. 'You can forget that right now!' she shouted. 'Don't you understand that you can't just help yourself to someone else's business? Is this your way of repaying me for friendship? For trying to help you with a job after George's death?'

Jane leaned back, distancing herself from Angelica's anger. 'Don't be a drama queen, Angelica. Of course I'm grateful for that job. It taught me how to run a party business. But look at the facts. When the lease runs out you won't have a catering business. You can hardly run it from the pub. I'll have the barn, and if you're sensible, you can still have a job. The only difference is the Frampton estate will be bearing the risk and taking the profits.'

Rage made Angelica fluent. She came round the desk and stood over Jane. 'How typical of you. Just when the business is successful and there are good profits and little risk, you think you can step in and grab what you want. All your life you've helped yourself to anything you've wanted without doing a stitch of work. Have you the slightest idea how hard we've worked to make the business successful?'

Jane's cool stare and slight shrug stoked Angelica's fury. 'You won't be able to do it, Jane. I will certainly *not* work for you, and I won't hand over any of the customer files, the records, the equipment – anything that belongs to us.'

Jane smiled. 'Oh, do calm down, Angelica. If you feel like that, I'll just have to start again, but I know nearly all the clients now anyway, and buying new kit won't be a problem. I'm aware I'll need to build a new kitchen behind the barn. I'd thought you might have liked that. It would take the pressure off the pub.'

Angelica strode to the door and yanked it open. 'I do believe we still have the lease of this building, so presumably I have the right to throw you out of my office. Please leave.'

*

Angelica longed to tell Silvano what had transpired. Longed for the comfort and wise words she knew he would offer. But she couldn't bear to see him. He'd find out soon enough, she thought. Meanwhile she'd just have to continue as normal, but take no bookings for the barn beyond the end of the year, when the lease would be up.

Over the next week Angelica felt she was slogging through a grey mist. She was working as hard as ever but not enjoying it. She found herself avoiding both Silvano and Rosemary. She didn't want to see them together, and they were together a lot. Well, thought Angelica, it's the end of the month, so there are the accounts to do.

She began to feel angry with him. If he was in love with Rosemary, or even attracted to her, why didn't he say something? She wasn't his mother, who would ask questions about the girl's bloodline or her child-bearing capacity. She was his friend. She felt shunned, excluded.

And then she saw them out together, in his car. Twice. Once on the road to Banbury and the next day on the Burford road near Icomb. It was, she thought, a bit much to take your girl-friend out in company time, especially when said girlfriend was her assistant, not his. This justifiable reason for irritation now stoked her anger. She was short with them both, but more so with Silvano.

In February Lucy, her agent, told her that the contract for her next television series was ready to sign. 'Are you happy with everything?' she asked. 'All the things that won't be in the con-tract? The format? The mood? The people?'

'Yes, I think so. I had a long lunch with the producer and we agreed the theme. Back to basics. You know, take an egg, boil it, fry it, scramble it, coddle it. Everything from a three-minute breakfast egg to a soufflé Rothschild or *crème brulée*. It'll be fun.'

'There's one thing I think you won't like. Did she tell you who was to direct the series?'

'No. Why?' And then she guessed. 'Oh, no! Not William O'Neill?'

''Fraid so. I sounded her out about the possibility of a different director, but it seems they've signed him up already. Does it matter that much?'

'God, yes. I can't work with that man again. Don't you remember? I'll never forget it. He's the ex-schoolmaster who likes to have everything on autocue. The one who thinks spontaneity is a deadly sin.'

'Is it a show-stopper?'

'Absolutely. It's him or me.'

'Angelica, you need to think hard about this. You don't want to get a reputation for being difficult. And your television profile is good for all your other activities – your catering, your journalism . . .'

'I'm sorry, but I don't care. I hated working with him last time – he made me feel wooden and unnatural. I'd rather not do it at all than do it with him.'

'Look, Angelica, you're making a big decision with your career here. Don't rush into a refusal you may regret. Why don't you take the weekend to think about it? Then let's talk again next week, and meanwhile I will see how committed the BBC is to O'Neill.'

'I won't change my mind,' said Angelica.

'You just might. Remember, you're more experienced now.

With more clout. He'll have to listen to you. And he might have mellowed a bit, learned to trust presenters more.'

That was on the Wednesday. On Thursday, she started to hesitate. She wanted someone to discuss it with. She wanted wise advice. Silvano's. But she couldn't ask Silvano.

And then, on Friday, Lucy rang to say BBC Education had decided that keeping the star of the show happy was their priority, and O'Neill would now be directing a show about home crafts – basket weaving, stencilling, and so on.

CHAPTER THIRTY-TWO

At the weekend Angelica decided to set off for London earlier than usual, leaving Penny and Simon to do the set Sunday lunch: roast lamb and *tarte Normande*. Rosemary and Silvano would be there too. As the restaurant wasn't busy, she thought sourly, they could have lunch together and gaze into each other's eyes. She rang her mother. 'Mamma, can I come to lunch instead of supper tomorrow?'

'Of course you can, darling. We're just having soup and pasta. But come to supper too. *Osso bucco*.'

'Thanks, Mamma, but no. I'm a bit tired,' she said, 'and since I can leave the lunch service to the others – we're not that busy – I thought I could come up this morning and have a really early night. It'll be a treat.'

In the event her 'early night' started in mid-afternoon. Her mother had made the *osso bucco* for lunch instead of supper, and of course it was delicious so she'd eaten a huge helping, followed by Giovanni's famous *Zuppe Inglese*, and she'd drunk two large glasses of Chianti.

After lunch and coffee, she sat beside her father in the deep comfy sofa. Soon Giovanni was snoring gently and she felt her eyes closing but she forced herself awake. What she wanted was a bath in her own house followed by a siesta. So she rose quietly and crept downstairs. Her mother, of course, was up to her elbows in the sink. She forbore to remonstrate with her about using the dishwasher. She knew it was useless. Laura always washed everything meticulously and *then* put it into the machine.

Angelica went to her house, climbed into a bath, turned the radio up and listened to Sibelius as she shampooed her hair. Then, fearing she was about to fall asleep in the bath, she forced herself out and into an ancient pair of her father's pyjamas. She turned on the electric blanket and went to bed.

An hour later someone was ringing her doorbell. She lay doggo for a bit, thinking that whoever it was would give up soon. But the bell kept ringing. Finally she staggered down and opened the door.

Silvano was outside, holding a big bunch of early daffodils, which he thrust at her.

'Good Lord, Silvano. What's this about?' She took the flowers, and led him upstairs. Oh, hell, she thought. He's going to tell me about Rosemary. The daffodils are the consolation prize.

'Are you ill?' he asked, concerned.

'No – why? . . . Oh, this?' She indicated the too-big pyjamas. 'No, I was just having a siesta.'

'At five o'clock?'

Her anger was returning. What had it to do with him? 'Yes, at five o'clock,' she said curtly.

'OK. Look, Angelica, if this is a bad time, just tell me. I'll go away.'

Did she want him to go away? No. 'It's fine. I'm just grumpy.

382

Half asleep.' Remembering her manners, she said, 'Would you like a glass of wine? Tea? Anything?'

He shook his head. She put the flowers in water and he followed her upstairs. 'Thanks for these,' she said formally, as she placed the vase on the coffee table. She sat deliberately on a chair. If she was on the sofa he might sit next to her and she didn't want that. 'Is there a reason for this visit?' That sounded rude, but she needed to get it over with.

'Yes, there is. Do you remember, when we'd just opened the pub restaurant, you came to my house demanding to know what was bugging me, why I was so cold to you? After that business with Mario in the bar?'

She nodded. Of course she remembered. Would she ever forget?

'Well, now it's my turn. I want to know what the hell is wrong. What have I done? Why are you avoiding me? Not speaking, not smiling. For two years we've been such great partners and until recently great friends too. What's up, Angelica?'

She was silent for a moment, considering. He sounded reasonable and calm but she could tell he was upset. Obviously he had no intention of telling her about Rosemary: he was leaving her to guess. What kind of a friendship was that? OK, then, she thought, anger rising. Let him have it.

'All right, I'll tell you. I'm upset with you because you've never told me about Rosemary, and nor has she. I find that strange behaviour from a supposed friend, and even from an assistant. But I blame you more than her. She's young and presumably takes her lead from you.'

He was staring at her, his face a complete blank. Oh, God, she thought, he's not going to deny it, is he?

'What are you talking about, Angelica? What do you mean, me and Rosemary?'

That did it. She jumped up from her chair and shouted, 'You know exactly what I mean. You and she are together. And it hasn't occurred to either of you to let me know what's going on. I expect you think it's none of my business. But I think it's an insult to our friendship. Why didn't you tell me? Did you think I'd disapprove? Tell you she's too young for you? Well, I wouldn't have. I'd have said she's absolutely perfect. Intelligent, beautiful, classy, fun. I'd have wished you well, joined in the general joy . . .'

Suddenly a great lump rose in her throat, choking her. She spluttered a hiccuping sob, then let out a wail. She made for the stairs and stumbled up them to the bedroom floor, into the bathroom and slammed the door. She sat on the lavatory seat and clutched a handful of loo paper to her face, trying to stem her tears.

After a minute or two she heard the bathroom door open and Silvano come in. She didn't lift her head but opened her eyes a fraction to peer through her fingers. She expected to see his shoes in front of her, but she found herself looking at the buttons on his shirt, the little bit of hairy chest in the V below his neck. He was kneeling on the floor.

He put his arms round her and clasped her to him. 'I love you, Angelica,' he said.

Silvano only knew that he'd said it. Said, at last, that he loved her. And she hadn't pulled away. She'd straightened her head to look at him. She'd sat there on the loo seat, solemn as a child, staring at him, her face tear-streaked.

He stood up, put his arms round her and pulled her up. He

could feel her ribs through the ridiculous pyjamas. She was far too thin. Then he wrapped his arms right round her and she pressed her face into his neck. He could feel her breasts, small and firm, through his shirt. Oh, God, she was delicious.

He picked her up and carried her to her bed, tucking her in like a child, and tenderly kissing her face. 'Sleep, darling. You need that siesta. I'll wake you later.'

My God, he thought, as he went downstairs. That was the hardest thing I've ever done. Oh, to have climbed in after her, undone her buttons, pulled the pyjama bottoms off her . . . Why didn't I do that? Because I need to be sure. I need to know that she loves me. Really loves me. That she isn't allowing me to make love to her because she hankers for comfort. Or sex.

He pushed the thought of Mario out of his brain. We need to talk first. And I need to understand this Rosemary business. What could have given her that idea?

He lay on the sofa and found hope and happiness trying to push in. She wouldn't have been worrying about Rosemary if she wasn't jealous, surely. And she'd nuzzled into his neck. And let him hug her, and kiss her eyes.

He woke her at seven with a cup of tea. Angelica couldn't believe she'd slept for two hours. She wanted to get dressed, but he said, 'Stay as you are. You look like an urchin in a grown-up's pyjamas. It's very fetching.' He took the hairbrush out of her hands. 'And leave your hair. I think this will always be my favourite Angelica look.'

She wanted to cuddle up to him on the sofa but he insisted she sit in the chair. 'We have to do some talking, darling.'

So Angelica, at first reluctantly, but then with more energy as indignation returned, asked the questions.

'Why was Rosemary in your house? She came out one day, and kissed you on the step. You watched her all the time she walked round to the pub door. I saw you.'

At first Silvano was baffled, then suddenly he gave a hoot of laughter. 'I remember! She'd been stung by a wasp, on the inside of her arm. We only had witch hazel in the first aid box, so we raided my medicine chest for the calamine lotion. Did she kiss me? I don't remember that.'

'Yes, she did, and you patted her arm. Like a lover.'

'If she kissed me I suppose it was by way of thanks, and if I patted her it was just to comfort her.'

'And then last week I saw you out together twice in your car. Once near Banbury, then near Icomb. I would have challenged her for taking time out of the working day, but I didn't want to be disloyal to you.'

'Darling Angelica. I couldn't tell you, but we've been looking for new premises for Frampton Feasts. Since we're losing the barn, and the business is doing so well, we need to find somewhere as good or better.'

'Oh, Silvano, that would have been wonderful but I don't know if it would work. I've been keeping secrets too. I was so upset by the Rosemary thing that I didn't tell you about Jane's plans. The reason she wants the barn is she's going to run her own party catering business from it.'

He listened to her tale of Jane's visit to her office, of Jane calmly expecting her to hand over the reins and then become her employee. His teeth clenched and a tic worked in his jaw as his fury increased. 'Right, that does it. What an ungrateful, greedy, spoilt woman she is! Your mother mentioned that Grace thought she had catering ambitions, but I didn't take it seriously. Stupid bitch! The party business requires nice people to reassure the clients. Don't worry about her, darling. Without you, she'll fail. For sure.'

'I wouldn't count on it. She can be very determined and she's extremely efficient. And she's got pots of money for marketing.'

'Well, I've always thought, like Giovanni, that competition is good for a business. We'll just have to be better than she is. And we will be.'

He watched her worried frown melt and her face lift into a smile. God, she was lovely. How had he resisted for so long? 'Did I tell you that I love you?' he said.

She laughed. 'What has that got to do with Frampton Feasts?'

'OK,' he said. 'Back to business. We'll beat the lady, I'm certain. Especially if we get the right premises. The Frampton Arms is a lovely pub, but it's a bit small. I got some of the local agents to start looking for properties. I didn't tell you because I thought it would be helpful if I sifted through the possibles and got it down to two or three for you and me to look at together. We've seen about six. None any good. I took Rosemary along because she knows what's needed in the way of space for kitchens, parking, van-washing and changing rooms.'

She looked long and hard at him, then said, her voice subdued, 'Oh, Silvano, I've been such a fool. All my life I've been a fool. I'm so emotional, and I behave so badly. How could I have chosen Mario? How could I have been so suspicious of you and Rosemary?'

He came over to her and pulled her to her feet. 'Maybe because you were a little bit in love with me so you were jealous. Not because you thought I was betraying friendship, but because you thought I might love someone else.'

She nodded, and he kissed her. This time on the mouth, deeply. He shut his eyes, his whole body longing for her.

He eased her away. 'Let's wait, my darling. I want you to be sure. I've been sure for months. In fact, I've been in love with you for years. But let's see if you can really love me. I want you to be in love with me. I don't want to be the boy next door, darling. Or Mario's replacement because you need a lover.'

Angelica tried to protest, saying she *was* sure, but he said, 'No, let's wait. Let's go out for supper. I know a place in Maida Vale that's open on Sundays and serves great haggis and neeps. Do you like haggis and neeps?'

'I don't think I've ever had it. It's what the Scots eat on Burns Night, soaked in whisky, isn't it? But I've no idea what it is.'

'And you a cook! Haggis is stuffed sheep's stomach, the filling made of liver and lungs, oatmeal and spices. It's delicious. Neeps are mashed swedes. But the whisky is a mistake. I like them with tomato ketchup.'

So Angelica got dressed and they went to the Unrepentant Scot and ate haggis and neeps. It was an extraordinary evening, like coming home to something familiar, to a long-held love. But it was also exciting, new, happy. He made her laugh, teasing her for her jealousy and for jumping to daft conclusions. He set out to woo her as a lover. It crossed his mind that obliterating his brother from her mind when they eventually made love might be difficult. But it would work out in time.

They made an effort to discuss ordinary things, slipping back easily into their former no-secrets friendship. She told him about the new TV series and how she'd escaped the controlling William O'Neill.

'I'm thinking of setting up my own little TV production company to make cookery programmes. Then I can call the shots. Is that a good idea, do you think?'

Silvano threw himself back in his chair, laughing. 'Darling Angelica, you're brilliant! Of course it's a good idea. It should make money with you as the star. But perhaps not quite yet. We have a pub to find, a business to move, a new catering venture to establish somewhere. And a love affair to conduct!'

They discussed the pros and cons of keeping the name Frampton Feasts when they left Frampton. 'We could take the name anywhere, couldn't we?' said Angelica. 'It's got a fair following now, and we've worked hard for our reputation. Throwing it away would be daft, wouldn't it?'

'But if Jane starts up her own company, what's to stop her calling it something with Frampton in it, say Frampton Parties, to piggyback on our success?'

'She couldn't do that, surely. It would be illegal, wouldn't it? We registered the name.'

'But we'd never go to court, would we? After all the years of George's friendship and help, that would be so sad. And expensive. Perhaps we should bite the bullet and change the name.'

'Maybe, though it seems so unfair.'

'The confusion could be bad even if she doesn't call it Frampton something. She'll be in Frampton and we won't. If we change it now, and tell all our customers, we could make a clean break.'

Silvano could see Angelica didn't like the logic of his argument, but, he thought, she's sensible. 'One more thing,' he said. 'If we keep the name, and she fails or does badly, she could do us a lot of damage. People will think it's us. She's so harsh with staff and curt with customers, and knows so little about food, I don't see how she can succeed.'

'Oh, all right, I give in.' She smiled. 'What are we going to call it then?'

'What's wrong with "Angelica's"?'

'It's not just me, that's what. 'Silvano and Angelica'?'

'Too long and difficult to remember. And, besides, I'm only the back-room boy. How about "Angelica and Friends"?'

They settled on 'Angelica's Angels'.

'Darling Silvano,' she suddenly said. 'I need to tell you something. No secrets now.' He watched her take a breath and then blurt out, 'I had an abortion in Paris, a back-street one. I may not be able to have children.

Oh, my poor love, he thought. 'How terrible for you. Why did you do that?'

'Mario wanted me to. But I think I always knew deep down that he'd be a terrible father, so I agreed.'

Silvano sent up a silent prayer of thanks. If she'd had Mario's baby, she might never have left him.

'And then,' Angelica went on, 'we were cousins. Like you and me.'

'I've been thinking about that,' he said. 'We could adopt, though?'

She gave him the happiest, most beautiful smile. 'Yes. We could.'

After coffee, Silvano reached over the table to touch her mouth with his fingers. 'OK, here's my plan,' he said. 'If we're right, and this is the real thing, let's get married in a month. I don't think I can wait for more than a month. Until then, we'll wait. No hanky-panky. No telling anyone. We can spend the month trying to find the right site for the catering company. And a new pub. It would give me unkind pleasure to hand the Frampton Arms back to Jane too.

'And then, let's say on St Valentine's Day, we'll sneak off to a register office, get married, come home, and I will make love to you until you cry for mercy. And then we'll tell everyone it's a done deal. Is it a deal?'

'No,' she said. His fingers were still on her face. She lifted a hand and pushed his forefingers into her mouth, her eyes on his. Then she sucked them briefly, and a shaft of such longing went through him that he had to shut his eyes. When he opened them, she was still holding his hand and kissing it, and still looking steadily into his eyes. 'You may be able to wait a month for hanky-panky,' she said, 'but I can't wait another hour.' She stretched her foot out below the table and ran it up his calf.

Why did he ever think he could resist her?

Her perfect face was deadly serious. 'So it's no deal unless you change that clause.'